Gingerly, Picard moved forward, climbing between the fallen beams. There, at the end of a wide, half-melted passage, lay . . .

What? There hardly seemed to be anything there at all. At first it looked like nothing more than a gray fog—but a fog would have movement. This was more a sort of blur, like a shape Picard's eyes could not bring into focus no matter how they strained. "Just as the ancient texts described," he breathed. "At once there and not there."

Coray grew tired of watching people stare at their instruments and moved in toward the field, ignoring the cautions of the others. As she approached, her extended hand began to meet with a gradually increasing resistance. "It's like pushing against the wind," she said. "It's getting stronger," she went on as she moved in closer, using both hands now. "My hands are starting to feel . . . slightly warm."

"Move away," Picard warned.

"It's . . . tingling now," she continued, ignoring him. By now she was surrounded by the fog, still visible but slightly hazed out. "The warmth is spreading through my arms. I . . ." Her voice rasped slightly, and she cleared her throat. "How embarrassing . . . I must be choked up with excitement."

"Coray, please be careful."

"Don't worry, nothing can get through the suit. Just a little farther—ahh—*ow!* My hands . . ." She started to pull back, but met with resistance. She called out, but her voice was choked again. "On . . . fire . . ."

# STAR TREK

## THE NEXT GENERATION®

# THE BURIED AGE

### A TALE OF THE LOST ERA BY
### CHRISTOPHER L. BENNETT

Based on STAR TREK®
and STAR TREK: THE NEXT GENERATION
created by Gene Roddenberry

**POCKET BOOKS**
New York London Toronto Sydney Centauri III

Pocket Books
A Division of Simon & Schuster, Inc.
1230 Avenue of the Americas
New York, NY 10020

This book is a work of fiction. Names, characters, places, and incidents either are products of the author's imagination or are used fictitiously. Any resemblance to actual events or locales or persons, living or dead, is entirely coincidental.

This book is published by Pocket Books, a division of Simon & Schuster, Inc., under exclusive license from CBS Studios Inc.

First Pocket Books paperback edition July 2007

POCKET and colophon are registered trademarks of Simon & Schuster, Inc.

For information about special discounts for bulk purchases, please contact Simon & Schuster Special Sales at 1-800-456-6798 or business@simonandschuster.com.

Cover art by Stephan Martiniere

Manufactured in the United States of America

10  9  8  7  6  5  4  3  2  1

ISBN-13: 978-1-4165-3739-7
ISBN-10:    1-4165-3739-2

*For Emmett*

When I have seen by Time's fell hand defaced
The rich proud cost of outworn buried age;
When sometime lofty towers I see down-razed
And brass eternal slave to mortal rage;
When I have seen the hungry ocean gain
Advantage on the kingdom of the shore,
And the firm soil win of the wat'ry main,
Increasing store with loss and loss with store;
When I have seen such interchange of state,
Or state itself confounded to decay,
Ruin hath taught me thus to ruminate,
That Time will come and take my love away.
    This thought is as a death, which cannot choose
    But weep to have that which it fears to lose.

—William Shakespeare, Sonnet 64

# PART I

## THE QUALITY OF MERCY

———•———

2355

# 1

---

DAIMON FLAX HAD HIT THE JACKPOT.

Each new mineralogy report bore it out further. The planets and moons of this system were richly endowed with dilithium, latinum, verterium, topaline, and other rare and precious minerals in abundant quantities. All just sitting there waiting for the Ferengi to claim it, since this system had no pesky inhabitants to argue ownership or resist stripmining operations.

This was the kind of haul that Ferengi dreams were made of, and Flax had come across it on his very first voyage as DaiMon. It boggled the mind. His father, Bok, had spared no expense in ensuring that his beloved son could follow in his footsteps—not only paving his path to DaiMonship with lucrative bribes in all the right palms, but hiring the most expensive tutors and driving Flax hard to ensure his skills were worthy of the position thus purchased. And that position was a prestigious one: commander of the Raider-class starship *Seventy-Fifth Rule,* a compact but high-powered scout designed to be at the vanguard of commercial expansion, racing far beyond known space to seek out new wealth and new opportunities and to claim them for his own—and for the greater glory of the Ferengi Alliance, by means of the sizable percentages which the Grand Nagus and the GuiMon in Chief demanded from every DaiMon's claims.

But even Bok had never expected that his son would make such a valuable strike so early in his career. *This is leverage,* he told himself. This kind of luck suggested that the Great River was flowing in his favor, and if he played his hand deftly, he could impress the Nagus and GuiMon enough to stand up to them and negotiate a larger share of the system's wealth.

*Careful,* he told himself, recalling the Forty-third Rule of Acquisition: "Feed your greed, but not enough to choke it." He could negotiate for more, yes, but if he demanded too much, the Nagus would see him as ungrateful and disrespectful, and that would hurt his chances for profit in the long run. Besides, this system was a big enough prize that even a fledgling DaiMon's share would make him rich.

*Yes, the River is generous,* Flax reflected, taking a moment to consider the larger picture. Even Ferenginar's best-paid scientists were still hard-pressed to explain how exotic compounds like dilithium and duranium could form naturally, and yet such valuable substances could nonetheless be found in the mineral strata of many worlds. Flax took it as proof that the River was flowing beneath the surface of things, creating wealth and depositing it where Ferengi could make the best use of it. In this case, where Flax could make the best use of it. Maybe it was arrogant to think of the River choosing to provide for him personally. But other Ferengi had been endowed with legendary luck over the ages, and if this find didn't prove that Flax was one of those blessed ones, it was at least evidence that he could be.

A proximity alert sounded, jarring Flax out of his reverie. "DaiMon!" reported tactical officer Gorp. "Our remote probes are detecting an unidentified vessel approaching the system at warp!"

"On viewer!" Flax cursed himself for his complacency, even while commending himself for the decision to send out the sensor drones (well, actually it had been on science officer Mench's initiative, but since Mench was on Flax's payroll, that made it his idea by the Twenty-fifth Rule). Right now the ship was conducting a mineralogical assay of a deep impact crater on a moon of the system's giant fifth planet, and the kelbonite and other minerals that permeated the crust were interfering with sensors. The drones had been launched to speed the survey of the system's planets, but they also served as sensor and communication relays, compensating for the ship's current blindness.

Indeed, Flax realized that they gave him an advantage over this potential claim-jumper: he could see them, but if his luck held, they hadn't seen him yet. And hopefully not the drones either. "Shut down all thrusters on the drones. Communication on tight-beam only. Gorp, can you identify the intruder?"

"I don't recognize the warp signature, DaiMon." Gorp paused. "However, I *could* run it through the database for a match . . ."

Flax grinned at his subordinate's initiative. In an imminent crisis, military crews had no time for negotiation and had to follow their DaiMon's orders without question. But at the moment, the crisis was just imminent enough to give Gorp leverage while not yet so imminent that his delay posed a danger. "Five slips if you do."

"Ten."

"Seven." *Don't push it,* his tone said.

"Done." As Gorp worked his console's interface hemisphere to run the search, Flax did the same with the smaller globe on his command chair's arm, appending the seven-slip bonus to Gorp's pay for the week. "Here it is," Gorp said, then sucked in a gasp. "DaiMon . . . it reads as Federation."

Flax spun to face the tactical officer. "Starfleet?"

"I think so."

"Two more slips."

"Yes, definitely Starfleet." Gorp didn't look happy about his extra profit. "DaiMon . . . what do we do?"

Flax shared his crewmate's anxiety. In recent years, the Ferengi had been hearing increasingly about this United Federation of Planets from various trading partners. They had sought to learn more, but carefully, clandestinely, as per Rule 194: "It's always good business to know about new customers before they walk in your door." Besides, these people claimed to be explorers, seeking only peaceful contact and discovery, with no interest in profit. They even claimed to have a society without property or money. That meant one of two things: they were lying, or they were insane.

So Grand Nagus Zek had chosen to pursue a cautious strategy, ensuring that when the time finally came, the Ferengi could face these bizarre beings from a position of strength. The Alliance had begun negotiating with new races from a distance, through intermediaries or over audio channels, in order to create an air of mystery about themselves. Zek had offered their earlier trading partners incentives to stay quiet about the Ferengi's true nature—particularly their small stature relative to most humanoids—and even to spread rumors painting them as a vicious, dangerous race, a people who blew up planets that got in their way and served up females and children as afternoon snacks. Zek had also been investing more funds into a military buildup, both to bolster the Ferengi's new, meaner image and to improve their ability to defend themselves for real if the Federation proved as dangerous as Zek suspected.

But it was too soon. Zek's master plan was still being put in place; it would be years before the Ferengi were ready to face the Federation. If this Starfleet vessel discovered the *Seventy-fifth Rule*, scanned it, and learned its technical capabilities and the life signs of its crew, all hopes for a safe and profitable first contact could be scuttled. That could not be allowed to happen.

Moreover, the ship might be coming to jump Flax's claim

on this system. That could *really* not be allowed to happen.

"Any sign they've detected us?" he asked Gorp.

"No, DaiMon. They still approach at a low but steady warp factor. The crater shields us well."

Flax studied their course plot on the viewer: it would bring them near the giant planet that this moon orbited. They seemed to be heading for a warp gravity-assist maneuver, banking around the planet's subspace gravity well to put them on course for the fourth planet without using thrusters. A smart, economical maneuver—further evidence that these Federation types weren't as unconcerned with profit as they claimed. But it would be their downfall, for it would bring them well within the *Seventy-fifth Rule*'s weapons range while never bringing them into line of sight with it, leaving them unaware of its presence until they were directly in its gunsights. Flax smiled. Maybe the River was still bringing him luck after all.

———

### Captain's Log, Stardate 32217.3

*U.S.S. Stargazer* on routine survey mission into the Maxia Zeta star system. Initial scans indicate twelve planets, none habitable. The third and fourth are in Maxia Zeta's habitable zone, and may therefore be candidates for terraforming. Our science teams are preparing for a full survey and surface scan.

"So . . . where do you want to go for your birthday?"

Jean-Luc Picard looked askance at his first officer, who leaned nonchalantly against the starboard bridge railing. "This isn't a pleasure yacht, Gilaad. I go where the mission takes me. No telling where we might be on that date."

Gilaad Ben Zoma threw his captain a skeptical look. "Come on, Jean-Luc. This is the big one! A couple more months, and you'll have made it a whole half-century!" His eyes went up a bit. "And with fully half your hair."

Picard smirked and stroked his ever-increasing expanse of bare scalp, his hand coming to rest against what remained of his graying brown hair. "Don't knock it, Gilaad. It makes me sleeker. Cuts down on wind resistance and excess weight."

"Planning on running more marathons?"

"Well, it never hurts to be prepared for the long run."

Ben Zoma winced. "We could always make a run back toward Federation space if you wanted. Give the crew leave, take some personal time . . . if there's anyone special you'd like to spend your birthday with." He sidled closer, lowered his voice. "What was the name of that JAG officer back on Starbase 32 last year? Phillipa . . . ?"

Picard glared. "The bridge is no place for gossip, Number One," he said, a bit of sternness entering his voice. Ben Zoma looked mildly taken aback. Normally Picard would not have been so bothered by a discussion of one of his liaisons; he was close to his crew, and they knew he was as romantic at heart as any Frenchman. This bridge had hosted banter about his love life before, most notably nine years ago when he had been ribbed mercilessly for his brief fling with Miranda Vigo, a human who coincidentally bore the same surname as his hulking, blue-skinned Pandrilite weapons officer. But his relationship with Phillipa Louvois had been . . . complicated. And it had come in the wake of Jack Crusher's death, reminders of which were still difficult to bear over a year later.

He shook off his mood, smiled at Ben Zoma to soften the rebuke, and rose from the command chair. "After all, we have work to do," he said to the bridge crew as a whole, his lively tone revealing that he didn't consider it work at all. "Why celebrate a birthday on some dreary starbase or prepackaged holiday world when new discoveries await us every day? Look out there," he said, eyes gleaming as he gestured at the viewscreen. "A whole new system beckons.

Until now, Federation science knew it only as the sixth-brightest star in the Berengarian constellation of Maxia. Now it's a sun with twelve unexplored planets—a dozen gifts just waiting for us to unwrap them and discover the surprises they hold."

Idun Asmund turned from the helm console. "A dozen lifeless balls of rock and gas? Good to know you're easy to shop for, sir."

He chuckled. "Come on, Idun, use your imagination. Every system has its own tale to tell." He strode toward the science station, gesturing at the system plot on its large display screen. "Look here—two whole planets in the habitable zone, but for some reason no life has arisen on them. Or has it? Look how similar their compositions are, how young and uncratered their surfaces. Maybe they were once parts of a single larger body that was shattered sometime in the distant past, its debris then coalescing into new planets. What could have destroyed that planet? Was it a natural phenomenon, or artificial? Might there be ruins of some ancient, doomed civilization waiting for us to find?"

"If the planet was shattered," observed Vigo from where he stood at tactical, "it's unlikely any ruins would have survived."

"Perhaps they settled one or more of the system's moons before the cataclysm," Picard countered.

"Or maybe they never existed at all except in our wishful imaginings," Asmund said, belatedly remembering to add, "sir." Though human, Idun had been raised by Klingon parents and thus tended toward the confrontational.

Picard chuckled. "Ever the pragmatist. Well, good. Keeps us honest. Even so, it'll be intriguing to study the geology of such young worlds with such a turbulent history. I may go down with some rock-climbing gear myself."

"So long as you don't forget the oxygen gear," Ben Zoma said. "And maintain an active transporter lock at all times."

Picard sighed. "Yes, mother. Honestly, Gilaad, where's your sense of adventure?"

"I have enough adventure trying to keep you out of trouble, Jean-Luc."

"Then where were you on Starbase 32 last year?" he teased.

Ben Zoma laughed. "Oh, no, Captain. That kind of trouble I trust you to manage for yourself."

Picard joined in the laughter, but Asmund remained all business, as usual. "Coming up on fifth planet," she reported. "Decelerating to warp 2 for gravity-assist maneuver."

"Acknowledged," Picard said with a residual chuckle before turning to the officer manning the science station. "Lieutenant Schuster, I want an intensive scan for life signs in the Jovian's atmosphere as we pass by. With luck the system might turn out to be inhabited after—"

A perimeter alert klaxon interrupted him. Vigo whirled to his console, which was suddenly lit up with warning lights. "Unidentified ship dead ahead, Captain! They're firing!"

Picard headed back for the command chair. "Shields up. Brace for—" But just then the first salvos hit. The deck convulsed, sending Picard stumbling across the chair. Schuster toppled over the rail behind him, landing on Ben Zoma, but the fall saved him from the shrapnel when the science station blew out. Picard could hear other explosions from the decks below. "Vigo!" he called as he took his seat, folding the safety restraints over his thighs.

"Shields damaged, sir!" the Pandrilite called. Of all the people standing on the bridge, only he had kept his footing. "They were only half-raised at impact."

"Warp field has collapsed, Captain," Asmund reported. "We're in the Jovian's gravity well, suborbital velocity."

"Full impulse, get us some distance."

Ben Zoma voiced Picard's question. "Where did they come from?"

"They just appeared over the crest of a moon," Vigo said. "They must have been hiding there."

"Hail them."

Vigo sent out a standard hail. "No response."

In the seconds it took the warp field to collapse, the *Stargazer* would have gained some distance from the attacker, but it could be closing in from behind even now. He had to assess their capabilities. "Can you identify them, Vigo? If they come in a second time with our shields damaged . . ."

"Sensors are offline, sir."

"Picard to sensor control. Retask planetary sensors for short-range tactical! Vigo, aft shields to maximum. Helm, evasive action, we're sitting ducks out—"

A mighty thunderclap drowned him out as the *Stargazer* was struck again. The deck dropped out from under him, and even Vigo lost his footing this time. Fires broke out from the nav console before him and the system status displays behind him, and caustic smoke stung his eyes. "Report! Why isn't fire suppression working? Engineering, re—" He broke off as the viewscreen cleared before him, showing an aft view. Through the smoke and tears, he saw bodies flailing in the vacuum. His ship had been hulled. His crew was dying.

Almost unconsciously, he rose and took a step toward the screen, reaching out as though he could somehow catch them, save them. His foot struck a heavy, yielding mass, bringing him back to reality. He looked down, recognizing the bulk and blue skin instantly. "Vigo!" The weapons officer's temple bore a deep gash, hemorrhaging purple-black blood. Picard knelt by him and felt for a pulse, reminding himself that head wounds always looked worse than they were . . .

But not this time. There was no pulse to find. "Picard to sickbay! I need a team here on the double!" If he could get help in time, maybe he could be revived. But Doctor Greyhorse's response over the intercom was too mired in static to decipher. Was help on the way? What was still working on this ship? Who was still alive? And who the hell was attacking them?

Picard shoved those questions aside. There would be

time for them—and for grieving—later, but only if he pulled himself together *now* and started defending his ship. "Idun, continue evasive."

"Impulse engines are down, sir."

"Thrusters, best speed," he told her, knowing it would be a token effort. "Engineering—"

Just then, the fire-suppression fields kicked in, flickering into place over the conflagrations. *"Sorry for the delay, Captain,"* came Simenon's gravelly voice from engineering, relatively free of static. *"The fusion reaction's surging, and the EM leakage is disrupting internal forcefields. I can't guarantee it won't—"* The intercom erupted in another burst of static and the suppression fields dropped out, leaving the fires smoldering.

"Warp engines?"

*"In bad shape, sir. I can give you ten, twenty seconds, no promise of more."*

"Get the fusion generators under surge control," Picard ordered, breaking down into a fit of coughing. He was dazed, off balance—air circulation was down, and the fires had consumed too much oxygen.

"Where are they?" Idun asked, searching her helm screen.

"Ensign Durand," Picard said to the navigator, "Man sensors. Find them. Schuster, take tactical. Ready weapons."

The young Austrian lieutenant rushed to take over Vigo's station, but frowned a moment later. "Weapons not responding, Captain!"

Ben Zoma hit his communicator. "Bridge to fire control, what's happening down there?"

*"We're working on it, Commander! Half the power circuits are down. We're rerouting now."*

Ben Zoma moved toward the blasted, abandoned science station so he could supervise that process over his combadge without distracting the others on the bridge. Picard left him to it and turned back to Schuster. "Open a channel." Even if they wouldn't respond to his hails, he could still talk *at* them. The lieutenant nodded once the channel was active. "Do not attack again!" Picard cried, rising from his seat and striding forward. "We are on a peaceful mission!" The only response was another weapons volley, but a weak one this time. Picard staggered, as much from his dazed, weakened state as from the impact. They must have been at some distance, taking potshots. At the speed they'd needed to catch up for the second strike, they would have overshot considerably. But if they came in for another close-range attack run with shields and internal systems in their current state, the *Stargazer* would be finished. "Give your identity!" he urged, struggling to put a coherent sentence together. "You force us to defend ourselves!"

To underline his seriousness, he turned to Schuster. "Phasers full up! Arm torpedoes! Shields to maximum power!" It was halfway a bluff; he could still hear Ben Zoma coordinating with fire control to get weapons ready, and shields would be limited in power if Simenon couldn't get the fusion reactor to cooperate.

More salvos struck the ship. Smoke began to fill the bridge again, the fires rising. He coughed, waving smoke from his face. The suppression fields still weren't working. "Vigo! Get a fire control party up here!" he called—only belatedly realizing that Vigo was no longer able to follow his orders.

But if anyone noticed the lapse, they left it unremarked. "Shields weakening, Captain!" Asmund called. Typically, she had taken it upon herself to monitor tactical status in Vigo's . . . absence. In other circumstances, Picard would have lectured her about letting Schuster do his job, but right now he was grateful for her warrior's eye.

Simenon's voice came over the intercom. *"Fusion generator online."*

It was the first good news in some time. Picard strode over to Ben Zoma. "Weapons report!"

"Phasers coming to full charge, sir. Torpedoes armed."

"Who are they?" he demanded one more time, returning

to stand by his command chair and study the viewscreen again. "Identify them!" Even as he asked, he knew it was a futile request. He had to stop giving in to desperation and focus. *Think!*

Durand noted something on his sensor panel. "They're turning for a third pass at us, sir!"

*"We can't take another hit, Captain!"* Simenon declared. *"We have a fire in engineering—we can't fight it and hold this crate together at the same time!"*

"Contain it if you can, evacuate if you have to, Phigus," Picard ordered. He checked the system status screens, but they were shorting out as the flames spread. He turned to tactical, trusting Schuster to have adapted his console to compensate. "Damage report!"

"Fusion generators under surge control, sir!" Schuster reported as Picard came forward and resumed his seat. Despite the panicked tone in his voice, the lieutenant maintained the good judgment to keep his report focused on the engineering situation. "Power systems failing!"

Picard had to act fast, before the ship lost any more power. He couldn't sit around and wait for the enemy—he had to take it to them, and fast. But how, with the impulse reactor unreliable?

*Ten to twenty seconds of warp,* he remembered. At this range, it would be more than enough. *At this range,* he repeated, the ramifications coming together in his mind. In all likelihood, the enemy was relying on short-range tactical sensors at this point. There was a good chance that meant optical imaging and ranging, lightspeed-limited. If the *Stargazer* suddenly made a short warp hop toward them, outracing the light they gave off from this position . . . *we could make them see double!* Of course, they probably had subspace sensors as well, letting them see through the deception, but if he could just confuse them for a few seconds, it would be all he needed to regain the element of surprise. Even using a warp maneuver during a close-in battle could catch them off guard. For most ships it was preferable to keep to impulse, since the buildup of energy for warp could divert power from shields and weapons for precious seconds. But the *Constellation* class's four nacelles gave it an edge in power usage; the same ability that let it "warp coast," extending its high-warp capacity by alternating pairs of nacelles, could allow it to build up warp power with no loss to tactical systems. The unfamiliarity went both ways; if these aliens had never been encountered by Starfleet before, they probably would have no knowledge of this ship's special abilities. That would give him the edge he needed.

But first he had to know where they were. He could barely see them through the static—a vague impression of a rounded vessel with a rust-colored hull, but with too little detail to make out the shape. *That doesn't matter*, he reminded himself. He needed to know the *where*, and the *who* could wait until after. "Sensor beam bearing on hostile ship," he commanded.

"Seven seven mark nineteen, sir!" Durand replied.

"Phasers, sir?" Asmund asked. "Sir?" she repeated when no answer was forthcoming.

But he had to time this just right. He waited another moment before ordering, "Ready phasers and lock. Stand by on warp nine. Heading . . . seven seven . . . mark twenty," he decided—just enough to compensate for the attacker's probable motion. Durand moved to enter the course. "Engage."

Over the crackle of flames came the rising surge of the warp engines initiating their field. A distant explosion sounded as the ship struggled to jump into warp, but Picard couldn't divert his focus to wonder what it was. "Steady," he said, as much a plea to his ship as a command to Asmund. Another second and the warp field engaged, the bow shock appearing on the viewscreen. A second after that, Picard cried, "Now! Reverse and stop!" Idun jabbed at the console, taken by surprise but reacting with lightning speed as always. The warp streaks dissipated to reveal the enemy ship rushing into their sights. He'd timed it right, placing the *Stargazer* right off its bow, or effectively so by the standards of starships hurtling toward each other at hundreds of kilometers per second. The enemy ship fired, but the *Stargazer* remained untouched. His gambit had worked; the enemy had chosen the wrong target, firing toward the residual light from where the ship had been. He had to strike before they realized their mistake. "Phasers fire! Torpedoes away!"

On the screen, four blinding beams and six swirling balls of light converged on the onrushing ship. At point-blank range, they were devastating. With the phasers draining the shields, the first three torpedo hits were enough to knock them out completely, leaving the enemy defenseless against the final three antimatter warheads. As the ship disintegrated before him, Picard realized it was smaller than he had expected, the six torpedoes perhaps being overkill. But he knew there had been no choice. The *Stargazer* had been in desperate straits, moments from destruction by an enemy that struck without warning and gave no quarter. Their only chance had been to hit back with everything they had.

And they had won. They had survived. Relief washed over Picard, bringing a smile to his face in spite of the lives he'd have to mourn on both sides. The losses had been profound, true, but the *Stargazer* was still here. They would rebuild, and they would go forward, just as they had done before when Lisuni was killed, when Jack was killed.

But then Picard registered the red alert klaxon and the heat that was rising all around him. Open flames were pouring from both sides of the bridge, from the nav console, from everywhere. "Fire," he murmured in disbelief, his victory going up in smoke around him. "Fire!"

He shot to his feet as Ben Zoma came down to his side. "Fires all over the ship, Captain. Sickbay, the labs . . . they're evacuating engineering. Fire control teams are overwhelmed, the fields still aren't working. . . ."

*Evacuating . . .* That was it. They needed to evacuate the whole ship, in both senses of the word. He slapped his combadge. "Picard to all hands. Abandon ship! Repeat, all hands abandon ship! Fire protocols—avoid the lifts where possible." As the bridge crew left their stations and headed for the emergency ladders, Picard threw a wistful glance at Vigo's body, reminding himself that with luck, they would be back for him. He hit his badge again. "Picard to Simenon. Fire emergency, blowback protocol. Rig to vent all compartments to space once the crew is clear."

*"I'll do what I can, sir, but control systems are iffy and we're working from tricorders and padds here."*

"Do your best, but get to the shuttles."

After that, it was an organized frenzy as the crew raced to the shuttlebays and escape pods. Luckily, the *Stargazer* was designed as a platform for intensive planetary surveys and was thus equipped with seven shuttlebays around the rim of its thick saucer and over twenty support craft of various sizes, in addition to dozens of fifteen-person escape pods. However, many escape routes were cut off by fire, debris, or vented compartments. Picard and his command crew remained behind as long as they could, racing through the ship to assist personnel who were cut off from the shuttlebays or pinned beneath debris. More than once, Picard came across a crew member who was beyond help. Maybe some of them, like Vigo, could have been saved with immediate medical intervention. But sickbay was proving hard to reach and Greyhorse wasn't answering the intercom. At times, Picard wondered if he would make it himself, given all the smoke he was inhaling.

Eventually all but one of the usable escape pods and shuttles had been launched, some packed beyond capacity, and the command crew came together in the forward bay where the captain's executive shuttle sat waiting. "The atmosphere purge is set up as well as we could manage, sir," Simenon reported as he entered the bay. "Ready on your mark."

Picard glanced at the engineer's padd, its thermal readout showing the fires spreading out of control. Sickbay was an inferno by now, as was engineering. And Greyhorse and

Cadwallader were nowhere to be seen, the last ones still un-accounted for. "Into the shuttle," Picard ordered with great reluctance. "Then start the purge. We can't wait any longer."

But just then, Tricia Cadwallader came limping through the door, bearing the much larger, barely conscious Greyhorse on her shoulders. Picard and Ben Zoma rushed to catch the doctor as he collapsed completely, and together the last four survivors rushed into the shuttle. "Open bay doors and purge atmosphere now!" Picard cried, not waiting for the shuttle's hatch to finish closing.

The outrush of air gave the shuttle an extra kick as Asmund launched it, and only her decades of skill kept them from colliding with the bay doors. Once they were clear, she spun the shuttle so they could see their wounded starship. All its hatches gaped open, spilling out the white mist of freezing atmosphere along with gouts of smoke and the occasional lick of flame, which dispersed oddly in the weightless vacuum. Other breaches were visible on the ship's underside, but no air or flame came from them; those sections had already emptied their contents to space, including the men and women within them.

Simenon made an unhappy noise in his throat. "As I feared, Captain. The purge is incomplete. Some of the hatches didn't respond—we still have fires burning in much of the engineering section and physics labs."

A thought struck Picard. "Can you shut down ship's gravity? Without convection, the fires would smother in their own smoke."

The Gnalish shook his gray-scaled head. "I no longer have control of those systems." It was the paradox of Starfleet gravity generators: under power, their superconducting stators could be braked within moments, allowing near-instant gravity shutdown, but in the event of power loss the stators would continue spinning on sheer momentum for up to four hours. It was a safeguard against power loss, but right now it was working against the ship's survival.

"Oh, no," Simenon said. "I've read an explosion in

nuclear physics. Atmosphere venting from those compartments . . . I'm detecting radiation spreading outward. Looks like . . . a canister of plutonium must have ruptured. No fission, but the plutonium dust is spreading through half the ship." He shook his head. "We don't have the equipment to decontaminate it."

Picard stared at his dying ship. "Then we can never go back."

After the crew had absorbed that for a time, Ben Zoma asked, "What if there are more enemy ships coming? Ships that do have decon equipment? Do we just leave her for them?"

"We never made a stable orbit," Asmund answered. "She'll spiral down into the Jovian's atmosphere within a week, two at most."

"Can we make sure she self-destructs?" Picard asked Simenon.

"The engine controls are unresponsive. And these shuttles don't have the armaments to take her out. The only way would be to remove one of the shuttles' micro-warp cores and make it into a bomb."

"But we barely have enough shuttles and pods to hold all the survivors," Ben Zoma said. "We can't afford to leave one without warp power."

"Push it," Idun suggested. "Thrust against it enough to decrease its orbital velocity, make it splash down faster."

Simenon shook his head. "Still too much of an explosion hazard. And decelerating a mass that size would use up more engine power than we can spare."

"So we just have to hope," Picard said grimly, "that the enemy doesn't send reinforcements within that week or two. Or that Starfleet finds us first."

It was too risky to remain in-system, given that it may have been claimed by hostile forces. Picard ordered the escape pods to use their emergency grapples to join together and hitch onto the shuttles, which would then tow them out of the system at low warp.

Once this was under way, Picard realized there was one more duty he had to perform before leaving his ship behind for the last time. He struck his combadge. "Picard to *Stargazer* computer."

*"Working."*

He resisted an irrational temptation to apologize. "Cap—" His voice dissolved in choking. "Captain's log. Final entry, stardate . . . three-two-two-one-seven point four." He noticed his crew members looking at him, and he held their gaze as he began to speak. But no great valedictory speech came to him, no stirring words to inspire hope. In all likelihood, the computer recording this entry would be burned away to nothing within two weeks' time. So all he said was, "We are forced to abandon our starship. May she find her way without us."

*I'm sorry.*


## Fifteen days later

Science officer Skwart came up to Bok uneasily, his reluctance to speak sincere rather than an invitation for a bribe. Bok had been in a simmering rage, quick to unleash his anger upon his crew since they had confirmed the destruction of his son's ship with all hands aboard. Worse, it had been no accident. He had been slain by the occupants of the battered, half-radioactive vessel that Bok's crew had salvaged from the fringes of the giant planet's atmosphere. The vessel they had identified as belonging to the Federation Starfleet.

Bok skewered the science officer with his gaze, impatient to learn all he could about the assassins. "Report! Is the ship a trap?"

"We do not believe so, DaiMon. Analysis of the scorch patterns on its hull suggests that it must have first fallen into the planet's atmosphere some days ago. By a thousand-to-one shot, its disk hit at just the right angle to skim off the atmosphere and bounce back out. That gave it enough velocity to remain in a decaying orbit long enough for us to find her." Skwart shook his head. "It was an amazing fluke of luck, DaiMon, the kind a Ferengi dreams of his whole life! We are truly blessed by the River to have such a valuable acquisition as this ship dropped into our hands!"

Bok glared at him. "Blessed, science officer? You dare to say that after the loss I have suffered?!"

Skwart cringed. "I meant no disrespect to your son, DaiMon. I simply meant that we can always find comfort in profit."

To Bok, the words rang hollow. The profit he could gain from this ship's technological secrets brought him no comfort, any more than did the mineral wealth of this system. His son, the only male heir his useless mate had ever spawned, was dead. Bok no longer had a legacy; upon his death, his wealth would be scattered on the waves of the Great River. So what was the point of wealth?

But Bok was too shrewd a negotiator to reveal such blasphemous thoughts; that could lead to his sanity being challenged, his command and wealth being taken from him. He might not care about those things for their own sake anymore, but they were still useful tools for pursuing the only goal that still mattered. He would keep this rage to himself, hold it inside him until he could find a worthy beneficiary to whom he would offer it . . . as a *gift*. The thrill of the obscene thought gave him the strength to continue.

The derelict was abandoned, its hangars empty. So the killers of his son had survived, no doubt escaped back to their Federation. That put them beyond his reach for now. But he understood how to let an investment mature. He would have the time he needed to prepare a suitable revenge, and be ready to spring it once open contact was finally made.

Gazing at the ship on the main viewer, he decided that it would be the instrument of his vengeance. Its crew must have thought it lost forever, doomed to destruction in a gas planet's bottomless atmosphere. Imagine its captain's joy when Bok found him and offered the ship to him again. It would be a precious item he would gladly reclaim, like the fabled treasure chest of Narj. And once he took the chest into his vault, then the trap would be sprung.

"Prepare for warp tow," he ordered. "We will take the ship with us."

Skwart grinned, the familiar light of avarice in his eyes. "Very good, DaiMon! We will profit handsomely from the technologies we can salvage from this ship."

"No! The ship is mine, Skwart, and I intend to keep it intact. Indeed, I want you and the engineering teams to work on decontaminating it and restoring it to operating condition."

"Ah . . . I see. You wish to sell it as a collectible?"

"It is for my own private use. Ask no further, Skwart. You will be well enough compensated for your labor."

"Thank you, DaiMon." Skwart hesitated. "But what of the Nagus and the GuiMon? They might have other ideas for the ship."

"I will offer them the mining rights to this system in exchange for letting me keep it."

Skwart gasped. "*All* the rights, sir?"

Bok realized he had shown too much of his hand. "I meant a suitable percentage, obviously, you idiot. Now proceed with the towing operation!"

Skwart acknowledged the command and hurried away to oblige. Bok resumed staring at the eyesore of a ship, memorizing its every line and contour. This ship had been used to murder his son, and now he claimed it as just compensation. But it was only a means toward his true compensation, a price that would not be paid until he found the commander of the vessel.

Days later, back in Bok's private shipyard, enough of the ship had been decontaminated to allow his crew to access the vessel's computer system. Bok listened to its logs, heard the voice of its captain. He learned the name of the man who had killed his son.

*Zhon Look Picard,* he mused. *What kind of man is he? And what will become of him between now and the day when I take my revenge? Will he be disgraced for losing his ship, or rewarded for destroying a defenseless enemy? Will I find him wealthy and flourishing, or destitute on the streets?*

*Where will the River take you, Captain Picard?*

# 2

———

THE NEED TO EXTEND THE SHUTTLES' WARP FIELDS
to encompass their trains of escape pods reduced their effective range. They made it only six light-years from Maxia
Zeta before one of them suffered drive failure, requiring the
rest to drop to impulse as well. Picard could only hope it
was enough to take them out of the territory of an enemy
who attacked without warning or mercy, for the next step
was to fire up the distress beacon and wait. At this range,
deep in unexplored space with no subspace relays to boost
the signal, it would be weeks before rescue could come.

In the first few days, the main order of business was arranging for basic survival—inventorying the shuttles' resources, rationing their power, repairing damage they had
sustained in the battle, treating injuries. Two of those who
had escaped the *Stargazer* died days later from burns that
Greyhorse could have healed easily in a fully equipped
sickbay. Picard reluctantly had their bodies beamed into
space, memorializing them as best he could before the
shuttle trains moved on. The words blurred together in Picard's mind with those he had delivered on the first day, in
tribute to the twenty-two others who had lost their lives at
Maxia Zeta.

For the next few weeks, the crew tried to keep occupied as best they could. Ben Zoma worked to keep them active and engaged, to shore up morale by trading stories and playing games. Many made a game effort to continue the *Stargazer's* mission of research, improving their star charts and studying the local phenomena. But all Picard could think of when he looked at the astrometric scans was whether they revealed any potential hiding places within the shuttles' limited warp range, in case the enemy attacked again.

Who were they? Why had they struck without warning? How could they have caught him so flat-footed, turned his stalwart steed and companion of twenty-two years into a flaming wreck in under five minutes? Why hadn't he had shields up as a precaution? Why had he been so hasty in authorizing the warp gravity assist that brought him so close to the Jovian's moon? Why hadn't he fought back sooner?

For Picard, no matter how much Ben Zoma and the others tried to keep him occupied, the weeks of waiting were an endless loop of questions. What could he have done differently? What would he do now if they came back? How could he face the families of Vigo, Stroman, T'Moni, Yojaleya, Suranyi, Ki'hiut, and all the others? He knew his self-recriminations were harming crew morale, but he could barely bring himself to put on a brave face and tell them everything was going to be all right. Not when all he could think to say when he met their eyes was *I'm sorry.*

As the weeks wore on, morale became a moot issue anyway as power, air, and food reserves began to thin, requiring the survivors to stay quiet and still to conserve energy. Sensors had to be shut down, astrometric studies of the sector deferred for future expeditions. Lights were kept dim, oxygen turned low, and the survivors were left with little to do beyond lying still with their own grief, fears, and self-recriminations. Fights began to break out, stifled mainly by the lack of space to wage them in or oxygen to fuel them.

These were the conditions in which Picard celebrated his fiftieth birthday, nearly two months into their ordeal. No one was in any condition to celebrate. *Serves me right for tempting fate,* Picard thought.

It took nearly ten weeks for a rescue ship to come: seven for the signal to reach a Federation transponder, another two for the Starfleet vessel *Ceres* to travel out so far from home, days more for it to track down a cluster of tiny shuttles and pods lost in the immensity of the void. Picard did not even remember being rescued. When he came to in the *Ceres* sickbay, they told him that he had weakly answered their hails and thanked them, but if so, he had done it in a semi-conscious state that left no imprint on his long-term memory. They let him sleep after that, tending to the injuries and malnutrition of his crew. They assured him that every survivor was on the way to making a full recovery. "Not all of us," he heard himself reply.

After ten weeks' experience with the true vastness of space at sublight speeds, it was surreal to cross dozens of parsecs and reach Starbase 32 in only twelve days. Picard spent most of that time working on his deposition for the inevitable inquiry, striving to remember every detail of the day he longed to forget, to mold a frantic jumble of perceptions into a coherent explanation for what had happened. He knew the others were required to do the same, but he had no wish to prejudice their recall with his own or vice-versa, so he declined to discuss it with them. He came forth and interacted with them at mealtimes to the extent that seemed obligatory, but mostly he secluded himself in his quarters, feeling it was a sham to act as though he were still their captain.

Seeing Starbase 32 again felt like history repeating itself. For the second time in as many years, Picard and his crew had taken refuge here after a disaster. Except that last time, they had returned missing only one nacelle and one crewman—never mind that the crewman had been one of Picard's dearest friends. Looking back now, it felt like a dress rehearsal for the real thing.

The flood of condolence messages from old friends scattered across two quadrants—Marta Batanides, Cory Zweller, Donald Varley, Walker Keel, Elias Vaughn, Bob DeSoto, David Gold, even his sister-in-law Marie (who often wrote him though they had never met in person, what with the state of things between the *frères Picard*)—simply drove home the magnitude of his loss. Of his failure to protect his crew. He could barely bring himself to open the letter from Beverly Crusher, for whom this must have been a brutal reminder of his failure to protect her husband. It proved an innocuous enough note of condolence, but through the detached, boilerplate words, he could tell that she still had not forgiven him for Jack. On that, they were in complete agreement, now more than ever.

The second memorial service was harder than the first. There had been time for the families of the dead to travel to the starbase, and Picard had to look them in the eyes and try to convince them that their loved ones' deaths had been meaningful in some way. He retained little memory of his words, but doubted they had been convincing.

Afterwards, Phillipa was there. She was waiting for him when he reached his quarters, looking as irritatingly lovely as ever, though not as endearingly smug. "I didn't want to come to you with everyone around," she explained. "In case you . . . wanted to talk in private. . . ." Then she looked closer, beneath Picard's reserved exterior, and simply took him in her arms. They did avail themselves of the privacy of his quarters, but did very little talking until the next morning.

It was history repeating itself once more. Picard had met Phillipa Louvois during the inquiry after Jack's death. She had been a friend of Jack's at the Academy, and they had spent hours trading stories that soon branched out into lively debates on any number of issues. Phillipa had spent much of her youth on Tellar and had definitely picked up the Tellarite fondness for a good argument. She saw Picard's dignified self-assurance as arrogance and his idealism as self-righteousness, and was irresistibly driven to deflate his pretensions. But their passionate debates had soon evolved into other forms of passion, and Picard had discovered that she could be a source of great comfort and kindness when she let her guard down. The time they had spent together had done much to heal his grief over Jack—and to distract him from his guilt at his unresolved feelings for Beverly. Showing Jack's body to Beverly at her insistence, listening to her claim to forgive him and thank him while he was racked with doubt over whether his jealousy had led him to save Pug Joseph instead of Jack, had been the worst ordeal of his life. By contrast, Phillipa had beaten some sense into him, using her most scathing forensic skills to convince him he was a fool for believing he had sacrificed his friend on purpose—and using other skills to convince him that maybe Beverly Crusher wasn't so uniquely remarkable a woman after all.

This time, though, Phillipa had less comfort to offer beyond the physical. "You know there's going to be a court-martial," she told him over breakfast, her normal bluntness back in full force.

He looked up in surprise. "A court-martial? I know a court of inquiry is routine when a ship is destroyed, but—"

"That's just it, Jean-Luc. The *Stargazer* wasn't just destroyed, it was *lost*. As in misplaced. As in, you just up and *left* it there in demonstrably hostile territory."

"It was spiraling down into the gas giant!" he protested.

"Did you actually see it fall in?"

"No, but it's simple Newtonian mechanics!"

"What if someone intercepted it before it crashed?"

"We saw no evidence of that."

"That doesn't prove it didn't happen."

"Phillipa, what the hell are you saying?"

She caught onto the anger in his tone and moderated her own. "Look. I'm not accusing you of anything. I'm just saying that in a case like this, there's cause for concern. Without knowing for certain what happened to the ship, a fuller examination of the evidence is necessary to compensate. A general court-martial is a way to do that on the record, to assure the public and Starfleet alike that no possibility of wrongdoing or negligence was overlooked."

"So I have to prove I wasn't negligent?" he shot back. "Guilty until proven innocent?"

"Of course not. Not legally. But let's face it, people are going to wonder. Be honest, would *you* trust a captain who came back without his ship? Who couldn't even confirm it didn't fall into enemy hands?"

"I'd give him the benefit of the doubt, surely."

*"Khrught!"* she cursed in Tellarite. "You're the most smug, condescending man I know. You'd be the first to judge him for falling short of perfection."

He glared. "If I believed he'd had no other choice—"

"Exactly. You'd need to be convinced of that. Everyone would. And a court-martial is a way to do that, because it gets the facts on the record for everyone to see. It's like I keep telling you—the adversarial system is useful. The skeptics want to see that their suspicions are being addressed, and if their side gets a full and fair chance to prove itself and still loses on the facts, then they're more likely to be convinced. Plus it's cathartic to get those doubts out in the open—not just for the spectators, but for the captain and crew as well. Hell, most captains in a situation like yours welcome a court-martial, even demand it." She narrowed her eyes at him. "And you should too, Jean-Luc—not just to convince everyone else, but to convince yourself. I know you—you've never been able to tolerate anything less than perfection from yourself . . . let alone from anybody else," she couldn't resist adding. "And now you've just had the biggest failure of your career. More than anyone else, *you* need to see Jean-Luc Picard face judgment and put any doubts to rest."

Phillipa was right. The court of inquiry, led by Starbase 32's commander Naomi Jerusalmi, found cause to deliver three charges against Jean-Luc Picard: *Through negligence, suffering a Starfleet vessel to be hazarded*, the specification being that he took the ship into an unknown and potentially hostile environment without the precaution of raising shields; *through negligence, employing excessive force*, the specification being that he used insufficient restraint in destroying the hostile vessel rather than attempting to disable it; and *culpable inefficiency in the performance of duty*, specifically the duty of ensuring that his vessel did not fall into enemy hands. All three charges could bring several months in the brig were he to be convicted, and either of the first two could lead to his dismissal from the service.

But Jerusalmi, a compact, salt-and-pepper-haired admiral with jovial features, reassured Picard in much the same terms Phillipa had, stressing that it was essentially a routine precaution whenever there was even the suggestion of negligence. "Hell, usually that suggestion comes from the captain's own deposition. Because good captains are their own worst critics." She gave him a wistful look. "I can see it in your face as well as your deposition, you're blaming yourself for this. And I find that very reassuring. It's the ones who *don't* blame themselves who are more likely to be guilty of wrongdoing."

Jerusalmi was free to say this because regulations forbade an accusing party from convening or sitting on a court-martial—a regulation instituted in the late twenty-third century to guard against conflicts of interest. She explained that the starbase's JAG division commander, Captain Sartak, was the convening authority. He would detail a panel of officers of at least commander's rank to decide the questions of fact in the case, a judge advocate to instruct the panel on questions of law, and JAG officers to serve as trial and defense counsel. Picard would have one Starfleet counsel detailed to him, but could bring in a civilian defender through his own efforts or request any reasonably available officer to serve as his counsel, either alone or with the detailed officer staying on as associate counsel.

# THE BURIED AGE

"Then I would like to request Commander Phillipa Louvois as my counsel, Admiral," he answered promptly. She was a tough and cunning arguer, as he well knew, and it would be a boon to have her on his side. Moreover, he wanted to do this with the help of someone he knew and trusted.

Jerusalmi checked her records and frowned. "I'm afraid that won't be possible, Jean-Luc. It seems that Commander Louvois is . . . not available."

It was clear she wasn't telling him everything. "Admiral?"

She sighed. "Our JAG office works fast. She's already been detailed as associate trial counsel."

He chose to be obtuse. "In which trial?"

"In yours, Jean-Luc. She's going to be prosecuting you."

He stared at Jerusalmi in disbelief. "But . . . Admiral, that can't be! Phillipa and I . . . well, we're . . . good friends." He could tell she saw right through him, but that only underlined his point. "Wouldn't that be a conflict of interest?"

The admiral chuckled. "So would having her as your defense counsel . . . *if* this were a civilian court. In that case, a personal relationship with the accused would be grounds for recusal. But we're officers, Captain Picard. We undertake the tasks we're commanded to perform, and we do them to the best of our ability regardless of personal concerns, or face charges of dereliction of duty. Commander Louvois has been ordered to be your prosecutor, so that is what she will be. And from this point on, you are to have no communication with her except for official court business. Whatever relationship you and Commander Louvois may have had before, for the duration of this court-martial it does not exist—had better not exist, if you want the commander to keep her rank and position, never mind your own." She softened her tone. "Whether it exists again afterwards . . . the two of you will have to figure that out for yourselves."

When Phillipa Louvois arrived at the home of Captain Thomas Salisbury for their second day of pretrial prep, she found him already busy reviewing the logs of the court of inquiry. At the moment, the *Stargazer*'s helm officer, Idun Asmund—*former* helm officer, Phillipa corrected—was on the screen. *"So you were still at warp when you made the maneuver around the fifth planet?"* Admiral Jerusalmi asked.

*"Yes, ma'am."*

*"What was the purpose of the maneuver?"*

*"It's basic helm doctrine. Altering warp field geometry to change direction while at warp puts stress on the vessel."*

*" 'Faster than light, no left or right.' "*

Phillipa recognized the mnemonic from first-year flight training. On-screen, Asmund clearly did as well, but frowned in disapproval. *"To put it crudely."*

*"This stress, is it dangerous to the vessel?"*

*"Under normal circumstances, no. In conditions of severe gravimetric turbulence it could fracture a ship's hull, but usually there's no immediate danger. The concern is more to do with the cumulative buildup of hull stresses over time. The Stargazer is—was—an older vessel, so the captain preferred to keep such stresses to a minimum when feasible."*

*"And in this case?"*

*"The Jovian's gravity curved space and subspace themselves. So the ship could simply follow that curvature around the planet without having to change its own warp geometry at all."*

"And why," Phillipa couldn't resist asking, "was Picard in such an all-fired hurry to get there?"

Salisbury turned, pausing the playback. "Ah, you're here. That's definitely one of the key questions we need to explore. Was it necessary to draw so close to the Jovian and its moons, when scanners couldn't rule out the possibility of an alien presence on those moons due to the refractory minerals?"

Phillipa pursed her lips. "That'll be hard to prove, Captain. The defense will argue that at that range, the sensors wouldn't have been able to distinguish refractory blind spots from null readings. What we need to press them on is why they had to be at warp that close to their destination. And most of all, why they didn't have shields up as a precaution."

The slim, white-haired Englishman thought it over for a moment. "Let's focus on the latter. Had shields been up, the former would not be an issue."

"But if they'd approached more slowly, they could've detected the blind spots and been more alert."

"The defense will counter that it's an incredible fluke of luck that a ship at sublight was even able to target a ship at warp in the first place. If it hadn't been coming at them head-on, it would've been virtually impossible. Under most circumstances, traveling at warp would make the ship safer from sublight attack."

"If Picard had been concerned about being safe, he would've had the shields up. We need to play up the warp approach *and* the lowered shields together. Along with Picard's comments from the bridge log just prior to the attack, they paint a picture of recklessness, of a hotheaded captain too eager to rush into adventure and not watching out for his safety."

Salisbury stared at her. "And I thought you liked the man."

That brought her up short. The reminder of her feelings threatened to overturn the careful compartmentalization she'd striven to erect. "That's beside the point, Captain, and I'd appreciate it if you left it out of our discussions. I know my duty, and I will not let personal feelings interfere with it."

"All right."

"And even if I do like him," she couldn't resist adding, "I've always believed that you don't do people any kindness by staying quiet about their mistakes. If he screwed this up, I have just as much obligation either way to convince both him and Starfleet of that."

"All right, I said. Don't overargue a case, counselor."

His quiet but firm chastisement made her flush. Knowing when to stop remained her biggest problem. "Yes, sir." She cleared her throat and changed the subject. "I almost for-got—I was just coming to inform you, they've selected the members of the court. Admiral R'Miia, Captain Gof, and Captain Sudarmono."

"I see. Thank you."

"Kind of a small panel."

"Not uncommon out on starbases, particularly when a captain is on trial. Only so many officers of sufficient rank within range. But they should be quite sufficient, especially with Judge Advocate Sartak there to advise them on the legal niceties."

"R'Miia will be a tough one to sway," Phillipa opined. "Caitians are hard to read—that whole feline enigma thing. It'll be hard to tell whether we're scoring points with her. But she's got, like, nine thousand great-grandchildren, so maybe if we play up the angle of a captain failing to protect the surrogate family of his crew, we could get somewhere. Gof will be easier. He's a seasoned veteran, spent years on the Cardassian front. A military man through and through." It was a symptom of how vast the Federation had become that most of Starfleet was still on an essentially peaceful footing even though intermittent war had raged along the Cardassian border for over a decade. But those who had served on the Cardassian front were a hardened, cynical lot, and Phillipa was glad to have one on the panel. Picard was a peace-loving explorer through and through, perhaps even to a dangerous fault, and this battle-hardened Bolian's perspective could help to expose that. "The excessive-force charge will be tough to sell him on," she went on, "but there's no way he'd sanction leaving a ship intact in enemy territory. As for Sudarmono—"

"Phillipa," Salisbury interrupted. "What are you doing?"

She cocked her head. "Sizing up the panel. Strategizing how to win."

His pale blue eyes pierced hers. "We're not here to 'win,'

Commander," he said, his frail voice gaining strength. "We're participants in a search for the truth. We 'win' by ensuring that the members of the court are provided with a full accounting of the evidence and arguments on both sides so that they may make an informed, responsible decision for themselves—not by manipulating them into taking our side whether the defendant is guilty or not! These are not the dark ages when prosecutors routinely framed innocent defendants simply to bolster their own win-loss records!"

She winced as anger filled his normally level voice. "Of course, sir. I understand that. I just want to . . ." She trailed off, not knowing how to finish. The simple fact was, she did want to win. *But not just for its own sake,* she assured herself. "I'm just trying to do my duty as conscientiously as possible. I don't want you to think I'm slacking off because of my past relationship with the defendant."

"That's commendable, Phillipa. But take care you don't overcompensate. Your first duty is to the truth. Not to proving a point or totting up wins on your scorecard." He paused to let his point sink in. "Make no mistake—this will be an aggressive prosecution. There were a number of very serious questions raised by the court of inquiry, and I intend to pursue those questions to the fullest. But if we are to prove our case, we shall prove it on the facts. A courtroom is a place to seek the truth, not an arena for lawyers to battle for dominance."

She looked down so he wouldn't see the anger in her eyes. "Yes, sir," she said simply. But she was thinking, *I'll show him.*

# 3

---

IN RETROSPECT, IT WAS PROBABLY JUST AS WELL
that Picard's request for Phillipa as his defense counsel had
been preempted. The JAG officer assigned to his case instead was Captain T'Lara, a centenarian Vulcan whose experience in the courtroom extended back before Picard was
even born. Her performance on the first day of the court-
martial quickly reassured Picard that he was in excellent
hands.

Captain Salisbury spent most of the first day calling
members of the *Stargazer's* bridge crew to testify to the
events at Maxia Zeta, his line of interrogation leading to the
suggestion that Picard had been negligent in approaching an
unknown star system without shields raised. This became
clearer when Salisbury called retired Captain Grev as an expert on starship procedures, evoking testimony from the
grizzled Tellarite about his years on the Tholian and Cardassian fronts, leading to his opinion that any unknown situation should be ventured into cautiously, with defenses
ready. But T'Lara dissected Grev's testimony easily on cross-
examination, forcing him to admit that his examples applied
to systems of known enemy affiliation and were not necessarily applicable to an exploration scenario. She moved suc-

cessfully to have Grev disallowed as an expert on the command procedures of explorer starships as opposed to combat vessels, though she commended his expertise in the latter. In redirect, the prosecution evoked testimony from Grev to demonstrate that any unknown system was potentially a hazardous one. In recross, T'Lara asked him: "Are you aware, sir, of any instances of Starfleet vessels encountering dangerous vessels or phenomena in interstellar space, as opposed to within the boundaries of a star system?"

"Of course," Grev replied. T'Lara then cited several examples of starships destroyed or crippled in what was thought to be empty space. In each case, he acknowledged his awareness of the incident, confirming it for the record.

"So life-threatening phenomena may be encountered anywhere in the galaxy, at any given moment."

"I would say so, yes."

"Tell me, Captain—is it feasible for a starship to have its full shields raised on a constant basis?"

Grev was forced to concede that this was impractical, and that regulations pertaining to shield operation only specified that they be raised at the moment a threat became evident. Later, in cross-examining Gilaad Ben Zoma, T'Lara would evoke the statement that Picard's very first order upon detection of the hostile vessel had been to raise the shields.

But first, Salisbury questioned Ben Zoma on the specifics of the battle, calling particular attention to the sequence of events. "So it was not until some time after the second attack that Picard first mentioned arming the weapons?" he asked the former first officer.

T'Lara raised an objection to this new line of questioning. "Irrelevant. Delay in arming the weapons is not listed among the charges and specifications against Captain Picard."

"It goes to demonstrate an overall pattern of insufficient readiness, Your Honor," Salisbury countered, "and is thus directly relevant to the charge of negligent hazarding." Sartak allowed the line of examination.

But again, T'Lara was able to dissect it with relative ease.

In cross-examination, she simply asked, "Are you familiar with Starfleet Directive Zero-One-Zero, Commander?"

"Yes, ma'am," Ben Zoma replied.

"Would you recite it, please?"

"'Before engaging alien species in battle, any and all attempts to make first contact and achieve nonmilitary resolution must be made.'"

"Indeed." T'Lara then took him through a restatement of Picard's actions in the battle, demonstrating that he concentrated first on evasion and damage control, second on attempting contact and identification, and on the use of force only as a last resort.

By the end of the first day, T'Lara had succeeded in making the prosecution's case seem rather weak. Still, even T'Lara's skilled defense could not entirely reassure Picard that he had not been too reckless or slow, had not let his ship and crew down in some way.

The next day, the prosecution ramped up its case. This time, Phillipa led the questioning, since the elderly Salisbury claimed his voice was failing him. However, Picard had to wonder if Phillipa had not been sent out as the attack dog, to hit hard in a way the genteel Salisbury was less suited for. She began by recalling Ben Zoma for redirect examination. "Yesterday you told us about Directive Zero-One-Zero," she said. "Could you tell us Directive Zero-One-Two?"

Ben Zoma paused before reciting the regulation. "'When engaged in combat with an unknown alien species, all attempts must be made to resolve said combat using minimum necessary force.'"

"Is there a discussion section following this directive in the manual?"

"Yes, ma'am."

"And does it speak to the reasoning behind this directive?"

"Yes, ma'am."

"Could you be more specific?"

"It points out the importance of achieving communication with the hostiles so that the conflict can be resolved through diplomatic means."

"So that the reasons for the conflict can be understood and resolved."

"Yes, ma'am."

"Because such things are often the result of misunderstandings—even territorial intrusions by the Starfleet vessel itself."

"Objection," T'Lara said. "Speculative and prejudicial."

But Ben Zoma was already voicing an objection of his own. "This was no territorial defense, it was an ambush! They made no attempt to identify themselves, gave us no chance—"

"The witness will restrain himself," Sartak ordered, keeping his Vulcan calm but speaking forcefully enough to get through to Ben Zoma. But Louvois was finished with him.

Indeed, it was young Lieutenant Schuster who bore the brunt of her interrogation over the hostile ship's destruction. "Why six torpedoes, Lieutenant? If it only took three torpedoes to bring down their shields, why did you fire three more?"

"Objection. Incompetent," T'Lara said. "The lieutenant has already testified that all six torpedoes were fired as a single volley."

"I'll rephrase the question. Why did you fire six torpedoes when you did not know that all six would be necessary to bring down their shields?"

Schuster was looking very guilty. "I followed the tactical computer's recommendation, ma'am."

"Because your training is in sciences, not tactical."

"Yes, ma'am. But I do understand computers and sensors. The recommendation was based on a sensor reading of the enemy ship's shield strength and hull composition."

"But didn't you testify that the sensors were damaged, their readings fragmentary?"

"Yes, ma'am."

"Then how did you know the scans weren't in error?"

"Objection. Prejudicial and calls for speculation. Starfleet does not expect omniscience from its officers," T'Lara added. "Only that they make decisions using the best information available."

"Are you objecting, counsel, or starting your closing argument early?"

"Counsel will direct all comments to the court," Sartak reminded Louvois. "However, the points on both sides are fair. Move on."

"So . . . the tactical computer recommended six torpedoes to cope with the shields."

"Yes, ma'am."

"With or without phasers?"

"Pardon me, ma'am?"

"Were those computations based on the assumption that the torpedoes would be fired alone, or were they based on the assumption that the torpedoes would be fired along with a phaser barrage?"

Schuster flushed, struggling to remember. "I'm . . . not sure, ma'am," he was forced to admit.

Louvois patted him on the hand. "That's all right, Lieutenant. You're a science officer, forced to take over a station you weren't expert in. Don't worry about it." She took on a quizzical expression. "Now—who was it who assigned you to take over tactical?"

"Cap-Captain Picard, ma'am."

"Why you? Why not a more experienced officer like Ben Zoma or Asmund?"

"Objection. Calls for speculation." As usual, T'Lara's objection came almost instantaneously.

"Sustained."

"All right, let's go back a bit. You fired full phasers and six torpedoes simultaneously, correct?"

"Yes, ma'am."

"Even though you weren't sure whether the tactical computer's recommendation was for both to be fired simultaneously."

"Uh . . . yes, ma'am."

"So why did you fire both?" Schuster was reluctant to respond. "Answer the question, Lieutenant."

"B-because Captain Picard ordered me to."

"He ordered both phasers and torpedoes fired?"

"Yes, ma'am."

"Do you think that was excessive?"

"Objection. Calls for a conclusion."

Louvois nodded toward T'Lara. "Let me put that another way. What happened to the hostile ship?"

"It was destroyed, ma'am."

"By 'destroyed,' do you mean that it was rendered lifeless and nonfunctional, or that it was actually physically destroyed?"

"It was physically destroyed. From what I saw and read on the sensors, I would say most of its mass was vaporized by the energy released in the annihilation reaction, and the remaining portions were probably mostly disintegrated or melted by the shock and heat of impact."

Louvois paused for a beat. "What would have been the minimum damage necessary to inflict on the opposing ship to save the *Stargazer* from destruction? In your opinion as a science officer."

Again, Schuster was slow to respond. "I would have to say . . . effective destruction of their weapons and propulsion systems. More realistically, knocking out their main power systems, since we didn't know the ship design well enough to target more specifically."

"So the level of destruction you did inflict was much greater than what would have sufficed to do the job."

"I . . . yes, ma'am."

"In other words, it was in excess of what was necessary."

Schuster winced. "Yes, ma'am," he said through clenched teeth.

"Why did—" She broke off, rethinking her wording. "Did

Captain Picard explain to you why he ordered both phasers and torpedoes fired?"

"No, ma'am."

"Do you know if he explained it to anyone else?"

"No, ma'am."

"Do you think he should?"

"Objection!" T'Lara was on her feet in a Vulcan heartbeat. "It is incompetent for trial counsel to insinuate that Captain Picard is obligated to speak in his own defense. I move for a finding of misconduct against trial counsel."

"Your honor, I did not offer any such opinion. I simply asked if the witness did."

"The insinuation remains either way."

The disruption was sufficient to make Sartak call for a recess while he deliberated. When the court reconvened after lunch, Sartak declared, in effect, that Louvois had just barely dodged a finding of misconduct by her wording, but that she was on notice and further irregularities would not be tolerated.

Afterwards, Phillipa changed her tack, concentrating on the third charge, Picard's alleged failure to ensure that the ship was scuttled. She called Simenon to the stand, and the engineer testified to everything Picard had attempted, first to save his ship, then to ensure its destruction once abandonment became inevitable. He explained why they could not have risked returning to the ship or sparing a shuttle warp core to destroy it, and stated that its descent into the Jovian's atmosphere was certain in any case. "And long-range scans saw no sign of hostile ships in the time it would've taken the *Stargazer*'s orbit to decay."

"You didn't exactly see the *first* hostile ship, though, did you?" Louvois countered, promptly adding, "I withdraw the question" before T'Lara could object. She went on to challenge the theory that the hostile had been hidden by refractory minerals rather than by some intrinsic stealth property, forcing Simenon to admit that he could not be certain no alien vessel had retrieved the *Stargazer* before its plunge into the Jovian. She also questioned his conclusions about the seriousness of the plutonium contamination, grilling him on whether one or two engineers in environmental suits could have withstood the radiation long enough to ensure the ship's destruction. Simenon insisted that it would have been too hazardous and that the controls most likely would have been too damaged by the fires. But she spun enough hypothetical scenarios for how it might have been done to leave him doubting his own certainty. On cross, T'Lara managed to show that her hypotheticals had too great a risk for too little probability of success. But Louvois argued on redirect that the probabilities were far from certain, and that Captain Picard had often taken on risky situations against his engineer's judgment and succeeded. Had Simenon been mammalian, he would have been swimming in his own sweat by the time she was finished with him.

Afterwards, a bit surprisingly, she called Doctor Greyhorse to the stand, taking some time to establish his credentials as an expert in space psychology. She called his attention to Picard's final log entry: *"We are forced to abandon our vessel. May she find her way without us."*

"Tell me, Doctor," she asked. "Is that a statement you would expect to hear from someone who intends or expects that vessel to be destroyed?"

"Objection. Calls for a conclusion."

"Hypothetically, I mean. In general terms, does such a statement seem consistent with the intention to ensure the destruction of the vessel in question?"

"No, it does not."

"Your witness, counselor."

Invoking Greyhorse's expertise in psychology, T'Lara questioned whether starship personnel were prone to anthropomorphize their vessels, and whether Picard's "May she find her way" constituted evidence of such anthropomorphism. After Greyhorse answered in the affirmative, she asked, "In your experience, do humanoids have a tendency to invoke belief or rhetoric pertaining to life after death when faced with the demise of an individual they care for?"

"Objection, relevance!" Louvois called.

"Overruled," Sartak said. "The witness will answer."

"Yes, ma'am."

"So even if they know an individual is about to die, might they not speak of that individual undertaking a metaphorical or spiritual journey beyond death?"

"Yes, ma'am."

"So in your psychological opinion, Doctor, if someone expresses hope that an individual about to die will undertake such a journey successfully, would that require the speaker to believe that the individual in question will remain literally alive in some way?"

"No, ma'am. It could simply be said for the sake of comfort, or ritual."

"And given that starships are often anthropomorphized, might not the same logic apply to an equivalent statement about a starship?"

"Yes, ma'am. It's quite possible."

"Thank you, Doctor Greyhorse."


At the end of the second day, the prosecution rested. T'Lara launched into the defense's case bright and early the next morning, calling Commander Lun Minsal, a veteran Atrean science officer with an A7 computer rating, to the stand. Minsal testified that he had run a thorough series of simulations of the events at Maxia Zeta V based on the sensor logs downloaded from the *Stargazer* and the shuttles. By asking Minsal to vary the simulation parameters slightly, T'Lara was able to show the remarkable fluke by which the hostile had been able to succeed in its sneak attack at all. Had the *Stargazer* been on an even slightly different course, the attack would most likely have been a clean miss, allowing the Starfleet vessel to gain considerable distance at warp before the hostile, now in open space and detectable, could have overtaken it. Further tweaking of the simulation showed that if Picard had been even one second slower in ordering shields raised, the first salvo—hitting head-on at warp, with only the navigational deflection field in its way—would most likely have inflicted massive casualties and critical systems failure, leaving the *Stargazer* helpless and leading to its destruction with all hands in the second attack pass. The simulations further showed that the *Stargazer* could not have survived another hit, so that Picard's inspired warp-jump maneuver, using speed-of-light latency to make his ship into its own decoy, had once again saved the lives of his crew. "Have you heard of this tactic being used before?" T'Lara asked.

"No, ma'am," Minsal said.

"Pardon me, I was not specific enough. Have you heard of it being used prior to stardate 32217.3?"

"No, ma'am."

"But did you hear of it before I requested your services as an expert witness?"

"Yes, ma'am."

"In what context?"

"It's been the talk of the fleet ever since the news came in."

"And when the members of the fleet discuss it, what do they call it?"

"The Picard Maneuver, ma'am."

T'Lara then moved on to Minsal's assessment of the hostile ship, based on the reconstructed sensor readings. She focused specifically on its shields and hull strength and whether there was any evidence that could have suggested in advance that the ship could not have survived both a phaser barrage and six torpedoes. Minsal could give no unambiguous answer; there were simply too many uncertainties about the ship's construction and power usage.

Minsal's simulations further showed that any attempt to return to the contaminated, burned-out ship and accelerate its plunge into the Jovian would have had at least a 70 percent probability of life-threatening failure. They also confirmed that atmospheric entry and burn-up within twelve days was a mathematical certainty.

Salisbury took the cross-examination, concentrating on the uncertainty in the strength of the hostile's shields and hull. He asked Minsal to adjust the parameters and showed that the torpedo barrage without phasers would probably have left the hostile ship intact and crippled. He also had Minsal repeat his simulations of alternate approach courses into the system, using them to question the wisdom of following a course that passed within essentially point-blank weapons range of an uncharted moon when a more cautious, distant approach would have given Picard plenty of warning. He had Minsal repeat the simulated attempts to retake the ship, emphasizing the nearly 30 percent probability of success, if not in restoring the ship to functionality, then at least in arranging for its total destruction without additional loss of life.

With the facts of the case examined scientifically, T'Lara saw no need to call any defense witnesses other than Jean-Luc Picard himself, at his own insistence. She had advised him that his testimony was not required, but he felt obligated to face his accusers and his crew, explain his actions, and face whatever judgment they warranted.

"How long were you captain of the *Stargazer*?" she asked him.

"Just over twenty-two years."

"In that time, were there any prior instances when your vessel came under threat of destruction when entering a system that appeared uninhabited?"

"Yes." T'Lara took him through each one. In 2339, the ship had explored a post-main-sequence star system containing technologically advanced but uninhabited remains on thousands of its planets, satellites, and asteroids. It had come under attack from an automated defense system that would have surely destroyed them had it not been eleven million years old and somewhat decayed, leaving a number of gaps in its coverage. Apparently—so science officer Valderrama discovered after they had managed to tap into the defense grid and override it—the inhabitants had abandoned their system when an attempt to halt their star's expansion into a red giant had backfired and led to massive solar eruptions. They had left their cities and habitats intact in hopes of solving the problem and returning later, and had installed the defense grid to repel any alien looters. But in their xenophobia they had programmed it too narrowly; when their descendants did return generations later, they had changed enough in language, culture, and appearance that the defense grid no longer recognized them, and they were driven away, never able to return.

"When you made your approach to this system, did you have shields raised?"

"No," Picard replied.

"What was the first sign of danger?"

"We detected a massive power buildup on an asteroid three million kilometers away, consistent with a charging weapon system."

"What was your response?"

"I ordered shields raised immediately."

"What was the result?"

"The attack came several seconds later. The ship was shaken, but damage was minor."

"I see." T'Lara paced for a moment. "You knew the system showed signs of habitation, but you approached without shields raised."

"Correct. There was no indication of current habitation, so no immediate cause for alarm."

"Did you believe there was no chance that the ship would come under threat?"

"No. I am always aware that any unknown environment poses potential risks. I and my crew remained alert at all times, and responded promptly as soon as danger presented itself."

T'Lara nodded. "At Maxia Zeta, did the system show any sign of prior or current habitation?"

"None that we could detect."

CHRISTOPHER L. BENNETT

They moved on to further examples. In 2341, the *Stargazer* had been studying an orbital irregularity in a binary system when it almost collided with the cause, a tiny quantum singularity in a chaotic figure-eight orbit around the two stars. Picard had ordered a warp jump away from the singularity, but the interaction between it and the warp field had created a time warp and quite literally blown the *Stargazer* into the middle of the next week. Picard had counted himself lucky that the ship had jumped ten days forward instead of back, thus avoiding a session with Temporal Investigations. However, subsequent attempts to engage the warp engines had subjected the ship to severe gravitational time-dilation effects centering on the warp nacelles and threatening to tear the ship apart with tidal stresses. It turned out that the warp engines were still in temporal synch with the singularity ten days in the past, pulling the ship between two different time frames. Finally, Jack Crusher had had the idea to position the ship ten light-days out from the singularity and make the engines emit a series of graviton pulses. The pulses traveled back ten days through the time warp and then spent ten days propagating through normal space out to the *Stargazer*. Once the ship was positioned at exactly the right distance (difficult to achieve with the ship trying to shake apart every time it moved), the pulses synchronized, effectively putting the warp drive back into the same temporal frame as the rest of the ship and allowing the engines to be shut down, severing the link.

"But you had some advance evidence of the singularity, did you not, due to the gravitational disturbance?" T'Lara asked. Picard acknowledged that they had, although the singularity's small size and chaotic orbit had made it impossible to pin down its exact position.

The next case was borderline: in 2345, the ship had been surveying a Neptune-like ice giant in a seemingly uninhabited system when it had taken fire from below. They had then received a transmission from the aquatic beings that inhabited its high-pressure water-ammonia mantle, beings that the sensors had missed due to their great depth. Their past interactions with Class-M-life forms had been mutually harmful due to their radically dissimilar biochemistries and psychologies, and now they wished only to be left alone. Picard had respected their wishes, regretting that he would not have the chance to study such a fascinatingly alien biosphere and culture. But, as T'Lara had him confirm, these "Polyphemians" (as Picard had dubbed them) had merely attacked as a warning rather than attempting his ship's destruction.

The final example had been in 2348. At this point, the *Stargazer*'s duties had been keeping it on patrol of the Federation's borders rather than at its usual deep-space exploration, since the Cardassians had been acting up again and drawing Starfleet resources away from other sectors. It had been during this year that Jack had married Beverly, and during the ensuing months spent close to home, Picard had seen much of the Crushers and grown closer to them both. He thus remembered it as a happy time in his life, and had given little thought over the years to the minor skirmish he now related to the court, in which several ships belonging to the Acamarian Gatherers had attacked the *Stargazer* when it stumbled upon their lair in a lifeless red-dwarf system. They had attempted an ambush, but Picard had already received reports of Gatherer raids in the area and was not taken off guard. The ships had possessed enough firepower to destroy the *Stargazer*, but Starfleet sensors and shields were better; Picard had lured them in close to the dwarf star just before it gave off one of its periodic x-ray flares, burning out their sensors and leaving them helpless. Doctor Greyhorse had treated their radiation exposure and the incident was resolved without fatalities.

"So in this case as well," T'Lara said, "you had some advance warning of danger." Picard answered yes.

T'Lara moved on to the ambush at Maxia Zeta V, focusing on why Picard chose to fire both phasers and torpedoes. "Were you not aware that an all-out attack might bring about the destruction of the hostile vessel?"

"I could not rule it out as a possibility, no."

"Did you wish to destroy the hostile vessel?"

"Not if I could reasonably avoid it. I would have preferred to incapacitate the vessel so that contact could be made and the reason for their attack determined."

"Then why did you choose to fire all your weapons at once on the first salvo? Why not begin with a phaser barrage and gauge the results before going further?"

"It was clear that their weapons were formidable—as were their sensors, to be able to strike us from impulse while we were at warp. It stood to reason that any ship with weapons that powerful would have shields able to withstand at least as much power."

"It stood to reason, but you could not be certain. Again, why not begin with a less forceful attack to confirm your assessment of their defenses?"

Picard took a deep breath and let it out in a sigh. "My ship was in flames around me. The fusion reactor was surging, interfering with ship's systems. The weapons were relying on jury-rigged power circuits. We were flying half-blind. Our weapons, our remaining shields or sensors, any of them could have failed at any moment. I knew that if we did not neutralize the threat with the first shot . . . we might not have a second. As I saw it, there was no option but to use the maximum possible force in defense of my vessel. I deeply regret that this resulted in the loss of all personnel aboard that vessel, and that the reasons for their attack may never be known. And I profoundly hope that this incident does not preclude the Federation's chances for future peaceful contact with their species, whoever they may be. But the commander of that ship left me with no other option. It was, quite simply, them or us."

"That is what your command judgment told you."

"What it told me then, and what it still tells me now."

"Thank you, Captain Picard. Your witness, counsel."

At the trial counsels' table, Salisbury began to rise, clearing his throat, but Louvois interrupted him and a hushed debate followed. Phillipa seemed to be trying to persuade Salisbury of something he was reluctant to accede to. Finally, he relented—and Phillipa came forward to the witness stand.

Picard was shocked. She had *wanted* to be the one to cross-examine him? To face him directly and try to prove his guilt? He couldn't believe it. She had been aggressive in plying her case with other witnesses, to be sure, but this . . . If she had been ordered to do it, that would be one thing, but she had actively fought for it. He stared at Phillipa as though he had no idea who she was.

"Captain Picard, how many previously uncharted star systems would you say you've surveyed in your twenty-two years as a Starfleet captain?"

It was an innocuous enough beginning, and he allowed himself a glimmer of hope. "I would say . . . close to three hundred."

"By my count, the number is actually three hundred and fifty-six. Not counting Maxia Zeta. Does that sound about right?"

"I suppose so."

"In fact, you have one of the fullest, most distinguished records of any explorer captain of the past century. Isn't that so?"

"I wouldn't presume to say."

"Will counsel stipulate to that characterization of Captain Picard's record?"

T'Lara narrowed her gaze, but since the proposition seemed innocuous enough, she gave a slight nod. "So stipulated."

"Three hundred and fifty-six systems in twenty-two years. That's an average of roughly one every three weeks."

"Nothing so regular as that. We might chart several dozen adjacent systems in the course of a month, then at another time be on border patrol duty or starbase layover."

"Of course," she said tightly. "Please wait until I ask the question. You're the defendant here, not a guest lecturer."

"Objection."

"If counsel has a question," Sartak advised, "she will please proffer it."

"After all those surveys, Captain, doesn't it all start to feel a bit routine?"

"I beg your pardon?"

"When you've been doing the same thing for decades on end, doesn't it by definition become a routine?"

Picard smiled, shaking his head. "Oh, no. Every system is different. There's always the thrill of wondering what you'll find."

Her voice hardened. "Captain, isn't it true that your own log entry of Stardate 32217.3 described 'a routine survey mission into the Maxia Zeta star system'?"

"Yes, it is."

"So in your own words, it was a routine experience."

"I was speaking procedurally, not emotionally."

"All right, let's take the emotional statement you just made about the thrill that's always present. If it's always there, doesn't even that thrill become familiar and expected?"

"I wouldn't put it that way . . ."

"If you always feel something, Captain, doesn't it there-fore become familiar and expected?"

He sighed. "In a sense, you could say that."

"Yes or no?"

"Yes, if you insist." He barely kept his irritation in check. Phillipa could always get under his skin.

She smiled, leaning in close. "There, was that so hard?" Resuming a normal stance, she continued, "So: you're enter-ing an uncharted system for the three hundred and fifty-sev-enth time. There's nothing particularly striking or exotic about the system. It's just another day in the life. The bridge logs show you joking with your crew about your birth-day . . . your hairline . . . even your past romantic involve-ments." She gave no outward acknowledgment of the fact that she herself was the "romantic involvement" in question. "You didn't exchange a single word with your crew about the need for caution and alertness as they entered an unknown system, did you?"

"I trust my crew. They don't need me to remind them of the obvious."

"In other words, you're confirming that you didn't specifically discuss those topics?"

"No, we did not."

"Indeed, you spoke of your enthusiasm at the adventure the system offered. You even spoke of going rock climbing on a world you hadn't even charted yet, and needed your first officer to remind you of the need for safety equipment, isn't that right?"

"I didn't 'need' him to remind me."

"Answer the question. Is that not what he said after you mentioned rock climbing?"

"Yes, it was."

"The truth is, you were eager for adventure. You weren't thinking about caution, you were looking for your next thrill, isn't that right?"

"They aren't mutually exclusive!"

"Isn't that right?"

"No, it is not!"

"You weren't hoping for excitement?"

"Not to the exclusion of caution!"

"Answer the question!"

T'Lara was on her feet. "Objection! Counsel is badgering the witness."

"Sustained."

Phillipa took a breath. "We've all heard the testimony that there was no way of anticipating that an attack would come from the Jovian's moon as you passed it. Would you say that was accurate?"

"Yes, I would."

"At this point I would like to play back the *Stargazer* bridge log at time index fifteen-oh-eight."

She worked a padd, and the log visual appeared on the courtroom screen. *"If the planet was shattered,"* came Vigo's words, *"it's unlikely any ruins would have survived."* Picard watched himself reply, *"Perhaps they settled one or more of the system's moons before the cataclysm."*

Phillipa turned back to Picard. "Approximately forty-five seconds later, the ship was attacked from one of the system's moons. Do you still wish to say you were unaware of the possibility of a threat from one of the moons?"

"I was speaking of the possibility of long-abandoned ruins, not an imminent threat."

"Didn't you tell the court earlier today of an incident where the *Stargazer* was almost destroyed by a defense system from long-abandoned ruins?"

"Yes, I did, but here we had no reason to think—"

"No, you didn't think at all, did you?"

"Objection."

"Sustained."

"You didn't evaluate the risk and judge it to be minimal," Louvois went on. "You didn't even contemplate the risk, did you?"

"There was no basis for more than routine alertness."

"So you don't feel there was anything wrong with your actions on stardate 32217.3?"

"Everything I did was in accordance with regulations."

"I'm not asking about regulations, I'm asking what you feel. Do you believe you did enough to safeguard your ship and crew?"

"I haven't been able to think of anything I could have done to prevent this."

"That's what you've rationalized after the fact. What do you *believe*?"

"Objection, badgering."

Sartak nodded. "The question has been adequately answered."

Phillipa reined herself in, going back to her table to take a sip of water before continuing. "Let's turn to the moments leading to the destruction of the unidentified ship. According to your own testimony, Captain, the bridge was filled with smoke and fumes during the attack. You were having trouble breathing."

"Correct."

Again, Phillipa played back a portion of the bridge log, though at this point the data were fragmentary and there were video and audio dropouts. But there was enough to support Phillipa's case. "Would you say that you show signs of disorientation?"

"Physically, yes."

"Weren't you confused mentally as well?"

"I was dazed for a moment."

"Do you think your command judgment was compromised?"

"No."

"Yet at one point you call for Vigo even after discovering that he was dead."

"It was force of habit. We served together for twenty-two years."

"So you didn't forget that he had died mere moments before?"

"I remembered it as soon as the words left my mouth."

"So you did forget!"

Picard glared at her, furious that she would use Vigo's death to score points like this. "An event like that can be hard to assimilate. Hard to believe. It takes time."

"What you're describing sounds like being in shock. Would you say you were in shock at that point?"

"No. I couldn't afford the luxury."

"How about denial? You just said it was hard to believe at first, even though you'd just seen it firsthand. That's denial, right?"

"I suppose so."

"What else were you in denial about?"

"Objection. Begs the question."

"I'll rephrase." Phillipa paced away, then turned back to

ask her next question. "You testified that you ordered both phasers and torpedoes fired because you believed the destruction of your ship was imminent if you did not stop the attacker then and there, correct?"

"That's right."

"So at the time, you were fully conscious of the likelihood of total defeat? Of your own death?"

"I have rarely been more so."

"Think back carefully. At that moment, did you truly believe your ship could be destroyed?"

"Of course I did."

She took a step away again, then spun and spoke quickly. "But after you abandoned ship, you said, 'May she find her way without us.' I submit that despite all evidence—"

"Objection!" T'Lara cried. "Beyond the scope of the direct examination of this witness."

"Sustained."

But Phillipa barreled on over their words. "—despite your obligation to destroy your ship, in your heart you could not believe it was truly possible that you could lose her. Isn't that true?"

Sartak spoke over her final words. "The objection has been sustained, counselor. You have been cautioned for your behavior before. Discipline yourself before you invite discipline upon yourself."

At the trial counsels' table, Salisbury stood and caught Phillipa's eye. Picard caught her mouthing *I can do it* to him, and after a moment he reluctantly sat down, but kept his eye on her. Phillipa simply turned back to Picard and resumed her questioning. "You are a student of ancient history, are you not?"

"I am," he replied guardedly, wondering where this was going.

"Can you tell the court how the first contact between the Menthars and the Promellians occurred?"

It was starting to become clearer. But T'Lara interrupted. "Objection. Relevance."

Louvois turned to Sartak. "The witness's awareness of historical precedents is relevant to establishing his state of mind."

"Overruled."

So Picard answered the question. "A Promellian ship unknowingly intruded into a Menthar holy system during a sacred time, and was attacked. It destroyed two of its attackers before being destroyed itself, and both sides declared war soon thereafter."

"What was the outcome of the war?"

"Both civilizations were obliterated."

Phillipa nodded. "Can you tell me how the first contact between the Federation and the Gorn occurred?"

Picard sighed. "The Federation unknowingly placed a colony in Gorn space, and the Gorn destroyed it in self-defense. The advanced Metron civilization intervened in the conflict, placing a Starfleet captain and a Gorn captain in single combat. The Starfleet captain injured the Gorn, but refused to deliver the killing stroke, thus helping to persuade the Gorn that the Federation was not an aggressor. A peaceful, if tenuous, relationship was established as a result."

"Now, then . . . in light of these examples, are you worried about the consequences of your actions at Maxia Zeta V?"

"I have no way of knowing if the situation was analogous."

"But you already said on direct that you hoped the incident would not damage our chances of peaceful contact with the species whose ship you destroyed."

"Yes, I said that. But we can only speculate what might happen."

"But we know what did happen at Maxia Zeta. Are you satisfied with your actions there?"

"I'm satisfied that I had no other choice."

"Do you consider the incident a success?"

Picard glared. "Of course not. I lost my ship and twenty-four good people."

"So you consider it a failure?"

"I consider it a tragedy."

"Don't you wonder every day if you could have done something differently?"

"Of course I do. But there was nothing else I could have done."

"You don't believe you were reckless and overconfident?"

"No."

"You don't fear your judgment was compromised?"

"No!"

"You don't wonder if you overlooked some way to save or scuttle your ship?"

"We did everything we could! You heard Simenon testify to that, you got it out of him yourself!"

"Of course I'd expect your crew to back up their captain's version of events."

"Objection!" T'Lara shot to her feet. "Improper impeachment of witnesses!"

"Sustained."

But Phillipa didn't break her stride. "You don't feel you failed your ship and crew?"

"No!"

"Then why do you still wake up in the middle of the night yelling for their forgiveness?!"

*"Objection!"*

Salisbury was on his feet too. "Commander!"

Sartak rang the bell that rested upon his bench. "Order!"

"Your Honor," T'Lara said, "the question assumes facts not in evidence and is unfairly prejudicial. I move for a mistrial and a finding of misconduct against the assistant trial counsel."

"I shall confer with the lead trial counsel and defense counsel in chambers," Sartak announced. "This court-martial shall stand in recess until 0800 tomorrow. Dismissed," he finished, striking the bell once more.

Picard barely heard it. He was still staring at Phillipa, stunned at her betrayal. It brought him some satisfaction that she was unable to meet his eyes.

# 4

———

PHILLIPA WAITED IN SALISBURY'S OFFICE FOR
what seemed like forever, bouncing off the walls of the compact space as she tried to imagine what was going on with
the judge advocate. Finally Salisbury entered, but for some
moments he simply stared at her in quiet anger. "I don't
know what came over me," she blurted out. "I know I
crossed a line there, but—"

" 'But'?" he fired back. "You'd best stop there." He took a
shuddering breath and let it out sharply before continuing.
"I managed to persuade the judge advocate that your . . . behavior did not irreparably prejudice the members. So we've
dodged a mistrial."

She sighed in relief. "Thank you."

"I did it for the case. *Not* for you. The only reason it
wasn't deemed irreparable prejudice is because you damaged your own credibility more than Picard's." He moved
behind his desk. "The compromise is that you are removed
from the case effective immediately. A letter of reprimand
will be placed in your jacket, and you will submit to a court
of inquiry to investigate whether a charge of dereliction of
duty should be brought."

Phillipa gaped. "What? On what grounds?"

"That you allowed personal feelings to interfere with the performance of your duty."

She scoffed. "Are you kidding? I just did everything in my power to prove the guilt of a man I have feelings for! That was the job I was assigned and I did it. How can you still doubt my objectivity after that?"

"You went beyond your job, Commander. What I saw up there wasn't a trial advocate examining a defendant. It looked more like the bickering of an old married couple. I daresay you even took pleasure from it."

"I resent that, Captain."

He sighed. "Very well, I withdraw the remark. But even aside from that, you still put a personal agenda above the case."

"And what agenda is that?"

"The one you've been harping on all along. Your desire to prove that you could do your duty despite your feelings for Picard. I warned you against overcompensating and that's exactly what you did. You didn't just strive to be objective, you actively *turned* on him. My God, Phillipa, you betrayed a bedroom confidence just to score points against him in court!"

"And I acknowledge that was an error," she said with a nervous laugh.

Salisbury's eyes narrowed. "I don't think you understand just what it was. What it means. We're all fellow officers, whether JAG, starship, S.C.E., whatever. We never know when we may need to depend on each other to stay alive. So we have to know that we can trust one another.

"Commander, you just turned on your own lover, exploited one of his most vulnerable moments, simply in order to prove a point about your own abilities. After that, how can any of us trust you?"

She stared wordlessly for a time, but then gathered herself and stood straight and proud. "So that's how it is, huh? I was ordered to put my feelings aside for the job, and now I'm going to be ostracized for doing it too well? Well, if that's the kind of double standard Starfleet uses, then the hell with it. I'll save you the trouble of an inquiry." She pulled off her combadge and tossed it onto Salisbury's desk. "I'm resigning my commission."

"Phillipa!" His voice stopped her when she was halfway out the door. "Don't overreact to this. It's a serious mistake, but it doesn't have to end your career. Face up to it and learn from the consequences, and it will make you a better lawyer and a better officer."

"Face a Fleet that looks at me the way you just made it clear you do? I deserve better than that." She turned back toward the exit.

"And what does Jean-Luc Picard deserve?"

It was a while before she answered. "Better than he got from me. Luckily he's got a better lawyer than you and me put together."


The remainder of the court-martial was more sedate. T'Lara conducted a brief redirect to counter some of Phillipa's insinuations, and Salisbury declined to recross. After that, T'Lara rested, and only the closing arguments remained.

Salisbury made the case for which Phillipa had overzealously sought to lay the groundwork: that even if Picard had not provably violated the letter of regulations, even if all his decisions could be rationalized away after the fact, his behavior demonstrated a pattern of recklessness and complacency that had exposed the ship to avoidable peril and left its crew unprepared for the consequences. He stressed that exploration was as dangerous as any combat situation—often more so, for the risks involved were impossible to anticipate. "It is the nature of humans, and of many other species, that familiarity breeds contempt," he said. "Do something for too long and it can become too routine. Perhaps twenty-two years is too long for any one captain, however gifted, to remain on an explorer ship. Perhaps rotating our captains to other duties after a certain interval is important to keep them fresh, to keep us all safe.

"For we must never let our fascination with the unknown blind us to its perils. We must never let it blind us to our overriding responsibility to the safety of those under our command."

In her closing argument, T'Lara stressed the point that no negligence or violation of regulations had been proven, and that no being should be convicted on the basis of vague generalizations about what might have been avoidable. "It is always easy to second-guess a decision after the fact, when certain knowledge of its results is available," she said. "But as every starship commander knows, the results of our decisions are usually impossible to know in advance. Given the quantum nature of the universe, even the use of time travel to see future events would only reveal one possible future, and the very act of observing that potential future would alter it enough to prevent its occurrence as observed. Any event will always appear different in hindsight than in foresight. So how may we fairly evaluate the judgment of an individual in a moment of crisis? We cannot, for only those residing in the moment can truly understand the context of their decisions."

She moved on to the question of caution, acknowledging the importance of protecting one's crew, but suggesting that it was too narrow a perspective. "Is it true that the safety of oneself and one's crew overrides all other factors? Consider Directive Zero-One-Zero. It specifies unambiguously that 'any and all attempts' to make peaceful contact with an alien race must be made before combat is engaged. This does not exclude cases where the aliens attack us. Logically, if crew safety is our highest priority, then in such a case the response should be to fight back first and attempt contact only after safety is assured—if any of the aliens remain alive to contact. But this is not the case. Our own regulations make it clear that peaceful communication with other beings is our highest priority—even at the risk of our own safety.

"Indeed, the very existence of Starfleet demonstrates this principle. Were safety our overriding concern, we would explore solely through unmanned probes. Rather than risk colonizing alien worlds, we would remain in our home systems, where dismantling their asteroidal and cometary bodies would allow us to construct artificial worlds with a sufficient combined surface area to support a hundred times the Federation's current population.

"We do not do what we do to be safe. We do it for the reasons spelled out by Zefram Cochrane centuries ago: to seek out new life, and to boldly go where none has gone before. To *seek out* new life, gentlebeings. Not to face it timidly with our defenses up, but to approach it with an attitude of openness, a willingness to trust. That means coming into their star systems with our defenses down, rather than appearing to them as a threat. That means staying our hand and trying to talk even when attacked. And it means seeing unknown others as potential allies who may simply be eager to learn, rather than mortal enemies who must be deprived of our technological secrets at all costs.

"It is true that this attitude contains risks. But that is the meaning of 'to boldly go.' We choose to take on those risks, because they are usually justified by the rewards. Offering trust always carries the risk of betrayal," T'Lara said, meeting Picard's eyes briefly, "but it is the only way to earn trust.

"Jean-Luc Picard has been charged, essentially, with not being defensive enough. With practicing the openness on which Starfleet is based rather than a more militant protectiveness. And yet, paradoxically, he is also charged with being too defensive, with using too much force to defeat an attacker. How can this be?

"Members of the court, I concede that Captain Picard placed openness and the desire to learn above the use of defensive force. But I submit that this is worthy of commendation, not punishment. And I submit that it is inconsistent and illogical for the United Federation of Planets to concede this behavior by putting him on trial for it and then simultaneously question his restraint in the use of force. The charges against Captain Picard are inconsistent and unfair, and must not be allowed to stand."

# CHRISTOPHER L. BENNETT

The members returned their verdict within just a few hours: not guilty of all charges and specifications. When the verdict was delivered for the final charge, the members of the *Stargazer* crew in the audience let out a cheer, and in moments they were huddled around Picard, shaking his hand and patting him on the back.

But Picard was simply numb. Throughout the court-martial, as he had gone through the motions, it had felt as though he had justified his choices well. But now that the verdict was in, Picard found it hollow. It could not bring back those twenty-four people who had trusted him with their lives. It could not change the fact that he had failed them. That he had failed to save his ship. That he had failed to find a way to spare the other ship's crew and achieve peaceful relations. The court-martial may have proven that, technically, he had done nothing wrong; but there was still so much that he had failed to do *right*.

On top of all that, he had failed to anticipate Phillipa's betrayal. How could he have misjudged her so completely? Perhaps she been right about him—despite all the careful rationalizations he'd constructed with T'Lara's help, perhaps he had simply been relatively lucky at Maxia Zeta, and his judgment had grown too sloppy.

The court-martial was over. Picard was free, his Starfleet status secure. But he had no idea what he would do next.

Picard begged off his crew's—*former* crew's—celebrations, pleading fatigue from the court-martial. But the next morning, Gilaad Ben Zoma showed up at his door to check on him. Picard greeted him cordially enough, but Ben Zoma could sense that an unwonted distance existed between them. "Are you sure you're all right?"

"I'll be fine," Picard said, a noncommittal answer. Respecting his boundaries, Ben Zoma changed the subject.

"They've offered me a ship. The *Lexington*. I plan to accept."

Picard brightened at that. "Well, it's about time. You'll make a fine captain, Gilaad. And the *Lexington*'s a fine ship."

"Well, it needs some refitting first. It's about as old as the *'Gazer*—they're looking into redesigning the fire safety systems in ships from that period, making them more reliable. Improving the fusion surge control too. What happened there, it may have cost us a lot, but it will make a difference in the future."

Picard nodded. He was at a loss for words for a time. "The others?"

Ben Zoma shrugged. "I've asked some of them about coming with me. Pug and Tricia have said yes. But Greyhorse has already accepted a ground posting at Starfleet Medical. And Phigus says he's thinking about going into teaching. Helping to get the next generation on its feet."

"Hm," Picard said. "You know, I could've been a teacher. Professor Galen offered me the chance to follow in his footsteps . . . but I was too impatient for the slow work of archaeology, too eager for the adventure of starships." He gazed out the starbase window, seeing nothing.

After a moment, Ben Zoma's reflection appeared in the window. "What's on your mind, Jean-Luc?"

"The truth, old friend, is that I don't know. I don't know what to do. What to think. What to feel. The *Stargazer* was my anchor, and I severed the chain. I don't know who I am anymore."

"You're Jean-Luc Picard. Finest captain in Starfleet."

"Am I? How often does Starfleet give another capital ship to a captain who's lost one? Do you think they'll ever trust me with anything larger than a tug? And I'm not even sure they should, after the way I fouled up out there."

"Your record speaks for itself. Twenty-two years of great accomplishments won't be forgotten."

"They only care what you've done for them lately."

"And that was a great accomplishment too. They're already writing the Picard Maneuver into the textbooks!"

"Alongside 'Pyrrhic victory,' no doubt. It was a flashy

trick, nothing more. They'll have me performing it at space shows to thrill the crowds. Just so long as there are no other lives depending on me."

Ben Zoma started to protest, but thought better of it. "I should know by now how hard it is to get through that stubborn hide of yours, Jean-Luc. I'll just leave you to your mood and trust you to figure out for yourself that you're being a self-pitying fool."

"Gilaad." Picard turned to him, apology on his face. "I'm sorry. We shouldn't part like this." He extended a hand, and he and Ben Zoma clasped wrists like old Roman soldiers. "The *Lexington* is in the finest of hands, my friend. I look forward to hearing of its adventures."

"And I look forward to hearing where fate takes you next, old friend. Good luck."

Picard smiled and nodded. But the smile evaporated as soon as Ben Zoma was gone. *Where fate takes me,* he mused. *Perhaps I should cast myself onto the winds of fate. Let them take me wherever they blow. I don't feel much like captaining anything anymore—not even my own soul.*

# PART II

## ROUNDED WITH A SLEEP

—◆—

2358—59

# 5

---

"ANCIENT HISTORY," SAID JEAN-LUC PICARD. "IT IS
a phrase we often use to describe a past very distant from
ourselves, lost to the mists of time. We think of it as connot-
ing a primitive time, before modern technology, often before
intelligence itself."

Picard looked out across the faces of the students arrayed
before him in the lecture hall. So far, only a few watched
him intently, while others looked on with only mild attention and many more looked bored. Understandably; this was
only an entry-level course, and many of the students were
here only to meet their classics requirement. It would be up
to him to try to inspire their interest in archaeology, as
Richard Galen had inspired his so long ago.

He smiled, moving casually away from the podium.
"And those assumptions are all well and good when dealing
with the history of a single planet. But when each of our
peoples moved beyond our native worlds, we began to discover that things were a lot more complicated. We have encountered civilizations that were roving the stars before

humans or Vulcans discovered fire. Sometimes we have only encountered their ruins.

"And these finds forced us to redefine our terms, even our disciplines. Archaeologists dealing with civilizations millions of years old must adopt the tools of paleontology, even evolutionary biology, as they attempt to chart the growth of truly long-lived civilizations." He smirked. "In fact, I oversimplify. A civilization usually lasts for a few hundred years, a few thousand, before either collapsing or transforming into something fundamentally different. Archaeologists studying the ancient species of the galaxy may have to chart the rise and fall of *thousands* of civilizations on a single world. Imagine how much more complex it grows when we take thousands of worlds into account."

Again he surveyed the large hall. The percentage of students really paying attention had risen, but not by much. He was tempted to call on his old Starfleet skills, the command voice that seized the attention of all listeners. But then he would not have earned their interest honestly, on the basis of the ideas themselves. Besides, that was a part of his life he had left behind—for now, at least, and possibly forever. No, he would simply have to accept that a third-year doctoral student had not yet earned the right to teach a more advanced class, and would first have to earn the attention of students like these. If anything, he had achieved lecturer status sooner than was usual under the University of Alpha Centauri's archaeology doctorate program, his maturity and discipline serving him well in his studies. At this rate, Professor Langford had said, he might be Doctor Picard within only another five years.

"Indeed," he went on, "our aspiring scholar of ancient galactic history may find it necessary to call on the skills of the engineer or programmer as well. For instead of burnt bones, arrowheads, and clay pots, a dig may turn up advanced technologies, even computer storage systems whose memories may still be retrievable. Such finds are rare on planet surfaces due to erosion, but the vacuum of space can preserve artifacts far better than any desert tomb. Thus bringing yet another discipline to bear, for it may take the skills of an astronomer to locate such relics in the first place."

He gave the class another self-deprecating smile. "Now, I know this comes as no surprise to many of you. We have all heard of such ancient civilizations, the great galactic empires of the past, the mighty beings who have evolved to near-godlike form and left devices we still struggle to comprehend." He paused and sharpened his gaze. "But I want to explore with you, today, the following question: Just how ancient is 'ancient'?"

He moved over to the "blackboard" screen that covered the wall behind the lectern, activating it and setting it to display a simple timeline. "I'd like you to do something for me now. I'd like you to name for me the most ancient civilizations you can think of."

The most attentive students toward the front of the hall spoke up first. "Galos Sigma!"

"Iconia!"

"The Sargonians!"

"Bajor!"

"Organia!"

Picard entered them and the other suggestions on the screen, positioning them on the timeline, sometimes with wide error bars to represent their duration or the uncertainty in their age. Naturally one of the native Centaurian students mentioned the ancient ruins of the extinct civilizations that had emerged and died out in this system over the ages. Soon after came the inevitable mention of Tagus III, well-known as the pet project of the UAC's archaeology department. An arrow on the far left of the screen appeared, indicating that its ruins were far too ancient to display on the scale shown.

"Any others?" he asked. More suggestions came: Kurl, Ma-aira Thenn, Talos IV, Clan Ru, the B'nurlac. Inevitably, there were one or two he'd never heard of; it was a big galaxy, and even an expert couldn't keep track of every civilization.

Eventually the suggestions slowed. "Aldea?" someone asked, provoking a laugh from those who dismissed it as legend.

"Any others?" Picard asked.

"How about El-Auria?"

Picard spun at the familiar voice coming from the side door. The enormous blue disk of a hat left no doubt—it was indeed Guinan! He wanted to break into a grin, run to his old friend's side, and ask her what she was doing here. But he had a class to teach, so he maintained his decorum, offering her only a small, private smile. "Well, since you're so late to the lecture," he said with mock sternness, "perhaps you could fill us in on who they were and when their civilization thrived." He had recognized the name of Guinan's homeworld, and was intrigued by the prospect of getting her to reveal something about her origins. He knew her world had been lost in some mysterious tragedy, but she and others of her kind had revealed few specifics. They saw themselves as listeners, and did not talk about themselves very much.

Unfortunately, Guinan reverted to form and simply gave a small, apologetic smile. "No, you're right . . . it's probably not ancient enough for this discussion. Never mind. I'll just take a seat in the back, if that's all right."

He concealed his disappointment. "Certainly."

Guinan made her way to the back unobtrusively, though the prominent halo of her hat—which, as usual, she left on even indoors—made sure she did not disappear into the crowd. Picard solicited more suggestions, but the class seemed to have run dry. "Well," he said, looking over the display on the screen. "We've got some impressively ancient cultures on this list. Ten thousand years for the Kalandans, the Fabrini, the Ky'rha. Thirty thousand for Bajor, fifty thousand for Cheron. A hundred thousand for the Shedai. Two hundred thousand for Iconia and the Mro, more for the Talosians. Half a million or more for the Sargonian Diaspora.

Five to ten million for Organia. Consider that," he said. "Civilizations that rose and fell while most of our ancestors were still swinging in trees. Surely these are the very embodiment of the word 'ancient.'"

He paused for a moment, looking out over the class, letting the idea sink in. Then he asked the question. "Now. How old is the galaxy?"

The students were nonplussed by the apparent change of subject. A Vulcan student near the front recovered swiftly, though. "Approximately thirteen point five six billion years," she said, "with a one-sigma uncertainty of point zero seven billion."

"Thank you. Let's put that on our timeline, shall we? And let's pull out a bit so we can see it." He input the commands, and the timeline shrank to fit. The array of civilizations that had stretched clear across the board were now concentrated in a tiny, dense speck at the far right, save for a sparse few scattered across the right-hand sixth of the screen. Picard waited a few seconds for the students to take in the drastic change of perspective. He had their attention now. "Hm. Well," he said, affecting a tone of curmudgeonly surprise. "Where did everybody go?" A chuckle ran through the audience. "I'd say this puts a different perspective on things, doesn't it? Thirteen point six *billion* years. And most of the so-called ancient civilizations known to Federation science occupy less than a tenth of a percent of that span."

He moved forward, letting his enthusiasm for the subject enter his tone. "This, my friends, is the challenge we face when we study history and archaeology on a galactic scale. There is simply so *much* of it that we will never run out of new things to discover. Even the attempt to construct a comprehensive history of the galaxy is an undertaking that would itself require an archaeological span of time to complete.

"Not to worry, though," he went on after a moment. "The situation is not as extreme as it may appear. The truth—and now we must bring astrophysics into our discussion—is that for the majority of its lifespan, the galaxy has not been capable of supporting life as we understand it. Stars of the early generations would have had fewer heavy elements to make planets from, since those elements are formed in supernovae and have become more common over time. The turbulence and radiation would likely have disrupted most protoplanetary disks before planets could arise. If some planets did form, they would probably have been too frequently irradiated by gamma-ray bursts for life to gain a foothold.

"The earliest evidence of complex, multicellular life in our galaxy dates back some five to six billion years. However, the worlds on which it could evolve were few and far between at the time, so sentient species would have been even more so. It's believed that tens of millions of years might pass between the evolution of one sentient race and the next, and few would survive the still-frequent cosmic cataclysms long enough to master spaceflight and ensure their own survival—particularly since the lesser availability of heavy elements would have impeded their technological growth. Even for those that did eventually develop interstellar travel, there would have been nowhere nearby to go. It is believed that most such civilizations would have turned their efforts inward, as the Taguans, the most ancient civilization of which we have firm evidence, appear to have done. Some may have chosen to build artificial habitats around other stars, expanding that way until they eventually found other planets to settle. These species may have had tens of millions of years all to themselves in the galaxy— perhaps undergoing divergent evolution into multiple different species. The research of Professor Richard Galen and others suggests several waves of galactic occupation, a single people expanding across the galaxy, meeting no one but themselves and their offshoots, and then, eventually . . . vanishing from the stage." Picard wished he could tell the story with the same passion and lyricism with which Galen had imbued it when the young Jean-Luc had studied under him at Starfleet Academy. There had been such poignancy in

Galen's voice as he had spoken of the total disappearance of these hypothetical races, of their ultimate failure to leave a legacy, a lasting imprint on the galaxy. Perhaps in time, the more Picard immersed himself in the research, the closer he could come to conveying the majesty and wonder of this work.

"Now, eventually, within the past two billion years, life was coming along often enough that an ancient civilization might occasionally meet a new one. The evidence is that the younger civilization was usually quite soundly overpowered or destroyed by a people unfamiliar with the concept of co-existence with—" Picard broke off, noticing that a Peliar student had raised his hand. "Yes?"

"Where do you think they went? The species that vanished. If they were spread across multiple worlds, how could they have all died out?"

"Maybe they didn't," said a human woman next to him. "They could've evolved to a higher plane."

The Peliar scoffed. "If you believe in such things."

"In fact," Picard pointed out, "there are a number of documented examples of species evolving into incorporeal forms. The Organians, the Molherian Firesouls, the Thasians. However, we do not understand enough about the process to say if it truly represents a 'higher plane' or simply a different form of being.

"As for how these species died out, it is impossible to say for sure in most cases. But the question does bring us to an interesting anomaly." He reset the screen to zoom in gradually toward the present epoch, allowing Tagus III to slide off the screen. "Over the megayears, as you can see, the number of civilizations gradually increased. The galaxy became more stable, massive gamma bursts less frequent. Stellar metallicities rose, allowing more planets to form. With civilizations encountering one another more often, earlier in their history, they appear to have learned to coexist more comfortably.

"But then, suddenly on the cosmic scale of things, something seems to have happened." He froze the chart at a point where a discontinuity was visible. From screen left to center, the scattered bars representing civilizations grew relatively more numerous, and then cut off. "Here, some two hundred and fifty million years ago or so, there is a gap. To date, nothing—literally no evidence of intelligent life—has been found which can be reliably dated to the period between roughly two hundred fifty and one hundred million years ago. After that, civilizations begin to emerge again," he said, his finger sliding toward the right of the timeline, "steadily increasing in number until we reach the abundance of civilizations we are familiar with from the past few hundred thousand years."

He stepped back to look at the graph, giving the class a moment to do the same. "Now, admittedly, our data set from prior to a hundred megayears ago is quite scanty. Very little survives from that far in the past; on such a time scale, planetary geology or erosion will generally destroy any evidence of technology. Most space-based facilities will have been thoroughly cannibalized by intervening civilizations by the time we discover them, or else will have been destroyed by asteroid impacts, knocked out of orbit, or what have you. The ruins on Tagus III have only survived so long thanks to the extraordinary durability of their materials and that planet's lack of tectonic activity. So this gap could simply be a statistical fluke, a matter of mere chance that we haven't discovered anything from that period.

"However, there are some compelling coincidences. For instance: starting some two hundred and fifty-two million years ago, the planet Earth underwent the Permian-Triassic Extinction Event. Also known as the Great Dying. It was the most severe mass extinction in the history of the planet, even surpassing that which was caused by humanity in recent centuries. In a remarkably short time, no more than a million years, as many as ninety percent of Earth's species disappeared from the fossil record. To this day, we are not entirely certain what could have come so close to exterminating all life on Earth. It seems to have been a combination of factors, including excessive volcanic eruptions and an asteroid impact, but even those are insufficient to explain the sheer magnitude of the extinction. Let alone to explain the similar die-offs discovered on other worlds at roughly the same period of time, including Centauri VII. True, the extinctions do not align exactly by any means. But there is enough converging evidence to create a great mystery. Where did everybody go?"

He surveyed the room again, realizing his time was running out. He looked to where Guinan sat, seeking to gauge her reaction, but she merely sat quietly and listened, as was her nature. "In any case, I hope I have managed to convey to you how much there is left to learn about the galaxy's past. Perhaps these mysteries may inspire you to make a career out of seeking their answers, as they have inspired me. At the very least, I hope I have succeeded in showing you that what we think of as 'ancient history' is really nothing of the kind." He paused. "The Federation today is so driven to expand through space, seeking out new life and new civilizations. But there is a far greater number of *old* civilizations that we have barely begun to discover. We should not overlook them in our haste to embrace the new."

He saw the students were getting fidgety now. "That's all for today," he said. "Thank you for your attention."

The latter sentence was drowned out by the noise of the students draining from the room. Before long, only one person remained seated, a wide-brimmed blue mushroom springing up from a field of desks. Picard grinned up at her. "Well, are you just going to sit there?"

One of Guinan's thoughtful little smiles appeared on her deep brown face. "Since I got here so late, I don't want to be in any rush to leave."

He chuckled. As always, Guinan had her own offbeat way of looking at things. Collecting his note padd, Picard came off the podium and began climbing the stairs toward her, but she rose and met him halfway. "It's wonderful to see you, Guinan. How long has it been?"

"Five years, six. I only just got back in the area." Guinan was an inveterate galactic traveler. The El-Aurians had come to Federation space some sixty years before as refugees. Yet rather than settling down as many of the others had done, Guinan had remained a wanderer, never staying in one place for more than a few years (a brief sojourn to such a long-lived people), and often taking lengthy jaunts to sectors of the galaxy that the Federation had yet to chart. Guinan claimed she had been a traveler since long before her people's refugee era, but her statements about her past, Picard had learned over the years, could not always be taken at face value.

At the moment, though, the concern in her eyes was quite sincere. "I heard about the *Stargazer.* I'm sorry I wasn't around then."

*So am I,* Picard thought. When they had first met, over twenty years ago, he had helped her through a difficult time, and in some way he still did not understand, meeting him had seemed to bring her new hope when she had needed it. Since then, she had returned the favor many times over with her patient attention and often-surprising advice. Her counsel might have helped him through the rough patch he went through after the court-martial. But he had found his way out of that before too long, with a little help from other friends. So he said, "It's quite all right. No way you could've known. So what brings you here?" He started back down the steps, and she followed.

"I'm thinking of enrolling in your class."

"Really?" He considered it unlikely, but played along, keeping a jocular tone as they headed out into the hallway. "You never seemed that interested in archaeology before."

She shrugged, making the hat wobble a bit. "All the more reason to start. Never hurts to try something new."

"Quite right."

"Besides, you've always been so interested in it . . . I guess I wanted to see what all the fuss was about."

They emerged from Carl Blegen Hall onto the grounds of the university's New Samarkand campus, and Picard squinted. It was a bright day; Alpha Centauri B was less than four years past periastron and shone in the daytime sky sixteen hundred times brighter than Earth's full Moon, though it was little more than a point. It was a pittance compared to the light and heat that Centauri III received from the A star, but it still had a psychological effect on the perception of brightness. Guinan's hat kept her eyes shaded, though, and she looked around the campus without difficulty. "This is a nice place. Looks like there's a lot of tradition behind it."

"Mm-hmm," Picard said. "Centauri III was humanity's first colony outside Sol system, and New Samarkand one of its first cities. Cochrane himself helped establish it. Everywhere you go in this city, you can practically smell the history."

"Isn't there a lot more history to smell on Earth? I remember some really great aromas the last time I was in Paris. The bread . . . the wine . . ." She looked at him. "Come to think of it, I remember there was a wine called Château Picard."

"Yes, well. Paris holds little fascination for me these days."

"You don't like the wine?"

He tried not to glare at her. She had an aggravating way of gently twisting a conversation to dig into people's hangups and fears, and an even more aggravating way of seeming to understand people better than they understood themselves. "Let's just say it reminds me of one of my more unsuccessful romances," he said. Having no desire to get drawn into a discussion of Jenice, let alone the family of winemakers he had turned his back on to go into space, he returned to the previous subject. "Centauri University has a fine archaeology program. Their work on Tagus III has been exceptional— considering that the Taguans have forbidden offworld access to the ruins for a century. And my graduate advisor, Dr. Miliani Langford, has done some impressive work reconstructing the history of the Iconian Empire from the ruins and legends left behind on their conquered worlds."

"Is that what brought you here?"

"Yes, along with Tagus. I've been fascinated with the Iconians ever since I took Professor Galen's classes at Starfleet Academy." He sighed. "My ideal would have been to work with the professor himself. Back then, he wanted me to leave the command track, maybe even leave Starfleet to become his protégé. I was sorely tempted, but the stars beckoned too brightly then."

"So you were hoping you could make up for that now. Go back and try the road not taken."

"Unfortunately, Professor Galen's researches have taken him far afield these past few years. I'm not even sure what he's working on now." Had it really been twenty years since he'd seen his old mentor in the flesh?

"But you took his advice anyway. You left Starfleet."

They had reached his favorite shade tree, its surround currently unsullied by students, and so he paused beneath it. "Well, technically I'm on an extended leave of absence. My commission's still active."

Guinan studied him. "Extended enough to take nearly a decade earning your doctorate."

He took a moment before answering, his gaze locked on nothing. "Let's just say I'm keeping my options open."

"I just figured, after the *Stargazer* and the court-martial, you might have . . ."

"Hm? Oh, that. No, I've hardly thought about it in years. Well, it bothered me for a time. I lost my confidence, despaired for my future, all that. But then I pulled myself out of it, regained some perspective. And then I got to talking with Elizabeth Wu. You remember her, she was my old second officer on the *Stargazer*." Guinan nodded, still listening. "Well, she had gone into civilian research, and it certainly agreed with her. It got me thinking that there were new possibilities worth exploring." He shrugged. "I had a good run on the *Stargazer*, but it came to an end, as all things do."

"The ship came to an end. Not your career."

"No, of course not," he said, maintaining a breezy manner in contrast to her solemn tone. He could understand her reacting this way to the loss of his old ship, since it was fresh news to her. But if she thought it still weighed him down, he wished to assure her that she was sorely mistaken. "But it seemed like a good opportunity to take a break, as it were. To try something different. And so far I'm loving it."

"I have to admit," she said, "you do make a very good teacher. It suits you better than I thought it would."

"You make it sound like a confession."

She furrowed her smooth brow. "I just mean that I never thought you'd give up being a starship captain." Her eyes lingered on the top of his head for a moment. "Not yet, anyway." Picard had to wonder what his increasingly gray hair—which he kept shorn close these days, since it was becoming very patchy on top, trapped between receding temples and a growing bald spot—had to do with anything. "I figured it was in your blood. You've always had such a . . . passion for exploration."

"Oh, I still do," he assured her. "But starship exploration is a cursory process, barely glancing at one planet before haring off to the next. Starfleet is so obsessed with moving outward at top speed. To really explore, you need to linger. To dig down, get the soil of a place in your fingernails, its dust in your pores. And then it takes long, careful analysis in the lab, taking your time to really get to know your discoveries, to live and breathe and dream them, before you can really claim to understand them. All starships do is pave the way for the real explorers." He gestured back toward Blegen Hall. "Look at our work on Tagus. Even today we're learning new things from relics collected over a century ago."

Her gaze remained on him, as calm as ever. "The Picard I knew wouldn't have had the patience to spend months in a lab poring over a few relics."

"Well, I was something of a hothead back then, wasn't I? I'd like to think I've mellowed with maturity."

"But don't you ever miss the travel? Getting to see new worlds, meet new peoples?"

"I've been on a couple of digs with Dr. Langford. Last year we visited the ruins of Ligillium on Vanlac V and actually *found* the Tomb of Zaterl."

"I thought that was just a legend."

"That's what they told Schliemann about Troy. But it's there."

"Even the Emerald?"

Picard nodded. "I held it in my own hands. We left it there, of course, out of respect for the Vanlaca's cultural heritage. And we've kept the exact location secret to deter grave robbers and pothunters. But we gained a much richer insight into Ligillian technology, art, and religious customs." His gaze went unfocused. "And just . . . being there . . . it was amazing."

"And you're okay with doing that just once a year or so. Spending the rest of it in the lab, or in the classroom."

"I want to be more than a tourist, Guinan. The thrill of seeing new places is one I still feel, yes, but there's a richer satisfaction in taking the time to understand a thing in depth."

Guinan studied him for a moment, then shook her head, seeming oddly frustrated beneath her surface calm. "I don't buy it."

"What?"

"What's that line people like to quote from that favorite author of yours? About protesting too much?"

"'The lady doth protest too much, methinks.' Queen Gertrude in *Hamlet*." He looked at her quizzically. "Are you saying I'm trying to convince myself of something? That I don't really love what I'm doing now?"

"Oh, I think you love what you're doing. I just think you love commanding starships more."

"Well, I'm not so sure anymore. That had its burdens as well as its rewards."

"'Uneasy lies the head that wears the crown.'"

He chuckled. Guinan, the old rogue, knew her Bard better than she'd let on. "You could say that. I certainly sleep better these days."

She shook her head. "Shakespeare said something about sleep, too. What was it? 'In that sleep of death'?"

"I'm still living, Guinan. I haven't given up on life just because I'm pursuing a different dream."

Guinan studied him. "Why didn't you pursue this dream the first time around? Why'd you choose to stick with starship command?"

"At the time, it was what I felt compelled to do. But I was a callow youth back then. A creature of impulse."

She thought about that for a moment. "You know what all the great leaders I've known have had in common?"

"What was that?"

"Their first impulses usually turn out to be right."

Picard smirked. "Well, then, I'm not among that august company. I've made some whoppers in my day."

"I said usually, not always. Especially when they don't listen to those first impulses."

He frowned at her. "Look, why is this so important to you? I'm entitled to make my own career decisions, aren't I?"

"If you're the only one affected by them."

"And what do you mean by that?"

She hesitated. "Just that there are a lot of starship crews out there that could use a good leader."

"Starfleet has no shortage of those. And they weren't exactly in haste to offer me a new command after I lost the *Stargazer*."

"They will. It may take a while, but they'll give you a ship again."

"It's not as simple as that, Guinan. You're a civilian, you don't—"

"You're not hearing me, Picard. I'm not saying that it's possible or that I think you should. You *will* command a starship again. I know that for a fact."

He was tempted to dismiss it as a mere platitude, but he knew Guinan too well for that, and he saw there was more to it in her eyes. "How could you possibly know such a thing?"

Her gaze held steady. "Because I know you, Picard. I know things about you that you don't know yourself yet."

Guinan's certainty was compelling, and Picard felt stirrings of ambitions he hadn't pursued in years. But then he felt his tangible responsibilities beneath his feet once more. "Maybe someday, old friend," he said with a smile. "But not just now. Perhaps in a few years, when I've earned my doctorate, Starfleet might give me command of a science vessel, the kind that takes on specialized, long-term survey missions. Then I could still do serious, in-depth research. But perhaps I could choose to teach at the Academy instead—share the benefit of my experience in that way. In either case, though, I want to see this through."

After a moment, she nodded. "I guess it's not your way to leave something half-finished."

"I'm glad you see that." Picard realized how much the shadow of the tree had moved during their conversation. "Walk with me to my office? I have some research I really need to get back to."

Guinan nodded, and they moved along once again. "Anything to do with what you were talking about in class? The mystery of what happened to life in the galaxy a quarter of a billion years ago?"

"No, much closer to home. I'm helping Dr. Langford analyze the artifacts recently unearthed in a new dig on Centauri VII." He gestured toward the bright orange star in the eastern sky; "Centauri VII" was actually the second planet of Centauri B, added to the five around the A star. "They're from the new stratum that was first unearthed about twenty years ago. We're still only beginning to learn about that civilization, discover how far it came before its cataclysm." As they walked, he told Guinan a little about the prehistory of this system. Proxima Centauri, the tiny red dwarf that circled the A and B stars at a much greater remove, had been both a blessing and a curse. Without it, the system's planets would have been bone-dry, all their volatiles seared away at the start by the heat of two newborn suns. Proxima's passage through the system's outer cometary cloud periodically knocked comets inward, over time replenishing the Centauri planets' water and atmospheric gases. Once life had arisen, the ongoing bombardments had stimulated evolutionary change, as biology rose to the challenge and found new ways to adapt. If anything, life had evolved faster on Alpha Centauri's planets than on Earth, and Centauri was two billion years older. So the paleontological record was rich, and more than one geological era in the histories of Centauri III and VII had boasted intelligent, tool-using life, humanoid or otherwise. Yet the ongoing bombardments had struck each of these civilizations or protocivilizations down in their prime, evidently before they reached the stage where they could migrate into space and deflect comets. It was a sad litany of squandered potential and broken dreams, but a treasure trove for archaeologists.

"And one of these civilizations died out a quarter-billion years ago, like so many others?"

"Well, yes, about the same time as the late Permian extinction on Earth. There could be a common cause there, given the proximity of the stars. But the idea of any galactic extinction event is much more speculative. And the archaeological record in this system is too inconclusive. The ruins we're studying are actually from an even—"

"Would it interest you to know that there are legends all over the galaxy of a great disaster from around that time?"

He stopped walking and stared at her, forcing a pair of students behind them to swerve around where they stood. "Yes, actually, it would. What can you tell me?"

Guinan shrugged. "Just stories I've heard here and there. Legends, as I said. True, there's not a lot of evidence left from back then. But . . . well, some beings live a *very* long time. I've met a few in my travels. There are tales, rumors . . . nowhere near firsthand, mind you. But cultures before yours have found the same mysteries and done their own digging—literally or otherwise. There are tales of mysterious objects or structures surviving from before the disaster, locked inside protective fields. Unchanging and immune to time."

"Tell me more."

She opened her mouth, but then shut it again. "Nahh. You wouldn't be interested."

"What?!" He barked a laugh. "What could possibly make you imagine I wouldn't be interested in this?"

"Because these stories, they're from very far away. Places the Federation's never been before. If someone wanted to follow up these clues, maybe look for one of these hidden . . . things, they'd need a pretty fast and powerful ship. Probably a ship that could defend itself, because you never know what's out there. And if they found one of these structures—" She chuckled, shaking her head. "Well, if their defenses are as advanced as the stories say, it'd take some really top-notch experts and equipment to have a chance of figuring out how to get in."

Picard threw her a look. "You mean a Starfleet ship. And Starfleet personnel."

"That would work."

He shook his head. "I'm no longer as quick as I once was to assume Starfleet is the best at everything. And this university boasts one of the finest archaeological institutes in the known galaxy. We have no shortage of resources at our disposal."

She pursed her lips. "I suppose so. That is, if you can convince someone to let you use them for this." She offered a small, self-deprecating shrug. "They are just legends, after all."

"You let me worry about that, Guinan." He probed her eyes. "That is, if you're telling me the truth about these legends, and it's not just some ploy to maneuver me back into Starfleet."

Her dark eyes held his unwaveringly. "I may have been known to prevaricate sometimes. But I wouldn't lie to you, Picard."

He accepted it. "Then will you tell me everything you

know about these legends? Where you heard them, where we can search to find out more?"

"It'll take a while. Does your busy research schedule allow time for dinner?"

Picard smiled. "Not always, but for you, old friend, it certainly does."

"Good. I know this great little tavern . . ."

"You always do."

# 6

———◆———

PICARD'S DUTIES KEPT HIM FROM DEVOTING TOO
much time to following Guinan's lead, but over the ensuing
weeks he began an investigation as a personal project. Fortunately, in archaeology of this sort, the first stage of "digging"
could be accomplished without leaving one's desk, so long
as one had subspace access. Students of ancient galactic archaeology benefitted from the fact that earlier civilizations
had had their own archaeologists. Instead of starting from
scratch, one could piggyback on what scholars millennia in
the past had accomplished. Over the centuries, Vulcan,
human, and other spacefarers had unearthed archives and
databases from long-extinct civilizations, vast treasure
troves of knowledge. Of course, it wasn't as simple as entering a question into a library computer and getting an instant
answer; if it were, Federation science would have jumped
forward thousands of years by now. These archives were
vast, containing the collected knowledge of whole civilizations that had encompassed dozens of worlds and endured
for dozens of centuries, if not more. Sifting through so much
accumulated information for a desired datum could be as ar-
duous a process as digging through soil strata in search of
ancient ruins. Even deciphering the encoding schemes used

by extinct civilizations could be the work of decades, and the indexing schemes of beings with alien minds and cultural contexts could be baffling and deeply opaque. Searches were largely a matter of trial and error, unless one knew precisely what to look for.

Compounding the problem was the fact that the older a databank was, the more its contents were eroded by quantum degradation. The probability of any given particle in a data storage medium undergoing a spontaneous change of quantum state was low, but over hundreds or thousands of millennia, more and more such errors would inevitably accumulate. Picard had little hope of finding solid information dating back as far as he needed to look; at most he might find fragments, or more recent retellings passed down from civilization to civilization, too far from primary sources to be reliable.

But soon he realized he was looking at it the wrong way. If these changeless structures Guinan had described actually existed, if they possibly even survived to this day (as he restrained himself from consciously hoping), then some might have been discovered by comparatively recent civilizations. He had found no records in the databases of the Federation or its allies, but some ancient civilizations from this part of the galaxy were known or believed to have stretched a good deal farther in their day.

He knew from Guinan that the tales she'd collected had their origin in the Beta Quadrant, somewhere antispinward and coreward of the Upper Scorpius OB association—literally "beyond Antares," as the old song had put it. Antares itself may not have been quite as remote today as when the song was new, but the regions beyond it were still largely unexplored. And Guinan's tales could not be narrowed to any specific part of it.

In time, Picard's database searches turned up some promising leads. Kalandan archives spoke of a mysterious structure existing "outside of time," at once there and not there. The Fer-Gruacch Library, what could be reconstructed of it, hinted at the existence of several such structures, though it seemed to say that their specific locations were impossible to pin down. And the Heritage Banks of Vormoreshinak related an incident wherein a mysterious spaceborne object had impacted a world on the Imperium's outer marches, destroying numerous coastal cities with the resultant tsunami, but surviving the impact completely undamaged and resisting all subsequent attempts to interact with it. Unfortunately, the Vormoresh had let it lie buried on the sea floor, where two million years of sedimentation would have left it essentially unreachable even if the specific location of the planet had not been lost to quantum erosion. Still, between them, these records at least allowed Picard to narrow the probabilities. But it wasn't enough yet to justify going to Miliani Langford and trying to persuade her to mount an expedition. As a mere doctoral student, Picard could not lead a dig on his own—and he would not wish to exclude his colleague and friend from such a discovery.

But the more he reviewed the records, the more he was able to narrow down a potential region for the search and to reconstruct at least some descriptions of specific star systems to search for within that region. A quarter-billion years was an enormous stretch in humanoid terms—longer than mammals or dinosaurs had existed on Earth—but a small percentage of the lifespan of most inhabited systems. The stars themselves would have completed more than one full orbit around the galactic core in that time, their differing orbital velocities and eccentricities spreading them hundreds of parsecs apart from one another. But all he needed was one or two clear descriptions of sites happened upon by (comparatively) more recent archaeologists.

Soon he came upon something more tangible, something that, while not a definitive link to the timeless structures Guinan had spoken of, might at least provide a solid lead. So finally, more than a month after Guinan's visit, he made his proposal to Langford during the morning jog they often shared. (He had made a few attempts to persuade her to go riding with him instead, but the energetic 51-year-old had seen no value in letting the horse do all the exercise while she just sat on it.)

"I found a reference in a B'nurlac archaeological database," he told her as they loped around the boundary of the park adjoining the university, "to a planet on which they found ruins approximately two hundred fifty million years old. From the era of the Great Extinction, and well-preserved. They described its star system specifically—a distinctive one with three inner Jovians and three red-dwarf companions. And it was right in the Trans-Scorpian region where the records of these mysterious objects overlap, roughly eight hundred light-years away."

"Calm down, Luc," Langford, an elfin woman with Polynesian features and subtly gray-streaked black hair, said with a chuckle. "I understand your excitement, but don't get ahead of yourself. For one thing, this so-called Great Extinction is just a legend."

"A legend shared by cultures from all over the galaxy, according to Guinan."

"And how much of the galaxy has your friend been to?"

"I would not care to put a limit on the extent of her travels. She's an El-Aurian."

Langford winced in sympathy. "Mmm. So she's traveled very far as a refugee."

"And even before that, possibly for many centuries."

"Sounds like I should hire her as a consultant. What do I need you for?" she teased.

"Well. Guinan is notoriously hard to pin down. If she stays somewhere, it's for her own reasons."

Langford shrugged it off. "Anyway, let's say we get a ship and spend months trekking out to this remote system in uncharted territory. Let's say we find this planet and unearth viable ruins. How do we know that civilization would've had anything to do with the artifacts you're looking for?"

"According to the B'nurlac, the civilization that left the ruins was a starfaring one, very advanced. It's likely that they had traveled widely in the region and encountered most of its major civilizations. There could be records of the beings who created the timeless artifacts, perhaps even indications of the planets they inhabited."

"Records reduced to Swiss cheese by a quarter-gigayear of quantum erosion."

"Even advanced societies leave information in other ways than computer storage. Paintings, museum exhibits, educational toys. Consider the mosaic star map on the ceiling of Starfleet Headquarters' main lobby."

Langford's sloe eyes widened with surprise, and she came to a stop. "You really must care about this. You usually don't like to talk about your days in Starfleet."

Picard frowned. "I have no problem talking about my Starfleet career. I just . . . it grew a little tiresome having people constantly ask me about it when I was busy working on a doctorate. That's all."

"Oh. I'm sorry, I guess I misunderstood."

"Quite all right." He smiled at her, realizing his tone had grown a little harsh. It was just that the incessant questions from others had gotten rather irritating. . . .

"So if we do find a list of places to look, how do we know what to look for?" As Langford spoke, she began doing some stretches to keep herself limber. Picard took a moment to appreciate the grace of her movements before answering. She came from a family of artists and stage performers, and could have easily held her own among them if she hadn't been drawn to archaeology instead.

"Well, if these objects are completely frozen in time," he said, "undergoing no change of any kind, then it stands to reason that they would absorb no light, no energy. They would reflect or scatter one hundred percent of any scanning beam. And they would emit nothing, so they would be blank spots on passive sensors."

"Didn't some of the records say it was impossible to pin down their location? What if they move somehow? Or aren't entirely within our continuum?"

"The more I study the documents, the more I think they're saying something else. Not that their location is indeterminate, but that their *boundaries* are. That they lack definite edges somehow. Perhaps it's an effect of the stasis fields. In any case, if we do locate such an object, I think we'd know it when we saw it."

"And if we did find one, what would be our chances of opening it up? None of the others who claimed to find them had any success."

"As far as we can reconstruct from their records. Perhaps some of them succeeded and classified the results. At least, perhaps we can build on what they learned, take the next step."

Langford pondered. "You said there were records in the Fer-Gruacch Library from three hundred and ten millennia ago."

"Yes."

"Wasn't that shortly before their civilization vanished?"

Picard cleared his throat. "Yes, well . . . we can't assume there was a correlation. And there's no evidence they fell prey to a cataclysm. It's as though they simply . . . went somewhere else."

She crinkled her eyes. "Like evolving to a higher plane? Are you hoping that maybe this discovery will give us the secrets of the cosmos?"

"I assume nothing," he told her with dignity. "I simply submit that this discovery could hold the answers to many mysteries."

Langford harumphed. She began to jog again, and Picard followed. After a few moments, she spoke again. "I don't know, Luc. It's awfully tenuous grounds for such a major investment of time and resources. And the Centauri VII artifacts still need further analysis."

"They aren't going anywhere, Miliani. And there's no shortage of experts to study them. I'm offering the chance to find something entirely new. To begin filling in a tremendous gap in our understanding of galactic history. Even if we don't find Guinan's artifacts, just locating that site in the quaternary star system could give us a wealth of new knowledge about an uncharted era." He craned his head, trying to catch her gaze. "I know you, Miliani. You find that prospect as compelling as I do. Your responsibilities here can wait."

"My academic responsibilities, perhaps," she admitted after a pause. "But we've been making plans for my family to come visit. It's been far too long since I've seen them."

"You talk on subspace all the time."

"It's not the same. You don't understand." She instantly showed regret. "I'm sorry, that was harsh."

"No, it's all right." The truth was, he didn't fully understand. He knew what it was like to be drawn away from home and familial tradition by an irresistible urge to learn. What remained strange to him was how she had managed to stay so close to her family, and they to her, in spite of it.

Picard had a thought. "Perhaps I could take on some of your teaching duties for a week or two. Give you the extra time to go visit your family. Then, when you return, we could begin to organize the expedition."

She came to a stop, staring up at him. "Luc, that's so— well, it may be for totally self-serving reasons," she laughed, "but it's still very sweet of you. But I couldn't ask."

"Miliani, I'm the one asking."

"But you work yourself so hard as it is. . . . Could you handle even more responsibilities?"

He smiled. "At the risk of invoking my Starfleet career again, this is mild next to the responsibilities of a captain or first officer."

Her eyes were darting around as she swiftly evaluated the possibilities. "Well . . . if I assign Rosa to assist you . . . oh, let's face it, you're far better at time management than I'll ever be, so if I can pull it off, it should be a breeze for you. Oh, Luc, you're a prince!" She pulled his shoulders down and kissed him on the cheek.

Picard gave a laugh that sounded a bit giddy to him. "So this means we'll go? On the expedition?"

"Beyond Antares?" she said with a smirk. "Sure, what the hell? It's been too long since I went haring off on a mad adventure. And the setting is too romantic to resist," she added with a wink.

Then she was off again, jogging back toward campus with a new spring in her step, and her sweet soprano, trained since childhood, wafted back to him on the winds. *"The sky is green and glowing . . . Where my heart is . . ."*

Of course it was nowhere near as simple as setting a course and saying "Engage," as Picard could have done on the *Stargazer.* The whole expedition had to be approved, organized, and supplied first. It took time for Langford to craft a proposal and persuade the university to invest in the project. Moneyless society or no, some resources—particularly the time and commitment of skilled experts—were still finite, and it was necessary to justify one's need for them. And this expedition would need experts. As Picard had told his class, archaeology alone could not do the trick. They would need a planetary scientist, an engineer, a linguist, and probably a physicist, as well as a medical doctor and assorted graduate students to provide general assistance. Grad students were to scholarly work what ensigns and enlisted personnel were to Starfleet: the ones who existed to do the tedious, mind-numbing chores so the decision-makers would be free to make decisions. Of course Picard was such a student himself, but Langford treated him more as a partner.

While Langford worked to recruit the personnel, Picard saw about hiring a suitable ship. With university backing, he arranged with Centauri III's leading civilian spacecraft firm to provide a custom vessel, high-powered for maximum warp speed—considerably less than Starfleet's fastest, but excellent for a civilian ship. Since the crew would be only a dozen or so, life-support needs were reduced, increasing the power available for velocity. The ship would also be sleek and narrow, like the rocketships of old, presenting a minimal cross section to oncoming space debris and radiation and reducing the power requirements for navigational deflection. For a Starfleet vessel, designed with the possibility of combat in mind, such a design was impractical since enemies could approach from any direction. But this craft was built purely for moving forward as fast as possible.

Even so, the journey into trans-Scorpian space would take months, and Picard was determined to shave off as much time as he could. Warp velocity was not a strictly linear thing; due to differing mass and energy densities and subspace geodesics, some areas of space allowed higher effective speeds for the same application of engine power. Navigators came to know these shortcuts intimately and use them as regular "space lanes," but only in charted territories. The civilian databases lacked information on the subspace topography out beyond the Upper Scorpius star-formation region.

So it was that Picard took a step he was reluctant to take: using his Starfleet connections for help. He was not eager to be lectured about how much easier this would be if he were still in the Fleet. He knew it was an empty platitude; had he stayed in the Fleet, they would have stuck him behind a desk and this would have been just as difficult to arrange—at least if he wanted to go himself.

But the man he chose to contact was one he trusted not to waste his time with platitudes—if only because he would be more interested in the quest itself. Donald Varley had taken Galen's archaeology classes alongside Picard; their friendship was forged through their common fascination with the mysteries of ancient Iconia. Indeed, as Picard had expected, the look in Varley's eyes when they spoke over subspace was one of thinly veiled envy. *"You're on the trail of something pretty amazing, Jean-Luc,"* the grizzled, brown-complected captain said in his ponderous tones, shaking his head. *"I would dearly love to join you out there, but unfortunately, things are far too tense right now."*

"Really," Picard said. "I thought with the Galen border conflict resolved, things would be quieting down."

*Oh, we're all friendly with the Talarians now, but the Cardassians have just been getting bolder, testing us for weaknesses. They may be building up for a war.* Varley shook his head. *"Forgive me, Jean-Luc, but you did not choose the best time to leave us."*

Picard shook his head. "I'm an explorer, Donald, not a warrior."

Varley smirked beneath his mustache. *"That's what I used to say. Duty takes you in strange directions sometimes."* Varley sighed. *"I apologize, Jean-Luc. I don't intend to make you feel guilty."*

"And you haven't. Starfleet has many fine officers. You don't need me."

*"I hope not. And if you find what you're looking for . . . well, that may be more important in the eyes of history.*

*"I'll have my navigator compile the most up-to-date charts we have on the Scorpius Reach, Jean-Luc. We've made a few preliminary surveys out there. And I think there's a major research mission being planned for next year, though it looks like you'll be getting out there first. I trust you'll give us a little* quid pro quo *and share whatever navigational data you gather."*

"I will. Thank you, Donald."

Once he got the data, Picard was able to plot the most efficient route for at least eighty percent of the journey. If the ship performed according to specs, the travel time would be less than four months.

But those months would be spent in rather cramped conditions—perhaps more cramped than Picard was comfortable with, he realized when Langford let him in on her choices for the expedition. Not that he had anything against the personnel themselves, but he was dismayed to learn that both Xian Chuanli, the expedition's planetary sciences expert, and Stefcia Janasz, their engineer, would be bringing their families along.

"These aren't Starfleet officers, Luc," Langford told him as they stood together in the compact bridge—little more than a cockpit, really—of the ship that Langford had decided to dub *Cleopatra's Needle*. "You can't expect them to go off for the better part of a year and leave their lives, their families behind. Besides, Stefcia's wife Jameela is a medical doctor, so that's another slot on the roster filled."

"And their child? What duties can a two-year-old perform aboard ship, hm?"

"They can't very well leave him to fend for himself, or foist him off on relatives at such a critical phase in his development." She stared at him. "Honestly, Luc, what's gotten into you?"

He had the good grace to look embarrassed. "I'm simply . . . not very comfortable around children."

"Why not?"

"I don't know. I simply . . . haven't dealt with them much. I don't relate to them well. When I try . . . well, the less said, the better." The one encounter with a child that loomed largest in his memory was from four years ago, when he had needed to tell a five-year-old boy named Wesley Crusher that his father Jack was never coming home. He had attempted to offer some words of comfort, and he remembered the lad had been very brave and stoic about it, but he had seen the anger, the blame, in those wide brown eyes and known that he had no inkling of how to reach the boy.

"Hm," Langford said. "I guess that comes from being the younger of two. I was the eldest of six. I *had* to learn to be good with children for the sake of sheer survival." They shared a laugh. "But don't worry. Little Bazyli is a darling child, you'll love him. And Xian Yanmei will be no trouble—she's a very smart, responsible fifteen-year-old. She can work as a button-pusher and gofer, save us one grad student."

Picard grimaced. "Well, it's up to you. It is your expedition, after all."

She clasped his arm. "It's ours, Luc. Formal schooling aside, you have far more experience surveying alien planets than anyone else here, myself included. And the whole thing was your idea."

"Still, a mission can only have one leader. And I'm content for that to be you."

"This isn't a mission, Luc. It's a research expedition. In academia, we collaborate as equals. We consult with one another and try to arrive at a consensus." Picard scoffed, having seen his share of academia, and she confessed, "Well, in theory. Let's just say that these are smart, independent people with healthy egos and they'll be more cooperative if asked rather than ordered." He nodded graciously, conceding the point. "Except where the grad students are concerned," she finished with a chuckle. "Them we can order around to our heart's content."

Picard laughed too. "I appreciate the warning." Then he sobered. "I suppose I shall just have to learn to cope with the children's presence on board."

Langford shook her head. "Honestly, *Captain* Picard. You've faced down Cardassians and Breen, and you're intimidated by a two-year-old?"

He straightened, determined to maintain his dignity, though it simply made her more amused. "It's simply that it is a very small ship. We will be in close quarters, and some of the . . . adjustments may prove difficult."

Langford looked at him for a moment. "On that subject, Luc . . . you're right, with the children on board it will be tighter than we expected, even with you serving as the pilot. Perhaps . . . it would be more spacious if you and I shared quarters."

He stared at her for some moments, speechless. "Miliani . . . I hadn't realized . . ."

"Oh, don't make such a thing out of it, Luc. We're both adults, we're both single, we like each other, and we'll be in close quarters for quite some time. It's the most natural thing in the world."

He felt relief tinged with regret—or maybe the other way around. "Nothing more than that?"

She flushed just a bit. "Well, not necessarily. Oh . . . maybe a little. Don't tell me you haven't . . ."

"Oh, I have. I have indeed, Miliani." He took her hand. "But . . . Rosa, the other students . . . I already sense some resentment from them, a belief that I'm getting special treatment."

"You're entitled to privileges they aren't. You've earned them."

"Yes, but if we were to . . . share quarters . . . it would seem I was earning them in another way, and that would inappropriate for a lea—for the well-being of the expedition."

Langford considered it for a moment, then sighed. "You're right. I should have thought of that, it was a foolish impulse. . . ."

He stroked her cheek. "Not at all. You would never act foolishly, Miliani. And I am deeply flattered."

She studied him. "Only flattered?"

Picard smiled. "No. Not only that."

"Then . . . this is only for the good of the expedition?"

"Absolutely."

She leaned up and kissed him. It was gentle, almost chaste, but far from brief. "Then you and I will have to revisit this topic after the expedition."

"I await it eagerly."

She gave a sharp sigh, shook herself, and stepped away. "Enough fooling around, then. Let's go see what's out there!"

# 7

———

Stardate 36338

AS IT HAPPENED, IT ONLY TOOK *CLEOPATRA'S NEEDLE*
a bit over three months to find its target world, and to Picard's mind it had not come a moment too soon. Despite
Langford's reassurances, the children had made the journey
a continuing ordeal for Picard. Bazyli Janasz had chosen the
occasion of their expedition to enter a state known in ver-
nacular as the "terrible twos." Picard had heard of this condition, but had always assumed the tales to be exaggerated;
he, of course, had been quite well-behaved at that age, regardless of what his elder brother may have claimed. But
Bazyli seemed determined to live up to the reputation of his
age cohort, alternately squalling at the top of his lungs and
bouncing around the *Needle* like a Jacinnan racing cat on
Scalos water, finding his way into every compartment that
wasn't doubly security-sealed, claiming delicate scientific
equipment as part of his personal cache of toys, and generally reaffirming Picard's commitment to bachelor status. On
top of which, the boy seemed to develop a paradoxical fixation on Picard himself, despite all his efforts to dissuade

such attention. Picard quickly learned to lock the bridge door when he was on piloting shift, but the boy would lie in wait for him just outside the hatch, the only thing he would devote his unbroken attention to for more than ten minutes at a time. At first, Langford was amused by this, but after two weeks she took mercy on Picard and began running interference for him, using her formidable skills with children to divert the boy's attention. To be sure, the boy's mothers were no slouches in the parenting department, treating him with what, so far as Picard could tell, was a finely measured balance of love and discipline. But both women had duties aboard the ship, and Picard doubted that even two full-time parents could successfully manage a force of destruction such as Bazyli Janasz without help. Whatever ancient African had coined the proverb "It takes a village to raise a child" must have had a two-year-old in mind.

The other child, Xian Yanmei, had fallen short of her press as well. At first Picard had been impressed by the fifteen-year-old's intelligence and skill and had begun to admit she could be a valuable addition to the team. But she soon developed an intense fascination with one of the graduate students, a young Argelian computer expert named Sorma, who was nearly a decade her senior and already involved in a passionate (and distractingly noisy) relationship with Rosa Payne, a xenoanthropology student more his own age. Yanmei had descended into a deep sulk at first, apparently due to her conviction that Sorma barely noticed her existence, and as a result she barely seemed to notice her responsibilities, given how cursorily she executed them. But then Allis, the Kobheerian linguist, made the mistake of mentioning Yanmei's crush in Sorma's earshot, and the Argelian—who, Picard had to remind himself, was simply being true to the values of his own extremely open and hedonistic society— had proven quite willing to extend his affections to Yanmei as well. Both Rosa and Yanmei's father had reacted to this with considerable vehemence before Sorma's flirtations could proceed very far, which was probably best for the girl in the long run; but the melodramatic fights that had broken out between Yanmei and Rosa, Yanmei and her father, Rosa and Sorma, and so on had made Picard want to stay in his cockpit, lock the door, crank up the Mozart, and not come out until they found their planet. As it was, he had pushed the warp engines to the bleeding edge of their safety margins and scanned aggressively for subspace geodesics that could shave precious hours off their travel time.

And finally it had paid off. The B'nurlac records had included spectral readings of the target star, not well enough preserved to allow an exact match by themselves, but enough to narrow the range to G7 stars of a certain metallicity. It was then a matter of searching among those stars for one with three red-dwarf companions. Once they drew close enough to allow detection of the dim red dwarfs, they were able to pinpoint the system, which bore a single M-type companion at fifty-three AUs and a co-orbital pair at two hundred forty. Using Starfleet's navigational data, it was a matter of only another month to complete the journey.

The B'nurlac records proved equally accurate about the spectacular arrangement of the inner system, practically a travelogue of the major known classes of "hot Jovian" planets, giants that had migrated to the inner regions of their star systems. The innermost planet was an extreme case, hugging its star so closely that its "year" was under two standard days in length. The stellar wind and radiation pressure from the star turned the Jovian into an immense comet, with a tail of outblown atmosphere streaming from its dark side and trailing off into a faint spiral; it was no doubt somewhat less massive than it had originally been, but still substantial. The star and planet had interlocking magnetic fields, combining to create a diffuse gas torus that linked the two in a plane perpendicular to the planet's orbit. Stellar prominences arced from the star and dissipated into the torus, looking like a pair of fiery pincers reaching out to clamp down on the Jovian world.

The second Jovian was a limpid and profound blue globe

of cloudless atmosphere as deep as the eye could see, the third a pale world swathed in brilliant white clouds of water ice. It was as though some deity had distilled the essences of clear sky and cloudy sky and poured each into a separate globe. Of course their appearances were a predictable function of their atmospheric temperatures, but that made them no less striking to behold. Surely this beauty had been what had drawn the B'nurlac here to begin with.

The fourth planet was terrestrial and M-class, a large, ocean-rich world with several asteroidal moons. The next two out were massive worlds with thick crusts of ice—one with a tenuous sheath of nitrogen and water vapor, the other with a denser atmosphere consisting mostly of hydrogen. Beyond were several icy dwarf planets and assorted cometary debris.

"The fourth planet doesn't fit," Xian Chuanli said as he looked over the scans. Picard, Langford, and Doctor Ruyao, the Caldonian physicist, clustered around him in the *Needle*'s compact science lab. "The inward migration of the Jovians should've churned up the protoplanetary disk and caused an intense cometary influx—and after that there would've been ongoing bombardment from comets knocked inward by the red dwarfs, like with Proxima. Habitable planets in hot-Jovian systems are usually water worlds, like Pacifica or Naiad. And with *three* inner Jovians . . . well, you can see how much water and ice there is on the other worlds. This planet should have . . . what, Ruyao, seventy, eighty times as much water as it does?"

The towering Caldonian shrugged—or maybe he was trying to work a kink out of his shoulders, hunched over as he usually was in the ship's confines. "There are many variables that could alter the exact figure, but judging from the $H_2O$ abundance on the other worlds, it would most probably be several dozen times what we see."

"Right. The highest mountain on the planet should be ten, fifteen kilometers beneath the surface."

"Evidence of terraforming, perhaps," Picard said. "A good sign. Can we determine the age of the surface?"

Xian called up the geological data. "Hard to be sure from this range. But I can make out erosion features that must be tens of millions of years old at least."

"So we know the water must have been removed long before the B'nurlac came," Langford said.

"Uh-oh," Xian interrupted.

"Uh-oh?"

"There are power signatures down there. I don't think we're the only ones here."

Picard moved in to take a closer look at the readings, localized to a continent that was only now coming into view as their perspective changed. "It could be a settlement . . . but the readings are oddly diffuse. No massive concentrations of metallic signatures such as a city, but some of these power emanations speak of a fairly advanced technology."

An alarm began to sound; Picard recognized it as a proximity alert. He rushed forward to the bridge, where Stefcia Janasz was taking her turn at the helm. "Report," he snapped out of reflex, drawing some stares. Langford threw Stefcia a look, wordlessly apologizing for Picard and asking her to tell them what she knew.

"There's a ship on an intercept course. It looks pretty big."

"Warp-capable?" Picard asked, concerned about Prime Directive issues.

"With that acceleration curve, they've at least got inertial dampers. And that kind of field control usually comes with warp, doesn't it?"

"Usually," Picard said. "Hail—that is, I think we should hail them," he amended, turning to Langford for approval.

"All right, look," Langford said. "You're the resident expert on first contacts and diplomacy, Luc. I'm happy to defer to you on this, and I recommend that everyone else do the same, okay?" There was quick agreement from those assembled—probably quicker than there would have been if a large ship of unknown intent were not bearing down on them. "So give in to your impulses and tell us what to do."

He sighed. "Stefcia, would you hail the approaching ship, please?"

The engineer complied. After a moment, the console indicated a return signal had been received and auto-translation was underway, as the two vessels' computers engaged in an ultrafast language lesson beginning with basic physics and mathematics and working forward from there. It was a protocol that most starfaring civilizations adopted to facilitate first contacts, and thus served as further evidence that this was a warp-capable, interstellar species.

Still, the *Needle*'s translation software was not on a par with Starfleet's, so a process that would have taken seconds on the *Stargazer* dragged on for nearly a minute. The first intelligible words spoken were: "Unidentified ship, deactivate your engines and state your purpose."

Picard had been studying the sensor readings in more detail. The ship's overall technology seemed on a par with the Federation circa 2200, well behind the *Needle*'s, but it still greatly outclassed the smaller ship in power and armaments. So he complied with the first demand and opened a channel to respond to the second. "Greetings. This is the research vessel *Cleopatra's Needle,* belonging to the United Federation of Planets. We are on a peaceful mission of scientific research."

A face appeared on the viewscreen. It was a humanoid male, bronze-skinned, with a small nose, wide chin, and horizontal ridges along the cheeks and temples. His head and upper body appeared to be encased in a form of armor that looked bizarrely like tree bark, and Picard could not tell whether it was something he wore or a part of his body. *"I am Nibro of the Tanebor Orbital Guard. We are unaware of the United Federation of Planets."*

"We are from a distant sector of this galactic arm. We are new to this region, and we are pleased to make your acquaintance. Is Tanebor the name of your species?"

*"Tanebor is the world you approach. We are Mabrae. Your Federation has no territorial claim here."*

"And we make none. As I said, we are here simply to conduct scientific research. We seek knowledge that we believe may be found on Tanebor."

*"What form of research is this?"*

"This is an archaeological expedition."

Nibro's skepticism was clear. *"We colonized Tanebor only two generations ago. There is nothing there for an archaeologist to find."*

"We have reason to believe that the planet may have been inhabited at least twice before. It is those civilizations that we seek to learn of."

*"This world is ours now!"* The bark in Nibro's words matched that upon his skin. *"We dispute any claim of prior occupation!"*

Picard raised his hands placatingly. "Rest assured, the peoples I speak of have been extinct for many thousands, even millions of years. There is no one left among them to dispute your claim. And we seek only to learn what we can of them and their way of life." He measured his next words with care. If Nibro was representative, the Mabrae were a people with a strong sense of territoriality. He had to demonstrate respect for that, to acknowledge their power over their own turf and to show that this small expedition offered no threat. "Please . . . we are far from our own homes, and have traveled long. If nothing else, we would be grateful for the opportunity to rest and recover from our journey—and to enjoy the magnificent beauty of your system while we are here. And perhaps then we could be allowed to petition the appropriate authorities for permission to conduct archaeological research on your world, in accordance with whatever laws would apply."

Nibro seemed mollified by his words, but still skeptical. *"There are no specific laws for archaeology, for there has been none here. We have found no ruins in two generations."*

"Then we may be able to help one another. Any ruins would be extremely ancient, perhaps buried deep beneath your surface by geologic processes. Our expedition has specialized equipment for finding such ruins." *Specialized* being his diplomatic term for *probably a century or two beyond anything you have.* "Naturally any knowledge we gain shall be freely shared with you."

Nibro considered for a moment. Picard tried to read his eyes; if his Starfleet instincts had not grown too rusty, he had to conclude that Nibro was inclined to accept that the small expedition posed no threat, but was still obligated to assert his territorial dominance. *"You will accompany us to an orbital facility where your request for entry will be processed. If all is in order, then you will know the bounty that is Tanebor."*

Once Picard and Langford had made their case to the local officials, they found the Mabrae to be a more agreeable people than they had appeared at first blush. Indeed, once past the initial suspicion of outsiders, they took considerable pride in the abundance their world could provide to guests. They were actually quite beautiful, like something out of a fairy tale. They were graceful and elfin, and instead of clothing, their bodies were adorned with actual live plants. It was a symbiotic relationship that had evolved on their cool, oxygen-poor homeworld, the plants providing the mammals with extra oxygen while the mammals provided the plants with warmth and nutrients, the latter supplied by microscopic root tendrils that penetrated their skin. The horizontal ridges on their cheeks and temples extended to the backs of their hairless heads and were found along their sides and limbs as well, providing anchor surfaces for the plants—terraces of skin on a millimeter scale.

Over their history, the Mabrae had learned to cultivate and eventually bioengineer their epiphytic raiments into a wide array of specialized types. Picard had already seen the armor of their defense forces, indeed an analog of tree bark, but engineered into a dense organic-polymer resin that could stop a bullet. Other Mabrae's bodyplants were less all-concealing, but still specialized to fit the jobs and social roles of their hosts. Some were functional; laborers had abundant leaflike pockets for holding tools and equipment, desert-dwellers had broad sunshades on their heads and fleshy succulents for water retention, athletes wore very little covering to facilitate free movement. The politicians and diplomats bloomed with colorful flowers of countless personalized types. It was unclear whether these represented lifelong social castes, or if a Mabrae could change professions by crop rotation, so to speak.

Although they used refined metals where such materials worked best, much of the Mabrae's technology was built of strong and adaptable resins, rubbers, and plastics, if not actual wood. Their homes were interwoven with living trees or coated throughout the interior with vines. Some of these "houseplants," as Langford dubbed them, were specialized to provide fruits and vegetables, others grew large, spongy leaves for seating, while others provided the equivalent of plumbing and sanitation. (The Mabrae slept in what were essentially beds of mulch. Perhaps their small noses were a survival trait, though the fragrances of their floral attire were generally quite pleasant.) Picard had rarely seen such advanced bioengineering, despite the Mabrae's technological limitations in other fields.

Their botanical symbiosis also explained their strong territoriality, at least in Rosa Payne's xenoanthropological opinion. "They've always lived so close to nature," she told the others, "to the plants and the soil they grow in, that they literally feel like a part of it. Their land isn't just where they live, it's an extension of who they are. And since they've always depended on it to survive, they've always been suspicious of rival populations, because they could invade their home soil, steal its nutrients and water."

"In other words," Langford quipped, "they have very deep roots."

Their attachment to their land—even this alien land they had adopted, highly prized for its wet lushness—made it challenging to negotiate for digging rights. The Mabrae insisted on controlling access to their land and asserting ownership of anything found beneath it, and required Langford and Picard to jump through many bureaucratic hoops in pursuit of permission. Yet at the same time, Picard sensed that their bond with their land made them insatiably curious to know what Federation technology could reveal about its secrets.

But the government liaison, Coray, was not inclined to make it easy. She was a stunning, graceful Mabrae with mahogany skin and large bright eyes. Her athletic body was lightly adorned in vines that sported flowers and leaves in a few strategic areas, and her head was coated in a mane of delicate-seeming, multihued blossoms. From the start, it was clear that her outward beauty was a weapon she wielded in pursuit of her agendas. "I'm sure you understand my . . . position," she purred with bald innuendo when he protested the restrictive guidelines she sought to impose upon the digs. "I want you to be able to find the ruins you seek, but I have to protect my people's needs too." She flowed out of her spongy seat and came around the tablelike growth between them, leaning on its edge right in front of Picard. "And come now. Would it really be so unpleasant to let us work *closely* with you?"

Picard stared at her, unmoved. Perhaps twenty years before, he might have been swayed by such tactics, but now he found them somewhat vulgar. "Madam Coray," he said to spare her further embarrassment, "as appealing as the enticement you offer may be, I would not presume to accept it, and I do not believe you would truly grant it if I tried. My hope is to establish a relationship of mutual respect between our peoples, one that requires no veiled agendas or playing of games."

She froze for a moment, looking mildly offended, but soon schooled herself to display a businesslike poise. "Of course," she said, returning to her seat. "An admirable response to my test of your intentions. It reassures me that we may proceed in an environment of mutual trust." Her delivery was just a tad too calculated to be convincing, but it was at least an improvement over crude seduction. "But surely, Captain," Coray went on, "you must see that having Mabrae observers participating in the dig is entirely appropriate, and indeed will make your work considerably easier."

"Indeed it could," Picard replied. "But under the specific parameters you propose, it would make it difficult for my team to gain enough ongoing access to any ruins to make real study possible."

"Our people are quite capable," Coray countered, though her tone remained smooth and charming. She might have dropped the frankly sexual approach, but the refined allure of a mature, intelligent woman was still very much present as a subtext. She hadn't abandoned her strategy of seduction, simply adjusted her methods.

"I have no doubts about the innate ability or intelligence of the Mabrae," he assured her. "But the simple fact is that no one among your people has had reason to specialize in archaeology. It will be to your advantage as well as our own if you allow us to carry the brunt of this investigation."

"We have experts coming in from Taredin," she said, referring to their species' native world. "Once they arrive, you will be allowed to assist them."

"And how long will that take?"

"Several weeks for them to arrive, several more for transplantation."

"Transplantation?"

"Replacing their Taredinian epiphytes with Taneborian ones. They must be compatible with the land." Picard could not tell if she meant this biologically or ideologically. Either way, at least it confirmed that bodyplants could be switched out for other types.

Unwilling to wait that long, Picard tried to sweeten the deal by offering the benefits of diplomatic relations with the Federation. As a Starfleet captain, he was empowered to represent his government in negotiations with alien civilizations—although, given his reserve status, any agreement he made with the Mabrae would be informal until approved by the Federation Diplomatic Corps. He sought to encourage Coray's enthusiasm at the prospect of alliance with a civilization somewhat more technologically advanced than their own (though not enough so for the Prime Directive to impede him). As they negotiated, however, he sensed Coray's hope that the ruins or relics the expedition might unearth—found on Taneborian soil and thus Mabrae property, as she repeatedly reminded him—could give them whatever technological advantage they needed, perhaps even over the Federation itself.

Picard considered that unlikely; any finds would almost certainly not be intact, whether because of the ravages of time and geology or because the B'nurlac had removed anything of value. Technological insights would probably be fragmentary and require decades to reverse-engineer—a task for which the Federation was probably better suited, provided Picard could successfully ensure their access to the data. He strove to convey this to Coray, but she proved very focused on her agenda and skilled at advancing it. He had to be wary of her attempts to lull and cajole him into concessions, to get him off his guard and lure him into disadvantageous bargaining positions.

In the hope that giving Coray a win might make her more inclined to ease off on other points, Picard and Langford chose to make one major concession: they would focus their efforts only on any pre-Extinction sites they might find. Any B'nurlac ruins would simply be marked and left for the Taredinian archaeologists to unearth once they completed transplantation. The concession did much to salve the Mabrae's pride, and negotiations proceeded more smoothly thereafter. It was only to be hoped that the Mabrae would abide by the agreement to share their eventual findings with the Federation; but if not, at least there were other known B'nurlac worlds closer to home.

It took several weeks, but ultimately Picard and Langford won permission to scan Tanebor for archaeological sites.

The proviso was that all their work would be overseen by a Mabrae team that would have to give clearance before they could excavate. Given that team's lack of archaeological knowledge—and the fact that Coray herself would head it up—it was clear that it would be difficult to convince them of anything. Picard sensed that this would be a long, difficult process.

Indeed, Coray's team gave little ground and watched the offworlders keenly as they methodically scanned the planet for ruins. Still instinctively seeing the archaeologists as trespassers, they remained aloof and suspicious, uninterested in social interaction with the team.

In particular, Coray soon showed herself to be a rose with thorns. When Sorma, struck by her beauty and acting true to his Argelian sexual frankness, made one advance too many, he ended up in the nearest Taneborian hospital with a fairly serious case of anaphylactic shock. Or so it seemed at first. Jameela Janasz was called in to assist due to her greater familiarity with Sorma's physiology, enabling her to conduct an examination of her own. "It wasn't merely an allergic reaction," the cocoa-skinned doctor told the others out of Mabrae earshot. "Sorma was poisoned by some kind of toxic pollen. It looked to me like it was engineered specifically as a bioweapon. If you ask me, Coray's flowers are more than just decorative. And from the looks of them, all those different types growing on different vines . . . I checked, and if you look close enough you can see resemblances to a number of indigenous toxic plants. So she probably has some more serious poisons she can spray if she wants to."

Langford exchanged a look with Picard. "Is she a spy?" she asked.

"A government agent," Picard confirmed. "More than she appears. Able to neutralize us if we become too great a threat."

Looking worried, Stefcia clasped her wife's hand. "Are we in danger? The children?"

CHRISTOPHER L. BENNETT

Picard held out his hands, palms down. "Now, let's not overreact to this. From their perspective, it's a reasonable precaution to take in dealing with outsiders. No different from Federation security personnel carrying phasers with both stun and kill settings. We simply must take care not to provoke further incidents. We've begun to earn their trust, such as it is, and so long as we do nothing to lose it, we should be all right."

"Well, I bet Sorma's finally learned his lesson," Xian said with a touch of satisfaction.

Coray herself, when they spoke later, was unapologetic about the incident. "Your aide suffered a more severe reaction than intended, no doubt due to his alien metabolism," she said with measured ease and questionable honesty. "But he brought it on himself with his crass advances. And really," she purred as though it were the most reasonable thing in the world, "how could he expect me to be attracted to naked, hairy bodies that must be draped in dead cloth to hide their barrenness?"

Picard ignored the slight and hoped the others would follow his example. "Please forgive him," he said. "His cultural values differ from yours or mine, and he is young and inexperienced at adjusting to alien value systems."

Coray gave him a look that was superficially curious, but by now Picard could read it as suspicious. "You appear the same as he."

He returned her gaze pointedly. "Appearances can often deceive, Ms. Coray."

# 8

———•———

THE REAL TEST OF THEIR TENUOUS ALLIANCE WITH
the Mabrae came after nearly two weeks of searching. The
*Needle*'s ground-penetrating sensors detected the signatures
of advanced materials in a shape too regular to be natural, in
a sedimentary layer over two hundred million years in age.
The structure was inside the wall of a vast chasm dug by one
of the planet's mighty rivers, and the sensors had missed it
until the *Needle* passed overhead at an angle giving line-of-
sight on the canyon wall. On closer inspection, that portion
of the canyon edge appeared very different from its surroundings, the sheer, stratified rock walls interrupted by a
sloping, jumbled grade that began well back from the surrounding edges and protruded out into the canyon floor. According to Xian, it looked as though the upper portion of the
canyon wall had been blasted into slag and debris that had
slid down and buried the ruins.

"The B'nurlac," Picard said to the others as they stood on
the far edge of the chasm, looking across at the blasted slope.
"They must have found the ruins in the canyon wall, exposed by megayears of erosion. And then, afterwards, they
must have blasted the rock face to bury them again."

Coray took a step closer to the edge, her garlands ruffling

in the wind. "Why would they have done that? Could they have found something dangerous in the ruins?"

"Not necessarily," Langford told her. "Their civilization was destroyed when their bioengineered slave races rose up to eradicate them. They may have buried the ruins to prevent the rebels from finding them. Or perhaps the rebels themselves did it as a terrorist act."

"If there are usable structures there," Picard said, "then given these readings, they may have been extraordinarily durable. Either side may have used the ruins as a bunker during the war, and been buried alive when the other side attacked. We may find bodies."

Langford grinned. "One site, two civilizations. How convenient."

The Mabrae were as eager as the Federation team to find what the ruins contained, so approval to dig came quickly—although a contingent of bark-armored security personnel (Picard was beginning to think of them as Dryads) soon arrived to complement Coray's team and keep close watch both on the ruins and on the aliens who would excavate them. But for once, the Mabrae's presence helped to accelerate the work, for the heavy excavating equipment they provided allowed the mountain of slag to be removed faster.

Past a certain point, of course, faster was not better. Archaeology was meticulous, thorough work out of necessity. Excavating a site usually destroyed it, or at least destroyed the context of its contents, and so every archaeologist had a duty to future generations to document everything—literally *everything* that was found, regardless of its importance to their specific investigation—because it might prove crucial to some future avenue of study generations hence. Even the blasted rock face was scanned in detail, layer by layer, before it was removed, in case it contained B'nurlac artifacts or remains. Chemical analysis of the rock itself could provide insight into the weapons used to shatter it, and thereby help explain who reburied the ruins and why.

Despite the help of the Mabrae equipment, Picard and

Langford still preferred to rely on the *Needle*'s transporter to beam away as much rock as feasible. A transporter could be a marvelous archaeological tool, for it documented everything down to the subatomic level even as it removed it. The data from its pattern buffer was routinely downloaded into computer storage for later analysis—at too low a resolution for precise rematerialization, but sufficient for gross analysis of the rock composition and structure. The ship's AI was sophisticated enough to identify artifacts and ecofacts, alert the team to the findings, and then, upon request, beam away only the matrix in which they were embedded, leaving them handily unearthed.

Still, they had only one transporter, and the gradual, meticulous process took weeks. Finally, after a month and a half on Tanebor, they unearthed the outer shell of what sensors read as an extensive structure stretching back into the rock as deep as they could scan. Potassium-40 and uranium-235 dating of the stratum it rested upon gave its age as 252.3 million years, an almost perfect match for the start of the Permian-Triassic extinction on Earth.

"Getting in won't be easy," Stefcia told the others as they stood together in the large notch they'd dug into the canyon wall, staring at the expanse of crumpled, dusty metal their work had exposed to sunlight for only the second time in the past quarter-gigayear. "That sucker's made of neutronium."

"Neutronium?" Coray asked.

"Well, hyponeutronium, I should say. The real stuff would sink to the center of the planet." Coray only seemed more puzzled, so Stefcia elaborated. "It's a name we use for alloys of heavy transuranic elements. Their nuclei are mostly neutrons, and with the right alloy mix they can become some of the densest materials outside of collapsed matter. Hence, 'hyponeutronium.' But sometimes we get lazy and drop the prefix."

"Whatever you call it," Xian Yanmei asked from where she stood behind them, "how do we get through it?"

"We keep digging," Langford told the teenaged girl. "If the B'nurlac did use this facility, they must have found or made an entrance." Yanmei groaned.

But Stefcia's engineering insights let them narrow the search, so it took only three more days to unearth an entry hatch. Or rather, what was left of one. Even its sturdy hyponeutronium construction had been partially squashed by the weight of gigatonnes of sandstone crushing down on it for a quarter-billion years. The hatchway was thus buckled outward, its original hatch missing and replaced with a new door custom-made to the shape by the B'nurlac, using more conventional duranium. That door was found inside, crumpled under the mound of compacted rubble that spilled in through the hatchway; no doubt it had given way to the pressure more readily than the surrounding walls had.

Before the team removed the rubble and exposed the interior to the outside air, a thin tube was driven through to sample the interior atmosphere. Tricorder readings told them what they needed to know about its composition and safety, but the "preserve everything" mentality of the archaeologist compelled them to take actual samples of the undisturbed air for future study.

To minimize atmospheric changes that might damage any remains inside, they put up a simple airlock, essentially a pressurized tent, before they beamed away the rubble blocking the hatchway. Then, finally, they were able to tiptoe around the fallen B'nurlac hatch and make their way into a facility older than the first proto-dinosaurs on Earth.

It wasn't easy, though. The ceiling had sagged, the supporting walls and columns crumpled, so that the clearance was no more than a hundred and eighty centimeters, less in many places. The corridors had relatively high clearance, but the larger rooms' ceilings sagged badly in their unsupported centers. This would not have been a great problem for the B'nurlac, with their low, ankylosaurian bodies. For the humanoids, though, it was rougher going. Ruyao was content to stay outside, saying that there was no need for a theoretical physicist to be present on the scene. Picard couldn't blame the Caldonian, who had bumped his high, bifurcated head quite enough times on the *Needle*'s door jambs.

Still, this was an archaeological site of a sort rarely found on a planet's surface—an open, air-filled chamber sealed off from the outside world over geologic time, not flooded with sediment, bowed but uncollapsed, protected from wind and rain and animals. Skeletal remains and many kinds of artifacts could survive indefinitely in such conditions. Indeed, there were B'nurlac skeletons lying here and there, no doubt where they had suffocated after the compound had been reburied. Their presence reinforced the theory that the blasting of the cliff face had been a military strike or terrorist act. The bones were covered in an organic mush, the remains of their flesh and organs eaten away by the microbes that had inhabited their bodies. But eventually, the microbes had run out of usable chemical compounds to digest and died out before they could eat away more than the outermost surface of the bones themselves. The worst damage the skeletons had suffered was from the weight of their bony dorsal carapaces slowly crushing the ribs, skulls, and leg bones underneath them. The forward arms and clubbed tails were the best-preserved bones aside from the carapaces themselves.

At any other time, Picard would have been fascinated to learn more about the B'nurlac, to investigate how and why they had died and what their remains could reveal about their behavior in death, and thus possibly their beliefs and values in life. He certainly wished the Mabrae archaeologists well in discovering those answers, and did his part to ensure that the B'nurlac remains were meticulously documented before being removed for further analysis. (The B'nurlac were now extinct, so there was no one to object to their removal. Still, Langford urged the Mabrae to treat the remains with respect. She doubted her words would be effective, though; the Mabrae were clearly eager to study a species more alien than any they had yet encountered.) But Picard's primary interest was the compound itself and the far more ancient race that had built it.

Yet no remains beyond the B'nurlac's were found; presumably the B'nurlac would have removed any earlier remains before adapting the facility to their use. Moreover, the original computer consoles had been torn out and replaced with B'nurlac equipment. Picard hoped that beneath the surface, some remnant of the original data banks would still be there, or that some form of hard-copy documentation survived. Unfortunately, it became clear over the following days that the B'nurlac occupiers, more likely soldiers than scientists, had stripped the compound of virtually anything that might give insights about its builders or their civilization. The only free equipment or documentation found was B'nurlac, and the original computer cores had been gutted and replaced.

Picard was deeply disappointed by this. "I'd been hoping the B'nurlac might have adapted the original systems to their own use," he told Langford. "They often did scavenge other technology."

She patted him on the back. "In this case, the technology was a quarter-billion years old. Maybe it just didn't work anymore. Sure, theoretically we could have extracted data from their systems if we'd found them, but we couldn't have expected them to just start up and work perfectly."

"With some sufficiently advanced technologies, it's been known to happen," Picard replied. Giving a heavy sigh, he went on, "This whole thing is starting to feel like a dead end."

Langford furrowed her brow. "I'm not so sure. Think about it, Luc: does this compound seem like it could've been self-sufficient to you?"

He stared at her. "Are you suggesting there could be other structures nearby?" She nodded. "We can't be sure of that. True, it doesn't have the facilities to be totally self-contained, but its needs and personnel could have beamed in from halfway around the planet."

"Why overcomplicate things, though? We could beam to the university from anywhere on Centauri III, but we still choose to live nearby. It's just more efficient." She smiled. "And we've found two hatches so far, and if the architectural pattern holds, there are probably others. More evidence that the people who lived or worked here had reason to go to other places nearby."

He came to his feet, buoyed by renewed hope. "We need to get our best ground-penetrating sensors in here. Against the outer walls."

"Right away," she agreed, rising with him.

But before she could move, he impulsively hugged her and kissed her forehead. "That's why you're the teacher and I'm the student. Thank you." He ran toward the airlock, belatedly realizing that it had taken her a few seconds to begin to follow.


Finding the next building over took hours, but digging a path took another week, even with the use of transporter relays to let the *Needle* reach down this far. Here, the original hatch was still present, but the buckling of the walls left openings that let the team pry it open and slip inside.

Here was a place the B'nurlac had certainly never reached. Its original equipment and furnishings were intact, their configuration suggesting a nonhumanoid but still bipedal form, willowy and long of limb, perhaps with some kind of dorsal crests or spines that fit into the open grooves in their seat backs. And yet there were no remains. There were piles of residue that may have been clothing, but nothing biological. A device like a data padd lay on the floor in one room, as though it had fallen there. It was nonfunctional. "It's almost like there were people here and they left in a hurry," Langford said.

A desklike structure turned out to be a computer console, and Stefcia was able to get it open and interface with its systems. Picard was hoping these beings had built robust data storage systems. But what Stefcia found was badly decayed. "It's worse than ordinary quantum erosion," Stefcia said, "or data corruption from the background radiation of the surrounding rock. If these memory crystals work the way I suspect, they should be very stable against quantum shifts, multiply redundant too. It's like they were hit by a massive discharge of energy."

"What kind of energy?" Picard asked, crouching beside her, for the ceiling was too low for him to stand up.

"Hard gamma, nucleonic radiation . . . probably tetryons too."

Langford frowned. "I thought those didn't occur in normal space."

"They're only stable in subspace," Picard said, "so evidence of their effects indicates that a subspace phenomenon occurred nearby."

Curious, Picard set his tricorder to scan for evidence of tetryon exposure in the materials of the room. He found several areas that appeared to have been so irradiated, with the loci at various places within the structure. One such locus was almost directly above where the fallen padd was found. "As though it came from the people," Langford said slowly.

Coray looked up sharply from where she crouched. "Some kind of weapon, disintegrating them?"

"Or a subspace transporter of some kind," Picard said. "One that their technology wasn't shielded against, however."

"You spoke of a great extinction event throughout the galaxy," the Mabrae went on. "Could this be actual evidence of it?"

"We can't assume that. We aren't even certain there was a widespread extinction at that time. If there was, then it would surely have been quite gradual on a humanoid time scale, not a single event." He shook his head. "We need more information to go on before we try to form theories about any of this."

And so, once they had completed the meticulous task of documenting and thoroughly scanning anything they might disturb, they again brought in the ground-penetrating sensors and searched for other structures. It took weeks more to excavate and document each of the ruins they found. The further buildings contained little evidence beyond what was in the second, at least pertaining to the specific questions Picard had; but still the team took its time documenting and sampling everything for the benefit of future researchers. Picard found himself beginning to grow impatient. He remembered telling Guinan, roughly eight months ago now, that starship exploration was rushed and cursory, and that it was careful, meticulous study over the long haul that revealed the deepest truths. But now he was starting to miss the Starfleet approach, to wish he could just go after the specific piece of information he wanted and leave the rest for a dedicated science vessel to deal with later. Still, he recognized that as a selfish, immature impulse. He had a responsibility to history to do this right, no matter how long it took.

Finally, after three more weeks of digging, they hit something better: a large, expansive structure, now mostly collapsed in on itself, containing numerous semihollow objects. "A ship hangar!" Picard practically crowed.

"What's so great about that?" the weary Yanmei asked in the infinitely jaded tone that only the very young could master.

He resisted glaring at her. "We've been hoping to find maps, databases that could lead us to other, contemporary civilizations. These ships would have them."

"But what if they're as decayed as the data in all the other structures?" Coray asked.

He grinned. "That's all right. There are over a dozen ships there, all of the same design. Multiple copies of the same database—and they can't all be eroded in the same places. All we have to do is fill the gaps in each with data from the others. With luck, we'll be able to reconstruct a full navigational database." He met Miliani's eyes and grinned wider. "And then our quest can really begin."

It took more long, hard weeks to excavate the hangar ship by ship. Not only had the structure itself been largely crushed, but many of its overhead launch doors had broken open, allowing earth and rock to pour inside. Many of the ships were badly crumpled, their data crystals shattered beyond repair.

But gradually, over the weeks, they accumulated a set of reasonably intact data crystals. Only a few showed the kind of damage observed in the residences' computers; going on the assumption that the radiation surges had been centered on the buildings' occupants, it suggested that most of the ships had been unoccupied at the time of . . . whatever. But a quarter-billion years of quantum erosion and geological background radiation had still taken their toll.

Eventually, with the help of Sorma and the Mabrae's computer skills and Allis's linguistic abilities, they were able to rebuild a partial navigational database. It proved fortunate that the database came from spacecraft. Mere positional coordinates would be useless after more than a full galactic orbit. But spaceships needed to do more than simply end up at the same point where a system was located; they had to match its motion through space as well. And of course stars' positions slowly changed over centuries, so navigational databases needed to keep up. Thus, the reconstructed data gave star coordinates based on the parameters of their orbits around the galactic core—semimajor axis, eccentricity, inclination, argument of perigalaction, and so forth. Tanebor's location provided a baseline for their definitions of galactic longitude and orbital plane, enabling the conversion of the other systems' coordinates.

Of course, the chaotic interactions of stars and gas clouds over hundreds of millions of years would have altered these orbits substantially. Luckily, Federation astrophysicists had extrapolated most of the large-scale interactions, and applying those algorithms to the reconstructed data let them narrow the probable current locations of these stars to within a few dozen parsecs. Spectroscopic and planetary-system data from the ancient navigational banks would let them home in the rest of the way, as the B'nurlac records had done with Tanebor.

Thus the team was able to select several candidate systems within a reasonable distance. With the Taredinian archaeologists having now arrived to take over further excavation here, Picard, Langford, and their team made plans to survey those systems. At the urging of the team, Picard agreed to focus on the three candidates closest to the Federation. "After all," Langford stressed as the team sat together in the *Needle*'s compact lounge, "we still have lives and studies back on Centauri. We've been gone seven months already; we have to start thinking about wrapping this up and getting back to other responsibilities." She met Picard's eyes. "Other things we'd like to do with our lives."

He smiled back. "Understood. If we don't find anything at these three sites . . . well, I can always come back once I've earned my doctorate."

"Maybe *we* can," Langford said. Breaking their gaze, she looked around at the others to include them again. "By now, we all qualify as the Federation's leading experts on the Proto-Taneborians," she went on with a chuckle. "Who better to mount a second expedition?"

The government of Tanebor insisted on participating in the search, adamant that they had a rightful claim to any discoveries arising from research conducted on their soil. Since they had no ships fast enough to keep up with *Cleopatra's Needle*, they insisted that Coray and an aide travel aboard her. The team members resisted this; not only was the ship crowded enough already, but few of them were happy with Coray's superficially warm but unrelenting oversight. But the Mabrae refused even to allow the *Needle* launch clearance unless they acceded to this demand.

And so, much to her dismay, Xian Yanmei had to share quarters with her father, freeing up an extra room for Coray and her aide. This "aide," Bilan, turned out to be one of the bark-armored Dryad soldiers. He constantly watched the Federation personnel with a harsh, suspicious glare, but was intensely loyal and obedient to Coray—leading to speculation among the team about just what the two of them did together in their shared quarters, and, if it was what many in the team suspected, just how Bilan's armor plating affected the logistics of the act.

Picard, of course, was above such gossip, and he passed the time working to improve the analysis of the reconstructed star charts, as well as assisting Langford and the others in the detailed analysis and preservation of the artifacts and remains they had been allowed to take with them. This leg of the trip added weeks more to their journey, as they trekked toward galactic south in the rough direction of Lambda Scorpii. But the work kept them occupied and made the time go quickly, despite the Mabrae's continual scrutiny.

Their first destination was a K6 star a hundred and fifty light-years from Tanebor—the nearest candidate they had found, though at the time of the original charts it had been a close neighbor. They were able to confirm its identity by its spectrum and the configuration of its planets. However, they found one major anomaly: the Class-M planet shown in the database was missing. All the other planets were there, although Xian's simulations showed their orbits to be consistent with what they would be if the third planet had disappeared sometime between 220 and 270 million years before.

"Disappeared?" Picard asked.

"Or been moved out of the system quickly enough that the gravitational effect on the others was minimal. Either way, whatever we might've been looking for is gone now, if it was ever here."

But the possibility remained that the inhabitants had

settled the other worlds in the system, though none were habitable without artificial aid. Scans of those bodies revealed a number of ruins, but closer exploration revealed that all of them had been stripped down to the superstructure sometime in the distant past. "By the B'nurlac?" Coray asked.

"Or someone else. We are dealing with a time span more than ten thousand times greater than your recorded history or ours. Many civilizations could have passed through here in the interim."

But with only mysteries to be found, there was no point in remaining in the system, so they soon left it behind and set course for their next target, a G4 star another hundred and twenty light-years away, bringing them somewhat closer to Federation space though still in unexplored territory. At least, it had been. According to a recent dispatch Picard had received from Donald Varley, the Starfleet vessel *U.S.S. Mary Kingsley*, under the command of Captain Onna Karapleedeez, was now heading into the Scorpius Reach on the first leg of a two-year Beta Quadrant survey.

Picard had politely thanked his old friend for the heads-up. But he had grown close to his teammates (the adult ones, at least) and shared in their confidence that they could achieve anything Starfleet could, perhaps surpass it, even if it took them longer to do so. He was determined not to call on Starfleet for assistance if he could possibly avoid it.

# 9

---

A SHADE OVER TWO MORE WEEKS OF TRAVEL brought them to their destination. The G star's third planet was a borderline M-class desert world, probably more temperate a quarter-billion years ago when its sun was less luminous. There were few indications of ruins on the planet, since its fairly active plate tectonics had recycled most of its surface in the interim. But on the fifth planet, they hit paydirt. It was a world roughly the size of Mars, but built more like a larger version of Europa or Enceladus: a rocky core covered by a deep mantle of liquid water and a thick crust of water ice. Its smooth, high-albedo surface, most of it bright as a pristine snowfall, showed it was geologically active, with cryovolcanoes spewing water into its thin nitrogen-methane atmosphere and coating its surface in what was essentially a very fine sleet. Sensors showed this cryovolcanism to be driven by the planet's internal heat, its core kept molten by the radioactive elements within it. Moreover, the splashes of red and brown around many of the volcanic vents read as organic residue, indicating the presence of life in the subglacial ocean. The *Needle*'s dynoscanners corroborated this, indicating numerous aquatic life forms, probably of the chemosynthetic type generally found in such environments. But scans showed no signs of the characteristic waveforms of intelligent thought or the activities and constructs of a technological civilization.

All of this would have been intriguing enough to Picard as an explorer, but it faded into the background when scans detected the signature they had sought for eight months: a spherical object roughly forty meters in diameter, reflecting a hundred percent of sensor emissions and giving off zero emissions of its own. It showed no distinct edges, with the readings instead seeming to trail off or blur into the background—exactly as Guinan and the ancient records had described.

The spherical phenomenon read as part of a larger construct buried deep in the icy crust, over fifteen kilometers down and two kilometers above the slush zone between the crust and the watery mantle. It was tilted at an odd angle, with the reflective sphere in the lower half of the structure. "How in God's name did it get down there?" Jameela asked as the team reviewed the readings in the lab.

"I have a hypothesis," Xian said. "It might have been the kind of research base we use to study subglacial life on Europa-type worlds like this."

"But wouldn't it have had to be at the bottom of the crust?"

"It probably was, originally. Remember how long it's been. The pattern of cracks and dead calderas on the surface suggests that the crust rotates slightly faster than the planetary core. After all, it's literally floating on the mantle, not actually attached to the core, so it doesn't have to spin at exactly the same rate. If this base had originally been at the bottom of the crust, imagine what would happen if it drifted over one of the thermal vents in the ocean floor. The heat would have melted the surrounding ice. If the base was airtight and built of light enough materials, it could have been buoyant and floated upward. Then, once that part of the crust drifted past the hot spot hundreds of millennia later, the water would have frozen again, trapping the base inside." Xian chuckled. "I guess we're lucky it wasn't heavier than water, or it would've been too deep for us to reach."

"Can we beam down through fifteen kilometers of ice, though?" Langford asked.

"Maybe," Stefcia told her. "Ice is a lot less dense than rock. And if we don't have enough power to beam there directly, we can drill into the surface, drop a relay down there."

Picard stared at the sensor screen's outline of the ancient base buried deep inside the ice. After all these months, had they finally reached their goal?

And what new journey would it start them on?


After a bit of discussion, the team agreed to name the ice planet Proserpina, after the goddess Ceres's daughter whose abduction into the underworld brought winter until she was allowed to return above.

The transporter barely had enough power to reach the base through Proserpina's crust, so Stefcia's relay plan was instituted as a precaution. Landing on the surface, setting up the mining phaser, and digging their bore hole took up more precious time, but after waiting this long, Picard chided himself for being so upset over a few more hours.

Once the relay was in place, the team began by beaming out a test sample of the air, as procedure dictated. It consisted almost entirely of nitrogen; no doubt most of the oxygen had been exhausted long ago in chemical reactions with the materials making up the base. It was also less than two hundred Kelvin—much warmer than the planet surface, but still lethally cold. So the initial team—Picard, Langford, the Janaszes, and Coray (at her insistence)—beamed down in full EVA suits to get the lay of the land.

Picard and the others stumbled and slipped when the

transporter beams released them onto a surface that was sloped at over twenty degrees and covered in a frost of carbon dioxide and water frozen out of the chill atmosphere. Langford fell against him and he caught her, being the quickest one to regain his footing. "Thanks," she said, smiling up at him through their visors. He returned the smile and advised the team to engage the adhesion pads in their soles. Even aside from the frosty slope, the gravity here was under a third of standard, providing little traction.

Suit lights dimly illuminated a wide cylindrical space. Stefcia angled her light downslope, roughly along the chamber's axis, but it illuminated no sign of a far wall. "Just as well if we don't know how far down it goes," Jameela teased her wife.

But Stefcia had other ideas. "Let's shed some light on the situation," she said, removing a cave illuminator from her pack. This was standard equipment for dig sites, a telescoping pole that expanded into a sort of torchiere with a brilliant white light source on top, bright enough to illuminate a decent-sized cavern but sheathed by a translucent funnel-shaped shade to protect any eyes that looked in its direction. Stefcia expanded the illuminator and secured it to the floor, angling its "lampshade" to compensate for the tilt, and setting it to brighten gradually to about medium level, adequate for a chamber this size.

As the lighting came up, Picard looked around to get a sense of how far apart the walls were. He was startled to discover that there were apparently no walls at all. The growing light showed that they occupied what appeared to be a perfect cylinder carved into the ice. "It can't be," Stefcia said. "Ice is too soft—it would've flowed and filled in this space by now."

Picard went over to the wall, scanning with his tricorder. The thin coat of frost along the walls, rapidly sublimating away under the heat from the illuminator, followed a contour some twenty centimeters inward from the visible curve of ice, as though coating an unseen surface. "There is a composite material of some sort here. But it's . . . perfectly transparent. Essentially invisible."

"A cloaking field?" Langford asked.

"It reads more like the kind of metamaterials that were used in early invisibility research," Picard said. "But metamaterials have limited applications because they can only be made perfectly transparent to a narrow range of wavelengths. They're useless in most lighting conditions. This . . . somehow, it's able to achieve the same effect over the whole visible spectrum—possibly beyond. That shouldn't be possible!"

"But it's beautiful," Langford said, her helmet slowly turning as she took in the room. "Look how clear and pure the ice is. It's like being in an Andorian fairy ta—" As her helmet tilted upward, she broke off and gasped. Picard craned back, trying to see what she had seen, and was struck just as speechless.

Embedded in the frozen crust above him was a vast crystal chandelier, thousands of linear stalactites hanging down from nothing, receding into the clear ice to form converging lines of perspective that stretched to the vanishing point. As the torchiere brightened and more suit lights pivoted up to scan the ceiling, the slender, ethereal columns shone even more brightly, sparkling as the lights played over them. *Mon dieu,*" Picard breathed. "What are we seeing?"

"I've seen this before," Langford said, "diving under the Centaurian icecaps to study the sunken ruins. They're tracks of bubbles—escaping gases that rose through the ice while it was still half-frozen." She laughed, moving underneath them to get a better view. "But these are so long, and they seem to go on forever! My God, it's beautiful!"

Once the team had gotten their fill of gawking at the scenery, Picard suggested they make their way toward the reflective structure. But as they headed downslope, carrying the torchiere with them, he and the others could not resist craning their necks upward to watch as the bubble tracks swept past, pivoting gorgeously around the vanishing point. "It's like . . . like warp streaks carved in crystal," he said.

Langford smiled at him. "I was going to say a forest of piccolos."

Picard let his imagination feed on the inspiration the magnificent vista provided. "Scepters of air. Signs pointing the way to infinity."

"A frozen meteor shower," Jameela suggested.

"A parade of magic wands," Stefcia countered.

"Anti-icicles!" Langford crowed, and the others joined in her laughter as the crystal sky continued to rain beauty upon them.

As they moved down through the compound, the structure of its walls began to change. The ceiling remained invisible, but the unseen walls gave way to patterns of large hexagonal cells with circular black openings within them. The beam-down area must have been some kind of observation lounge, Picard supposed. Soon, he realized that the circular openings were beginning to flicker with faint images, and a cool blue light was beginning to shine down from the ice, a fairy-castle illumination apparently refracted from a source behind the honeycombed walls. "It's like . . . like the material of the walls is drawing energy from us," Stefcia said, studying her tricorder screen. "From our body heat, our sensor emissions . . . the impact of our feet, even the kinetic energy of the sounds we make. They're using it to regenerate their power. Amazing!"

"Can you get a sample of the wall material?" Langford asked. Stefcia extracted a small phaser drill and cut a sample free from the edge of one of the hex cells. But no sooner had she put it in a sample tube that she noted activity from the hole she'd left. "There's some kind of fluid or gel seeping out of the cut edge." She scanned it more closely, setting her tricorder to high magnification. "Damn . . . it looks more like a wound clotting. I think it's trying to heal itself."

"Could it be organic?" Picard asked.

"Or nanotech so advanced it might as well be."

As they proceeded, they found a variety of hex-cell types in different parts of the compound. Some were larger than others, some smooth without the central black disks. Some of the disks were blank and flat, others patterned with three-dimensional protrusions in concentric rings, perhaps controls of some sort. Some of the rooms had furnishings of wildly varying shapes, as if to accommodate a variety of body types, and there seemed to be a rough correlation between the hex-cell and furniture styles in the different rooms. "Maybe each was specialized for a different species," Langford suggested.

As they drew nearer to the sensor-blind area, the walls began to show signs of wear. The shape of the corridor ahead seemed distorted. "Maybe compressed by the expansion of the ice freezing around it," Langford proposed. "I'd wondered how it stayed so intact."

"But if it's self-regenerating elsewhere . . ." Picard began.

She nodded. "Then why not here?"

The deterioration continued, with even the invisible ceiling growing cloudy and dark. Soon they came to a rift where the floor had given way, leaving only bare, slender support beams. It opened into a large chamber whose floor was a level below them. "Thank goodness for low gravity," Langford quipped.

Looking around, Picard moved over to the side wall, which extended down to the floor below. He got a grip on one of the hex cells and wedged his boot on the rim of another, finding to his surprise that the black "screen" material within gave way to the pressure of his toes like firm gelatin. The outer rim was rigid enough, however, and he found it supported his weight. Following his lead, the team cabled their suits together and carefully made their way down the wall. Picard studied the damage to it as he moved down. "It's as though it's partly . . . melted," he said.

"If the whole thing's a nanostructure," Stefcia observed, "maybe it can be programmed to change shape. If the mechanism breaks down, then it might lose cohesion."

"Let's make very sure of our footholds, then," Picard advised. In the low gravity, a fall would not be too dangerous by itself, but there was rubble below that could potentially damage their suits.

They made it to the lower level without incident and proceeded forward. The source of the null readings was very near now, in the blackness behind the ruins of the fallen ceiling, a clutter of beams and half-melted metamaterial that formed a partial wall before them. Picard spotted a break in the rubble. He started toward it, but stopped and turned to Langford. She smiled. "This is your quest, Luc. Go ahead."

Gingerly, he moved forward, climbing between the fallen beams. Stefcia came up behind him with the torchiere to illuminate what lay beyond. There, at the end of a wide, half-melted passage, lay . . .

What? There hardly seemed to be anything there at all. At first it looked like nothing more than a gray fog—but a fog would have movement. This was more a sort of blur, like a shape Picard's eyes could not bring into focus no matter how they strained. It had a sense of permanence to it, of tangibility, despite its elusiveness. "Just as the ancient texts described," he breathed. "At once there and not there."

Remembering himself, he stepped farther into the passage to allow the others clearance and began scanning it. But his tricorder revealed little more about the . . . shape . . . than long-range scans. It read more like a kind of spherical interference field that gradually trailed off with distance from its central mass. After a time, Coray grew tired of watching people stare at their instruments and moved in toward the field, ignoring the cautions of the others. As she approached, her extended hand began to meet with a gradually increasing resistance. "It's like pushing against the wind," she said. "It's getting stronger," she went on as she moved in closer, using both hands now. "My hands are starting to feel . . . slightly warm."

"Coray, move away," Picard warned.

"You are too cautious," she said with a teasing lilt. "How will we understand this if we don't confront it?"

"Look how damaged this structure is by increasing proximity to the zone," Picard told her. "We don't know what its effects on living flesh might be."

"It's . . . tingling now," she continued, ignoring him. By now she was surrounded by the fog, still visible but slightly hazed out. "The warmth is spreading through my arms. I . . ." Her voice rasped slightly, and she cleared her throat. "How embarrassing . . . I must be choked up with excitement."

"Coray, please be careful."

"Don't worry, nothing can get through the suit. Just a little farther—ahh—*ow!* My hands . . ." She started to pull back, but seemed to meet with some resistance. She called out, but her voice was choked again. "On . . . fire . . ."

Picard knew better than to risk going in after her and possibly giving the others a second victim to cope with. He tapped the comlink on his suit. "*Needle,* can you lock onto Coray and beam her out?"

"*I'm trying,*" Sorma's voice came back. "*There's some kind of interference.*"

Looking around, Picard spotted the illuminator pole that Stefcia held. Grabbing it from her, he pushed it into the field, feeling the increasing resistance as he pushed it in deeper. The field swallowed up its light, and by the time it reached Coray, the emitter had flickered and shut down, leaving only the suit lights to illuminate the scene. Picard tapped it against Coray's shoulder to make sure she noticed it. She reached for it, but her hands were twisted claws, unable to close around it. Finally she managed to hug it with her forearms and Picard and the others pulled her clear. "Medical emergency," Picard called. "Beam us up now!"


Coray's hands were swollen and inflamed, her arms not much better off. Her lungs were also inflamed, as though she had inhaled an excess of dust, but there was no dust in them. Her flowers and vines were dying, their petals falling off. This mortified Coray worse than her other injuries. It was more than just being humiliated, more even than being stripped of her defenses; she reacted to it like losing part of her body.

But Coray's injuries, along with the damage to the illuminator, her EVA suit, and their samples of the damaged base structure, gave the team the evidence they needed to determine the nature of the field. The medical database turned up similar symptoms resulting from early transporter accidents where the confinement beams had failed to expel the air from the target zone before rematerialization. It was as though something had been inside Coray's body, sharing space with it—even though there had been nothing there except the blur field. It had pervaded the suit and the illuminator as well as her body, not only getting through the surface layers of the suit but getting *within* them as well, uniformly throughout. But nothing was left behind except the evidence of a presence. As Picard had said below, it was as though something had been there and not there at the same time.

And that gave Ruyao the clue he needed to piece it together. For something to be in two states at once, it had to be a quantum phenomenon. And before long, the towering Caldonian had a theory for what could cause it. "The tales say these . . . phenomena are frozen in time, do they not?" Picard nodded. "Let us assume, for the sake of argument, that an object could be completely suspended in time. It would then have exactly zero motion, yes?" Again, Picard and the others in the lab indicated agreement. "But that would mean it had exactly zero momentum as well. And by the uncertainty principle, if its momentum could be determined so precisely, with zero uncertainty, then the uncertainty of its position would become infinite."

"What?" Yanmei asked.

"You must have covered quantum theory in class," Xian chastised his daughter. "Position and momentum. The more accurately you can measure one, the more uncertain the other is. The Heisenberg principle."

"Indeed," Ruyao said. "This positional uncertainty would effectively cause the waveforms of the particles to expand outward and overlap with surrounding particles—not unlike the way a Bose-Einstein condensate can form when matter is cooled to near absolute zero, its particle motion reduced to an extreme degree. However, in this hypothetical case, the reduction of momentum is far more extreme than is conventionally possible, allowing the particle overlap to manifest on a macroscopic scale."

"In other words," Picard said, "we're seeing the quantum uncertainty of its position. It's literally in many places at once."

"Correct."

"But how does it get through the suits?" Stefcia countered. "Even a spread-out quantum wave should still be blocked by a potential barrier like a solid surface."

"But its waves are already present in the space, fixed and unchanging. The suits and their occupants move into it."

"If its uncertainty is infinite," Langford said, "wouldn't it be *everywhere* at once? Throughout the whole universe? Not getting denser the closer you get to it."

"Essentially, the wavefunction of *every* particle has a nonzero probability of being anywhere in the universe," Ruyao replied. "However, in practice this probability is arbitrarily close to zero at most positions and may be discounted." He pondered, his massive brain working in that towering skull, much of whose volume was dedicated to cooling chambers to keep the powerful cerebrum from overheating. "You have a point, though. The uncertainty observed here is consistent with a momentum infinitesimally above zero, rather than exactly zero."

"Then perhaps the field is not completely frozen in time after all," Picard said with rising hope. "Perhaps there is a way to effect change within it."

"Perhaps," Ruyao replied. "Assuming that the uncertainty halo is caused by the mechanism under discussion. However, such a mechanism is purely an ad hoc postulate at this point; I can offer no theory as to what could produce such an effect. Known methods of temporal distortion do not behave in the manner observed here. There is usually a subspace gravimetric component. Yet this phenomenon seems just as causally decoupled from the subspace domains we can observe as it is from normal spacetime."

Picard looked around the group. "Any other theories? Assuming this is a temporal field of unknown type, how do we penetrate it? How do we alter it?"

Stefcia shrugged. "We could try beaming a probe into it, if we could penetrate the interference. If it is some kind of . . . quantum uncertainty field, it would be hard to get a lock on anything inside . . . but if we're just beaming a probe in instead of out, I could use a strictly positional lock. As long as the probe's inside the ACB, it'd still be in our time flow long enough to materialize . . . though after that, no promises."

But when they attempted the maneuver with the help of the relay, there was no result at all. The matter stream simply bounced off the outer edge of the zone, although the diffuse nature of the "bounce" caused the matter stream to lose cohesion, and the probe rematerialized on the pad as a pile of metallic slag. "Okay, I'm an idiot," Stefcia said as she and the others stared at its remains. "I should've known that would happen. If there's no time and no change, how do you even get a confinement beam to penetrate it?"

"So have we confirmed it is frozen in time?" Langford asked.

"Hard to say for sure. Either frozen or close enough that it'd take years or centuries for a nanosecond to pass inside."

"Is there anything else we can try?" Picard asked. "How can we affect the field itself, alter its time flow?"

Stefcia stared back. "Don't look at me. I'm not the theory guy around here."

Picard resisted snapping at her. It was just the nature of

CHRISTOPHER L. BENNETT

her profession. The Starfleet science officers he'd worked with for over twenty years were trained as generalists, adept at both theory and practice. Civilian scientists like Stefcia and Ruyao were more specialized in their expertise.

But that was the whole point of having this multidisciplinary team—so the specialists could fill in the gaps in each other's knowledge. So Picard asked Stefcia and Ruyao to brainstorm together on finding a solution.

Meanwhile, the base itself continued to regenerate its power. The longer the team spent within it, feeding it with the waste energy of their bodies and devices, the more alive it became. An artificial gravity field had formed, countering the slope and allowing the researchers to walk "upright" in the base's reference frame. Oxygen had been produced and risen to a breathable level, again somehow seeming to come from the walls themselves. The screens within the hex cells had become active, many displaying computer readouts or morphing solid controls out of their surfaces while others remained on standby or displayed abstract patterns of swirling color. The computers were clearly far more intact and functional than those they had found on Tanebor, but they were so massive and intricate that Allis and Rosa had trouble determining where to begin their efforts at decipherment.

Still, it gave the team another possible avenue, which Picard assisted Allis, Rosa, and Sorma in pursuing. If whatever—or whoever—lay inside the field was completely frozen in time, or near enough as made no difference, then there was no way of altering its state from the inside. That suggested that the occupants could have been relying on some external mechanism, perhaps something in the ice base's equipment.

However, the effect of the stasis field on the surrounding structure argued otherwise. Further observations confirmed that the decay was a result of the quantum field, the base's integrated, nanoscale technology thoroughly disrupted by the overlap of particles almost, but not quite, existing in the same space. Indeed, its systems, so dependent on fine atomic structure for their function, were even more vulnerable to disruption than humanoid flesh, which was why the damage extended so far beyond the visible quantum haze. Once power was restored, the base began attempts to repair itself, but the healing proceeded slowly and was seen only on the outer fringes of the decay zone. Over the next several days, Picard and the others became increasingly convinced that the ice base's computers had no more idea what the stasis zone was than they did, and were struggling to cope with the disruption in their midst. Whatever had created it, it was evidently not an intended part of the base's design, and that meant the base itself would provide no answers.

But Ruyao and Stefcia could do no better. The two of them went back and forth for days, tossing out ideas and proposals, but it soon became clear that instead of converging on a solution, they were just going in circles, increasingly arguing over their divergent worldviews. Stefcia was a nuts-and-bolts engineer uneasy with abstraction, and Ruyao was a pure theorist who saw the attempt to bend his theories to serve practical goals as an act of intellectual vandalism. Perhaps, given a few years, Ruyao could reason out a theory and devise a means of verifying it experimentally, and then others could develop new technologies based on that theory, whereupon Stefcia could apply them. But Picard was unwilling to wait that long. He was too close to the answers to quit now. He needed someone who could merge theory and practice, who could size up an unprecedented situation and whip up a solution on demand.

Loath though he was to admit it, he needed a Starfleet science officer. And he knew where he could find one.

*"Jean-Luc Picard! I wondered if we'd be hearing from you."* On the monitor, Onna Karapleedeez smiled, her eyes crinkling up beneath the column of violet-hued keratinous

scutes that covered the middle third of her forehead. The captain went on in her famous, booming voice. *"I knew you couldn't resist the smell of Starfleet for long."*

Picard smiled politely at the venerable, gray-braided Kreetassan. "I apologize for not contacting you before, Captain," he said diplomatically. "I've simply been so caught up in our explorations."

*"I know the feeling, Jean-Luc. We deep-space explorers, we are a breed unto ourselves. Even out of uniform, you still end up pushing the frontiers."* Karapleedeez laughed. *"And now you find there are some things you can't do without a uniform, no?"*

Picard resisted wincing, annoyed that she could read him so well. But then, Captain Karapleedeez was famous for her keen perceptions. Many people joked that she was half Betazoid, though she chalked up her prowess to her species' innate attention to detail, the meticulousness that gave the Kreetassans their reputation as a prickly, easily offended people. Of course, Karapleedeez, like many of her species, had learned to accommodate the relative chaos of other cultures in order to function as part of the larger interstellar community. But she was famous for running a tight ship and demanding perfection from those who served under her. It made her one of the most hated and admired captains in Starfleet.

Picard explained his situation to the captain, and soon she was nodding sagely. *"A fascinating find you've made, Jean-Luc. Potentially of galactic importance, if we can pierce it. Luckily, all we have scheduled is a brown-dwarf survey of the region. I can leave a shuttle crew behind to complete that while we come rendezvous with you. We can be there in three days."* Picard was surprised; he would have simply postponed the survey. But that was the Kreetassan way— everything in its proper time, place, and manner. *"I'll lend you my second officer. On the command track now, but she came from sciences, and excelled at it. I think you'll like her. And when you can spare the time from your busy research, come aboard and I'll give you a tour."* Typically, she didn't offer to share a meal, something her people considered a private, even intimate practice.

"I look forward to it. Thank you, Onna."

Stefcia was not pleased with Picard's decision, though she was angrier with herself for failing to find a solution than with Picard. Langford did her best to convince the engineer that it was not her fault, that this was simply beyond anyone's expertise and it would take more minds to solve it. The rest of the team members were eager enough for answers that they accepted the help readily. Ruyao was largely unconcerned one way or the other, content to play with permutations of his theories. Coray was still sulking like a lily in her tent, dejected at being defoliated and forced to wear dead cloth upon her skin, and made it known that she would have nothing to do with the discovery unless a way were found to shut off the quantum field. Bilan the Dryad was vigilant as ever, though, and insisted that the Starfleet officers be made fully aware of the Mabrae's claim to any discoveries that resulted.

Three days later, right on time, the *Kingsley* arrived. The *Hokule'a*-class starship was the first Starfleet vessel Picard had looked upon for over three and a half years, and the sight filled him with a mixture of nostalgia and discomfort, both of which were stronger than he had expected them to be after all this time. As he and Langford stood before the *Needle's* transporter stage, ready to receive their guests from the *Kingsley*, Picard wondered how he would react to the sight of Starfleet uniforms again, and braced himself.

The transporter keened, and three officers coalesced on the pads. Two were male ensigns, a human and a Vulcan, in the teal blue of sciences. The other was a dainty lieutenant in command burgundy, her long auburn hair tied back in a ponytail. She was young and elfin in appearance, but radiated an undeniable air of authority and competence.

Striding forward smartly, she extended a delicate hand to Picard and smiled as he took it. "Captain Picard, it's a privilege to meet you. I'm Lieutenant Kathryn Janeway. These are Ensigns Wright and Sabar."

"Lieutenant," he replied. It was a bit unusual for a lieutenant to be second officer, but the *Kingsley* had a small crew, mostly scientists. Picard guessed this was the young woman's first command assignment. "Allow me to introduce Doctor Miliani Langford, the head of this expedition."

Janeway looked startled, but quickly recovered and extended her hand to the professor. "Of course, Doctor Langford, I'm terribly sorry."

"Quite all right. Old habits die hard. And to be honest, this really is Jean-Luc's expedition. My name's on the paperwork, but he's the *éminence grise*."

"Well," Picard demurred, running a hand over his remaining hair, "not too *grise* yet."

"But very distinguished," Janeway said with warm humor. Though there was obvious respect in her manner toward him, there was no trace of intimidation or undue deference. Picard found that refreshing.

"Now." Janeway clapped her hands together. "Where's this puzzle we're here to solve?"

# 10

———

PICARD TOLD LIEUTENANT JANEWAY NOTHING about the vista of bubble tracks before they beamed in together. Once she arrived, though, she seemed unimpressed by the beauty of the ice; if anything, she seemed disturbed for a moment before she regained her professional mien. Picard briefly wondered if she was claustrophobic. But then a memory resurfaced from a bit over a year ago, a news item about the death of Admiral Edward Janeway. If he recalled correctly, it had been in a crash in the polar region of Tau Ceti Prime. If this Janeway was related to the admiral, it would explain her reaction. But Picard was not inclined to pry.

If the environment did trouble Janeway, she gave no further sign of it. However, she reacted with considerable interest when they reached the decayed portion of the base and came upon the quantum field. The fallen ceiling had been cleared away and a ladder placed at the corridor breach, allowing easier access. "Oh my," she whispered when it came into view. "Now there's something you don't see every day."

"Take care not to approach too closely," Picard advised her. "The quantum bleed is still present even where it isn't clearly visible."

"Of course we're within the edge of its waveform even

now, as the damage to this facility shows," she said, waving a hand to encompass their surroundings. She chuckled.

"Lieutenant?"

"It's a little ironic, Captain. Here we are trying to get inside the thing, and in a way we already are."

"Not in a very useful way, though."

"You never know, sir."

He gave a self-deprecating smile. "I'm not in uniform, you know. You can call me Jean-Luc."

She smiled back. "I know. But I'd rather call you Captain."

Janeway continued to scan the field, drawing closer than Picard had recommended. "Lieutenant—"

"It's all right, sir. I know my limits. And you don't get the job done by holding back." Was there a subtle chastisement in her tone? He was probably imagining it.

After a while, Janeway retreated, switching her tricorder to her left hand and shaking the right as though it had grown numb. "I'd like to take these readings back to the *Kingsley*, run them through our main computer," she said. "Your party is welcome to join me." She gestured to the ensigns. "All right if Sabar and Wright stay here to run some additional tests?"

"Certainly. And we will accompany you."

Bilan, who had been standing watch under Coray's orders, strode forward. "I insist on observing as well."

Janeway looked over his sturdy, bark-armored frame. "Yes, I imagine you . . . *would*."


Once aboard the *Kingsley*, Picard exchanged the expected pleasantries with Captain Karapleedeez, but was eager to get on with the data analysis. It was just as well that the captain did not insist on sharing a meal.

As Janeway led him, Langford, Stefcia, Ruyao, and Bilan to the ship's physics lab, Picard noted that many of the crew were watching him as they passed by. Janeway noticed his unease. "Sorry for the stares, sir. People in Starfleet still talk about you often."

He grimaced. "The man who had the *Stargazer* shot out from under him."

Janeway stared at him in disbelief. "The *Stargazer* was lost because it had a lousy fire-suppression system. You're the man who saved the ship when its captain was killed, led it through twenty years of expanding the frontiers of knowledge, and then staved off total annihilation with a brilliantly unorthodox manuever that won him the Grankite Order of Tactics and ended up as part of the textbooks. These men and women are wondering if they'll ever have the chance to serve with you, sir."

He studied her face. "Starfleet didn't seem to mind when I chose to take an indefinite leave of absence."

"Absence makes the heart grow fonder, sir."

"So that's it, eh? I'm the kindly old uncle of Starfleet. A relic of the past. Fine, let it stay that way. They'll appreciate me more." He pulled ahead to end the conversation.

As a result, he almost missed the lab, but soon enough he was deep in analysis and discussion with the others. "You were right, Doctor Ruyao," Janeway said after a while. "This has got to be a Heisenberg effect resulting from the zero momentum of the particles within the stasis field. Uncanny, to see a quantum effect with the naked eye!"

"But as we discussed," Ruyao said, "the finite extent of the wavefunction suggests a nonzero time flow within the field."

Janeway shook her head. "No, it's inconsistent. There is a complete and total lack of readings from inside the field. There are some particles that form and decay in an almost immeasurably short amount of time; if the interior were even marginally above zero entropy, there would be some faint particle emissions detected in the days you've been scanning. Or some profoundly redshifted EM emissions."

"Then how do you propose resolving the discrepancy?"

"If the interior is at exactly zero time, it must be inside an event horizon to prevent the paradox of an object that's everywhere at once and is totally unaffected by surrounding phenomena."

"But then we would see only the horizon."

"*If* it dropped off abruptly. But what if there's a gradient? A narrow dropoff from zero to normal entropy at the very edge of the field. What we're seeing would then be just the fringe effects, the outermost rim of whatever's inside." She looked up sharply. "And that could be our ticket in."

"How so?" Langford asked.

"It's a quantum effect, so it could penetrate an event horizon as easily as it penetrated Ms. Coray's environmental suit. The object's waveform doesn't have to physically move into the zone, because it has a finite probability of being there already. The quantum bleed would overlap both our time continuum and the one inside, and that could provide a link."

Ruyao contemplated her proposal. "In theory. What you describe is a quantum entanglement of the interior and exterior spaces. Entanglements do allow bypass of conventional space-time barriers, whether the speed of light or an event horizon." He mused further. "If we could entangle something else with the quantum boundary, it would be entangled in turn with the interior, and perhaps allow interaction."

"Yes!" Janeway cried. "It could work."

"But how?" Stefcia challenged. "We've been saying all along, zero time means zero change. Even if we can connect with what's inside, how can we possibly affect it?"

"Remember, we're talking quantum physics," Janeway said with a wry grin. "It's all about probabilities, not absolutes. We don't have to change it from a zero-entropy state to a nonzero-entropy state. It already has a finite, if minuscule, probability of already being in that state. We just need to tap into that probability and persuade it to express itself."

"If we entangle an object within our temporal frame of

reference with one in its," Ruyao elaborated, "then they will share a common waveform. Our temporal frame will be an inherent part of its. And this will not be a change. Consider: if there is zero timeflow inside, then within its reference frame, whatever we do to it now will be occurring at the instant of its creation. In effect, it is already part of its wavefunction, and always has been."

"Retrocausality," Janeway said. "We'd be bootstrapping our own solution into existence."

"I'll just take your word for it," Stefcia said. "So what do we have that can entangle with it?"

Janeway grinned. "The same thing we usually entangle things with. The Heisenberg compensator in a transporter. It's a Bose-Einstein condensate, not too different from the field down there. It entangles with every object being transported and lets us bypass the uncertainty principle, essentially preserving the position and momentum information in a way that doesn't require us to measure either one directly and thereby lose the other."

"So," Picard said, "you propose that we attempt to lock a transporter onto the quantum field itself."

"Maybe not as simple as a standard target lock. As you found out, the transporter reads it as an interference field." But her eyes were darting back and forth as she visualized it in her head. She paced the room, her left hand on her hip as she gestured with her right. "We'd have to do some rewiring of the transporter circuitry . . . essentially hook the targeting scanners directly into the compensator to create a link between it and the quantum field, create the entanglement that way. Then we could hook the molecular imaging scanner into the compensator to read it. With luck, that could let us get a reading on whatever's inside. And once we measure it in our frame of reference . . ."

"Then it converges with the quantum waveform of our continuum," Ruyao finished. "It becomes part of the normal flow of time and space once again."

CHRISTOPHER L. BENNETT

"Well, that's the theory, anyway." Janeway smirked. "But before we take it to the captain, we need to figure out all the ways it could go horribly, horribly wrong."

Somewhat to the team's surprise, Janeway and the other scientists were able to identify few failure modes in her plan, and were confident they could prevent or otherwise cope with every one. Although Picard could only halfway follow it and Langford was entirely lost, the simulations confirmed that Janeway's proposal should work. Once Captain Karapleedeez was briefed, she granted the team permission to proceed using the *Kingsley*'s transporters, which were more advanced and powerful than the *Needle*'s.

Monitoring from the *Kingsley*'s transporter room, with Langford at his side, Picard watched the viewscreen with barely contained excitement as, down in the base, Ensigns Wright and Sabar carefully nudged a pair of transporter pattern enhancers into the quantum fog, a refinement Stefcia had proposed to improve the odds of a successful entanglement. Bilan stood near the two ensigns, watching but contributing nothing as usual. The *Kingsley*'s chief engineer, Dan Legato, manned the transporter console, with Janeway at his side. This transporter had been heavily retooled and half its guts were still exposed, lashed together by opti-cable and power conduits that sprawled across much of the floor, but Legato assured them that it would work much better than it looked. Karapleedeez glowered at the disorder as she came in, but accepted it as a necessary evil for the moment. "We're ready to proceed, Captain," Janeway told her.

Karapleedeez nodded, and Legato engaged the console. "Targeting scanners activated . . . locking onto pattern enhancers. Heisenberg compensator engaged. Scanning . . ." After a moment, he shook his head. "I'm not getting anything."

"Retune the compensator," Janeway told him. "We need to find a resonant waveform."

Endless seconds passed. The transporter room felt as

frozen in time to Picard as the quantum field itself. "There's . . . something," Legato reported. "But it's very tenuous. It comes and goes."

"The scanner frequencies," Janeway said, sounding irritated with herself for missing it. "Vary them in synch with the compensator's waveform. Think of it as music class, Dan—we need to find a three-part harmony."

"Aye, Lieutenant." His hands played across the console. Picard watched the monitor—the dull gray field still showed no change. Except . . . did it flicker, or was that a trick of his eye motion?

"I'm getting readings now," Legato said. "A large space . . . dozens of life forms, multiple species . . . technological devices . . . No, it's fluctuating!"

Picard could see that. The quantum fog seemed to be expanding outward, becoming more diffuse yet more tangible at the same time. It seemed to come in overlapping surges. "We're losing the lock," Janeway said.

"No, ma'am," Legato countered. "*They're* losing cohesion. The whole thing is coming apart!"

Karapleedeez stepped forward. "Beam out every life form you can! Transporter room three, beam out the team on the surface!" There was no certainty they were in danger, but given the way the fog was surging, it seemed a wise precaution.

But before anyone could acknowledge her orders, the quantum field exploded outward. Not in the conventional sense, though—rather, its already diffuse presence seemed to lose all cohesion and just *become* far more widely distributed across space. It engulfed the three men on the surface and swallowed up the camera a split second later. The feed from the surface flickered and blinked out, cutting off the screams. A second later, Picard felt *something* surge through his body, leaving a wake of soreness, and an alert klaxon began to sound.

"What happened?" Karapleedeez barked the question a split second before Picard could.

"The whole thing destabilized," Janeway gasped in horror. "Its particles . . . their waveforms collapsed randomly. They've materialized scattered throughout this whole volume of space. Inside us, inside the ship's systems . . . not critical, but enough to hurt."

"Did you get a lock on anyone?" Karapleedeez asked Legato.

"Only four," he said. "They're in the buffer . . . there was so much degradation, I'm running data reconstruction now . . . they're coming through!" But he did not sound confident about the results.

Five pads lit up and four beings began to materialize, one large enough to span two of them. Only one was humanoid. One seemed to have a pear-shaped body with four legs and a swanlike neck on top; one had a kangaroo-like body and an angular head with bulging eyes; and the large one had a long, horizontal body cantilevered on a central pair of legs.

But none of them materialized intact. Four hideously torn, bloody figures solidified on the pads and promptly slumped to the deck. *Mon dieu!* Picard cried as the stench washed over the room.

"Bolus," Karapleedeez cursed under her breath. "Beam them to sickbay, now! Captain to sickbay, prepare for extreme transporter failure victims, four species, all unknown!" It was probably a futile effort, but it had to be tried. *We're responsible for this*, Picard thought. *I'm responsible*.


The three men on Proserpina were retrieved promptly after the four aliens had been sent to sickbay. The *Kingsley*'s full medical staff and Jameela Janasz split their energies to tend to both groups at once. The ensigns and Bilan had suffered the equivalent of confinement-beam failure, with a dangerous number of particles materializing inside their bodies when the field had collapsed; but the transporter's biofilter had removed the contaminants upon beam-out, and it was simply a matter of repairing the damage. They would all live, and Bilan's armor bark seemed to be made of sterner stuff than Coray's vines at the cellular as well as the surface level.

Apparently the particles making up the stasis bubble (and its occupants, Picard reminded himself grimly) had been scattered over billions of cubic kilometers, but had been more likely to materialize closer to their point of origin, which was why the men on the surface had gotten a much larger dose than the scattering of single particles that had interpenetrated the *Kingsley* and its crew. (The alert had been triggered by a few isolated particles of matter that had materialized inside the ship's antimatter pods. The resultant annihilations had been far too feeble to breach containment, but the gamma rays had been enough to trigger the klaxon.) Many of the aquatic life forms within several kilometers of the base had no doubt been injured or killed by particle incursions, and Picard could only pray that the scans had been accurate about the absence of sentient life. Sensors showed the base itself to be badly damaged, its power systems failing, its hex cells and surfaces exploded outward from the inside. A sphere of ice around the compound had melted from the heat and pressure of so many particles materializing within it, and the water had breached the damaged walls of the base and flooded it. When the ice eventually solidified again, it would have nowhere near its former clarity, muddied as it now was with the subatomic remains of the ancient facility whose destruction Picard had brought about—and the remains of its builders' very bodies. Their ashes had been strewn across half this system, some of them becoming a permanent part of the *Kingsley*, of *Cleopatra's Needle*—even, Picard reflected, of his own flesh. *And all great Neptune's oceans will not wash it clean.*

The four aliens retrieved from the stasis bubble were hardly any better off than their peers. They had already been dissolving into quantum mist when the transporter had locked onto them; it was not simply a matter of removing contaminants from their bodies, because much of the mass of their actual bodies was missing. Two of them were dead on arrival, and the big, long-bodied one expired within moments, even as the *Kingsley*'s Doctor Lenama scanned its anatomy and tried to get a sense of where to begin.

But astonishingly, the humanoid lived. "I can take no credit for it," the Lorini physician told his captain and the others an hour later in the briefing room. He switched the monitor to a live feed from the sickbay isolation chamber, where the humanoid hovered in weightlessness to protect her ravaged skin and tissues (she was barely recognizable as female). The others quailed at the sight of the being, a bloody ruin seemingly farther gone than the worst burn victim Picard had ever seen. "By all rights, any known humanoid species would be past any hope of recovery with damage this extensive. Even my Fabrini ancestors at the peak of their medical sciences could not have made a difference. And yet her life functions are still hanging on at a minimal level. What is more, I believe her cells are beginning to regenerate."

"How is that possible?" Langford asked.

Lenama mercifully switched the display to a sensor readout of his patient. "As far as I can reconstruct, her biology is extraordinarily robust and adaptive. Her organs are multiply redundant and largely decentralized; for instance, she has several small hearts distributed throughout her body, secondary respiratory channels bypassing the trachea, and so forth. Her genome is so intricate I can barely begin to sequence it, with multiple coding layers. We have two basic levels of genetic coding, the genes within the DNA strands themselves and the nucleosomes that expose or block different segments of the strands from being accessed by the transcription enzymes that read the genetic instructions. Her genome shows at least three levels of coding that I can identify and multiple families of transcription factors, microRNAs, and support proteins, most of whose functions I cannot even speculate about yet.

"And there is more." He switched to a closer, cellular-level scan. "Her entire body is pervaded with nanotechnology. At first I almost missed it, for it is largely organic and wholly integrated into her cellular structure. Instructions for its replication are even written into her genes, with transcription nanites that parallel the action of natural enzymes. I daresay she was literally born with this nanotechnology, that it is an inherent trait of her species."

Lenama looked around the table. "Whatever this being is, I suspect she comes from a civilization far more advanced and ancient than our own."

"What is the prospect for recovery of her personality, her memory?" Karapleedeez asked. "Could she remember who she is, where she came from?"

"Hard to say. Her brain is regenerating too, and has complexities that elude my analysis. Yet the brain is a most delicate organ. Even when damage to it can be repaired, the original memories are scattered to the winds. And this is an extremely damaged brain. Given what we see of her regenerative abilities and redundancies, I would not care to rule out the possibility of her regaining some degree of higher function. But I doubt she could remember much of her past."

"Then all of this," Picard muttered, "all that we have done, is for nothing."

Langford clasped his wrist. "No. We've learned a great deal from this. We've learned there were very advanced beings living back then. We've learned that they apparently coexisted in a community with multiple other species. We've learned about their technology, and now we're learning about their biotechnology. Studying this woman's regenerative powers could save countless lives in the future."

"But at what cost to her? To the others?"

"Frozen in time like that, they weren't living anyway. None of them would have ever lived again without outside help. Think about it," she went on. "They must have known they'd be completely frozen, completely helpless. They were totally dependent on the kindness of strangers, and had no way of knowing how advanced the technology of those strangers might be, thousands or millions of years down the road." She shrugged. "They were buried deep under the ice. If they, maybe, went into stasis to protect themselves from some great cataclysm, they must have known the chances of rescue were slim, and that their eventual discoverers might have trouble achieving it. It's remarkable that we managed to save even one of them. That we've given her the chance to live again."

"Assumptions," he countered. "We don't know they intended it to last this long. What if it was some routine experiment, and the people outside who were meant to shut it down were caught in the catastrophe?"

"Then they would've still been lost forever if we hadn't found them."

"There's another possibility," Karapleedeez said. "What if they were never meant to be released? What if the system was deliberately designed to be impenetrable? Perhaps these were prisoners. Dangerous beings locked away for the good of everyone else."

"Then why not just execute them?" Picard countered. "Freezing them in time forever with no hope of escape is no different from that."

Langford squeezed his wrist again, smiling wistfully. "That's my point, I think."

Picard held her eyes, beginning to smile back ever so faintly, while Karapleedeez went on. "Different cultures have their own values, their own ways of rationalizing different punishments. They might have felt there was a difference. Or perhaps they simply kept the prisoners around as an object lesson, frozen in amber for the moral edification and amusement of future generations."

Janeway cocked her head and asked her captain, "Are you suggesting our guest should be under guard?"

"Until we know more about her, definitely."

"And if she does prove dangerous?"

Picard spoke up, feeling a surge of protectiveness toward this being. "You heard the doctor—even if she does recover some higher function, her memory is most likely gone. Whatever her past, it's been wiped clean now. She'll be dependent on us, not a threat to us."

"Some life forms," Karapleedeez pointed out, "can be threats without knowing it. Indeed, their own ignorance of the threats they pose can make them far more dangerous. Remember your training, Captain."

"My training, *Captain*," he told the Kreetassan, "is to seek out new life forms and attempt to make peaceful contact with them. I fear we've already tragically failed at the latter, and this woman will have to bear the cost. And my training tells me that we owe her dearly for that."

He stood. "So post your guards and take your scans if you must. But if your military judgment tells you that her presence on this ship is unwelcome, then we will take her to ours and tend to her there. You can ride herd on us if you want to make sure she doesn't go off on some rampage from her sickbed. But after what we have inflicted on her and her companions, I will not see her treated harshly when she awakens lost and confused in our world." And with that, he strode from the briefing room.


Once Picard calmed down, he realized he had been too hard on Karapleedeez. The captain insisted that all the forms be followed and precautions taken, as dictated by her training and her species' instincts, but beyond that she was not unsympathetic to the alien woman's plight, and was as curious as Picard to learn about this very new yet very old form of life. But when Picard apologized, the captain told him it was unnecessary; his high dudgeon had done no worse than make her nostalgic for home.

Their guest continued to regenerate with incredible speed, the process accelerating as her body grew stronger. Over the next few days, her limbs and torso filled out into a lanky, athletic frame, subtly different in proportion from the baseline humanoid shape—the limbs and feet slightly longer, the shoulders a tad wider, the breasts more upswept and wide-set, the hips narrower—but still aesthetically pleasing to the human eye. Her face was slim and delicately tapered, her eyes and lips wide in proportion, her nose aquiline. Her skin grew in with a remarkable texture, its epidermis consisting of scales as fine and iridescent as those of a butterfly's wing. Their base color was a light golden hue, but as her scales grew in, more colors began to manifest on her temples, cheeks, and neck and down her back, flanks, and limbs. They grew into an intricate set of fractal stripes and sworls, reminding Picard variously of a tiger, a snake, or a Mandelbrot set, depending on how he looked at them. The patterns were predominantly reddish but contained all the colors of the visible spectrum (and perhaps beyond) in their intricate curves—yet subtly enough to avoid garishness. The patterns on her temples grew inward across her hairless brows like elaborate eye shadow and tapered down to points at the sides of her nose, forming a broad, gently curving V shape bisected by her nasal bridge. Along with her wide eyes and cheek stripes, they gave her face a feline quality. Her hair grew out reddish gold—if you could call it hair. It was more like a variant of the butterfly scales, as iridescent as they were and as fine as spider silk. It was hard to see where her skin ended and her hair began.

"Of course she's beautiful," Langford said when she caught Picard staring at the woman for too long. She lay on a normal sickbay bed now, healed enough to be taken out of free-fall isolation. "She's a wholly engineered organism, every system of her body enhanced by technology. Her people could probably make themselves look however they wanted. It's synthetic."

"Perhaps," he replied. "Or perhaps they simply enhanced what was already there."

She looked at him askance. "Don't tell me you're smitten by outward appearance alone."

After a moment, he looked at her in surprise. "What? Oh. No, of course not." He turned back to the sleeper. "It's what she represents that I find compelling. A link to the greatest mystery of our time. A sentient, humanoid being who lived so long ago that . . . that flowering plants had not even evolved on Earth. And here she lies, right in front of us, alive and breathing." His voice grew solemn. "The only one of her kind left in existence."

"Unless there are other stasis fields. The records did speak of more than one."

"But we don't dare risk opening them. Not until our technology has advanced a good deal more." He fell silent for a moment. "I can't stop thinking of the cardinal rule of archaeology. Preserve everything. Record everything exactly as you found it, and if possible, leave it as you found it. Do not destroy a site for future generations in the narrow pursuit of one selfish prize.

"We were too reckless, Miliani. We pushed too far, too soon. And the cost . . ."

Her hand was on his shoulder. "We archaeologists rarely find ourselves dealing with decisions that can affect living beings. I think maybe I'm still in denial about it. I haven't let myself face it yet. I just try to focus on the fact that we saved one life, at least." She smiled without real humor. "In our business, we thrive on death, in a way. Nothing rewards us so much as finding a tomb, a crypt, an execution site. Finding a whole city and its occupants buried whole in a single catastrophe fills us with excitement. We get philosophical about death, or at least pragmatic, because we're so removed from the event, because they all would have been dead by now anyway, whatever the reason. Everything dies, and all you can do is try to extract some meaning from it."

She gestured at the bed. "There's your meaning, Luc. A living, breathing person. That's more than most ruins produce."

He gave her a grateful smile. Their gaze held for a moment—and then something shimmered in the corner of his view. His head snapped back toward the bed. Yes, the woman's head was definitely moving! Her narrow lips parted and a faint moan escaped. "Get the doctor," Picard told Langford. "And the captain. I'll try to talk to her."

"What are the chances she'll understand? Even if her brain is functional, the translator would have no referents . . ."

"She's humanoid. Hopefully her brain structure's close enough that the translator can adapt. If not . . . well, I'll do what I can."

Langford looked between Picard and the alien once more, then headed off for Lenama's office. Picard gingerly approached the bed as the woman's eyes fluttered open, her silky golden lashes parting to reveal wide irises of midnight blue. They drifted for a time, unfocused, but then came to rest on Picard and held there. The chevron of her brows furrowed in distress. "It's all right," Picard said, keeping his voice as reassuring as he could. "You're safe here. No one will harm you." She tried to pull herself up on her elbows, legs kicking feebly under the bedsheets, but her strength gave out and she fell back, panting, her eyes still locked on him. "You've been badly hurt, but you're healing. You're in a medical facility. We are tending to your needs." Did she even still possess the capacity to comprehend language? Or were her actions only animal reflex?

But after a moment, she seemed to calm herself and looked around, sizing up her surroundings and her situation. She met his gaze again and waited, as though inviting him to speak. "There. That's good." He gestured to himself. "I am Jean-Luc Picard. Picard," he repeated. "You are in a sickbay," he said, his hands taking in the room, "aboard the starship *Kingsley*."

Her eyes stayed locked on him as he spoke, but then darted behind him as Langford, Lenama, and Karapleedeez entered. "It's all right," he told her, palms out placatingly. "This man is a doctor. He's here to help you."

"Hello," Lenama said, bedside manner fully engaged. "I am Doctor Lenama. May I approach and examine you?" Her initial alarm faded more quickly than it had with Picard, and she simply held a curious gaze on the doctor, not resisting his cautious approach or his measured, hands-on inspection. "You are healing remarkably well. Can you speak?" He gestured to his mouth as he spoke, then to hers.

She opened her mouth, and a dry rasp came out, choking off in surprise. "Of course," Lenama said, and hurried to the replicator for water. Picard moved forward and helped her to sit up as the doctor returned. The woman looked at the glass, sniffed its contents, sipped it cautiously, then gulped it down with gusto. Then she pulled herself straight, regaining her calm poise, and tried again:

"Hhhh . . . Ehh . . . Ello. Hello."

Picard stared, trading a look with the others. They had heard it too. That was not the translator; she had spoken the English word. After only one example, she understood its use.

As if to remove all doubt, her eyes locked on Picard again. "Hello. Pi-cahd." Her voice was low and rough.

He took a step back so she could see him more clearly. "Hello. Yes, I am Picard. Can you understand us?"

"Yes. Can understand . . . I. I can understand. Speak." Again, there was no question that her own lips and tongue formed the words he heard. "I am . . . in starship?" She pronounced it as he did.

"Yes, that's correct. This is the starship *Kingsley*. We represent the United Federation of Planets."

"Am I . . . United Federation? Am I of this?"

Picard's heart sank. "Do you not remember who you are? Where you come from?"

"I . . . no. Not of Fed—not of the Federation?"

He shook his head. "No, I'm sorry. We . . . found you. We do not know . . . who you are. Who your people . . . are." Now was not the time to put that in the past tense. "We were hoping you might remember . . . something." Her head sank.

"Is there anything you remember?" Lenama asked. "Even your name? Picard, Lenama," he elaborated, gesturing to both of them in turn, and then to her with an inquisitive look.

Her vivid brows drew together as she tried to remember.

"Ih . . . Ri—rieh . . ." She trailed off and gave a heavy sigh. "No. I do not remember." She sagged, lost and forlorn.

"Ariel," Picard said. She looked at him curiously. "For now, we could call you Ariel. If you like."

"What is Ariel?"

"Ariel is a character from . . . a story my people tell," he said; under the circumstances, his initial impulse to call it a very old story seemed rather ridiculous. "Ariel was a magical being . . . a delicate spirit of the air. She defied a powerful being and was imprisoned for it, condemned to suffer torment for many years." Shakespeare had left Ariel androgynous, so the feminine pronoun was as valid as any. "The captor died while Ariel was still entrapped, and so she might have remained for eternity had a wise man not found her and used his arts to release her from her torment."

Her deep blue eyes bored into his. "I was imprisoned," she discerned. "For many years. And you released me."

Picard looked away. "We did. Although you were in no torment where you were. You were . . . frozen in time. Time did not pass for you."

"And so I might have remained for eternity." She smiled at him. Her hand reached out weakly and brushed against his; he clasped it with care. It felt like cool satin. "Yes. I like Ariel."

# 11

—◆—

WITH THE QUANTUM FIELD GONE AND A SURVIVOR recovered, Coray had emerged from seclusion and regained much of her former assertiveness, though some of her confidence was lost along with her floral adornments and defenses. While aboard the *Kingsley*, she wore as little clothing as Starfleet propriety would allow, but still seemed uncomfortable in it. She insisted on being allowed to see Ariel and speak to her, pointing out that the Mabrae's agreement with the archaeologists gave her people a share in any knowledge gleaned from this discovery, whether by Ariel's personal recall or by study of her unique regenerative physiology. But Karapleedeez stood firm, promising to keep Coray fully briefed on their findings but insisting that their guest was still too weak and disoriented to be interrogated.

However, that was largely a ploy to keep Coray at bay. In fact, Ariel continued to recover at incredible speed. Her regrown muscles and tendons needed physical therapy to regain their strength, but that was occurring at over twenty times the rate it would take for a human. Ariel's psychological recovery seemed just as swift. She had rapidly adjusted to her situation and showed little sign of denial or panic, according to the ship's counselor. Her grasp of English had become rapidly fluent; it had not been long at all before she was using words that she had never even heard before, according to subsequent review of the sickbay logs.

"Is she telepathic?" Karapleedeez asked at a subsequent briefing. Seated with her were Picard, Langford, Janeway, Doctor Lenama, and Counselor Subramaniam.

"Not fully," Lenama answered. "Our scans show some psionic activity, but only in the language and empathy centers of the brain—the regions dedicated to communication, whether verbal or nonverbal. She seems to be virtually a living universal translator, a born communicator."

"I wouldn't say that, exactly," Janeway said. "She isn't decoding our speech analytically, but reading its meaning directly from our minds. It's deeper than what a translator does, and potentially much more powerful."

"I suppose," Langford said, "that the proper Greek term would be *logopath*—one who senses speech and meaning."

Lenama nodded. "But there's no indication that she can read our unverbalized thoughts or influence our minds in any way."

"Says the man who has been in her proximity for hours," Karapleedeez pointed out.

"Her brain was horrifically damaged. We were all aware of that well before she gained consciousness. She has no memory, no agendas, no reason to deceive us."

"Deception can be an instinct. Especially in an unknown environment."

"But such a precise telepathic illusion?" Janeway countered. "That would require specific knowledge of what to falsify and how. That couldn't be instinctive."

"Could she take it from our minds?"

"Not without knowing what to look for and how," Lenama said. "Again, not a matter of reflex. I am confident of my findings."

"Ariel seems calm and curious," Subramaniam said. "I believe she senses that we mean her no harm, and that we are her only hope of learning anything about herself, where she came from, or where she is now. It is in her own interest to be truthful with us," he added, "so that we may learn more about her and help her learn as well."

*But is it in our interest,* Picard wondered, *to be truthful with her? When she learns why she is the only survivor, will she be as willing to trust us?*

After the briefing, Picard received a message from Ariel, asking him to meet her in the ship's gym. Wondering what she might need, he made his way there in haste. He found her in, of all places, the swimming pool. Her head was beneath the surface as she swam laps, so he waited to speak. She wore a forest-green one-piece suit that left her back bare, exposing the near-symmetrical splash of rich color that spread across it like an *irezumi* tattoo.

Soon she came up for air and spotted him. "Hello!" she called. "Look what I can do!"

"Yes. You do it quite well."

"Apparently I learn fast." Her voice had filled out into a clear, throaty alto. Her accent was an amalgam of the people she'd spoken with so far, but owed the most to Picard.

"Or perhaps," he suggested as she swam toward him, "your body retains the memory of an ability you had before. It's possible there could be other latent memories you could regain in time."

"I'm not so sure I want to," she mused, climbing the ladder out of the pool. Her fine hair was plastered to her skull like a shimmering cap. "All I know is the way I am now—and what I'm starting to become. Old memories might just confuse me. And what if I don't like who I was?"

"There is something to be said for a fresh start," Picard agreed. "Oh!" He realized she was dripping wet, and hastened to get her a towel.

But she waved him off. "Never mind. Look." Ariel held out her arm. Picard watched as the drops of water seemed to be sucked in beneath the fine scales. "It seems my body can absorb the water and use it."

"Remarkable."

"Yes, isn't it? I keep discovering new things I can do. It's rather an adventure." She grinned.

"I imagine so." He smiled back, impressed by her aplomb and positive attitude. "So . . . what did you want to see me about?"

"Why, this! All of it. I'm having an adventure being Ariel, and I wish to share it with you, my Prospero."

He looked up at that. "You've been reading."

"I asked the computer. I didn't like talking to it, though. Hardly anything there beneath the words. I'd rather hear more about him from you." She looked down. "Except my suit is still wet. I suppose it doesn't work like my skin. One moment." She began to pull the suit off, making his eyes widen in alarm, but then she stopped. "Sorry. I'm still learning your social boundaries. As far as I know, I've never had a nudity taboo."

"I'm not surprised," he said in a courtly tone, "with skin such as yours."

She smiled. "Give me a moment to change, all right?"

"Of course."

Perhaps unsurprisingly, when she returned it was in a deep blue halter top that bared her back as fully as the swimsuit had, tucked into a pair of loose slacks. Now dry, her hair was fuller-bodied and visibly longer than it had been the day before. "Well?"

"Charming. It brings out your eyes."

"Well, that's disturbing. I'm still getting used to them being where they are."

Picard laughed. "Astonishing. In two days, you've not only mastered our language, but learned to pun in it."

"Really? Hm. I suppose that's another talent I've discovered. Oh, this amnesia is exciting!"

"So what other skills have you discovered?" he asked as they strolled out into the main gym.

"Well, I've learned Fabrini and Kreetassan. I can see in the dark. I have eidetic memory—there's a charming irony— and an uncanny sense of direction. I can tell you exactly where Proserpina and its sun are relative to us at this moment." She pointed to them in turn, or to the wall and floor beyond which she alleged them to be.

"I suppose I shall have to take your word for it."

"Well, Ariel was a sprite of illusions. I could be lying, you know." She brightened. "Ah—here's something I can prove I've learned." She jogged out onto the gym floor and began to dance. She began awkwardly, but her grace improved by the moment. Her light, strong build and long legs made her a natural.

Picard applauded. "Wherever did you learn that?"

"From Miliani."

"She showed you all this?"

"Not quite," Ariel said, going into a spin and keeping her head pointed in his direction as much as possible, speaking between head rotations. "We talked—about it. She showed me—a few moves—and I sensed—the fundamentals—in her mind. Whoo!" She came to a stop, tottering a bit. "Apparently I'm not immune to dizziness. No nausea, though, that's good. It doesn't sound pleasant."

Picard looked at her, puzzled. "I thought you could only sense communication."

Looking back with equal puzzlement, she skipped toward him, reached out, and pulled him onto the floor to dance with her. "How is this not communicating?"

"I suppose you have a point," he said. "Or en pointe. But I fear this is not a language in which I have any fluency."

"Let me teach you."

He disengaged himself. "No. Thank you, but . . . you must be tired. You're still healing, and . . ."

She studied him for a moment. "Perhaps I should rest. Will you walk me to my quarters?"

"Of course."

They strolled through the *Kingsley*'s narrow corridors in

companionable silence for a time. Then Ariel started as a klaxon briefly sounded. *"Yellow alert. Stellar flare warning. Radiation crews to ready status. Standard protocols under-way. Stand by."*

"What is it?" Ariel asked, concerned but not panicked.

"Nothing to worry about," Picard said. "A routine precaution when a star gives off a radiation flare. The captain will raise the shields, possibly move the ship behind the planet if the flare is intense enough. But it's probably the last we'll hear about it."

"Oh. Thank you." She let out a tense breath. "It's just that 'alert,' 'warning,' and 'radiation' are words that do not connect with pleasant emotions in your people. I suppose you are used to such announcements in context, but for me . . ."

He smiled at her. "'Be not afeard,'" he said. "'The isle is full of noises.'"

She frowned at the odd usage, then smiled. *"The Tempest?"*

He nodded. "Some of Shakespeare's finest poetry, paradoxically in the mouth of a monstrous villain—Caliban, son to the witch who imprisoned Ariel. 'The isle is full of noises—

Sounds, and sweet airs, that give delight and hurt not.
Sometimes a thousand twanging instruments
Will hum about mine ears; and sometime voices,
That if I then had wak'd after long sleep,
Will make me sleep again, and then in dreaming,
The clouds methought would open, and show riches
Ready to drop upon me, that when I wak'd—'"

He hesitated, seeing the look in her eyes. "'That when I wak'd,'" he finished softly, "'I cried to dream again.'" When he said it, a tear fell down her cheek. "I'm sorry. I didn't mean to upset you."

"No, Jean-Luc. You said it beautifully." She moved

closer. "And I don't mind the sadness. Even that is a new adventure for me. And I cherish the gift from you, my Prospero." She nestled her head on his shoulder, her arms folding around him.

Delicately, he pushed her away. "Ariel . . . I am very flattered, but I do not wish to take advantage."

She respected his wish for separation, but her gaze pierced his. "That is not the truth, Jean-Luc. Not in full, at least. There is something that makes you pull away from me. Something you hide beneath your words. I know you wish only to help me—I can feel this—but there is a secret you are all keeping from me. A lie of omission that you fear I will discover. How do I reconcile this with my certainty that you mean me no harm?"

He struggled for words, and soon realized that the only words he could give her were the truth. "You deserve to know," he told her. "But not out here."

She led him to her quarters and sat expectantly, waiting. He struggled to express it. "We have told you that you were suspended in a stasis bubble, frozen in time."

"Yes."

"What we have not told you . . . is that there were others. Dozens of others, of your own kind and other species as well. We . . . found your stasis bubble, and we were stymied by it. We had never come upon anything like it before. So we put our best minds to work on finding a way to open it, to deactivate it. We came up with a theory, one that we believed would work." He wanted to look away from those huge, receptive eyes, but he owed it to her to meet her with this head-on. "But we were far beyond our abilities. We caused the whole thing to destabilize. We tried to beam out as many of you as we could . . . but we failed. Only you survived, and only because your regenerative abilities are so extraordinary. Everyone else—your colleagues, your friends, maybe your family for all we know—they died. We killed them."

Straightening up, he took a step closer. "Ariel . . . *I* killed them. I almost killed you. This was my quest, my ambition, to find these stasis bubbles and unearth their mysteries. In my greed for knowledge I destroyed dozens of lives . . . some of whom may have been the last of their species in the universe." She merely watched him, still waiting, not reacting. "I do not deserve your gratitude, Ariel. Or your friendship."

Two tears rolled down her cheeks and dripped onto her breast. Her skin reabsorbed them. "You have no choice." He looked at her, questioning, and her face grew wistful. "My nature is . . . to connect. To commune with other beings. I sense this at my core. And you, Jean-Luc Picard, were the first being I connected with in my new life. The first who spoke to me, and gave me a name. That is a bond I cannot break even if I wished it."

She rose and stepped toward him. "And I do not wish it, Jean-Luc. Do not ask me to join you in hating yourself, for I cannot feel that for you."

"But what I did—"

"Was a tragedy. But it hurts you more than it hurts me. Did you think I didn't realize I was not the only one in that stasis field? That I didn't divine the likely reason why no others were present? I feared something shocking when I asked—but what you've told me is nothing more than I'd already surmised. It's actually something of a relief.

"I have no memory of those others, Jean-Luc. I grieve their loss, but it's abstract. You are my reality." She took his hand, cradled it in hers. "I live because of you. Because you felt a need, a craving to reach out and connect with beings from your past.

"To me, there can be no nobler motive. Whatever mistakes you and your people may have made, whatever variables you were unaware of, your purpose was a beautiful one. A loving one."

"It was selfish. We placed our curiosity above the good of others."

"But that curiosity was an expression of respect, of empathy for others. You wished to know them, because you cared about them. You wished to make them live again. Yes, it was for yourself, but it was for them as well. That is the nature of communion, of togetherness. Self and other become one."

Ariel took Picard's face in her hands. "Until you came, I and the others had no existence. We were not ourselves, and we could not commune with others. Now at least some vestige of them is part of you, through what you have learned of them, what you can communicate of their lives to others.

"And I am here . . . alive again . . . through you. With you. And I forgive you." She embraced him, stroked her head against his cheek and shoulder. Her hair was the softest thing he had ever felt.

But then she pulled away, stepping back, lowering her eyes. "But it is too soon for more. I suppose you should go."

He averted his eyes as well. "I understand. You need time."

She gave a wry laugh. "Ah, no, Jean-Luc. I'd love for you to stay. I'm always most content when you are near. It's you who need the time. I'll let you go . . . and when you're ready, you will let me know."

She embraced him once again, and escorted him to the door without another word. It wasn't until he was halfway back to his quarters that he realized she'd spoken those last lines in flawless iambic pentameter—right down to the rhyming couplet at the end. "Astonishing," he breathed.


Kathryn Janeway sighed, rubbed her eyes, and got up from the console she'd been hunched over for longer than she could remember. Stretching a kink out of her back, she strode toward the replicator. "Coffee. Black," she demanded. The elixir brought her much-needed relief, but did not remove the weight on her shoulders. She carried the hot cup back to the console, her mind still darting around the equations of the stasis field as she strove to understand why her oh-so-brilliant plan had gone so brutally wrong.

The tragedy had been a wake-up call to Janeway, more so than a sea of coffee. She had to be more responsible, more aware of the real-world consequences of her actions. If ever again she faced a choice between her own interests and the good of an alien people, she would err on the side of the latter, no matter what it was she had to give up.

At first she thought the image of shimmering red-gold in the corner of her eye was a part of the thoughts that preoccupied her. But then she realized it was the genuine article, standing in the doorway. She almost spilled her coffee. "Ariel!"

"Lieutenant Janeway. May I come in?"

"Of course. Uhh, would you like some coffee? Or—"

"No, thank you. I've been sampling foods and drinks all day and I think I've reached my limit."

Janeway couldn't quite muster the same casual, chatty attitude. "Ariel . . . I gather you've been told the whole story. About . . . what happened with the stasis field."

Ariel anticipated her, smiling. "Please, don't make me go through this again. It was an accident, you had no way of knowing, it's a miracle I'm alive at all after all this time, I'm grateful and I forgive you. All right? Can we go on to the next bit now?"

Janeway blinked several times, her vision blurring a bit, and cleared her throat. "Thank you. I appreciate that. So . . . what is the next bit?"

Ariel moved into the room and leaned on the edge of the table. "Yesterday I told Jean-Luc that I wasn't sure I wanted to know about my past . . . that I was happy just to get to know myself and the new people in my life. But . . . after last night . . . well, I realized that I need more than that. It's my nature to connect with others, and although I am enjoying getting to know you all, something inside me yearns to connect with others of my own species."

"Oh," Janeway said softly. "Under the circumstances, that could be a problem."

"But Jean-Luc tells me there may be more stasis bubbles elsewhere in the galaxy. More of my people could be in them."

"Ariel . . . even if we could find them, we don't dare risk trying again."

"Not unless you learn more about their technology. I may

be able to help with that, as well as with the search for other bubbles. I want to work with the data you recovered from the ice base's computers before the explosion. Maybe I can help interpret some of it. It's far less easy for me when there's no mind behind it, but I'm still good with language. And there might be something in it that strikes me as familiar."

"Even if there is . . . it might be years before we can find a solution, if not longer. This technology is millennia ahead of ours. And these bubbles are said to be scattered across half the galaxy. It could take a lifetime to find more of them."

Ariel gave a small smile. "The doctors are still going crazy over my regenerative abilities. They tell me my cellular metabolism has attributes they've seen in species that were extraordinarily long-lived, races called Platonians, Dlascru, Omegans—but perhaps even more so. They're not even certain I'm capable of dying of natural causes." She laughed. "Can you imagine how that feels? To be three days old and told you may be immortal?"

"No, I surely can't."

"I can barely wrap my mind around it. It feels so . . . imbalanced, to have all that future and no past. I want a past, Kathryn. I want to feel more settled in the heart of my life, not dangling at one extremity."

Janeway pondered that. "I . . . *think* that makes sense."

"I'm relieved to hear that," Ariel said, and they shared a laugh. "Also . . . I want to do it for you. You and Jean-Luc and the rest. You all feel so bad about what happened to the others in the bubble. If I can help you find a way to save the rest of my people, maybe that will even the scales."

"That's very kind of you, Ariel." She narrowed her eyes. "You say 'my people.' What about the other species?"

Ariel tilted her head. "Must a people be one species? Your Federation isn't." Her brow furrowed. "I hadn't really considered the question. I just took it for granted that I was including everyone. Hey, that's noble of me. I'm glad to know that."

Janeway chuckled. "You are a highly social being by nature.

CHRISTOPHER L. BENNETT

You connect with others very easily. I suppose it stands to reason that you'd think of everyone as your people." She smiled. "You're like an embodiment of the Federation's ideal."

"Oh, no," Ariel demurred. "That honor goes to you. To humans, and those like you. It doesn't come nearly as easily to you. Your instinct is to pull away from those who are different. And yet you choose to embrace them. That's far more admirable."

"Well, on behalf of humanity, I thank you." Janeway finished her coffee and worked the console. "I'm calling up what we obtained from the base's computers. You can have a seat here."

Ariel moved to the seat, but her eyes were on Janeway. "What is it?" the lieutenant asked.

"May I ask a personal question? Not about you in particular, but about matters personal to your species."

Janeway lifted her brows. "Certainly."

"Is it common for humans . . . to pull away from those they have feelings for? To desire intimacy yet feel compelled to resist it?"

Janeway stiffened, feeling ice in her veins. "It can be," she said at length. "If we have lost someone dear to us. Or if they've hurt us. There can be . . . a fear of trying again." Lord knew, it had been like that in the early days with Mark, with the ghosts of Justin and her father still looming. "But it's something we can overcome . . . if the other party is patient enough." She realized it had been too long since she'd written to Mark.

"I think that must be it. He's been hurt before—betrayed, I think. But I sense he's more worried about hurting me. Isn't that sweet?"

Did she mean Picard? Well, it was none of her business. "Sounds like he's worth being patient with. But maybe for now we could get to these computer files?"

Ariel nodded, clasping her shoulder briefly. "Of course. Thank you, Kathryn."

# 12

---

WITH PROSERPINA'S SUN ENTERING A FLARE CYCLE
and the subglacial base essentially destroyed, Karapleedeez
gathered the archaeologists and raised the question of
whether there was any need to remain. The *Kingsley*'s life-
science department had been happily studying the animal
life beneath the planet's icy crust while Ariel's rescue and
recovery had been going on, but the data they already had
would take years to analyze properly, and the ship had only
two years in which to explore several hundred assigned sectors. Moreover, Coray was beginning to demand that Ariel
accompany her to Tanebor as a "guest"—though it was clear
she saw the ancient refugee more as a prize, the one tangible
discovery this expedition had produced. Karapleedeez
shared Picard's reluctance to accede to that, but proposed
that setting course for Tanebor to return Coray and Bilan
would help to settle them down for now, and that they could
negotiate the matter further along the way. Picard and Langford agreed, and so *Mary Kingsley* and *Cleopatra's Needle*
left the frozen globe behind them.

Langford offered Ariel the hospitality of the *Needle*, but
Ariel demurred, explaining that so long as the ships were
traveling together, she would prefer to remain in the more

familiar surroundings of the *Kingsley,* since she was still finishing up her physical therapy and since the starship's more powerful computers and larger staff were of use to her in attempting to decode the base's computer files. Picard also chose to accept guest quarters aboard the Starfleet vessel so that he could assist Ariel.

Meanwhile, Ariel had already begun a search of Federation archaeological records, determined to find anything that could connect to her own era. When Picard came to her quarters in response to a summons, he found her wide-eyed (more so than usual) with excitement. "I think I've found something," she said, hustling him over to the console where the image of an eldritch alien ship, somewhat like a bunch of grapes as painted by Dali, appeared on the screen. "An ancient pod ship discovered ninety years ago, in orbit of an anomalous neutron star called Questar M-17," she explained. "It had hex cells and energy absorbers not unlike the ice base. And it dates back *three hundred million* years! There was an incorporeal entity aboard, and the ship's crew destroyed themselves to prevent its escape. A Starfleet crew found it alive and almost lost their ship to it, and unfortunately it destroyed the alien derelict before it was banished to the neutron star's surface. If it's still alive," she went on, barely pausing for breath, "maybe it knows something about my era, what happened to my people."

Picard took some time to review the data. "It's very tenuous, Ariel. The technologies have as many differences as similarities . . . the ice base doesn't have this woven-metal construction, and its energy accumulators were passive rather than actively draining our equipment. It could simply be coincidence."

"Or it could be a precursor culture to the ones who built the base."

"Even so, the entity would have been trapped fully fifty million years before your time. Your species, your civilization might not even have evolved yet."

"They might have. Who knows how long a society of immortals could endure?"

Picard tried to keep his tone gentle, reluctant to dash her hopes but aware that her enthusiasm was getting in the way of her judgment. "But it would have had no knowledge of galactic events fifty megayears after its imprisonment. Anyway, it says here that the pod ship's crew encountered the creature near the rim of the galaxy and destroyed themselves to keep it from reaching populated sectors. This creature probably never interacted with anyone in our galaxy aside from that ship's crew." Ariel sagged, her enthusiasm fading. "Besides, it is reportedly a very malevolent and aggressive entity," he told her. "And it's trapped by a hypergravity effect that would make it too dangerous to approach. It would be too great a risk for no meaningful gain."

"Damn," Ariel said. "It's the only thing in your records that even hints at a connection to my time."

He smiled. "Well, let's not give up on the ice base records. At least we know they *are* from your civilization. It's just a question of deciphering them."

The translation proceeded slowly. The files they had were fragmentary, random screen captures and downloads of files whose contexts and subjects were unknown and which seemed to be written in a variety of languages. It was hard to know where to begin without any context, and Ariel's hope that she would find familiar resonances in the data seemed fruitless at first.

But then, after two long days of study, Ariel spotted a recurring pattern that she realized was familiar. It was a proper name that she rendered as "Manraloth," rhyming with "oath." "It's a species name," she said. "I think it must be my species' name. I am a Manraloth!"

The name provided more than just a comforting sense of identity for Ariel. It was a clue as well. Like the names of pharaohs in the Rosetta Stone, it provided a target string to search for, a recurring pattern that could be a seed for crystallizing their understanding of the languages in the ancient files. And Ariel hoped as well that finding references to the name, whether in the ice base's files or those from the ruins on Tanebor, might help identify star systems where other Manraloth had lived, and where other stasis bubbles might therefore be found. Although the ice base's population had been multispecies, the transporter scans showed the Manraloth to have been the majority group within the stasis field, suggesting that it may have been their technology.

And so this brought Picard to a point of decision. He went to Langford's quarters on the *Needle* to discuss it with her. "Ariel is becoming more determined by the day to track down other Manraloth," he said. "I think we should help her. We owe it to her."

Langford studied him. "Of course we do, Luc. I'm sure the Federation will do everything it can to help her."

He frowned. "The Federation? Why not us?"

"Because I'm tired, Luc. We all are. We've been at this for nine months, ten counting prep time, and it'll take three more to get home. We've made an amazing find in the field, and now it's time to go back to Alpha Centauri, reconnect with our lives, and take our time evaluating what we've found. Of course Ariel is welcome to join us at the university if she wants, to help us with our studies."

"That won't be enough for her. She needs to keep searching. She's lonely, Miliani. Even though she's bonded with us, she still feels a need to connect with her own flesh and blood."

"And you think I don't?" Langford asked. "I have a family back in the Federation, one I'd really like to see again. So do most of the others. And what about little Bazyli and Yanmei? They've been away from children their own age for nine months, and that's not good for their development."

"Fine. We can take a rest at Centauri, let some of the team members go, recruit fresh ones."

"Luc—you're not hearing me. I'm going back home to stay. This is the longest dig I've ever been on, and I need time to recuperate. I have duties back home to catch up on, responsibilities to the university, journal articles I'm committed to write." She stepped closer, tapped his chest with a finger. "And lest you forget, so have you. What about your doctorate? What about your studies of the Taguan relics? What about your teaching?"

"There will always be time to finish those. And surely I can earn experience toward my doctorate if I help Ariel unearth more ruins, learn more about an uncharted era of prehistory."

"To some extent, yes, but there's work you have to do back home as well. And who knows how long Ariel's search could be? The nearest Manraloth site we know of took us nearly a year to find. What if the next closest one is out in the Perseus Arm? Or the Gamma Quadrant? Ariel may be immortal—you're not."

"If there was one this close, odds are there are others within a few years' travel at most." He spread his arms, inviting her to look at him. "And I'm still in my prime. I can always come back to finish my doctorate later."

She sighed, paused a moment before speaking. "But why does it have to be you?"

"Because . . . because I was the first person she met in this era. It's as though she . . . imprinted on me. There's a bond between us. She needs me."

"Oh," Miliani said very softly, her eyes trembling.

Picard realized what he was saying, what it was doing to her. He stepped toward her. "Miliani . . . I'm sorry. I didn't plan this. I never would have wished to hurt you. But . . . it's not as if there were any promises between us."

She gave a nervous laugh. "No—of course not. It would've been foolish of me to think of it as a promise."

"Miliani . . ."

She gathered herself. "No, you're right. Like I said all those months ago, we're both grown-ups. We're friends. Colleagues. It would've been nice to have more, but these things happen."

"Exactly. I would have been happy to explore that, but things . . . just didn't go that way."

"And she's certainly worthy of it."

His eyes widened. "What? Oh—this is about helping her . . . about what we owe her. I—" He stopped. "No. Why am I prevaricating with you? You deserve better." She smiled. "Maybe I'm prevaricating with myself. You could always see right through me."

She squeezed his shoulder. "The best friends always can." They fell into an embrace. But when it ended, she held him by the shoulders and probed his gaze. "Are you sure you're making the right decision, Luc? I'm as romantic as the next archaeologist, but . . . are you sure you're doing this for the right reasons? You do have other commitments. And it's not your way to leave something unfinished."

He smiled sadly. "Which is why I can't abandon Ariel now. Why I can't abandon the quest we started. It's already cost so much. . . . I have to give it meaning. And as you yourself said, she is the meaning."

She pulled away, turned to face the wall. "You're a fine man, Jean-Luc Picard. I just wonder if I'm ever going to see you again after we get home."

He came up behind her and held her by the shoulders. "We'll have plenty of time before then."

"No, we won't. You'll be busy with Ariel." She lifted his hand from her shoulder and brought it to her lips. "Go now. Be with her. I hope . . ." She sighed, and turned to meet his eyes once more. "I hope you find what it is you're searching for."

Coray was grateful that the Manraloth woman had agreed to meet her in Coray's own guest quarters aboard the *Kingsley.* Not only did it give her some sense of being in control of the territory, but it spared her the need to cover herself in more dead, synthetic fibers than she had to. She was most comfortable in something called a *bikini,* a sort of crude approximation of her old vines, with a few colorful "leaves" of cloth bound in place by woven cords. Still, it was painful to

be draped in a thing that hung lifeless and gave her no feed-
back, that only reminded her of what she'd lost. By now, by
all rights, her vines should have at least started to regrow,
some residual root tendril in one of her skin ridges starting
to sprout again. But the Federation people said the damage
had been done throughout, to the roots as well as the exter-
nals. And while they had the means to heal animal bodies,
their botanists had met with no success restoring her vines.
Perhaps it was because of the barbaric segregation they
maintained between floral and faunal life, their inability to
grasp the symbiosis. Or perhaps it was simply that she had
been away from the sun and rain of Tanebor for too long.
She felt as though she herself was starting to wilt.

In contrast, Ariel seemed bright and lively and perfectly
at home when she arrived at the door, and Coray had to
struggle to match her air of confidence. "I welcome you to
my soil," she said—not merely figuratively, for she had managed to sweet-talk the ship's quartermaster into coating the
floor of her quarters with some leftovers from the arboretum.

"Oh, thank you!" Ariel said, looking over the floor with
an intrigued expression. "Hang on." She took a moment to
slip off her foot coverings, placed them on a small table by
the door, and came in barefoot, kneading her toes in the dirt
and grinning at the sensation. "That feels lovely."

Coray suddenly had to resist liking her. Maybe that
could come later, but not until she had achieved her objective. "Thank you, Ariel," she said, her tone polished and
diplomatic. She offered her guest water, and the offer was
accepted graciously. Once they had taken their seats, Coray
began. "I asked you here because I wished to implore you
once again to accompany me to Tanebor. It is a lovely
world, advanced, peaceful, and wealthy. Anything you
wished, we would be glad to offer. And all we would expect in exchange . . . is that you tell us of yourself. That
you let us share in your research into your past, your study
of your own abilities, and allow us to benefit from it even
as you do."

# CHRISTOPHER L. BENNETT

She got a polite smile in response. "That's a very benevolent offer, Coray, but I really have to say no. I'm sorry."

Coray leaned forward. "Ariel, do not say no just yet. There is more I can tell you of what our world offers."

"And I would love to visit it someday, truly. But I have too great a need to find others of my kind."

"We would gladly help you with that."

"I'm sorry, but I'm afraid your ships simply aren't fast enough to accommodate my needs. Otherwise I'd welcome your help, really, but Federation ships are much faster, and it's as simple as that."

"But somewhere in you, or in the archives we have discovered in searching for you, may be the knowledge to improve our drives a thousandfold. And you may be the key to decoding that knowledge."

Now Ariel leaned forward and put a reassuring hand on Coray's mahogany-brown knee. "And I promise that any such breakthroughs will be shared with the Mabrae as well as the Federation. I am truly grateful, Coray, for the role your people have played in bringing about my rescue, and I am wholly cognizant of the debt I owe to you. I will respect that debt no matter where my travels take me. And I trust the Federation to honor its treaty with you as well."

Coray kept her face still, but inside she was seething. Ariel had deftly pulled the roots out from under her, preempting the next two arguments she'd intended to wield. And Coray knew as well as Ariel must that the whole thing was a pile of fertilizer, that the Mabrae had contributed nothing to this venture beyond grudging indulgence and self-interested meddling. "Very well," she said, rising to her feet. "I know when there's no point in pushing further. You're just too good."

"Too good at what?"

"At saying just what people want to hear. At making yourself what they wish you to be. I must concede to the master—you have them all coiled around you in a way I couldn't have managed with these aliens even in fullest bloom. And I had to train for years—with you it's a natural talent." She paused. "Assuming you're telling the truth about your loss of memory."

"Coray, I don't understand what you mean."

"Don't think you can seduce a seducer. Play the game all you like with others—you have to keep in practice just as I do—but let's show each other professional courtesy, shall we?"

Ariel shook her head. "You misunderstand, Coray. I'm a communicator. It's my nature to connect with others. To understand them. That's all you're sensing."

"To understand is to control. Knowing what others want tells you how to get what you want from them." She sighed. "So what do you want, Manraloth? I can't read your eyes, your scent, your body. So tell me what I can offer to get you to come to Tanebor."

Ariel looked sad. "Nothing, really. Not for a long time, anyway." She perked up. "But maybe there's something I can offer you that will satisfy you and your superiors."

Again Coray was impressed. She'd somehow read what Coray had been suppressing even from herself—her fear of the consequences to her career if she came back naked and empty-handed. "What could you offer?"

Ariel looked her over. "The others told me about the vines and flowers you had. I would've loved to see those. And I bet you'd love to have them back."

Coray guarded her reply carefully, restraining herself from jumping at the offer. "What do you propose?"

"Well, it's not a sure thing, but— May I use your console?" Coray nodded. Ariel went to the desk and worked the controls for a few moments. "Lenama and Jameela have been continuing to study my regenerative abilities. They're still a long way from figuring out how to adapt them for other humanoids . . . but plants are simpler and generally more robust, much easier to restore. We've actually been running experiments on some plant samples, and the results are promising." She waved Coray over to the screen, showing her some readouts that Coray promptly memorized but only pretended she could follow the bulk of. "Let me get a root-cell sample from you, give me a few hours in the lab, and I bet that with a little help from Starfleet's finest, I can whip up something that could work on Taneborian epiphytes."

"So you're a botanist now too?"

"Apparently so. Comes as a surprise to me, too." She winked. "Among other scientific disciplines. I seem to be picking up most every skill I try within a matter of hours or days. Maybe it's some aspect of my logopathy, or maybe I actually knew these things before. Who knows? I may have been incredibly old and had plenty of time to learn them all." She furrowed her brow. "I imagine one gets tired of one career after a century or so—so I'd expect immortals to be polymaths."

Coray chose not to conceal her covetousness this time. "How can you tell me this and expect me to accept the idea of going home without you?"

Ariel rose from the console and put an arm around Coray's shoulders, walking her toward the door. "Think of this as a down payment. If it works, you could have your flowers back within weeks, maybe days. And the formula might be adaptable to solve many medical and, well, botanical problems on your planets. I hear Taredin is growing rather arid; maybe this could help reforest their world. That should keep your people occupied for now.

"And," she added, leaning in conspiratorially and lowering her voice, "consider this, my friend: if I find what I'm looking for, there will be a lot of Manraloth around, and maybe other very knowledgeable species as well. Plenty of us to go around, not just one poor foundling. Tell your superiors that letting me go is an investment—and the regeneration formula is proof of the potential return."

Coray was starting to realize she was right. Maybe this was an expert manipulation, but it was the best kind, the kind that could satisfy everyone. Indeed, that was how negotiations between canny rivals usually ended—with both sides maneuvering each other until they reached a state of mutual bribery they were both satisfied with. And this—the chance to have her beauty and her bite restored—was a bribe Coray was eager to accept. "I think those terms are very fair," she told the Manraloth. "And I thank you for your willingness to help me with my . . . personal loss."

"It's my pleasure." She picked up her foot coverings and the door slid open, but then she stopped and turned. "But I should be very clear—this is an experimental therapy, so you shouldn't rush into using it. You should probably wait until you get home, have your people run some tests on unattached Taneborian flora, just to make sure. You understand?"

"Yes, of course. A wise precaution. Thank you again." Ariel wiped her feet on the mat that the captain had insisted be placed outside Coray's door, then headed down the corridor still barefoot. As soon as the door closed, Coray's diplomatic smile became wider, more giddy. *To have my vines back!* There was no way she would wait for that—no way she would let her superiors or, even worse, her "friends" in the intelligence department see her return stripped bare and humiliated. Not when there was even a chance of being in bloom again. Maybe it was a deft manipulation on Ariel's part to subvert her government's wishes—rot, of course it was—but Coray would come out of it looking and smelling good in more ways than one, and she was fine with that.

Picard was waiting outside Ariel's door when she returned that night. Her hair was down past her shoulders by now, its wispy strands so light they wafted and flowed behind her even at walking speed. She was carrying some sort of vial, studying it with a critical eye. But before he could ask her about it, she tilted her head and asked, "Have you come to see if I'm all packed? We don't leave for another couple of days, you know."

"Actually," he said, "I was wondering . . . if I could come inside."

A smile slowly blossomed on her face, growing huge. "Always."

But once they were inside and she stood there facing him with that wide-eyed, piercing, expectant look he knew so well, he found himself unsure how to proceed. So he retreated into small talk. "Doctor Lenama and Lieutenant Janeway are saying they'll be sorry to see you go. Lenama thinks you may provide insights into the future of humanoid evolution. Aside from the nanotech, that is."

"Well, who's to say nanotech isn't part of your future evolution? The Manraloth clearly thought it was a good idea, and it seems to have turned out all right with me."

"I suppose you have a point. Maybe that's just one more taboo we have to overcome." Considering that he already had an artificial heart, he supposed there might not be any real harm in adding a few more cyborg components here and there. Although Ariel's nanotech was much more like part of her biology, organic in composition and so integrated into her cells that it could hardly be called mechanical.

Ariel stepped a little closer. "To be honest, I'm starting to grow tired of being poked and prodded like a lab specimen. That's part of why I can't go back to your university with you. I can't just sit around and help others answer their questions, I have to go out there and pursue my own."

"I understand," he assured her, closing the gap a bit more and stroking her arm lightly. "I have to admit," he added with a grin, "the prospect of going back to a classroom, or spending weeks in a lab poring over artifacts and data, has lost its appeal for me. I'd rather be in motion, out among the stars, searching for new discoveries." He took one more step toward her, and she matched it. He could see flecks of brightness in her eyes now, like stars beginning to emerge from a gloaming sky. "You've awakened parts of me I'd forgotten were there."

She grinned. "Parts? Plural? Tell me, Prospero . . . what else have I awakened, hmm?"

He returned the grin. "I think you know."

"No, I need you to show me," she said, her arms going around his neck. "There's a whole dimension of human communication that's been sorely neglected in my education so far."

"Then we must remedy that," he said. He leaned in toward her, tilting his head for a kiss. She tried to follow his movement and their noses collided, evoking a shared chuckle. "No, here—"

"Oh, I understand now." Her hands went to the sides of his head and held it there as her lips found his. He returned the kiss, showing her, and she followed his lead. As always, she had an extraordinary learning curve and soon raced ahead of her teacher. His arms roved over her body, pulling at her clothes, and she quickly surpassed his lead in that as well.

They made love with the lights on. How could they not, the way she shimmered? And there was so much about her to explore, so many colors, so many stripes and sworls and fractals, so many ways the contours of her body could catch the light as she moved. He could not bear to close his eyes as he made love to her. But she engaged all his senses. Her flesh was satin with the grain of her scales, velvet against it. Her hair was spider silk and will-o'-the-wisp. She purred like a cat and he felt it in her chest. Her scent required words no living language had.

And above all, there was her joy, a joy with facets beyond any he'd ever felt in a lover. The joy of sexual union and the joy of love, to be sure, but also the joy of discovering new abilities within herself, and the joy of finding a new way to communicate—perhaps the most profound and pure communication she had yet known. For him, there was the joy of letting go, of sloughing off the baggage of his past and starting life anew, as new as she.

The next morning, when he went to bathe, he found himself asparkle with a light dusting of butterfly scales. He laughed long and hard, and it saddened him to wash them off. But he winked at himself in the mirror. *There are many more where those came from, my friend.*


After *Cleopatra's Needle* headed back to Federation space and took Ariel with it, Coray remained aboard the *Kingsley* as it raced toward her home sector. The regeneration formula the Manraloth had given her was a powerful lure, but she reluctantly held off on using it, since Ariel recommended it would work best in her indigenous lighting, atmosphere, and biochemical conditions. A Mabrae ship was coming to rendezvous with the *Kingsley,* bringing envoys to negotiate with Captain Karapleedeez for passage in their space, so she could still restore her dignity and beauty before she reached home.

Once the *Seblos* arrived after sixteen long days, she arranged to be beamed directly into a private suite so no one need see her. As soon as she was there, she ripped off her cloth coverings and threw them in the mulcher. Then she poured Ariel's formula into the mister above the bed and lay down in its fertilizing embrace, letting regeneration rain gently down upon her.

Two days later, her vines were growing out of control, betraying her, binding and choking her, digging roots into her muscles and organs, draining nutrients from her body faster than she could replenish them, pouring toxins into her bloodstream at levels her own immunity could not cope with. The *Seblos*'s doctor struggled to save her, but it soon became clear there was nothing he could do. "The Manraloth," she rasped to Bilan as he stood sad vigil by his mistress's deathbed, in which the vines had taken root, pinning her there. "I underestimated her. More off my game than I realized. Should never have told her . . . I knew of her manipulative powers. Signed my own death warrant."

"We must tell the Federation what they have among them," Bilan said.

"No!" she gasped. Despite the pain, she grinned. "Leave

them unaware. Let her have her way with them. My . . . revenge." But the momentary pleasure of the thought faded, driven out by the awareness of what she needed to avenge. "I was . . . so beautiful."

At least, when they buried her on Tanebor, she would live on in the plants. She would be one with its soil again.

Ariel was devastated when the news of Coray's death reached them on the *Needle.* "I thought it would help her," she said through her tears. "I wanted to give something back to her, to her people, for their help in rescuing me. I was such a fool, to think I understood what I was doing!"

Picard held her close, rocked her gently. "It's not your fault, Ariel. You told her it was experimental, warned her not to try it without more tests. You couldn't have known she'd be so reckless."

"I should have. I'm supposed to be good at reading people."

"You are. You're very good at it. But some people . . . are very skilled at using language to obfuscate rather than communicate. Coray was such a person, and the first you've ever met." He leaned back to meet her eyes, clasping her bare, trembling shoulders. "I will tell you what you once told me. Whatever may have gone wrong with your results, your purpose was noble. You must forgive yourself."

Her lip trembled. "It's not as easy as I thought it was."

"No. But you helped me to do it. Now let me help you." She smiled sadly and fell against him once more. "Remember you have a purpose, Ariel. To save your people."

After a while, she spoke, her words muffled by his shoulder. "Do you really think we can ever find them? That we can save them if we do?"

"We will find a way," he told her. "I will see to that . . . if it takes the rest of my life."

# PART III

## BRAVE NEW WORLD

———•———

**2360**

# 13

———

IT WAS IN ARIEL'S FIRST WEEK ON CENTAURI III that the full weight of her situation finally hit her.

During the long trip back, Ariel had worked with Allis on translating the recovered data from the ice base. They had made considerable progress, but still achieved only limited results, due to the nature of the data. The computers had stored information in some decentralized way that made it nearly impossible to scan any files except those that were active on the hex screens, so the findings were fragmentary. Much of it pertained to scientific research into Proserpina's aquatic life forms—which had apparently included an intelligent species in that era, if not today—but there was relatively little about those who researched them. There were status reports, news updates, recreational programs, personal journals, and the like, but these were written for and by beings already familiar with their cultural context, and were thus obscure and unrevealing even after they had been thoroughly translated. William Shakespeare could have read the sentence "A Cardassian cruiser suffered a warp-injector failure on approach to the Trelka system on stardate 36849.6" and understood much of its syntax and vocabulary, but would have had no clue what it was describing. Much the same was true here; without knowing the underlying assumptions, the things the creators and intended users of these texts took for granted, there was no way to gain more than the most fragmentary understanding of the world they depicted.

Ariel had not been much better off, despite having lived in that world. Some of the things she read had triggered vague recollections or sensory impressions; she could remember, for instance, that the Toraak were the pear-bodied quadrupedal species from the ice base or that she had once gone ballooning in the atmosphere of an inhabited Jovian planet that might have been one mentioned in the files. But no matter how hard she had tried over the many weeks of their return journey, she had been unable to place those fragments in context. After a while, she had stopped trying and had chosen to concentrate on making the most of the here and now, in a very visceral sense that Picard had benefited from greatly.

Once back in New Samarkand, the expedition members had said their good-byes and returned to their respective homes to recover from their yearlong journey before eventually reconvening to evaluate their findings further. Ariel had moved in with Picard in his small apartment near campus, taking up little space since she had no possessions beyond a few sets of clothing. (She had shown no interest in wearing jewelry; it would have been rather redundant.)

Over the next few days, Picard had shown her the city—the campus, the cultural district, the market square, the museum, the park, the nightclubs. She had drunk it all in with her usual lively curiosity. But soon Picard had begun to sense a change in her. Dark moods would come over her and she would ask to return home. She would become distracted for long moments and be unaware of it afterwards. She would gaze out the window for long stretches with that wide, unblinking feline stare of hers. She would toss and turn in bed, moaning in her sleep.

One morning, Picard woke her from a nightmare and for several moments she could not remember where she was or who he was. She soon reoriented herself, but still seemed distracted and weary. Hoping some fresh air would do her good, he took her out to breakfast at a sidewalk café in the public square, a place whose lively, diverse crowds had appealed to her from the first day. But no sooner had they sat down than she began to grow agitated, her head darting around like a bird's. "Ariel, what's wrong?" he asked, growing concerned.

She stared at him, bewildered. "Who? No—no, it's not—*No!*" She shot to her feet, knocking the chair and table away, looking around her in a panic. Picard stood and came to her, reaching for her shoulders, but she struck his hands away. *"Get away from me!"* She backed away as if in terror, eyes glistening with tears. Then she spun and ran away, shoving a Tellarite couple aside.

Picard ran after her, calling her name, but the male Tellarite got in his way. "Hey, what did you do to her?"

"Let me through, I need to help her!"

"Looks like she feels different, mister."

*"Stand aside!"* It was his command voice, and it worked. The Tellarite got out of the way, and Picard dashed after Ariel's receding figure.

But it was too late. She was running twice as fast as he could, or at least it seemed that way. Soon she was swallowed up by the city and he could no longer spot her. Pulling his personal communicator from his pocket, he contacted the local police and requested their help in finding her. Within minutes, he was informed that other reports matching Ariel's description were coming in—reports of a seemingly deranged woman racing across streets and disrupting traffic, shoving people aside and screaming at them to leave her alone. Soon, an officer came onto the comm and apologetically told Picard that it would be necessary to phaser-stun the woman for her own protection—only to report a moment later that the beam had been ineffectual. *"We don't want to hurt your friend, Mr. Picard,"* the officer said, *"but something has to be done."*

"Where is she heading?"

*"Into the woods north of town."*

"Then please, let her go there. She is . . . a unique being, and I mean that in a very literal sense. If she's asking to be left alone, that may be the best thing we can do for her right now."

*"Are you sure of that, sir?"*

"She would not harm anyone else—and I'm confident that she couldn't seriously harm herself." *Even if she tried.* "I think . . . she's having a delayed stress reaction to a very serious trauma. Coming into the city seems to have started it. Maybe all she needs is some room. At least for now." He asked the police to clear a path for her, to keep her on sensors and monitor her vital signs, and to alert him of any major change.

Half an hour later, the police summoned Picard to the outskirts of the woods, where they had found Ariel's clothing strewn out over a long stretch of path, appearing violently torn. An Arkenite policewoman reassured him that she was safe, though. "She seems to have settled in at the top of Timur's Peak," she said, referring to a high, craggy hill at the heart of the woods. "We were afraid she might jump for a moment, but she's just sitting there now. Naked and sitting and staring up at the sky." She fidgeted. "We, ahh, still have an active transporter lock on her, just in case." Picard thanked her, though he believed it would not be necessary.

Ariel spent four days atop the crag, not moving, not eating, barely metabolizing. Police sensors showed her to be in a kind of trance state, but her vital signs remained stable. Rain fell on the second day and her body absorbed it; Picard would not be surprised if it was drawing nutrients from the soil as well. Threads began to show up in the city's web asking about the origins of the remarkable new golden statue on Timur's Peak. Sightseers came to look at her, but the police deterred them from getting too close.

Finally, she moved again, startling the sightseers, and came down from the crag of her own accord. The police met her with a blanket and coffee and took her to the nearest hospital, where Picard came in response to their summons. Once a doctor had examined her (and come out shaking his head in astonishment) and the police had taken her statement, Picard was finally able to see her again.

"I'm sorry," was the first thing she said. "I gather I caused something of a mess." In contrast to her breezy words, she was preternaturally calm and quiet. Perhaps *numb* was the word—numb after feeling too much for too long.

"I've taken care of it," he said. "Rank hath its privileges, even on reserve."

"And my naked rampage through the park?"

He gave a dismissive shake of his head. "This is a university town. Very cosmopolitan. No one minded. Least of all the men," he quipped, but it evoked no response.

"I should explain. I . . . have been remembering," she said, the words coming slowly as if chosen individually with careful thought. "Not all . . . but enough. I'm not sure what triggered it. Perhaps it was associational. Being within a large multispecies civilization again may have reminded me . . . of . . . past experiences. Or perhaps the mental stimulation of so many different languages to process had the effect of jump-starting my brain, triggering a cascade of new connections and reassembling much of my mind. Apparently my neural anatomy contains even more redundancies than Doctor Lenama realized."

"How much—"

"Wait." He held his curiosity in check and waited for her to continue. "It is still partial. Incomplete. Isolated fragments . . . of a life that I believe may have spanned thousands of centuries, if not more." Picard's eyes shot wide. The woman before him may have existed as an individual for longer than humanity had existed as a species.

But what Ariel said next drove that from his mind. "But I have remembered people. People I loved. Homes I built. Planets I spent centuries getting to know as intimately as you know your home neighborhood. Works of magnificent art and music and literature that had resounded down through the ages and that we believed would enrich the universe forever."

She was quiet for another long moment. "I remembered all those things. And I had to face the fact that all of them . . . everything I ever knew or loved in my life . . . every last trace of it . . . is gone from the universe. Completely. And irretrievably."

Picard sat with her in silence, trying to absorb the enormity of it. If it weighed so heavily on him, how much harder had it hit her?

Eventually she spoke again. "Once that hit me, I simply . . . could not bear to face the galaxy that had replaced mine. All these species I never knew, worlds that bear no trace of my beloved cities . . . evolving on the ruins of my world, blissfully ignorant that it had ever existed. I despised you all." Her tone was still deliberate, clinical, tightly controlled. "I had to get away. I . . ." She clutched the front of her hospital gown. "I could not bear the touch of anything from this time."

His heart sank. "I . . . see," he said at length. "That is . . . perfectly understandable." He began to rise.

To his immeasurable relief, her hand came forth and took his, stopping him. "So I . . . retreated into myself to deal with it. A natural healing mechanism, I suppose. They tell me it was four days. It felt more like a year. I . . . processed all my grief. My rage. My guilt at being the sole survivor. I do not pretend I have fully overcome these things. But I . . . am coping." She stood, pulling him up with her by his hands and not letting go. "And I have reached a stage in my coping process where . . . I could really use your support." She smiled slowly, her lips trembling a bit. "You are my anchor in this life, Jean-Luc. If life in this new world is to be worth living for me, it will be you who make it so." They fell into a long embrace, chaste but profound. "I love you, Jean-Luc."

"And I love you, Ariel."


Before releasing her, the doctors called in Jameela Janasz, the closest thing Ariel had to a personal physician, to consult. Their scans turned up something surprising. Ariel's genome had changed slightly since her original scans. Her overall genetic code was still the same, but the nucleosome structure had changed, causing different parts of it to be expressed. Her metabolism and biochemistry were shifting to be more compatible with human-digestible foodstuffs and with the standard shipboard atmosphere and gravity she had experienced aboard the *Kingsley* and *Cleopatra's Needle*. Her skeletal structure showed a slight variation as well, coming closer to a shape suited for standard gravity. Picard was surprised not to have noticed her proportions shifting, given how much time he spent in close acquaintance with Ariel's body, but she forgave him, saying it had happened too gradually for him to notice yet.

"How much more do you think I'm capable of changing?" Ariel asked Jameela and the staff doctors as they and Picard stood together in her hospital room discussing the findings.

"I have no way of knowing," Jameela said. "Your genome is very complex, and the changes manifesting here have resulted from only minor changes in its expression. I suppose all that cellular nanotech plays a role too, aiding in the gross anatomical restructuring." She shook her head. "It's as though you can evolve within your own lifetime. Which I suppose is a very adaptive trait for an immortal species—otherwise you could find yourself becoming ill-suited for a changing environment."

"And how much faster might this 'evolution' be than the more conventional kind?" Picard asked.

Ariel cocked a colorful brow at him. "Concerned I might change too much to be . . . compatible?"

He smiled, for the retort showed some of her old wry wit, though she was still far more subdued than before. "My curiosity is purely scientific," he riposted.

One of the research scientists, Doctor Denis, answered Picard's question. "That's hard to define," he said, "since the rate of evolution is largely proportional to the length of a species' generations, and this is all taking place within a single generation. But compared to a typical humanoid species, it might be a few hundred times faster, maybe a thousand. Assuming we're talking about the kind of rapid evolution that can occur on transition to a new environment, where noticeable change can occur within a few hundred or thousand years. Ariel could probably make the adjustment in months or years, depending on how great an adjustment it is."

"So she's not a shape-shifter," Jameela said.

"Not in the usual sense. What we see now is how she'll look for years to come, aside from minor variations. But if she is hundreds of thousands of years old," Denis said with a touch of disbelief, "who's to say how much she could have evolved since her birth?"

Ariel kept her thoughts to herself at the time, but once she was back home with Picard, she told him, "I think this could explain some of the things I've remembered. I have sensations, recollections of being in a body very different from this one." She smiled, the first real smile he'd seen since her breakdown. "I remember living in the ocean beneath the ice of Proserpina. Not just swimming through it in some sort of suit—*living* in it like a native. I remember having wings or membranes down the sides of my body, flying through the skies of a world where the air was so dense I could float on it. I have memories of not even being humanoid . . . of being some things I can't even describe."

"Do you think you could transform yourself that much?"

"It doesn't seem likely, from what the doctors said."

"Could these be . . . sense memories from other species you've communicated with telepathically?"

She shook her head. "I only get communication and meaning, not personal experiences."

"Then perhaps some form of virtual reality."

"No. Deeper than that." She sought her memory. "I think . . . in my day, we may have had devices that let us transfer consciousness between minds. We could actually go on vacation from our lives, become other beings. Yes," she said, smiling again. "I think it was quite a fad for a few millennia. There were . . . yes, there were fewer humanoids back then. They weren't as ubiquitous as they are today, for whatever reason. So borrowing other species' bodies could be quite an adventure."

Picard had perked up at that. "Hold on." He went to the terminal and ran a search. "Yes, I thought so. We have found consciousness-transfer devices in archaeological ruins on several worlds. Eris Alpha, Camus II, Kandoge. They're highly restricted, due to the dangers of abuse." He smiled ruefully. "I suppose your civilization was able to use them more responsibly. We've always wondered what they were for. You may have just answered that."

Ariel stared at him intently. "How old are these ruins?"

He checked, and his heart sank. "Oh. Only ten thousand years." Ariel sagged, and he looked at her apologetically. "I keep forgetting that what is the remote past to us is recent history by your standards. Even the Iconians or Vormoresh would have still been chittering away in the branches and picking nits from their fur when you were . . ." He noticed the distant look in her eyes and hated himself. "I'm sorry. That was callous of me."

"No, it's a simple truth," she said. "I'm learning to accept it. I was just thinking . . . I want to know more about those ancient civilizations. The oldest, most advanced ones that are still around today. They may be far closer to your age than mine, but surely some of them must have explored the mysteries of the galaxy's past. Perhaps they've found some of the answers we're looking for. The locations of other Manraloth stasis fields, at least."

CHRISTOPHER L. BENNETT

Picard pondered it. "That would be difficult. The most advanced civilizations we know of have usually evolved or . . . transformed into an incorporeal state. They can be rather hard to locate," he said with irony. "Even those who stay in a known location, such as the Organians, are notoriously reluctant to interact with beings such as ourselves."

"A policy analogous to your Prime Directive, perhaps?"

"Well, in the Organians' case, I'm not so sure. They didn't hesitate to meddle when they stopped the Federation-Klingon War of 2267. But since then they've shown no interest in our affairs." He grinned. "I suspect the only reason they intervened in '67 was because the war intruded on their home territory. Essentially they just wanted the neighborhood children to stop raising a ruckus in their front yard."

Ariel frowned. "How can you be so light-hearted when talking about a war? All that violence, all that destruction."

He was taken aback. "Believe me, I did not intend to make light of the war itself or the losses suffered in it. I have seen my share of combat and I know that loss very personally."

She came over to the desk and stroked his head. "I'm sorry, Jean-Luc. I didn't mean to sound judgmental. It just took me by surprise. Perhaps it's because you have seen so much combat that you can . . . compartmentalize it so. But for me . . . the idea of it is rather shocking."

"I haven't really seen that much combat." He was puzzled. "But in all your millennia of existence, you must have seen much worse. At least heard about it."

She shook her head, brow furrowed. "You know, I don't think I did. Maybe I'm just having a harder time retrieving the more unpleasant memories—I still recall nothing of what precipitated my enclosure in the stasis field—but I don't recall any wars. I think . . . in my galaxy, we had been at peace for a very long time. We had found ways to live together, ways of understanding each other and heading off conflicts. We . . . yes, we. The Manraloth were communicators, bridges between species." She smiled. "I think that was our role in the galaxy, Jean-Luc. We used our gifts to facilitate understanding and unity among its civilizations."

"A diplomatic corps."

"More than that, but yes, basically. It wasn't just us, though. We were part of a whole ancient community, a system that had been in place for mi—yes, I think it may be accurate to say millions of years."

"A single civilization, existing for millions of years? How is that possible?"

"Well, being immortal helped, I'm sure. But it wasn't a single, unchanging culture. More an . . . evolving community of civilizations. I'm sure we went through changes, of course. Yes . . . I remember different civilizations and factions rising and falling in prominence, different political values or cultural ideologies jockeying for influence, languages and belief systems evolving with the times. Although I suppose the pace of change would've seemed glacial by your standards. But we had a rich network of support structures, mechanisms for keeping the whole system stable—for resolving disputes peacefully, smoothing out transitions, heading off crises before they escalated. The Manraloth were key players in that process, though we were far from alone in it, I'm sure. And after all that time, it ran very smoothly. So the galaxy as a whole was at peace for as long as I can remember."

"That is . . . a compelling vision," Picard said. "And enviable."

She smiled down at him. "You underestimate yourself, my dear human. I think I understand why seeing your world, your Federation in all its glory, triggered memories of mine." She moved away, gazing out the window, so he could not see her face. Her voice was thoughtful, subdued. "What I see in your society—different races coming together, choosing to coexist in peace and promote harmony, reaching out to bring others into your fold—it reminds me of what we had. Keep going the way you're going . . . and you could become us one day."

He moved up behind her, wrapped his arms about her

waist. "It means a very great deal to me to hear you say that. To be told that it may one day be possible to eliminate war and strife from the galaxy . . . and that we may already be on the right track."

She clasped his hands against her for a time, then moved them away and began to pace the room slowly. "Still," she said, "there are so many others still in such distress. Whole civilizations knowing nothing but war and conquest and pain. These Cardassians I keep hearing about. The Talarians, the Tzenkethi, so many others."

"Well, things are improving with Cardassia. We may still be technically in a state of war, but there's been no fighting since the truce Sarek and Riva brokered last year. And the peace talks may be going slowly, but at least they're still at the table."

"But what about all the others affected by them, like those Bajorans living under their occupation? There must be more that can be done for them."

"It is a topic of the talks, but there is little more we can do. If we tried to intervene directly, the Cardassians would retaliate with force, it would escalate into a war in the Bajor sector, and the Bajorans and their neighbors would be far worse off."

Ariel shook her head. "We have got to find more of my people, Jean-Luc. We could help you. We could find ways to bring the sides closer together. To help them understand each other." But then she sighed, her shoulders falling. "No. I'm being unreasonable. We'd be out of touch in your world. We wouldn't have the galaxywide mechanisms in place to work within, we'd be starting over from scratch . . . I overestimate the good we could do."

He moved to her again and took her hands. "Even the knowledge that galactic peace is possible could be a powerful motivator. And any additional hands working toward that goal are always welcome." He stroked her cheek. "Besides . . . I promised to help you find your people, and that remains my goal. Whatever it takes, I will help you to reunite with them."

She cocked her head at him. "Even if I want to go to Organia? Will you take me?"

"I can certainly try. Whether they let us approach or simply teleport us halfway across the sector is up to them."

"Well . . . maybe I should do the talking, then," she said. "I do have *some* experience talking with geriatric intelligences." They shared a laugh.

"All right, Ariel. I'll—" He broke off. "It just occurred to me—with all these memories returning, I've completely forgotten to ask if you recalled your real name."

Her gaze grew abstracted for a moment. Finally she shook her head. "It doesn't matter. I like being Ariel. I can change my body, why not my name?"

"Why not indeed?"

Ariel then invited Picard to assist her in examining her body in detail for further changes. Their results were inconclusive, but highly satisfactory to them both.

Ariel's initial attempts to contact the Organians over subspace met with no response. In the meantime, she and Picard continued to search the retrieved records for Manraloth worlds. She had found a number of candidate systems, several within territory controlled or at least explored by the Federation. At Picard's request, Starfleet conducted sensor scans of all those systems, but found no evidence of stasis fields and no viable ruins.

Still, their research did provide insight into another mystery. Most of the worlds in the database were ones with large natural deposits of substances such as dilithium, tritanium, and duranium—either nonelemental compounds or stable transuranic elements that were not found naturally on the majority of worlds and whose methods of formation were still elusive after centuries of study. Moreover, they were often found only on one or two planets in a system, requiring miners to cope with the difficulties of digging them out of a planet's surface rather than the ease and convenience of asteroid mining. Many had theorized that they had been artificially created by ancient civilizations, but their widespread, seemingly natural distribution in many planetary crusts seemed to argue against that. The correlation between former Manraloth worlds and the planets where these deposits were found added weight to the theory of artificial creation. The strata containing these substances were found to have ages ranging from two hundred fifty to over six hundred million years. Ariel, however, expressed doubt that her species had been around quite that long; they may have inherited some worlds from older tenants.

Meanwhile, with the list of reachable candidates growing very thin, Ariel renewed her efforts to contact Organia, still meeting with silence. Picard suggested trying other known incorporeal races such as the Thasians or Molherian Firesouls, but they were all too young for Ariel's standards. "Perhaps they might be worth a try," she told him. "If nothing of my galaxy survives on the physical plane, something might on another dimensional level, and perhaps they have heard something of it. Still, the Organians are far older and closer, so they're still my first choice."

Picard shook his head in wonder, staring at her. They were strolling through the campus, and the efforts of sun and breeze combined to make her hair a fiery corona around the scintillant golden star of her head. But that was not the only thing that astonished him. "You speak so casually about incorporeal intelligence. We are still struggling to understand how such a thing is even possible."

She shrugged. "I suppose I simply got used to it. I have memories . . . impressions, mostly, but several times over my life, a people I knew would make the transition."

"Is that the fate of all sentient beings? To . . . sublime or ascend to that state?"

"I don't think so. There are other paths available. I was aware of species that had undergone 'introdus'—downloading their minds into computer mainframes and living in virtual universes. Some changed themselves into robotic or holographic form. I think there were some worlds where the people just chose to . . . regress. To forget all they had accomplished and start over at a primitive level."

"Why would they do that?"

"Who knows? Maybe they believed in a cyclical view of the universe. Maybe . . . maybe they felt they'd lived their lives wrong and wanted to try again."

"And they never subsequently reached an incorporeal level?"

"Hm?" she asked after a moment, as though her mind had been elsewhere. "Oh. Some may have, on their second go-round. I don't exactly recall."

He studied her. "Ariel, were you a biologist? A xenologist? Your knowledge of other species seems considerable . . . and we did find you at an aquatic research base."

"It's possible," she said after a moment's thought. "I've probably been many things in my life, but that may have been the most recent." She tilted her head at his wistful sigh a moment later. "What is it?"

"It's foolish." At her prompting, he continued. "A few months ago, you were always so excited to discover something new about yourself. Now, you've grown more . . . stoic about it."

"I suppose I'm getting used to it. Still, you're right," she said, mustering a smile. "Anything new we figure out about me is good. I should find it exciting. I suppose I'm just a little numb still." She hugged his arm. "Thank you for being excited for me, Jean-Luc. I'll try to follow your example."

He stroked her lambent hair. "Take your time, my love."

They kissed, but after a few moments, she pulled away, sensing his heart wasn't in it. She laughed. "You still want to talk about incorporeal beings."

"I'm sorry," he said, blushing and sharing the laugh. "It's just . . . it's a paradox. Evolution is driven by genes propagating themselves. So how could any biological organism evolve into a state where the body, and therefore the genes, no longer exist at all? By definition it isn't a pro-reproductive trait."

"Neither is immortality," Ariel pointed out.

"But in your case that may not have been a naturally occurring state."

"True. But there's a good analogy. Evolution can give us traits that allow changes having nothing to do with the genes. Evolving opposable thumbs allows the use of technology to change your world or your own form in ways that genes never could. I think a brain of sufficient complexity could easily produce other emergent changes as well—changes not a part of biological evolution, but made possible by its products.

"We know some brains can harness psionic energy fields to interact with others or manipulate the world around them, in the same way that hands let us interact and affect the world. Perhaps when this connection to the universe's energy fields is strong enough, the mind can exist as a pattern within them and no longer needs the body—perhaps is even slowed down by the limits of biochemical communication within neurons."

Picard pondered this as they walked. "But even so . . . no species evolves in lockstep. By all rights, there should still be corporeal Organians or Firesouls somewhere, or at least their descendants. There's no reason why a whole species would make the change at the same time, is there?"

She fell into thought for what seemed an inordinate length of time. Finally he squeezed her shoulder gently. "Ariel?"

She turned to him. "No," she said. "There is no sense in that at all. No reason."

He was concerned by the heaviness of her tone. "Are you all right?"

She shook off her sudden mood, waved his concern away. "It's nothing. I was just . . . all this talk of the fate of species . . ."

*And her being possibly the last of hers. Damn.* "I'm sorry. Let's change the subject."

"No, I'm fine now. You're right, it's a good question. I suppose they usually wouldn't go all at once. But maybe over a great enough expanse of time, most of them would eventually. Others might choose other paths, such as introdus, or maybe evolve into a corporeal form so different they no longer remember their connection."

Picard studied her. "Did any of your species ever make the transition?"

She gave him that unblinking, evaluating stare again for a long moment. "I don't remember it happening. I don't think it did."

"But you have psionic abilities. So the . . . affinity for it must be there. Given how swiftly your species can evolve, surely some branch . . ."

*"No."* She softened a moment later, smiled to apologize for her harsh tone. "Well, maybe. I can't remember, really. I think it's just a prospect I find personally unattractive." Smiling wider, she eased closer to Picard. "I think I simply enjoy the benefits of corporeal existence far too much to contemplate giving them up." She demonstrated her point with a kiss.

"That," he said between subsequent demonstrations, "strikes me as . . . a very wise . . . and enlightened . . . philosophy."

In time, Ariel decided that if the Organians would not return her calls, she'd simply have to show up on their doorstep. To that end, Picard chartered a private yacht and they set off toward the Federation-Klingon border.

When they approached Organian orbit two weeks later, Ariel hailed them, identifying herself and repeating her request for an audience. They met with no resistance as they settled into orbit, so Picard parked the yacht above the most likely beam-down coordinates—the site of the "capital city" visited by Kirk and Kor ninety-three years before, now reading as just vacant grassland—and joined Ariel in the transporter booth. A moment later, Ariel shimmered (not in her usual way) and faded from view—while Picard stayed exactly where he was. He made another attempt, with identical nonresults. He couldn't raise Ariel on the comm, though sensors showed her life signs stable and active at the beam-down point. "Very well, then," he muttered. "I'll stay here and keep the motor running." It occurred to him that he had not yet introduced Ariel to the wonders of Dixon Hill. Although on second thought, the raw violence of twentieth-century detective fiction would probably be unappealing to her.

He decided to reacquaint himself with the tales of his favorite private eye, having time to work through more than half of Tormé's oeuvre before Ariel materialized aboard three days later—without assistance from the yacht's transporter. He was delighted to see her at first, but she was hardened, closed off, eyes roiling with emotion. He knew by now to give her space. "How did it go?" he asked simply. She gave a long sigh, made her way slowly to the copilot's seat, and lowered herself into it. "Were they unhelpful?"

Her gaze held him, still and unwavering, and he was reminded of the day they had met. At length, she spoke. "They . . . were cooperative. They did not find me as juvenile as humans or Klingons—no offense." He nodded. "Indeed, I think they were astonished to meet a corporeal being of my age. They saw me as a bit eccentric, not unlike the way you would see a grown man who still plays with teddy bears, but they were intrigued enough in their politely condescending way to converse with me."

"And was the news . . . not good?"

The stare again. "They had no news, Jean-Luc. Not the kind I hoped for. They have never encountered a survivor from my time."

As that slowly sank in, Picard began to understand why she appeared so devastated. "Then . . . nothing at all survived."

She blinked, trying to shake off her mood. "Not as far as they were aware, anyway. They were vague about it—probably reluctant to admit it—but I gathered that there are levels of existence even they are not fully aware of. Beings that are perhaps as far above them as they are above y—us."

He shook his head. "Don't worry about insulting me. You're far closer to their level than I."

"Perhaps other incorporeals are more involved with those levels, but the Organians are a stay-at-home sort—well, most of them. I gather there's a small offshoot of their civilization that goes around studying other species by temporarily possessing their bodies. But the homeworld Organians don't like to talk about them and never have them over for dinner." Her words were playful, but her tone was dry and cynical. "Anyway, I can't entirely rule out something from my time surviving on some unknown dimensional plane. I just have no way of finding such beings, and I might not have been aware of them even in my own time."

"Did you learn anything of value at all?" Picard asked, hoping for her sake that the trip would not have been a total loss.

In fact, Ariel visibly brightened, though her underlying sadness remained. "Yes, there was one bit of good news. It actually came courtesy of that explorer branch. I had to prod them into consulting those records despite their embarrassment, and I'm not sure whether they ultimately did so out of pity or just to get me out of their figurative hair. But they turned up something useful. The Organian explorers have come across other stasis fields exactly like the one I was in."

Picard leaned forward. "Did they find a way to open them?"

"They didn't try. It wasn't the sort of thing they were interested in exploring, apparently. But I think one of them may be within a few months' travel of the Federation. The other two they've found are years away at least."

"You have coordinates, then?"

"Approximately. I need to check them against the database."

A few minutes later, the results were on the screen, and Picard grunted in dismay. "They could hardly have picked a worse place for it. If I recall my Starfleet intelligence reports, that region of space is disputed between the Breen and the Sheliak."

"I'm not familiar with either."

"They're both very mysterious to us, in fact. But one thing we do know is that they're both very forceful about defending their territorial claims. And neither would respond well to Federation intrusion, even in a border zone." The region in question, out past Albireo, was in fact well beyond the far border of the Breen Confederacy, but they had been establishing "protectorates" there for decades, expanding aggressively to spinward since their antispinward expansion was blocked by the Federation. The Sheliak's borders and buffer zones were well defined by the terms of the Treaty of Armens, but the Breen had not signed that treaty and did not honor it.

She stared at him. "You mean it could precipitate a war?"

He laid a comforting hand on hers, moved by her great compassion for sentient life. "I don't think they'd go that far. But if they caught us intruding, the consequences would most likely be terminal. You may not be easy to kill, but if they put their minds to it—"

"Never mind me." She clasped his hand in hers. "I wouldn't throw away your life. Not even for this."

"It's a risk I'd be willing to take, Ariel."

She studied the map display, thinking. "Maybe. But not alone."

He sensed something in her tone. "What do you mean?"

Ariel turned back to him. "Reason with me, Jean-Luc. This site is rather far away, requiring a fast ship. It's in dangerous space, requiring a ship that can defend itself. And if we do find a stasis field, we'll need the best scientific minds if we're to have any chance of opening it. You know what that adds up to, Jean-Luc."

With a heavy sigh, he nodded. "Starfleet."

# 14

—◆—

ADMIRAL GREGORY QUINN LEANED BACK IN HIS SEAT,
pondering the request Picard and Ariel had made. Through
the window behind Quinn, Picard could see the towers of
Starbase 20's historic groundside complex, tall, slim, and
ziggurat-topped in the style of mid-twenty-third-century
Federation architecture. The sky was a deep greenish-blue,
and Picard could see the slowly moving lights of some of the
starbase's orbital drydocks, large and bright enough to be
seen even in daylight.

But then Quinn spoke and Picard forgot about the
scenery. "It's quite an intriguing prospect you offer us, Jean-
Luc. Ms. Ariel," he added with a courteous nod.

"Just Ariel is fine, Greg," she answered. At Picard's
harumph, she added, "Sorry—Admiral." It was Ariel's nature to be on a first-name basis with the universe, and formal
detachment did not come easily to her.

But the white-haired admiral smiled, looking for a moment like the grandfather he was. "It's all right—I can forgive it from a civilian." His kindly mien faded as his eyes
darted in Picard's direction—specifically at his collar, where
the rank pins would be if he were still in uniform. "Of
course you understand my problem with what you propose.

Relations with the Breen are tenuous at best and—well, we've had no actual relations with the Sheliak for a hundred years, and I wouldn't like our next contact to be a military one, let alone one we precipitated."

"But this could be our only chance to save other survivors from my civilization," Ariel told him. "There is so much knowledge we could offer you, so much good we could do."

Quinn studied her. "Certainly I'd be glad to rescue beings in distress, as well as solve a great galactic mystery or two, if it were as simple as that. But the stakes are too high. We can't just barge into the disputed zone, and we have no diplomatic relations with either government through which we could negotiate for access." He softened a bit. "You said there are other possible sites some years' travel away. You might be better off trying for them."

Ariel shook her head. "Without ships as fast and powerful as Starfleet's, it would take well over a decade to get to either one. And I'd have no guarantee of finding a civilization there with the same level of scientific advancement as the Federation, not to mention the same degree of benevolence. Please, Admiral. Starfleet is my best hope by far."

Quinn shook his head sadly. "You have my sympathies, Ariel, but I'm simply not convinced it's worth the risk."

She held him in her catlike gaze for a moment. "Perhaps I can offer another incentive, then."

Picard looked to her, curious. So did Quinn. "Go on," said the admiral.

Ariel took a breath. She took Picard in with her gaze as she explained. "I've recently been sorting through a great many memories about my old life. There's a lot I haven't really had a chance to think about much yet, let alone tell anyone about. One of those things is a memory of . . . of how our civilization's memory worked," she finished with a smile. "That is, how we stored data for long-term access. As you can imagine, the Manraloth thought very much on a long-term scale."

"Are you offering some sort of computer technology?"

"Not exactly technology. Yet more than that. There's only one way to store information in a truly permanent way, a way that will never erode or be erased, at least not for trillions of years. And that's to store it in the event horizon of a black hole."

Quinn frowned. "You'll have to explain that to me. Physics wasn't my strong suit."

"Well, sir, if something falls into a black hole, everything about it is theoretically lost from the universe, right? No light, no information about the object can ever be retrieved on the outside."

"So I've been told."

"But it's not that simple. Information is energy. All information is encoded in energy patterns of some kind, be it the quantum states that define a particle or the electrochemical memories in your own brain. And it's a basic law that energy can't be destroyed or removed from the universe."

Quinn nodded. "I'm aware of that much."

"So the information that falls into a black hole isn't truly lost. It's still in there, preserved."

"How?" Picard asked. "Wouldn't everything that fell in just be crushed against the singularity? Then all its information would be converted into mere thermal noise, even if it could escape the horizon."

"In its reference frame, yes. But to an outside observer, anything falling into a black hole never actually makes it in. Gravitational time dilation makes it appear to slow as it draws closer, eventually freezing altogether once it reaches the event horizon."

"It sounds like what happened to you," Quinn said.

Ariel frowned, considering that. "No, not exactly. Anything falling into an event horizon would be torn apart by the tidal stresses long before. The information that would be preserved would be quantum-level—the atomic states, momenta, and so on of the particles themselves."

"So you're talking about some kind of quantum information storage?"

"In a sense. In short, all information that falls into a black hole is encoded on the event horizon. You could say that it leaves an imprint of itself, a ghost image, on the horizon as it falls through. Like a . . . like a club where they take a picture of everyone who passes through the door and put it up on the wall. Except the picture lasts forever. That information is preserved in time as perfectly as I was."

"So this is your long-term storage system," Picard said.

"Exactly. The Manraloth, and our sister civilizations, used black holes as data archives. We would feed encoded data into their event horizons, where they would be perfectly preserved for future civilizations to use throughout eternity."

"But how did you get the information back out again? Nothing can get out of an event horizon."

Ariel smiled at Picard. "The same way you and Lieutenant Janeway—who really deserves a promotion, if you ask me," she added to Quinn, "—got through the stasis bubble's event horizon. By using quantum entanglement. We essentially 'teleport' the data out and get around the barrier."

"And that doesn't destroy the data?" Quinn asked delicately.

Ariel gazed at him for a moment, registering the analogy. "Some of the physics may be universal, Admiral, but the details of the stasis field technology were very different from a black hole. Yes. The information can be retrieved, but that imprint on the event horizon is there forever and can always be read again."

Quinn saw where she was going. "So you're saying that everything your civilization ever learned . . ."

"Is out there still," she said, nodding. "Tens, maybe hundreds of millions of years' worth of knowledge about the universe. The answers to every mystery of physics and cosmology. Technological advances millennia beyond your level." Her eyes glistened. "Works of art and music and literature that I feared were gone forever, achievements of astonishing beauty waiting to live again.

"And more. Not just information, but *experience.* Precedents for every kind of political, economic, or social crisis ever encountered on millions of worlds over millions of years. For any given problem that would arise, you could find a solution or approach that had worked for someone, somewhere, in a very similar situation, and adapt it to your own needs. You could benefit from the experience of others' trial and error rather than having to repeat the same mistakes. It's part of how we avoided wars—we could usually find ways to head off problems before they escalated to that level.

"And all this knowledge is out there, in multiple black holes throughout the galaxy. Not erased, not eroded, not corrupted—perfectly intact and waiting to be read by someone who knows how. And the Manraloth know how." She leaned forward. "Admiral . . . this is too important *not* to pursue."

Picard had listened to this with growing fascination, excited by the prospect of so much knowledge. But Quinn still appeared wary. "I do appreciate what you're offering, Ariel. But . . ." He shook his head. "The explorer in me isn't comfortable with the idea of just having the answers to all the universe's mysteries *handed* to us. Maybe you'll find this the conceit of a juvenile species, but I'd rather we did the work to find it out ourselves."

She examined him. "Would the rest of your people feel that way?"

"Perhaps not," he conceded. "But that is another of my concerns, ma'am. I have to wonder about the Prime Directive implications here. Except that this time, we're the primitive civilization being offered the knowledge of a more advanced power. Are we really ready for that? Are we intelligent enough, mature enough as a people, to handle what you offer, to use it with care and resist its temptations?"

"I think you underestimate yourself, sir," she told him.

"The fact that you ask that question at all speaks well for the maturity of your culture."

"Thank you," Quinn said, "but you'll pardon me if I find that response a bit glib."

"You're a cynic, Greg," Picard said.

"It's served me well, Jean-Luc."

Ariel thought a moment. "Consider this, Admiral. The store of knowledge I'm offering you is orders of magnitude fuller than the entire collected information stores of the Federation. You could not gain all that knowledge overnight. Searching through the contents of such a database, reconstructing the knowledge it gave you about the universe, would itself be enough to keep you busy exploring for millennia. It would be as challenging and rewarding an adventure as traveling through space, but without the threat to life and limb."

Picard was torn by that. The prospect of exploration without loss of life was compelling, but he wasn't sure he could settle for a lifetime of exploring files in a database. Still, a loophole occurred to him. "And the archive would only be current up to a quarter-billion years ago, Greg. If we wanted to learn about the more recent history or current inhabitants of the galaxy, we'd still need to explore physically."

"But with vastly improved engines and defenses," Ariel added. "And access to countless precedents and problem-solving strategies that could help you find peaceful resolutions to any crises you encountered."

Quinn peered at her. "And do you have the experience to offer a peaceful solution to our little problem with the Breen and Sheliak?"

She pondered for a moment. "If they would let me talk to them, get to know them, perhaps in time. But not by past precedent. I don't actually remember all that the archives contained—how could I, even if my memory hadn't been scrambled? I just remember that they exist."

"And you hope," Quinn said, "that if we can rescue the

people from the stasis bubble you think you've located, then they can tell you where to find an archive, and this archive can then tell you where to find the rest of your surviving people."

"You're very perceptive, Admiral." Her words did not come off as flattery. Picard heard great vulnerability in her voice, fear that Quinn was about to reject her request for the final time.

But he thought of something that might change that. "Greg, there's something we need to consider. We know the stasis bubble is near Breen and Sheliak territory. We know they're both advanced civilizations. And the news of these bubbles' existence is not secret; it's been published in the major archaeology journals. What if the Sheliak or the Breen were to find this stasis bubble? What if they could find a way to retrieve its occupants intact? What if *they* got hold of one of these black-hole archives first?"

Quinn held up his hands. "All right. All right. I see your point. This is a security issue for us." He thought a moment. "I'm inclined to agree at this point. But, Jean-Luc, there's something I'm going to need from you in return."

Picard frowned. "What is it?"

"I'd like to discuss that with you in private. If you don't mind," he added to Ariel.

She looked them both over, then smiled. "Of course, Admiral Quinn. I really appreciate your willingness to help." She shook his hand and left, smiling at Picard as she passed.

Picard caught Quinn gazing after her once she was gone, and he knew Quinn too well to dismiss it as an old man's lechery. "What is it, Greg?"

"As I said, Jean-Luc, I'm inclined to authorize this based on the security concerns you raised. But I'm still not sure about these Manraloth. How much do we really know about them, after all? It all comes from her."

"I trust her implicitly."

The admiral gave him a small smile, missing nothing. "I don't have that luxury, old friend. I have to look at her as a

CHRISTOPHER L. BENNETT

member of an alien species of potentially great power and unknown intentions and morality." He frowned. "One thing we do know is that she's genetically engineered."

Picard stared at him. "I had thought, Greg, that we were well past the point of judging people on the basis of their genetics."

"The laws against genetic engineering—"

"Are starting to bend. The Darwin Research Station—"

"Is a test case that should never have been authorized! It's only a matter of time before it produces something disastrous—or some*one*. The laws are there for a reason."

"Ariel's no Augment, Greg. Her people thought of genetics as a functional tool, not a means to moral superiority or domination."

"Can we be sure of that? Think about it. You beamed members of four species out of that stasis bubble—and she was the only one physiologically equipped to survive the damage. Why didn't her people share that gift with the others?"

"We don't know that!" Picard countered, putting his hands on Quinn's desk and coming to his feet. "They were closer to the fringes of the field, more badly damaged. Maybe they could have regenerated otherwise."

Rather than reciprocating, Quinn sank back into his chair and spoke gently. "Calm down, Jean-Luc. Don't misunderstand me—I'm not accusing your ladyfriend of anything. I'm simply pointing out that there are questions we need to be aware of. We have to maintain a clear and objective view on this, no matter our personal feelings."

Mollified by his tone, Picard sat down again and calmed himself. "You're right, of course, Greg. That's as important for scientists as for officers."

"I'm glad you agree." He leaned forward. "Because if I'm going to authorize this mission for you, I need to be sure of where your priorities—and your loyalties—lie. I need you to put your uniform back on—*Captain* Picard."

It was some moments before Picard could reply. "I . . . appreciate the invitation, sir. I'll consider it, but—"

"No, Jean-Luc. This is something like the fourth time you've asked for our help with your pet project in the past two years, and now you're asking us to mount a secret mission into hostile territory. Now it's your turn to give us something back. You want this mission to succeed? Fine. Then you'll need the experience of a top-rate, veteran starship captain. And you've got one sitting right there," he said, pointing at Picard. "This is your quest, your area of expertise. You're the best man for the job, dammit, so stop pussyfooting around and start doing your job again." He held Picard's gaze. "I'd rather not make it an order, but I can recall you to active duty any time I want."

Picard fell silent for a time, thinking. He had always left this option open, placing himself on reserve status rather than retiring, but had not seriously considered returning to Starfleet. His top priority right now was helping Ariel . . . followed closely by simply *being* with Ariel, sharing his life with her. He could not imagine leaving that behind.

But then, there were plenty of married Starfleet officers. Indeed, the new *Galaxy*-class starships currently under construction at Utopia Planitia were designed to have families onboard. It was a concept he had always objected to strenuously, and the thought of having children underfoot filled him with dread. But love could make a man reconsider many things.

"May I have time to discuss it with Ariel before I reply, sir? I think she deserves to have a say in this decision."

Quinn's brows rose. "It *is* serious between you, isn't it?" He smiled. "Go ahead. But get back to me by morning."

Picard rose. "I must say, sir—I never expected Starfleet to offer me a ship again. I know I was cleared, but . . ."

Quinn nodded. "There are politics, of course. When a captain loses a ship, many are reluctant to trust him with another. But only those who don't know the score. You have a lot of friends in Starfleet, Jean-Luc, and we know you did nothing wrong. The heart of Starfleet isn't its ships. Ships are replaceable. People are not. And you saved most of your people against all odds, even when your ship itself turned on you. The way I see it, that makes you a damn good captain—and as long as I've got these pins on," he said, tugging at his lapels, "I can order others to see it that way too."

He chuckled. "Besides—it's not like I'm handing you the keys to the *Galaxy* or the *Yamato*. You're starting out small this time, a fast, well-armed scout, a couple of dozen crew. Bring it back in one piece and we'll see about trading you up."

Picard laughed. "Thank you, Greg. You're a good friend."

"You're welcome—Captain Picard."

"I haven't said yes yet."

Quinn winked. "But you never stopped being a captain."

When Picard told Ariel of Quinn's offer, she accepted it more readily than he did. "I think it's an excellent idea," she said. "As a Starfleet captain you'll be in a much better position to help my people. You can assemble your own crew, recruit the best scientists. And once we do find a way to free my people, you'll be in a position to speak for us."

"In what way?" he asked.

"Come on, you know I can read people. Admiral Quinn doesn't trust me. It's all right," she assured him. "In his position, he has to be cautious. But there will be others like him, and it will help to have a voice supporting us on the inside." She took his hands. "Because as advanced and powerful and immortal and all that as we may be, we will still be foundlings, out of place, unfamiliar with your galaxy. We'll need the help of a friendly power while we get back on our feet. I can't think of anyone better than the Federation."

Picard smiled. "You're very optimistic. Talking about the rescue of the Manraloth as if it were a sure thing."

Some of her sadness showed through. "I can't afford not to be optimistic at this point. Hope is what's keeping me going. Well," she added, smiling, "hope and you."

They kissed for a while, but then he asked, "And what

about afterwards? Once this mission is over, even if we succeed, Starfleet will have other duties for me. What will that mean for us?"

She stroked his head. "We can survive the occasional separation, my love. I'll be busy too, helping my people adjust. But we will find time. And no career lasts forever," she added with a smile laden with promise.

He harumphed. "But will you still find me desirable when I'm old and gray and you're as perfect as you are now?"

Her arms went around him. "'But flowers distill'd, though they with winter meet, / Leese but their show; their substance still lives sweet.'"


Rather than a scout ship, Picard's new command turned out to be (perhaps auspiciously) a *Miranda*-class frigate, the *U.S.S. Portia*. Although its crew complement would be small, Quinn had reasoned that if its mission were successful, it would return with an unknown number of passengers, so it made sense to send a ship able to support hundreds if necessary. The vessel was outfitted in a science configuration, lacking the "roll bar" weapons pod of the classic *Miranda* and bearing two large "sensor cannons" at the sides of its extended-saucer hull. Although the ship was heading into potentially hostile territory, it was on a scientific mission, and Picard's orders and preference were to avoid combat rather than engage in it. The emphasis was thus on speed and stealth. The starbase refit crew strove to maximize the *Portia*'s shielding and warp efficiency and minimize its energy emissions, and the lack of a power-hungry weapons pod (and the more compact profile that resulted) aided in both goals. Also, the less aggressive configuration at least made it possible that if they were discovered, the Sheliak or Breen might be slightly less inclined to shoot first. If they were attacked (which seemed more likely), the *Miranda* class's sturdy construction improved their chances of a relatively clean getaway.

## CHRISTOPHER L. BENNETT

To help Picard get back into the swing of starship command, Quinn assigned a veteran officer, Commander Quetzalxochitl "Sally" Vejar, a tall, sturdy Nahuatl woman in her late forties, as his second-in-command. She had more experience in administrative postings than on starships, but her knowledge of the tactical and political details of their target region and its players was exhaustive. Picard left her to staff the bulk of the crew while he hand-picked the best science team he could assemble. His choices were primarily enlisted specialists, skilled scientists who had joined Starfleet to take advantage of the cutting-edge research opportunities it had offered—including the quantum physicist Doctor Angus McCarthy, the temporal mechanicist Doctor Kimiko Jones, and Questor Deb'ni of Algolia, the renowned expert in transporter information theory. Qr. Deb'ni had already authored a paper analyzing the failure of Lieutenant Janeway's transporter-entanglement method and proposing possible solutions; the paper had been coauthored by veteran transporter chief Shawn Rider, whom Picard was also able to bring on board. For chief engineer, he requested Ryallen Colla, a Napean lieutenant commander whose experience with the Starfleet Corps of Engineers gave him the flexibility and ingenuity to deal with the technological challenges of this mission.

But he still needed an expert in probability mechanics, as well as a skilled enough generalist to take the post of chief science officer. In reviewing Starfleet's personnel files, he came upon one individual who might provide both. But the lieutenant's file was unusual enough that Picard felt the need to size him up in person before offering him the assignment. In some ways, his record was exemplary, his skills unequaled; yet after fifteen years in the fleet he had accomplished little of note. Had it been anyone else, Picard would have dismissed the individual as a slacker or a dreamer, brilliant but ill-suited to Starfleet responsibilities. But there were factors that made this officer unique, and perhaps uniquely qualified to contribute to this mission. Conventional assumptions simply could not apply.

So it was that Picard found himself on Starbase G-6, a small, general-purpose space station in the Betazed Sector, several days' travel from Starbase 20. The officer he sought was assigned to the records division, where he had been working for the last several years as, essentially, a file clerk. But the base commander insisted he was a particularly gifted file clerk—so gifted, in fact, that she had been able to transfer the department's other personnel elsewhere. "You mean he works there all alone?" Picard asked in astonishment.

The commander, a bovine-featured Grazerite, hesitated before responding. "It is . . . a comfortable arrangement for everyone, sir."

"Have the lieutenant report to me immediately in your briefing room," he ordered. "I'll speak to him alone." He could sense the commander's discomfort with her records officer, and wished to get the other side of the story unadulterated.

The briefing room was just across the hall from the commander's office, so in mere moments Picard was there, pulling out a seat to await the lieutenant. But no sooner had he begun to sit than the door chime sounded. "Enter," he said once he was settled.

The doors slid open, and the records officer entered the room. "Lieutenant Data, reporting as ordered, sir."

Picard looked him over, trying not to stare. Whatever he had expected the only android in Starfleet to be like in person, this was not it. Certainly there were aspects of him that seemed artificial—the stiff, slicked-back hair, the golden eyes that took in the room with a darting, methodical saccade, the pearlescent white skin that caught the highlights from his mustard-hued uniform. He bore no scent save that of a freshly laundered garment and a hint of bioplast sheeting. Nonetheless, he looked uncannily human, down to the pores of his skin. He did not stand mannequin-still, but held himself loosely, subtly shifting his balance, and expanded and contracted his chest in simulated (or actual?) breathing.

His features were not model-perfect or even particularly average, with a slightly beaked nose and a soft chin with a slight underbite. His build was unremarkable. His voice was a pleasant but nasal tenor, his delivery precise and formal but not mechanical. Whoever had created him had done a meticulous job simulating humanity, yet nonetheless had chosen to leave his android nature clear. Picard had to wonder why.

After a moment, he realized that Data was still watching him expectantly. "My apologies, Lieutenant. I did not mean to stare."

"Thank you, sir. However, I am accustomed to it. And I am incapable of taking offense."

"Well . . . good." He gestured to a chair. "Have a seat, Lieutenant."

"Aye, sir." The android complied, yet somehow even when seated it—*he*—appeared to stand at relaxed attention. He had taken it more as a motion to be performed than an invitation to rest.

Picard observed Data for a moment, but the android made no attempt to speak. Finally Picard said, "I suppose you're wondering why I've asked to see you."

Data tilted his head in a birdlike motion. "Yes, sir. Possibilities include: a request to perform a special records search; a performance appraisal; a notification of reassignment; a notification of promotion or demotion; a notification of injury or death to a close associate or family member. However, since I have no close associates or family members, the latter is highly unlikely." He enumerated each possibility in the same detached tone, as though the prospect of a radical life change were merely an abstract intellectual problem.

"I wanted to interview you," Picard told him. "I'm assembling a crew for a special mission, and I wish to determine if you are a suitable candidate for the post of science officer."

"I see. Accessing." Again that birdlike head motion, as though he were consulting charts floating in his field of vision. "At the current time, there are eighty-seven available

Starfleet personnel on active duty who have more experience and/or qualifications for the post of starship science officer than myself. Would you like a list of their names and locations, Captain Picard?"

Picard studied him. "Is there some reason why you would rather not accept this assignment, Lieutenant?"

"No, sir. In fact, I find the prospect intriguing and feel it would be a better use of my training and abilities than my current assignment."

"Then why was your first reaction to offer me alternatives to your own name?"

Data frowned. "Because that is my job, sir. I wished to provide you with the most comprehensive information available so that you could make the best possible decision."

"I see." Picard folded his hands before him on the table. "Did you consider that I already reviewed the potential candidates and chose to seek you out?"

"Yes, sir. I have a linear computational speed of sixty trillion operations per second. I was able to consider many possible scenarios between the time you asked the question and the time I gave my response. However, I could not conclusively assign that scenario a higher probability than the one in which you were unaware of the alternatives."

Picard gave him a look. "So you thought you'd hedge your bets?"

That brought another head tilt and a confused expression. "I am not engaged in gambling, sir. Inquiry: How can a wager be enclosed or confined?"

After staring for a moment, Picard waved it off. "Never mind that, Mister Data. We're getting off the subject. Now, what I need in particular is an expert in probability mechanics."

"Ah!" Data said, his voice going up nearly an octave on the word. "I understand, sir. I hold honors in probability mechanics and exobiology from Starfleet Academy."

"Yes, and if we're lucky on this mission, an exobiologist may be of use as well."

"Inquiry: What is the correlation between fortuitous happenstance and exobiology?"

Picard frowned. "Mister Data, are you trying to be funny?"

"No, sir," the android said, looking mildly surprised. "Humor is a phenomenon of which I have extremely little comprehension." Another curious head tilt. "Are you attempting humor, sir? That might explain our difficulty with communication."

"No, Mister Data, I am not. I am simply trying to learn more about you."

"I see, sir. I am a sentient android possessing a positronic neural network. I was discovered on the planet Omicron Theta by the *U.S.S. Tripoli* on stardate 15090.2. I am composed of a tripolymer substrate over a molybdenum-cobalt polyalloy skeleton and—"

"Data, stop!" The android's mouth snapped shut. "I can read all that in your service record. I came here in person because I wished to learn something about you that I couldn't read in a file. Something about the kind of person that you are. I wish to learn about the man behind the machine." With a puzzled frown, Data turned to look behind him. Picard ran a hand over his scalp, which seemed to be losing more of its few remaining hairs the longer he participated in this conversation. "Mister Data, explain something to me."

"If I can, sir."

"You have been living among humans and other species for twenty-two years now."

"Twenty-two years, thirteen days."

"Yes, yes. So how is it that with all your ability for accumulating knowledge, you have learnt nothing about idiomatic speech?"

"Apologies, sir. It is a difficult concept for me to grasp. According to my research, the capacity to understand idiom is dependent upon the capacity to empathize with the speaker and understand the emotional or social subtext behind the words. I lack the capacity for emotion and am therefore impaired in processing that aspect of human language." Picard was reminded of all that Ariel had taught him about the many levels beyond words on which communication existed.

"But surely you can look up the meanings of idiomatic phrases in a reference text."

"I can, sir, but it remains difficult to grasp without an understanding of the social context. There is a difference between having factual information about a thing and having working knowledge of how it is applied in practice." Picard was struck by Data's words; despite everything, they showed unusual insight. And despite his claim to possess no emotion, he seemed wistful about his lack of working knowledge.

"But surely after twenty-two years, you've had plenty of opportunity to observe your colleagues using figurative language, to master it through interaction. You are able to learn and adapt, correct?"

"Indeed, sir. However, such learning is contingent upon the opportunity for observation and interaction. I have had relatively few such opportunities since my graduation from Starfleet Academy."

This jibed with Data's record, one marked by a succession of solitary assignments, generally in tasks too tedious, isolated, or hazardous for other beings to perform. "Have you deliberately sought to avoid such interaction, Lieutenant?"

"On the contrary, sir. I wish nothing more in life than to understand what it means to be human."

That raised several questions. Picard chose the most immediate one. "Why?"

"I was constructed in the form of a human, sir. Thus, I conclude that I must have been created to emulate humanity. In order to fulfill my purpose, therefore, I must learn all that can be learned about the human condition, and emulate it as precisely as possible."

"So . . . essentially, you wish to become human."

"That is not possible, sir."

"Figuratively, Lieutenant. Human in every way except the biological."

Data nodded. "That would be accurate, sir."

"Then tell me, Lieutenant: if you crave to understand humanity so much, why have you made so little effort to interact with other Starfleet personnel?"

"I have attempted to do so, Captain. However, my fellow personnel have shown little interest in such interaction, and my superiors continue to assign me to solitary tasks."

"And you are satisfied with this?"

"No, sir, I am not. It is a continual impediment to my efforts to understand humanity, as well as my motivational imperative to acquire knowledge in all forms."

"Then why have you not objected to the assignments you have been given?"

Data seemed confused. "I am obligated to obey orders, sir. Am I not?"

"Yes, but . . ." Picard leaned forward. "That doesn't mean you're forbidden to express initiative. Starfleet does not want its personnel to be . . . unthinking drones." He'd almost said *robots*. "Officers should be able to assert themselves. To let their commanding officers know what they're interested in, what they're capable of. It's part of the information that a good commander uses in deciding what orders to give, what duties to assign. Yes, once an order is given you're expected to obey it, but you're entitled to express dissatisfaction, to try to persuade your commander to offer you different opportunities in the future. Do you understand?"

Data had that far-off look again. "Uncertain, sir. I am unsure how to reconcile the conflicting responsibilities inherent in the problem. This appears to be another example of social dynamics which I lack the experience to evaluate." His brows went up. "And yet it is a problem I would have to solve in order to gain such experience to begin with. It is a paradox, sir."

"Sometimes, Lieutenant, you must simply be willing to venture into a situation without prior experience or understanding. To be willing to learn as you go, and to risk making mistakes in the hope of gaining success. This is as true in the realm of social interaction as in the realm of Starfleet duties. Taking initiative—seeking out new opportunities, showing confidence in your own worthiness to attain them—is frequently rewarded. You cannot simply wait for new opportunities to be given to you."

Data tilted his head. "But, sir . . . are you not currently giving me a new opportunity that I did not seek out on my own?"

"Well—I mean as a general rule . . . Naturally, there are . . ." Sighing, Picard gave up trying to psychoanalyze an automaton. "Just one more question, Mister Data. Are you able to keep a secret? If assigned to a classified mission, would you understand the need for silence about it?"

Mercifully, Data did not point out that he had asked two questions. "Yes, sir. If ordered never to divulge information about a mission, I would be compelled to remain silent."

He studied the android—no, the lieutenant—for a moment longer. "Mister Data . . . I am not going to ask you to accompany me on this mission."

"Of course, sir. I understand." Data began to rise.

"Mister Data!" The lieutenant froze. "What did we just discuss about expressing initiative?"

Data opened his mouth as if to parrot back the specifics, but then stopped; perhaps he was able to grasp the concept of rhetorical questions, at least. After another moment, undoubtedly representing an extensive process of calculation and simulation within that positronic neural network of his, Data rose to attention. "Captain Picard, I hereby volunteer to accompany you on your mission."

"Is that what you want, Lieutenant?"

"Very much, sir."

"Then convince me. Explain to me why you are the right man for the job."

Data sat down and began to speak. An hour later, Picard left the starbase with Data at his side; the android had no possessions to pack. The base commander lamented only the loss of a records officer, but Picard pointed out that she had several other officers capable of doing the job. "And I think," he told her, "that all of you could stand to brush up on your sense of responsibility."

# 15

———•———

AVOIDING BREEN SPACE MEANT TAKING A ROUND-
about path. The *Portia* spent the better part of two weeks angling south from the galactic plane, roughly toward Kitalpha
and beyond, before beginning to curve gently north again toward Albireo. In all, it would take at least a month of travel
to reach their destination—longer if the need to dodge Breen
or Sheliak ships became an issue.

The long travel time gave Picard plenty of opportunity to
readjust to starship command. However, he found himself
falling back into the familiar patterns quickly, as though he
had never been away. The main adjustment lay in getting to
know his new crew. Sally Vejar proved a capable first officer,
quite efficient at managing the small crew and keeping him
briefed on their progress. Perhaps she was more by-the-book
than Picard was used to in a first officer, but that gave him
the freedom to be more relaxed and informal in his approach. Since this was largely a crew of scientists, he felt
comfortable treating them much the same way he had
treated his colleagues at the university or on *Cleopatra's*

*Needle*—as fellow explorers and scholars rather than military subordinates.

Ariel, naturally, bonded with everyone in the crew right away. True to her Manraloth instincts, she fell quickly into the role of an informal counselor or morale officer. Yet at the same time, she pulled her weight in the science department, engaging in long discussions with the Starfleet experts about the physics of Manraloth stasis bubbles and how they might be deactivated safely. It was not a field in which Ariel had any specific knowledge that she could remember, but she hoped that what she did recall about Manraloth technology in general could provide some insight. She also simply enjoyed the company of the scientists, who apparently shared a common love of music. She spoke to Picard of how much she enjoyed listening to McCarthy, Jones, and Deb'ni chat away about their disparate musical tastes and their common sentiment that the patterns and mathematics of music reflected something fundamental about the universe. She had told them what she could remember about the great works of music preserved in the Manraloth archives, the songs and sounds of a galaxy of worlds, along with all their ancient civilization's insights into physics and cosmology. According to her, it was a toss-up which prospect had intrigued the scientists more.

The one member of the crew who had the hardest time meshing with the unit was Lieutenant Data. And perhaps it was not primarily the android's fault. Picard noticed how the other members of the crew avoided him. On the surface, they were polite and professional toward Data, but there was a general sense of unease toward him, or at least uncertainty. "The fact is," Vejar told Picard in private, "they don't know what to make of Data. Neither do I, to be honest, sir. Is it—he—a piece of hardware or a fellow crewman?"

"He wears the uniform, Commander," Picard said. "He's a fellow officer and is entitled to be treated as such."

"I know that, sir. Intellectually, we all do. But it's one thing to know that in the abstract and another thing to have to deal with it on an everyday basis." Picard supposed he could understand their reaction. He hadn't known what to make of Data himself until he'd sat down and talked to the— the man. *And clearly I'm still working on it,* he thought. Prejudice, or at least caution toward the unknown, was a normal human trait, even an adaptive one up to a point. Humanity had little experience with sentient androids; its own research into the field had been terminated following the use of android impostors as assassins in the Third World War, and the alien androids that Starfleet had encountered since then had usually turned out to be hostile or dangerous themselves. None of that experience made it easy to take the idea of an android as a fellow Starfleet officer in stride.

"And to be fair, sir," Vejar added, "he doesn't make it easy. He's such a—a *child*. All he can contribute to discussions is incessant questions about every little niggling detail—it grinds just about any conversation to a halt. And if it isn't that, he's droning on forever with these detailed reports and doesn't know when to stop."

"Then simply ask him to stop. He won't take offense. And he won't learn these things unless he's told."

"Maybe. But that's not a task anyone here is particularly eager to seek out." Vejar shrugged. "With respect, Captain, does it really matter? I mean, if he isn't offended by it . . ."

"He's a member of a starship crew. That means he needs to be able to rely on his crewmates and they on him."

Vejar took his point and nodded. "Should I instruct the crew to take Data under their wings, sir?"

Picard considered the question. "I'm reluctant to take that step. Commanding them to do it would not resolve the underlying problem. And I have no wish to coddle Mister Data. If he is to learn to function as a part of human society, he needs to learn to take the initiative for himself. This is something that both he and the others need to learn by doing. The problem is how to nudge them in the right direction without taking away that autonomy."

Vejar pondered. "I think this is a bit out of my league,

Captain. I deal with procedures and regs. I generally leave problems like this to the nearest counselor." She perked up. "Maybe you could ask Ariel if she has any ideas. She's pretty good at bridging gaps, so I hear."

Picard smiled. "Number One, that is an excellent suggestion."

Vejar looked pleased with herself. "Well, what do you know? I'm Number One."


On stardate 37175.5, at 0537 hours shipboard time, Data was alone in the quantum physics laboratory on deck 7, sector 03, compartment 02 of the *U.S.S. Portia,* conducting simulations on the use of the Jahn-Teller effect to modify the Cooper pairs in the Bose-Einstein condensate of a standard Starfleet transporter Heisenberg compensator unit in order to minimize disruptive interference between its quantum waveform and that of a Manraloth stasis field's fringe zone of positional uncertainty. Shortly after he began running the 3,547th simulation run, the door slid open and Data turned to obtain visual identification of the individual who was entering. It proved to be the Manraloth female known as Ariel. "Hello, Mister Data," she said. "Am I disturbing you?"

He recognized the query as one commonly used by humanoids in similar situations. At Starfleet Academy, he had quickly learned that failure to solicit such information upon entering a room and initiating conversation could lead to negative reactions from those occupied with other tasks. Therefore, this was one social situation, at least, in which he was aware of the correct response. "Not at all, Ariel. I am capable of multitasking. Please enter."

"Thank you." She came into the room, her locomotion unusually efficient for a humanoid. There was very little wasted energy or uncertainty in her motion. Data recalled that her estimated age was on the order of ten to the fifth power standard years at minimum. Although this was anecdotal, analysis of her biology did support the hypothesis that her species was possessed of extraordinary longevity. He had heard her referred to as "immortal," a term which he found imprecise, since it was impossible to prove that a being could live for an infinite period of time without observing that being for an infinite period of time. Still, an extended lifetime would have provided Ariel with abundant opportunity to refine her physical movements to the degree he observed. He wondered what other areas she might have gained comparable experience in, and concluded that they must be numerous. He found himself wishing he could be at a comparable level of experience and insight. *Intriguing. Is this envy?*

Ariel came to within what was regarded as a typical social distance among many humanoid species and spoke further. "It occurs to me that I've been remiss in getting to know you better."

"Indeed. I have noticed that omission." Given how gregarious she had been in her interactions with the rest of the crew, it was an omission that had particularly stood out.

"And I apologize for it, Data." Her left hand applied gentle pressure to his right shoulder for 1.73 seconds. "It's my fault. I'm not as comfortable communicating with artificial intelligences as with organic ones, since there's no empathic connection. But that's not fair to you. You're as much a person as anyone else here."

Although few people had ever said anything along these lines to Data, he was aware of the proper response. Indeed, he had often simulated scenarios in which others would treat him in this way and had practiced how he would respond. "Thank you, Ariel. I accept your apology, and I would welcome the opportunity to converse further. Please proceed."

Ariel laughed, though Data did not understand why. "Well, all right. . . . Tell me, where did you come from? Who created you?"

"I was discovered on the planet Omicron Theta by the *U.S.S. Tripoli.* My creator or creators are unknown."

"You don't know who made you?"

"That is correct."

"Why not?"

"The colony on Omicron Theta was destroyed by unknown means prior to my discovery. I was the only survivor. The crew of the *Tripoli* found me in an inactive state on a slab of stone near the colony. Their arrival triggered my activation. That is my first memory."

"Did they attempt to find evidence of your origins on the planet?"

"Yes, but they found nothing. They subsequently chose to take me back to Starfleet Command for further study."

"Did you ever go back to Omicron Theta?"

"No."

"Did you ever consult the Federation's databases to attempt to find evidence of who might have created you?"

"No."

Ariel stared at him for a moment and blinked—something she typically did only 41.6 percent as frequently as an average adult human female. "I'm a little confused, Data. I thought you were curious about everything."

"I am curious about my origins. I simply have chosen not to investigate them."

"Why not?"

Data took several thousand processing cycles to formulate his explanation, a process which took 1.21 seconds. "I consider it my purpose in life to emulate humanity. To approach it as closely as I am able."

"Yes."

"Many humans believe themselves to be the creation of a higher intelligence. While no educated human would believe this to be true in a direct and literal sense, many do believe that their evolutionary process was somehow guided by a conscious mind, or that they were imbued with their human souls by such a consciousness."

"Go on."

"When I have questioned these humans about the inconsistencies and paradoxes inherent in their beliefs, they have . . . not always reacted positively. However, the consensus among them has been that awareness of their creator is a matter of faith—something accepted as true in the absence of direct factual knowledge."

Ariel slowly raised her head and lowered it again. "I think I understand. You fear that if you knew who had created you, and how, it would make you less human somehow."

"Correct. Having certain knowledge of my origins would give me an experience no human has. I believe this would further separate me from humans."

"Maybe that's true if you think of your creators as gods. What if you were to think of them as parents instead? Every human has parents."

Data processed her suggestion for 2.48 seconds. "I am unsure of the applicability of that analogy. It is unlikely that my creators are of the same 'species' as myself. And unlike a human offspring, I am incapable of repeating the procedure by procreating."

"Could you build another android if you wanted?"

"In theory, I could construct a body on a similar plan to my own and transfer my neural-net pathways onto a duplicate brain. However, the technology for such a transfer does not exist."

"Not yet. Maybe you could invent it."

"In time, perhaps."

"Well, you're a durable sort of fellow. How long do you suppose your life expectancy is?"

"No upper limit for my life expectancy has been determined, allowing for suitable maintenance and parts replacement. My systems are largely self-repairing. Barring catastrophic events, I may expect to live for several thousand years at the very least."

Ariel pulled her head back and widened her eyes. "Well! You and I should definitely be friends, then, Data," she said, returning her hand to his shoulder, then pulling and pushing gently upon it. "You may be the only person I currently know who will still be alive in a thousand years. You can never have too many old friends."

Data realized that this conversation offered an unprecedented opportunity to ask a question that he had often contemplated. "Inquiry: What is it like to be extremely long-lived?"

"Well, could you be more specific? What aspects of immortality are you curious about?"

"I have conducted extensive research on the topic of . . . 'immortality,'" he said, accepting the inaccurate usage for the sake of convenience. "Most of the references are fictional, though there are several documented cases of effectively immortal individuals or species. A prevailing theme in the literature seems to be that of tedium. Immortals are often said to grow tired of life or to welcome death, either because they have run out of new experiences or because they have wearied of repeatedly experiencing the deaths of loved ones." He paused briefly. "While I am incapable of grief, and have no loved ones to lose, I am concerned at the prospect of running out of new experiences."

Ariel's eyes ceased to focus on anything in the room for several moments, and Data occupied the time with further Heisenberg compensator simulation runs; a fractal analysis of the color patterns within Ariel's facial pigmentation; an analysis of vocal inflection dynamics among the various species within the *Portia*'s crew; a simulation of warp reactor performance under accelerational stress in the *U.S.S. Galaxy* starship prototype; a cross-comparison of anecdotal descriptions of a species called Ferengi or Varangi, reputed to be active in this region of the galaxy but not yet documented by Federation observers; and the modeling of an improved algorithm for extrapolating present-day spatial coordinates from Manraloth-era navigational records. "Well . . . there's some truth to that, Data," she finally said. "I remember quite a few immortal races from my time. Eventually, most of them did . . . grow tired of existing on this mortal coil."

The allusion to *Hamlet*, Act III, scene i, line 66 would have been lost on Data, but his association with Picard had led him to review the complete works of William Shakespeare, and thus the reference was readily accessible in his active memory. "Did they . . . choose to die?"

"Usually not. I don't think it's quite so simple as growing 'weary of existence.' Some beings are very comfortable in a rut; they welcome familiarity and routine. And if you do crave new experiences, there are always ones to find. Besides, the longer you live, the more you yourself are changed by your experiences. We all become different people as we age—even when we don't age physically. Even familiar experiences can become new, because the way you perceive them changes.

"But if you live long enough, you can . . . outgrow the physical universe. Many beings, sometimes whole cultures, come to find it limiting and move on to other things. They may retreat into virtual reality and live lives of pure imagination, unbound by physical laws and limits. They may move themselves to other universes where the physics are different and adapt their physiology to fit. Or they may choose to give up physical form altogether and become beings of pure thought, in the belief that it can enable them to access higher planes of existence that the anchor of the flesh prevents us from reaching."

"Intriguing. Inquiry: Did any of the Manraloth ever undertake such ventures?"

Ariel's eyes went unfocused again for a time. "That wasn't really our style," she finally said. "We liked being part of the physical universe too much. And we could evolve our own bodies, change ourselves over time, so there was always something new to discover about ourselves. And there were always new civilizations emerging that we could connect with, new ways of thinking we could learn. I never understood those beings who got bored with this plane of existence. It's the best one there is."

He contemplated her words for several thousand cycles.

"You speak of the relationships you formed with other species. Were these species mortal?"

"Usually, yes. When they started out, at least."

"Then did you not have to deal with the problem of seeing valued companions die on a recurring basis?"

Ariel's face took on an expression which usually represented a degree of sadness, though it did not seem to be a pronounced degree. "Yes, that's something you have to face. I think that . . . you have to learn to focus your affections on the species as a whole, more than on any one individual. To cherish watching a civilization grow and learn and mature, and to value its individuals for what they inherit from those you knew and what they can pass on to those you will know. It's still sad when you lose them, but that sadness is balanced by the joy of meeting new people, discovering how different they all can be from one another. Cherishing what they share as a people while delighting in what makes each one unique."

Data found this intriguing, but somewhat paradoxical. "Inquiry: How does this attitude reconcile with the close bond you appear to share with Captain Picard?"

Her eyes locked on him, with no blinking this time. After 5.88 seconds, she said, "I suppose I haven't really been thinking about that. What I have with Jean-Luc is . . . unusual. When we met, I had no memory, no past. He was the center of my universe. The bond we formed . . . it was—it is very special."

"Then how will you deal with his eventual death?"

"I'm not sure, Data. It will be hard. But . . . I'll survive it. I'll have to. I think I'll be able to cope because I'll have the memory of who he was a permanent part of me. So much of what I've learned of your era, your society, I've learned through him. So he will live on in me." She gave a small smile, but paradoxically did not seem happy. "And until then, I'll just have to try to make the most of the time we have together. Give myself as many lasting memories as I can."

Data would have liked to continue the conversation, but his internal chronometer was signaling. "Excuse me, Ariel. I must report for alpha shift duty in fifteen minutes." He rose to leave, but remembered there were further social niceties to consider. "I appreciated our conversation. It was most enlightening."

She smiled more widely this time. "We'll have to do it again sometime."

"Yes, we will. Particularly since no one else in the crew seems willing to converse with me socially."

"It just takes practice, Data. On both sides. Trust me, you're better at communication than I would've expected."

"Thank you." Given the Manraloth gift for communication, Data judged that to be a reliable assessment, and valued it accordingly.

Subsequently, upon reviewing the conversation while he locomoted along the corridor toward turboshaft 3, it occurred to Data that if he wished to improve his communications skills, perhaps he could emulate the techniques employed by Ariel. She had initiated their conversation by asking him about himself and listening to his responses. In the past, he had initiated many conversations by asking questions, but the subsequent conversations had not gone quite as well. Perhaps the difference was a function of the way he asked the questions, or of the lesser patience of humans compared to himself. But perhaps, he considered, the difference might have something to do with the topic of the questions: specifically, Data himself. Perhaps if he asked his crewmates to talk about themselves and their origins, the resultant conversations would proceed better. It was an experiment he would have to conduct at the next opportunity for social interaction.

The turbolift door opened, revealing Captain Picard inside. "Mister Data. Good morning." The captain stepped out of the lift and looked around. "I was just looking for Ariel."

"Yes, sir. I left her in the quantum physics laboratory. We had a most stimulating conversation."

Picard smiled. "Good, good. She has a veritable gift for conversation, doesn't she?"

Data contemplated his syntax. A gift was an object or possession given as a reward or a gesture of affection. At first, he did not see the relevance of the term to Picard's statement, but after a moment, a possibility occurred to him. "Yes, Captain. I did consider her conversation with me to be a gift." He recalled his new insight about directing conversations toward the listener. "At the end of our conversation, Ariel and I were discussing you."

Picard's eyes moved quickly to focus on Data's. "Really. What were you discussing?"

"How Ariel would respond to the inevitability of your death."

Picard widened his eyes as his head moved back slightly. After 2.03 seconds, he reverted to a more normal expression. "And what did she say on that subject?"

"That she believed you would live on in her through the influence you had upon her, sir. And that she wished to make the most of the time she did have with you."

A smile spread slowly across Picard's face, and his chest inflated. But then the smile froze and diminished somewhat, while his eyebrows rose at their inner corners. "I suppose that's an issue I had been avoiding, Mister Data. I hadn't thought about what losing me would mean to her. I'm . . . grateful for what you've told me."

"I am glad to be of assistance." Again he remembered to focus on the other participant in the conversation. "Inquiry: How do you react to the prospect of Ariel outliving you considerably?"

Picard looked uncertain, eventually settling on a partial smile similar to his previous ambiguous expression. Data's attempt at a pattern match turned up the word "wistful," though that only raised more questions. "I actually find it somewhat reassuring, Mister Data. How many people are lucky enough not to have to worry about death taking someone they love?"

"Accessing . . . I do not have that information, sir."

Picard chuckled, then grew quiet again for 2.38 seconds. "And I'll be happy as long as I get to spend the rest of my life with her."

"Then it is your intention to make a permanent commitment to her? Would this involve marriage?"

Picard again took a moment to formulate a response. He seemed somewhat surprised by it, though that was an inconsistent result and Data assumed his facial-recognition protocols were in error. "I think it very well might. Imagine that. Just five years ago, I thought I'd never want to settle down with one woman. Now I think there's nothing I want more."

After another few seconds, Picard's eyes darted back and forth and he cleared his throat. "Data . . . do you recall our conversation about keeping secrets?"

"I recall all conversations with perfect clarity, sir. Would you like me to repeat it back to you?"

"No, just . . . I would appreciate it if you would keep this conversation confidential. Just between us. You understand?"

"Aye, sir."

"Aren't you on duty?"

"In twelve minutes, eight seconds, sir."

"Very well. Carry on, Lieutenant." Data acknowledged the order and moved toward the lift. "And, Data?"

"Sir?"

Picard smiled. "It was nice talking with you."

"Thank you, sir. And you as well."


As the *Portia* came within a week's travel of the estimated location of the second stasis bubble, long-range sensors turned up an unexpected discovery. At first, they detected what seemed to be a single micronebula, one of the thousands of compact, dense clumps of gas and dust that pervaded interstellar space. There was nothing surprising about such a find. Such diminutive nebulae were common, and because of their small size, generally mere AUs in diameter rather than light-years, they were hard to detect or study from a distance. Indeed, humanity had been totally unaware of the existence of micronebulae prior to the mid-twenty-first century, and many of the early ones to be found, such as the Arachnid and Paulson Nebulae, had been mistaken for anomalous red or brown dwarfs at first.

The surprise came when more thorough scans of the region ahead revealed the first nebula to be just one of a cluster of more than two hundred micronebulae occupying a volume some ten parsecs in diameter. Data hypothesized that they may have been dense clumps within a larger nebula, perhaps a stellar nursery, that was blown away by the supernovae that had cleared most of the interstellar medium from this region several million years ago. Stripped of most of their matter, the residual micronebulae had been too small to collapse into stars. In several hundred thousand years, they would probably coalesce into rogue Jovians or brown dwarfs.

For now, though, they were security risks. The *Portia* was well within the region that the Sheliak claimed as a buffer zone and the Breen claimed as their manifest destiny. To date, they had been successful at avoiding detection by ships on either side, heading promptly in the other direction on the two occasions when they had registered warp signatures on long-range sensors. But the micronebulae added a new factor to the equation. "Breen have been known to hide in nebulae, Captain," Vejar told him. "And these are dense and charged enough to blind our sensors."

Data turned from the science station to address Picard. "But that level of internal electrostatic charge makes them extremely hazardous. I am detecting periodic electrical discharges in the one-hundred-gigawatt to one-terawatt range." That stood to reason, Picard supposed. Micronebulae could be as dense as terrestrial or Jovian atmospheres, unlike the near vacuum of major nebulae, and thus would be subject to the same electrostatic processes that spawned the immense lightning storms of Jupiter-type planets.

Picard turned to Lieutenant Kilif, his tactical officer. "Could Breen shields survive such discharges?"

"Unknown, sir," the young Bolian man replied. "We've had few direct encounters with the Breen. The ships we've met, I'd say no, but they could have something a lot bigger and stronger."

Picard stroked his chin. "So do we risk going through or take the longer way round? Will this shield us from Breen and Sheliak sensors, or leave us as sitting ducks for hunters in the blinds?" He looked around at his bridge crew. "Opinions, please."

No one replied at first. Vejar looked at him oddly. "Sir," she said sotto voce, "the decision is yours."

"I'm well aware of that, Commander," he replied in a normal tone. "However, we have a group of intelligent, capable professionals here, and I value their input as a factor in my decision." He gave her a small grin. "Call it a habit I picked up in academia."

"Well then, sir," Vejar said after a moment's thought, "I recommend we go around. No point in taking chances we don't have to."

"But going around could bring us closer to Breen or Sheliak space," Kilif said.

"If we take a z-axis course," Johanna Kolbe suggested from the conn station, "loop around the south side of the formation, we can keep our distance. But . . . that would be the longest course around them. It would nearly double our travel time from here."

"Do you have a recommendation, Ensign Kolbe?"

"I'd take the long way around. Sir. That stasis field isn't going anywhere."

Picard turned to the science station. "Mister Data?"

"I consider it unlikely that Breen ships are hiding in the micronebulae, Captain. The levels of electrostatic discharge are powerful enough to destroy any known Breen vessel even with full shields raised. A shielding mechanism powerful enough to deflect such discharges would most likely give off energy readings sufficient to penetrate the sensor interference. Therefore, I believe the protection offered by passage through the micronebula cluster outweighs the risk of Breen ambuscade."

"That's all well and good as a probability calculation," Vejar countered. "But Breen aren't driven by mere machine logic. If they're hungry enough for this space to risk fighting the Sheliak for it and believe they can win, then they're hungry enough, or crazy enough, to risk getting struck by lightning if it improves their chances of blitzing a few Sheliak ships in return."

On reflection, Picard decided that he took her point, although he would have a talk with her in private about how she had chosen to express it. "Very well," he said after a moment. "Conn, set course around the nebular cluster as per your recommendation. Warp factor four." It was not a decision he was happy with, since it delayed the attainment of his goal, as well as Ariel's. The crew would not be happy either; Ariel had gotten all of them excited with her tales of the Manraloth and the brave new world their archives could usher in, so they were all eager to locate the stasis bubble and solve its mystery.

But as Kolbe had said, the Manraloth were not going anywhere. It was a poignant irony that their two hundred and fifty-two million years of waiting weighed less upon their frozen minds than another two weeks would weigh on Picard's.

But the more Picard listened to Ariel, the more convinced he grew that the galaxy needed the Manraloth.

# 16

---

ONCE LONG-RANGE SENSORS DETECTED THE NULL
signature they sought, it took some doing to locate its source.
Rather than a typical star system, the stasis bubble was in
orbit of a dim, T-Class brown dwarf—a body only twenty
times as massive as Jupiter (but roughly the same diameter,
since the gravitational compression of its core made it far
denser), an aborted protostar glowing on residual heat from
the fusion it had briefly attained in its youth. Contrary to its
name, the "brown" dwarf glowed with a cool magenta light,
since the atomic sodium and potassium in its atmosphere absorbed the green portion of its spectrum. "'Even as the sun
with purple-color'd face / Had ta'en his last leave of the weep-
ing morn,'" Picard murmured at the sight on the viewscreen.

Next to him, Ariel smiled. "More Shakespeare?"

He grinned back. "I know, I'm becoming predictable. But
it fits. 'Rose-cheek'd Adonis hied him to the chase.' First
lines of *Venus and Adonis.*"

"Well, Venus is taken. Shall we call it the Adonis system?" Picard found it an ironic proposal for such a small
and unmanly protostar. But since Adonis, like Proserpina,
was a deity of rebirth, he accepted her proposal as a symbol
of hope.

Adonis bore its own miniature planetary system, a smattering of small planets and planetoids in orbits whose periods were measured in days, like a slightly larger version of a Jovian planet's moon system. And, like many Jovians, it had rings. The innermost ring was a diffuse gas torus like Jupiter's, generated in the same way by eruptions from its furiously volcanic inner planetoid. The second and third worldlets, larger than the first, orbited close together in a clear, wide gap in the ring system. Beyond that were several distinct rings, larger and less dense than Saturn's but similarly delineated and shaped by the gravity of the worldlets that orbited within them. The icy rings glowed dimly in the magenta light of Adonis, highlighted by the more vivid red of a micronebula just two dozen AUs away. The nebula's disrupted shape and the faint trail of hydrogen and dust that stretched from it suggested that Adonis had collided with the nebula a few thousand years before, splashing it out of shape and supplementing the rings with new matter. Whatever the cause, it was an unusual and beautiful system.

The collision had caused the nebula to dissipate somewhat, making it less effective as a sensor shield. At the very least, if there was a Breen ship hiding there, it would have to be smaller and less powerful than the *Portia*. Picard judged the risk to be worth taking, though he chose to ease into the system just below the plane of the rings to use them as cover.

The second planet was more or less L-class, with a tenuous atmosphere of nitrogen, oxygen, and hydrogen sulfide held by a gravity less than half of Earth's. It rotated in resonance with the third planet, with one sunrise coming every other "year"—although its years were just over two standard days in length. Its vegetation appeared mostly black; since the light from Adonis was so faint and mostly in the infrared, photosynthesis had to be achieved by other means than chlorophyll.

Perhaps the local life got some of its energy from the intense radiation belts that surrounded Adonis and engulfed the second planet. However, humanoids were not built the same way, so the radiation created a serious problem. The planet lacked enough of a magnetic field to protect a landing party from the intense bombardment, which included a middling amount of hyperonic radiation in addition to the usual types. Simulations showed that even full EV suits would provide only limited protection. "So how the hell do we get down there?" Picard asked the bridge crew at large.

Data rose from the science station. "Allow me, sir. I am immune to most forms of radiation, including protonic, beta, and hyperonic. I will be able to conduct reconnaisance and determine if the stasis field is part of a larger complex, as the first one was. If so, it stands to reason that said complex would be shielded from the radiation."

It made Picard uneasy to contemplate just how Starfleet might have determined Data's resistance to radiation. Still, if Data asserted it as a fact, it must be true. "Very well. Take a shuttlecraft to the surface," he said, remembering that transporters and hyperonic radiation didn't mix. He realized he'd have to consult with the science team about whether the radiation field would interfere with possible rescue operations.

"I think I should go too," Ariel said.

Picard frowned. "Do you know for certain you're resistant to such radiation?"

"Given my regenerative rate, I doubt it would be fatal. If I wore an environmental suit, I'm sure I could hold out for a few hours at least. Besides," she added, "I never got to see the first one with my own eyes. If I'm going to help figure out a way to open this one safely, I feel I need to experience it up close, get a sense of exactly what I'm facing."

Picard sighed. "Very well. But don't take any chances. Mister Data, if Ariel shows any signs of radiation sickness, you are to get her back to the ship as quickly as possible."

"Aye, sir."

Ariel pouted. "You worry too much."

"That is a captain's prerogative."

She gave him a skeptical look, then moved in and kissed him on the cheek. "You old softy," she whispered in his ear.


Picard monitored from the bridge as Data and Ariel made their way to the surface of Adonis II. They described a dim, purple-lit landscape inhabited by flat, spongy plants (to maximize the infrared they received on their surfaces) and various low-built, slow-moving creatures resembling trilobites or ancient sea scorpions. The few oceans were acidic and localized over geothermal hot spots, and contained significantly more life than the land. Away from the hot spots, much of the surface was barren or glaciated. Picard recognized the inevitable fate of brown-dwarf planets; whereas yellow stars grew hotter over their lifespans and red dwarfs stayed much the same indefinitely, brown dwarfs grew progressively cooler, their planets freezing over. It was why so few brown-dwarf systems had intelligent life even though they were far more abundant than main-sequence stars.

For now, the life forms of Adonis II were still getting by on its internal heat, produced by the regular back-and-forth kneading it received from the third planet's gravity as they orbited in resonance. But Data's analysis suggested that millions of years hence, the surface life would be gone, the oceans frozen over, and only the deep-sea vents would remain viable habitats.

But the habitat that concerned Picard today was of a different type, and soon the shuttle reached it. *"I can see the quantum blur from here!"* Ariel reported while Data brought the shuttle in for a landing. *"Amazing. It's out in the open, just a sort of spherical fog bank frozen in place. There's . . . yes, there's a sort of tail of stone stretching out behind it, tapering off with distance."*

*"Most intriguing,"* Data added. *"It is on the opposite side of the stasis field from the direction in which the prevailing winds originate in this region. Conjecture: The stasis field was originally underground, and two hundred and fifty-two*

*million years of erosive action have exposed it, leaving an uneroded wedge of stone in the region which the stasis field itself would have shielded from the wind. Although the more tenuous atmosphere would have reduced the erosive action of wind, the time interval in question is sufficient for it to have had an effect of this magnitude."*

"Then if this stasis field encompasses only part of a larger compound, like the first one did," Picard told them, "there may be other parts of that compound exposed as well. Maybe a way in."

*"I can confirm that now, Captain,"* Data replied. *"Several exposed shapes around the compound are unmistakably of artificial construction. They do show evidence of weathering, although to a considerably lesser degree than the surrounding geologic matrix."*

*"It looks like they have a hexagonal cross section,"* Ariel said. *"Maybe a design similarity to the other base."*

*"I am now detecting faint, periodic power emanations from within the base. It would appear to have still-functional technology within."*

*"Not surprising, with all this geothermal energy to draw on."*

*"In fact, Ariel, this region of Adonis II has no geothermal vents close to the surface. It is possible, however, that the builders of this facility drove a tap into the planet's mantle."*

*"I'd bet on it, my friend,"* Ariel said. *"We Manraloth always planned on the long scale."*

Landing on a patch of bare rock near the stasis field (but not too near), Ariel and Data made their way to the exposed ruins and began searching for a way in. Most of the walls they found were solid and unbroken—which came as no surprise, since they had originally been underground. But closer to the quantum aura of the stasis field, they found the wall material becoming more brittle and damaged, though to a less extreme degree than in the other base. *Because this facility has retained sufficient power for self-repair,* Picard wondered, *or due to a difference in material?*

*"I believe I can force an opening in the wall, Captain,"* Data reported.

"By what means?"

*"The application of mechanical force with my fist, followed by the use of both my hands to tear the resultant opening wider."*

Picard was taken aback for a moment, but remembered the notations in Data's file about his great physical strength. Nonetheless, another concern arose in his mind. "Data, we've seen that the quantum aura can have a disruptive effect on sensitive technology. Are you sure your systems can tolerate getting so close?"

*"Extrapolating from the intensity of the field effect at my current distance, and the point-zero-zero-zero-two percent decrease in my neural net performance, I am confident that I could withstand a brief exposure at the necessary range."* He paused. *"But . . . I appreciate your concern for my well-being, Captain."*

"You're a member of my crew, Data. Your well-being is as important to me as anyone else's."

*"Thank you, sir."* Despite his professed lack of emotion, Data sounded truly grateful.

A few moments later, Picard heard a loud report followed by the sound of a strong, nonmetallic material being ripped through. Moments after that, Data said, *"We are now inside a corridor of the base."* The ambience of his voice had noticeably changed to an indoors sound, reminding Picard that the android had gone down without an environmental suit.

Ariel and Data proceeded through the base, describing a facility with a different design from the Proserpina ice base. Instead of hex cells with circular screens, this facility had rooms and corridors with hexagonal cross sections, bearing what appeared to be control panels on the lower halves of the slanted walls and display surfaces along the upper halves. Still, the underlying technology had many similarities.

The common origin was confirmed when Ariel activated

a computer interface and reported seeing text in one of the languages from the ice base's recovered data. *"The memory banks are damaged, though,"* she reported after a moment. *"Basic operational software is intact, no doubt highly self-repairing, but records and factual information are more fragmentary than I'd expected."* Picard could hear the intense disappointment in her voice, and winced.

*"I would surmise that exposure to Adonis's radiation belts has damaged the contents of the database,"* said Data. *"Although the facility is sufficiently shielded for short-term humanoid occupation, the cumulative exposure over millions of years could have done considerable damage to the computer systems."*

*"Now, this is interesting,"* Ariel said.

"What is it?"

*"I've found a transporter system, Jean-Luc. Data, have a look at this."*

A few moments later, Data reported, *"If I interpret these readings correctly, Captain, this transporter mechanism is considerably more sophisticated and powerful than our own. It should be able to transport parties from the* Portia *without risk of disruption from the radiation belts."*

*"And it could greatly improve our chances of freeing my people from the bubble,"* Ariel added.

Picard thought it over for a moment. "I'm reluctant to rely entirely on an untested alien transporter system. If we lock our own transporter onto its pad, would that give us a sufficient safety margin to beam down?"

*"I am confident that it could, Captain."*

"Grand. Let's run a test first to make sure. But if it works . . . then, Ariel, I'll see you shortly."


The transporter link worked perfectly, and before long, Picard was down on Adonis II with the science team and security chief Kilif. However, as the scientists fell into an involved consultation with Data and Ariel on how they might adapt the base transporter and other systems to assist their efforts to access the stasis bubble, Picard became aware that he had nothing to contribute at the moment. So he set off to explore the base along with Kilif.

Like the Proserpina ice base, this seemed to be a scientific facility, with plenty of labs and observation stations in addition to residential and recreational facilities. The control panels in the lower chamber walls worked by projecting holographic images into the air above them, semitangible shapes and symbols that the operator could manipulate and modify. Based on the Manraloth translations provided by his tricorder and on the design of the lab facilities, Picard came to the conclusion that this was also a biological research center. "Interesting," Picard told Kilif, "how both the stasis fields we've found have been in research bases located in unusual, even hostile planetary environments. I wonder if there could be some correlation."

The Bolian contemplated the idea. "Facilities in hostile conditions might need special shielding. Could the stasis fields be modified shields of some sort?"

"Possibly. But there are plenty of shields to be found on more civilized worlds, in high-security facilities or undersea bases, for instance. Why do we find nothing on the former Manraloth worlds we've identified?" But Kilif had no answer.

The viewscreens revealed it to be early in the planet's day, the vast but dim magenta disk of Adonis low in the east, climbing up the purple-white spine that bisected the nearly black sky—the system's rings seen edge-on. By the time the dwarf reached its zenith—the next morning by ship time—the science team had a working strategy, and assembled in the *Portia*'s briefing room to lay it out.

"Our theory on why the first stasis bubble collapsed," Kimiko Jones explained, "is that it was forced to entangle directly with our time continuum. The transition was too abrupt. Like pouring boiling water into an ice-cold glass. Call it temporal shock."

"To be more specific," Angus McCarthy said, "when the entanglement was formed, the outside universe was able to 'see' inside the bubble all of a sudden, and it 'saw' the interior virtually frozen in time—that is, with near-zero uncertainty of momentum."

"And that," Picard interpreted, "translated to a very high uncertainty of position."

"Exactly," the Scottish quantum physicist replied. "The wavefunctions of the particles inside the field were thereby forced to decohere into random positional states. They tunneled in all directions at once, disintegrating the entire structure."

"The problem, however," Data said, "is that this should not have happened. Theoretically, the quantum state of nonzero entropy should already have been latent within the stasis pocket's wavefunction."

"What he means," McCarthy explained, "is that the merger of time flow between the outside universe and the bubble should've been instantaneous, as Lieutenant Janeway theorized. There should have been no temporal shock. The only explanation is that the stasis field is . . . *resisting* change, for lack of a better term. As though it's somehow repressed the part of its wavefunction that allows for nonzero time flow. And we have no theory that could've predicted that, let alone one that can explain it now."

"So there's no way Kathryn could possibly have avoided the collapse," Ariel added. "She didn't overlook anything she could've known about."

"I'm grateful to know that, of course," Picard said. "But how do we avoid a repetition of the problem?"

Chief engineer Colla responded to that one. "By modifying Janeway's process to avoid the direct entanglement," the Napean said.

"So you believe the basic procedure is sound."

"Up to a point, sir."

"Explain."

Data elaborated. "The plan is to encase the transporter's

Heisenberg compensator in a subspace field which will be tuned to exist out of phase with our temporal continuum. This way, when the compensator entangles with the quantum aura and in turn with the field interior, the combined quantum state of those three entities will remain isolated from our temporal stream."

Rider stepped in. "We'll use a phase transformer to communicate with the compensator inside the field, sir," the balding, auburn-haired transporter chief said. "With information filtered through the transformer, there'll be no direct entanglement between our time continuum and the field's."

Picard frowned. "What about the temporal difference between the compensator and the stasis field interior?"

Jones fielded that one. "The subspace field will be configured to impart a substantial time dilation on the compensator, sir," she said. "To go back to my heat analogy, it's only going to be a tiny bit 'warmer' than the field interior. We know that the quantum aura, which is only slowed to near-zero time, can entangle with the zero-time field without destroying it, so there may be just enough wiggle room in the field's resistance to let us peek in a crack, if we use a very minor time differential. Sort of like sliding a pin into a soap bubble without breaking it.

"In short," Ariel said, "we think we'll be able to start time moving again inside, but only at a very, very slow rate, maybe a millionth of a percent of normal."

Picard did a quick calculation. "That would hardly do us much good. We'd have to wait years for a second to elapse in there."

"Three years, sixty-one days, sixteen hours—"

"Thank you, Mister Data."

"Fortunately, the subspace field will be in a different time continuum," Jones said, "and its time flow relative to ours is variable. We can adjust the field to introduce a gradient, essentially step up the time flow by another factor of a thousand relative to our reference frame. Essentially a second in there will take a bit more than a day out here."

"Well," Picard said, "that's still an enormous step forward from zero seconds in a quarter-billion years."

"And it's enough to allow communication, after a fashion," Ariel said. "Hopefully, once we give them enough freedom to move again, they can arrange to deactivate the field on their own. Since they're presumably the ones who made it, it's better to leave that stage of it up to them."

Picard furrowed his brow. "But at a second a day, how long would it take to establish meaningful communication with the people inside? The longer we remain here, mind you, the greater our risk of detection by Breen or Sheliak."

Ariel folded her hands. "I believe I can establish faster communication with any Manraloth inside the bubble. We've determined the base contains equipment designed to interface directly with the logopathic centers of the Manraloth brain. There should be similar equipment within the bubble. If I place myself into a trance state, slow my thought processes down, I can send a signal through this equipment—enough to let someone inside know that they need to connect to it as well. Once connected, they may be able to speed up their thought processes to meet me in the middle. Or perhaps they have equipment allowing them to transfer consciousness into the computer systems. If so, that would accelerate their speed of thought greatly and faster discourse would be possible."

Picard met her eyes. "So . . . you're saying you might need to be down there, incommunicado, for days. Even weeks."

Her brow stripes rose in the middle, like a bird shrugging its outstretched wings. "I'm afraid so, Jean-Luc. Don't worry, though—as long as you water me every few days, I'll be fine." She smirked.

Picard cleared his throat, trying not to fidget at the prospect of her extended absence. A thought occurred to him. "What about the entanglement problem? As I understand it, telepathy is a form of quantum entanglement. Doesn't that create the risk of collapse?"

"No," Ariel said. "Any communication will be relayed through the base systems, which will interpret them from one time flow to the other. There will be no direct quantum connection between anything in there and anything out here."

"Just in case, though, sir," Colla said, "we'd like to use the base's transporter system to do this. It's based on the same principles, but it's a lot more advanced and powerful. It can scan and dematerialize almost instantaneously. If worse came to worst, then at least we could beam out a lot more people a lot more quickly, before they suffered any serious damage."

"But not everyone," Picard said.

Colla shook his head. "Depends on how many people are inside, but if it's more than several dozen, no."

"We'd also like to recover any technology, personal possessions, cultural artifacts and so forth that might be in the bubble," Ariel said. "Who knows what they might have wanted to bring with them, what valuable resources they may have preserved? So the goal is to establish contact and hope they have a way to turn the damned thing off safely."

"What about the internal damage the base transporter will suffer if the stasis field disintegrates? Not to mention any personnel in the vicinity?"

"We have devised a theoretical means of shielding a localized area from particle incursions in such an event," Data said. "Although its execution is beyond current Starfleet technology, the base's shield systems do possess the capability." He tilted his head. "The primary shield system is unresponsive, suggesting its generator is inside the stasis bubble and was most likely used to create it. However, there is a backup system we can employ."

Picard looked over the team's faces, gauged their level of confidence—and his own. "Very well," he finally said. "You may proceed. But take all possible care. Dismissed."

The science team filed out, but Ariel remained, looking wistful. "I know," she said. "I hate the idea of this forced separation as much as you do."

"Really?" he asked, keeping his tone light. "It'll pass in no time for you. I may be sleeping alone for a week or two."

"You've done that before," she pointed out.

He clasped her hand. "This is different. It wasn't you before."

Smiling, Ariel stroked the side of his head. "That's very romantic, my love. But we're both adults, you and I, and we both understand the need to defer our desires for the sake of our duties." She stood, taking a step closer and gazing down at him. "This is only the beginning, you know. If I free the people in there, find the information I'm looking for, then I will only get busier. Helping my contemporaries adjust to your world. Searching for the black-hole archive, searching for the rest of our kind. And then showing the Federation how to use the archive, working to help promote peace and cooperation. . . . Jean-Luc, it is the work of lifetimes."

"And I would gladly share in all of it."

"You have duties of your own. Starfleet will have other assignments for you."

"Once Starfleet is no longer useful in helping us recover the Manraloth, I'll resign. My future lies with you, Ariel."

"Ohh, Prospero . . ." She held him for a time. "I know you better than that, darling. I see you in that command chair, hear your voice on the intercom, and I can sense it, I can read it in you—this is where you belong. You're a leader, Jean-Luc Picard, not a follower. You're happy in command, and I would not take that from you."

"But to have you taken from me—"

She took his hand and held it to her breast with both of hers. "You never will. You know the bond we share. No matter where our paths take us, we will always have one another."

She pulled him to his feet, and they kissed. "Now if you'll excuse me," she finished with a smile, "I'm needed down below."

It took surprisingly little time for the team to set up their apparatus. Instead of having to rearrange the transporter components physically, all they needed was to program the Adonis base's transporter to reconfigure itself as instructed. More time was spent confirming with tricorder scans that it had actually completed the task than the configuration itself had taken. Next came the emplacing and activation of the subspace field generator and the confirmation that it had functioned as intended. This was the longest part of the process, taking upwards of half an hour.

As the moment of activation neared, all hands were alert and ready for anything. Colla manned the transporter below in order to beam out survivors should the stasis field collapse, while the *Portia* moved into a low forced orbit over the base with Rider manning the ship's transporters to pull the team out if their untried shield failed to protect them. The radiation made transporter use risky, but it was worth chancing in an emergency.

But the activation itself proved anticlimactic. After a few minutes of tuning the time-dilated Heisenberg compensator, the team reported a successful entanglement. Sensors showed no outward change in the quantum aura, but now registered a faint, profoundly redshifted energy flux from inside it, where before there had been a complete void. The event horizon was no longer absolute; time was crawling forward again inside the bubble. But it was not until the quantum integrity of the interior was confirmed to be stable that the cheer went up.

Scan data from the interior trickled in slowly and had to be corrected for redshift, but in time it was possible to read a large chamber inside the bubble, possibly subdivided, containing nearly a hundred and fifty individuals of roughly a dozen different species. Only two of those species were humanoid, though several were erect bipeds. Maybe thirty of the occupants read as Manraloth, albeit with wide variations, reflecting their capacity for individual evolution. Scans also showed a fair amount of equipment within, including what appeared to be a small space vessel.

But it was all frozen in amber, at least as far as the human eye could detect. The next step was for Ariel to attempt contact. With the *Portia*'s CMO, Doctor Bowman, supervising, Ariel laid herself out on an interface couch (as she described it), activated it with a mental command, and began to sink into her trance state. Picard held her hand as she began the process, and she squeezed his hand and smiled at him before closing her eyes and retreating inside herself. Her hand grew slowly limp and then, over the ensuing minutes, began to cool. But Bowman reported that her vital signs remained stable, simply slowed.

And then there was nothing to do but wait. How many seconds, each corresponding to a day or more outside, would it take for someone inside to receive Ariel's signal and enter the necessary state to respond? They could be here for weeks. The lack of warp signatures in the sector was comforting, but it was not a comfort Picard was willing to take for granted.

As Ariel communed, Data sought and received Picard's permission to study Adonis II's native life forms. Picard was curious about how a biosphere driven primarily by infrared and geothermal energy would function, and glad for something to distract him from the waiting.

Within a day, however, Data alerted him to a discovery that complicated their situation. As the purple pseudo-sun hesitantly sank below the horizon, a group of largish organisms was detected crawling toward the ancient base. Data called Picard down to observe them in one of the base's labs.

Like the holodecks Starfleet was beginning to install on newer starships, the lab gave them the ability to perceive the scene outside as if they were actually standing within it, without the need for environmental suits—although the image was amplified to allow Picard to see it, since the only light in the sky aside from background stars was from the gibbous O of the nearby third planet and the diffuse arch of the system's rings. Data pointed the creatures out to Picard. Like all this planet's life, they lived low to the ground, where the air was least thin. Roughly one and a quarter meters long, they looked somewhat like trilobites with crab claws and wide, flat tails that suggested beavers as much as lobsters. Picard saw that many were carrying burdens with those tails—round stones ranging from fifteen to twenty centimeters across. "Harvested from a river, perhaps?" Picard asked. "Rounded by the action of water and sand?"

"Perhaps," Data replied. "But the nearest river above ground is rather distant."

The creatures—*trilobeavers?* no, too facetious; perhaps *platycauds,* for their flat tails—were converging on the southern side of the base. Here, a sizable portion of the base's superstructure had been laid bare by erosion, the exterior of a large chamber that shared the hexagonal cross section of the rest of the base but on a significantly larger scale. From the inside, it appeared to have been the gym or recreation center, but from the outside it was simply a large, smooth, sloping surface that faded into the quantum aura of the stasis field, that eerie globe of frozen fog that dominated the scene. The rock-bearing platycauds were coming up to the edge of the exposed section, bracing themselves—and flinging the stones up into the quantum mist, using their tails as catapults. The stones flew far in the low gravity, but as they moved deeper into the mist, the bizarre friction of half-there matter slowed them and their parabolic arcs were truncated. The rocks came to land on the exposed, sloping shell of the gym, whereupon they bounced and began to roll slowly back down, picking up speed as they moved farther out of the quantum aura. Once the projectiles rolled off the edge and came to a stop on the rougher ground below, the platycauds moved in, used their pincers to retrieve the stones, and placed them on their compatriots' tails, whereupon the whole process was repeated.

"Note that the creatures always throw the stones approximately the same distance," Data pointed out after a time.

"Any deeper into the field, and they might be prevented from rolling back. Their procedure is very well calibrated."

"But what purpose does it serve?" Picard wondered.

"That will become evident once I overlay a thermal scan, sir." A moment later, the glow of infrared radiation was superimposed on the scene, making the platycauds gently luminous. Picard saw that the stones glowed as well, brighter with each pass through the haze. "As you can see, the friction of the stones' passage through the quantum aura is generating internal heat. Hypothesis: In the absence of local geothermal activity, the organisms are using the stones as an alternative heat source to facilitate survival during the forty-nine-point-one-hour nocturnal period."

Indeed, as they continued to watch, the platycauds laid many of the hottest stones around the perimeter of their group, presumably to ward off predators, while placing the others in piles that they huddled around for warmth. When a stone grew cool, the platycauds would repeat the catapult procedure to heat it once again.

"Mister Data," Picard said at length, "are we seeing a form of intelligent behavior? The use of tools?"

The lieutenant pondered the question. "Not necessarily, Captain. Many complex behaviors can be wholly instinctive. Examples of tool use such as the building of shelters or the use of stones to break open shelled creatures are observed in subsentient species on many planets. In this case, the stasis field and the exposed sloping wall would have been present in this region for many millions of years, allowing sufficient time for this behavior to have evolved stochastically among the platycauds." Picard had, of course, shared his suggested name with Data earlier.

Picard crouched down, getting a closer look at the platycauds as they huddled around the rock piles. They seemed to communicate by striking their claws and tails upon the ground, a better medium for transmitting vibrations than the thin air. As far as he could tell, the signals they exchanged seemed basic and repetitive, but who knew what he might be missing? "Still," he said, "if there's even a chance that we are seeing intelligent behavior here, then the Prime Directive comes into play. If we deactivate the stasis field, it would cause a massive disruption to their culture."

"There is insufficient data to suggest the creatures are intelligent, sir."

"Starfleet prefers to err on the side of caution in such cases, Mister Data. And even if they are only animals acting on instinct . . ." He shook his head. "What a truly elegant instinct it is. A testament to what life can achieve even without the sentience that we egotistically ascribe such weight to. Just because they aren't as intelligent as we are, that doesn't give us the right to destroy something so remarkable—let alone to deprive these animals of the means of their survival."

Data considered the problem. "Suggestion: We could rig a force field calibrated to produce an equivalent thermal effect to the stasis field."

"One that could last for millennia or longer, without maintenance?"

"Then perhaps we could reactivate the stasis field once its occupants have been evacuated."

"Perhaps. If such a thing is even possible."

"Once communication is established with the occupants of the bubble, they will probably be able to answer that question for us."

"And there's another issue here, Data. If that bubble decoheres, the particle incursions would kill all these platycauds. We may be placing them in mortal danger as long as we continue this experiment."

"They do leave this area during the local daytime, Captain."

"Could we shut the entanglement down for the night, resume in the local morning?"

"Doubtful, sir. The connection is stable for now, but we do not know if we can safely restore the stasis field to zero entropy." Data tilted his head in puzzlement. "Besides . . .

do we not have a greater obligation to the occupants of the field?"

"Equal, perhaps," Picard said. "But they have waited this long already." He shook his head. "Staggering."

Data cast his eyes toward Picard's feet, as if to confirm the stability of his balance. "Please clarify, sir."

"To think that these people and their technology have been waiting here so long that entire species have evolved in response to their presence. It drives home a sense of temporal scale that has been largely abstract to me before."

Data frowned. "The temporal interval remains two hundred fifty-two million years, sir."

"Lieutenant, maybe that extraordinary mind of yours is able to grasp exactly what that number means. For a mere human like myself, it's a different matter." He reflected that Ariel had lived long enough to witness evolution taking place. Would he ever be able to comprehend the universe on her level? Was he foolish even to try?

In any case, he realized that she would not be the only one with something interesting to report once she came out of her trance.

# 17

—◆—

OBSERVATIONS OF THE PLATYCAUDS CONTINUED over the next several days, but failed to produce conclusive answers about their intelligence. Above a certain threshold, conscious thought could be unambiguously observed, but there was a wide gray area where it came down to how one defined one's terms. The platycauds did exhibit various complex behaviors and interactions, but the universal translator could make nothing of their signals and they showed little evidence of tool use beyond the rock throwing. Still, even if they were not sentient now, Picard was not willing to deprive them of the opportunity to reach that level in the future, perhaps someday to achieve the capacity for spaceflight before their world froze over completely.

But when Ariel finally awakened after five and a half days, he deferred his news until later. "That didn't take long—relatively speaking," he told her as he helped her to sit up from the interface couch and handed her a glass of juice. "Were you unable to make contact?"

She beamed. "Quite the contrary. One of them had already done a personality upload into the interface system. They anticipated this problem might arise and had someone standing ready to communicate with the outside world just before they established the field. Very clever of them, I'd say."

"So this individual was able to communicate with you at a proportionately accelerated rate? You had more than five seconds' worth of conversation?"

She sipped from her cup while he spoke, then said, "Yes, but not immensely more. It took a while for us to, well, find each other, and a while longer to get synchronized. And the relay system slowed our communication further. We really only had time to cover the basics."

"And what did you learn?"

She finished her juice and cleared her throat. "There was . . . some massive cataclysm, as we theorized. He didn't have time to go into specifics, and my priority was naturally to ask about the stasis field." She sighed. "I'm afraid they don't exactly know how to deactivate it."

"How could that be?"

Ariel grew somber, presenting him with that unwavering, opaque stare of hers, yet not quite looking at him. "Whatever happened to them . . . it was sudden. They tried to use their standard shielding, but it wasn't enough. They were desperate, and they concluded—I haven't learned why yet—that the only escape was to jury-rig the shield system into a stasis field. Apparently the trade-off was reducing the size of the shield envelope, which is why only part of each base was enclosed. But although they were able to devise the stasis fields, they weren't sure of how to deactivate them again. They—*we* were relying on rescue from outside."

"From survivors of whatever the cataclysm was?"

She stared a moment more. "Or from someone more removed from it. Unaffected by it."

"Well, we can determine more later. For now, the question is, what are our options? We were relying on them to liberate themselves, but it seems they were relying on us."

"But we are better off than we were, Jean-Luc. Now we're in contact with the people inside, and some of them have scientific knowledge far beyond your own. They may be able to devise a solution." She gave him a wistful look. "*If they coordinate with the base computers and transporter outside the field. Which means I have to go back in for a few more days."

"Perhaps I could be of assistance," Data said. "If I interface my positronic net with the base's systems, I may be able to coordinate with the Manraloth scientists in devising a solution."

"That's not necessary, Data," Ariel said. "Your sentience is a marvelous thing, my friend, but when it comes to raw computing power, our systems are rather more advanced."

"Still," Picard said, feeling a sudden urge to stand up for the home team, "sentience can offer something raw computing power cannot: imagination."

Data looked at Picard. "I do not believe I . . . have an imagination, sir."

Picard smiled. "You can't have conscious thought without the ability to conceive of the unreal, Mister Data—to extrapolate beyond raw information and anticipate the unseen. 'We are such stuff as dreams are made on.' Even you, Lieutenant."

"But . . . I do not dream."

Picard stared at him. "Mister Data, were you specifically programmed to lack faith in your own abilities?"

"I do not believe so, sir. Perhaps I simply cannot . . . imagine abilities beyond my documented ones."

"Well, you'll never discover them unless you try." He turned to Ariel. "And it never hurts to have another set of eyes looking over a problem. I'm authorizing Data to attempt the interface."

"Very well," Ariel said. "I welcome the company. Oh, and there's one more thing," she added. "I think we need to notify Starfleet of what we've found."

He frowned. "From out here? It'd be risky."

"I think if you let me tie in the base computers to the *Portia*, we can tweak the subspace carrier wave—make it ten times faster and bury it so deep in subspace that the Breen will never notice it."

"Intriguing, if it works," Picard said. "But why the urgency?"

Ariel took his hand and beamed. "Jean-Luc . . . I've just been in contact with one of my own again. I have my brothers and sisters back. And they're trapped and in need. I just want to make sure they're taken care of. If the worst happens to us, if the Breen or Sheliak show up and we can't escape them . . . I want to know that someone knows my people are here, knows they're waiting. And I want to make sure Starfleet has all the data we've gathered, so they can use it to devise a solution if . . . if they're needed."

After a moment, Picard nodded. "You're right, it's a prudent precaution. Get to work on compiling a report and coordinate with Commander Colla on the subspace link." He stopped himself and smiled. "That is . . . in the morning. You must be tired."

She returned his smile with interest. "Actually, I've been resting for five days, and I could use some physical exertion."

"I think that can be arranged." He held her hand as she rose from the couch and did not release it. "Mister Data . . . you're dismissed."

The base transporter was on standby for emergency rescue, so Picard and Ariel returned to the ship by shuttle. Fortunately Adonis II's small size made for a low orbital radius and a shorter trip. Along the way, Picard told Ariel about the platycauds and their dependence on the stasis field. "Surely you're not saying we should leave my people there?" she protested.

"Certainly not. But we will have to find a way either to free them without destroying the stasis field or to restore the field after they're gone. And any attempts that risk collapsing the field must be performed in the local daytime when the fewest platycauds are nearby."

Ariel thought it over. "Maybe a thermal field could be

rigged, as Data suggested. If we use the base's shield equipment, it should be self-sustaining indefinitely."

"Well, there we go," Picard said lightly. "That was easy."

She chuckled. "Well, I've been around the block a few times."

"What would I do without you?"

Once they were back aboard and in his quarters, their communication was mostly nonverbal for some time. But later, as they lay together in bed (the lights were on as usual, and after days apart she seemed to shimmer more brightly than ever), Ariel looked at him and spoke seriously. "About what you asked before . . . what you would do without me . . ."

"Ariel, what are you saying?"

"When we free my people, I need to go with them. The ship they have in there, it's far faster and longer in range than anything Starfleet has. We'll need it if we're to find our archive and free the rest of our people."

"But the other Manraloth—"

"Will need me to help them reacclimate. We've discussed this."

He sighed. "I could come with you."

"Your crew needs you."

She was right; they had discussed it before. But now that it loomed as an imminent prospect, it was more difficult. "Ariel . . . I love you. I don't want to be without you."

She took his hands. "Jean-Luc . . . the bond between us has meant a great deal to me. And I want you to remember what we've shared with happiness . . . not filtered through the pain of loss."

"I fear it will have to be both." He stroked her hair, marveling as ever at its ethereal softness. "Is there any way I can talk you out of this?"

Her incarnadine brows furrowed. "I fear I will have to talk you into it, my dear."

And so they talked through the night as they held each other close. Her voice soothed him, and he drifted into twilight, still hearing her gentle words. And when he woke in the morning, alone in his bed, he was grateful for the special closeness he had shared with an extraordinary being for a time, but recognized that it was time for them both to move on with their separate journeys, enriched by their time with one another but no longer restrained.

That was Picard's way, after all—to be a free spirit, a wanderer, never content to settle down for long. And he did not imagine that would ever change.


Data watched as the entire crew of the *U.S.S. Enterprise* suffocated and died one by one. *Intriguing,* he said to himself.

For weeks, Data had been running simulations on the performance of the *Galaxy* class of heavy explorers under a wide range of conditions which they might be expected to encounter once they were placed into active service over the next several years. He had expected to postpone the effort during his period of interface with Ariel and the Manraloth, but his attempt to achieve such interface had proven unsuccessful. He could not slow his cognitive processing to the necessary level, and proved capable of communicating only with Ariel herself; for undetermined reasons, he could not interface with the uploaded mind within the stasis field. As a result, it had been determined that his energies would be better spent performing his standard duties and receiving periodic updates from Ariel.

Thus, over the past two days, he had continued his *Galaxy*-class simulations. In that time, he had noted a remarkable upswing in the percentage of simulations that terminated in catastrophic failure within ten years of launch, not only for the *Enterprise,* but for the *Galaxy, Yamato, Odyssey,* indeed every planned vessel of the class whose parameters Data had in memory. This was strange, since simulations with similar parameters had not produced catastrophic results with such regularity over the preceding weeks. The possibility existed that it was a statistical fluke, but Data had already initiated a thorough self-diagnostic to determine if some fault in his neural processors might be implicated.

In the meantime, however, he had other matters to occupy his primary level of cognitive processing. Ariel had revived from her second trance after 46.79 hours and had requested his presence. As he entered the chamber where her interface couch was located, he shunted the *Galaxy* simulations to a sublevel of his consciousness and initiated verbal interface. "Lieutenant Data, reporting as requested."

Ariel smiled. "At ease, Data. I'm not part of your chain of command, you know."

"I am aware of your civilian status. However, you did request that I come here, and I have done so. In what way was my statement in error?"

"Never mind. I have something for you. An upload from my friends inside." She patted the head of the interface couch. "Intact navigational data from the base computer. The best map yet of the pre-Cataclysm galaxy. With this, we can find a black-hole archive and the rest of my people!"

"In theory," Data told her. "However, it will still be necessary to adjust for orbital drift."

"Of course. And that's where you come in, my friend." Data turned to the door, since that was where he had come in, but he could see nothing about it that related to the topic of Ariel's conversation. "I gather you've been working on an improved algorithm for those orbital corrections. If we're to find a black hole, we'll need the most accurate mapping data possible."

"Not necessarily. If the black hole in question is currently in proximity to a star, nebula, or other matter source, it will possess an accretion disk and be detectable by its x-ray emissions."

"But if it's dormant in empty space, with nothing to swallow up, it will just be . . . a black hole. A very evocative name the humans came up with. Minimalist, inelegant, but bluntly accurate."

"You are correct: a dormant black hole would be difficult to localize except by gravitational lensing of background radiation. An accurate calculation of its orbital trajectory would be most helpful in the search. I will upload the data and apply the correction algorithm."

"Thank you. You're a treasure, Data." He supposed that could be technically correct; unique items were often regarded as precious, and he had been discovered in a hidden location. But before he could discuss the characterization with her, Ariel sighed. "Now I really ought to get back inside. There's so much more to learn from them."

This did not match with his expectations based on current models of her interpersonal behavior. "Inquiry: Do you not wish to speak to Captain Picard before you return to your trance state?"

"Jean-Luc is a busy person, Data, and so am I. Besides . . . they're my people. I never knew these individuals before, but now they're all the family I have."

"Then . . . you do not consider Captain Picard a potential member of your family?"

"He's a friend, Data. That's just not the same. Now, don't you have some navigational files to upload?"

"Affirmative."

"Then please do so."

Data transferred the files to his tricorder while Ariel returned to her interface couch. Meanwhile, in the back of his mind, the crew of the *Odyssey* died in flames. . . .


"There." Vejar pointed out the blip on the long-range sensors. "It's consistent with a Breen battleship's warp signature."

"Damn," Picard said. "The longer we spent here, the more inevitable this became." Ariel was now in the tenth day of her slow conversation with the Manraloth, and apparently still no closer to finding a way to free them and their fellow temporal refugees. "What's their heading?"

# CHRISTOPHER L. BENNETT

"Two-oh-eight mark forty-seven, at warp four. Not directly for us, but if they continue on this course, they could be within range to detect us within three days. Less if we have to increase our power expenditure."

Picard counted his blessings that they were in a brown-dwarf system, small and dim enough to be easily overlooked. Adonis would only be of interest to scientists, and Picard doubted very much that the Breen ship was on a research expedition. "If necessary, we may be able to conceal ourselves in the rings. If we tractor several large ice boulders in close against the ship . . ."

"That would only fool EM-based sensors. If they did an active gravimetric or tachyon scan, we'd be detected."

Picard mulled over the possibilities, gazing at the striated magenta globe on the viewscreen. "Could we hide inside the dwarf's outer atmosphere?" he asked the bridge crew at large.

"The convection currents would be way too intense," Kolbe answered from the conn. Of course. A methane dwarf might be far cooler than a star, but was still far fiercer than its Jovian cousins.

"Then we must either risk hiding in the rings," Picard said, "or be on our way within three days."

Vejar sighed. "I'll be glad when the Manraloth find their archive, sir."

"Commander?"

"Having all the answers at our fingertips? Just sitting back in a nice comfy chair and exploring a galaxy's worth of knowledge the easy way? No attacking Breen or Tholians or Ferengi—whoever the hell they are. Call me unambitious, sir, but that's the life for me."

Picard smiled. "No, Number One, I understand. It may lack the romance of starflight, but perhaps it's time we outgrew our need to buckle our swashes and became wise enough to learn from our elders."

"That's not a sentiment I would've expected from Jean-Luc Picard, sir."

"Jean-Luc Picard is not a young man any longer, Commander." He turned back to the sensor display. "But if I wish to continue aging gracefully, first I need to deal with our immediate problem." He tapped his combadge. "Mister Data, report to the bridge."

Data acknowledged, and was on the bridge within a minute. "Lieutenant," Picard said once he had explained the situation, "I want you and your team to redouble your efforts to deactivate the stasis field safely. We can no longer afford to wait on Ariel."

"Acknowledged, sir. But there is another matter I need to bring to your attention."

"Proceed."

"Over the past weeks, on my own initiative, I have been conducting a series of long-range performance simulations on the new *Galaxy* class of starships now under construction at Utopia Planitia. In recent days, those simulations have taken an alarming turn. Specifically, every simulation I have run within the past three days, fourteen hours, ten minutes, and forty-seven seconds has resulted in the destruction of the simulated starship within one-point-six to eleven-point-four years of its commissioning. The cause varies from simulation to simulation, but is almost invariably due to some unanticipated malfunction or system failure rather than a strictly external phenomenon. For instance, the transfer of power from engines to shields in a threat scenario may be critically delayed due to unexpected systems slowdowns."

Picard frowned. "Why was no evidence of this discovered before?"

"I wondered that myself, sir, and I ran the same simulations on the ship's computer. In those cases, with the exact same simulation parameters, the ships performed without critical malfunction in all simulation runs. When destruction did occur, it was always due to external stresses well beyond the vessels' design parameters, and occurred in only twelve point two percent of simulation runs."

"Then perhaps the problem is . . . internal?"

Data did not seem as troubled by the prospect of a malfunction within his own brain as Picard was. "I considered that as well, sir, and ran a thorough diagnostic on my positronic matrix, which I then repeated with the assistance of Chief Engineer Colla. No malfunction was indicated.

"I was therefore left with the hypothesis of external intervention as the cause of the anomaly. I noted that the catastrophic simulation runs began occurring within six hours of my interface with the Manraloth systems, on the date that Ariel transmitted an update of our findings to Starfleet Command."

Picard frowned. "Are you implying that Ariel or the other Manraloth somehow tampered with your brain, Mister Data?"

"I do not believe I was the target of the tampering, sir. In fact, I do not believe I was intended to become aware of this problem at all." He moved to the science station and called up a set of statistics. "This display gives the results of the simulations as run on the *Portia*'s computer operating in its standard mode. As you can see, the starships survive the simulation runs without critical malfunctions." He brought up a second display. "Since the computer and I arrived at disparate results using the same data, I considered that a difference in our design might have been a factor in the discrepancy. I therefore modified a subprocessor of the *Portia*'s main computer to employ heuristic neural network algorithms analogous to those within my own brain. In this case, the simulations consistently produce catastrophic failure." Data gave Picard a significant look. "The algorithms programmed into the ship's computer are based on my default performance, Captain. This is not the result of a malfunction within my neural network. Rather, the software parameters of the *Galaxy* class itself—those employed in its main computers and subsystems, of which I have identical copies within my own memory—have been tampered with in a way that is undetectable to standard analysis, but which my specific neural architecture was able to discern."

"Are you saying some sort of virus has been introduced?" Picard couldn't believe what he was hearing. "Data, Starfleet conducts scans for hidden viruses as a matter of course."

"True, sir. But such scans would be unable to recognize infiltration technologies of types never before encountered in Federation history." He worked the console some more, brought up more displays. "I have been conducting an exhaustive analysis of the software codes on all levels, and I have discovered these. Minute quantum variances distributed throughout the code, seemingly at random. Individually, they would be dismissed as incidental fluctuations or copying errors and corrected for. But I have detected traces of a pattern underlying them."

He turned back to Picard. "It is my belief, Captain, that these quantum irregularities are the components of a modular delayed-action virus: a program which is delivered in numerous, individually innocuous chunks of data over an extended period of time, but which, upon achieving critical mass within a system, self-assembles into a destructive program."

"Like smuggling in a bomb one piece at a time over the course of weeks," Picard said, his voice hushed.

"I believe so, sir. Except that the 'bomb' assembles itself once all its components are united. And rather than a single explosive device, it is more analogous to an infection that causes cumulative damage to the body.

"I have analyzed the contents of Ariel's transmission to Starfleet, sir. I have detected these quantum variances hidden within it. And I find that they have infiltrated both the *Portia*'s computer and myself, and presumably are spreading through Starfleet's computer systems even now.

"I must conclude that Ariel herself has sent this modular virus to Starfleet with the goal of sabotaging the *Galaxy* class, sir. Once the modular virus infected their systems, the vessels of that class would accumulate subtle system errors gradually over the course of years, building to the point of catastrophic failure. The time and circumstances of the failure would be different for each ship, thus concealing the existence of the sabotage."

Picard took several moments to absorb the lieutenant's words. "Mister Data," he said at length, "for someone who claims to have no imagination . . ."

"Sir?"

"I mean, the very idea is absurd! What possible reason could Ariel have to attempt to sabotage Starfleet vessels? We're the ones who rescued her, who helped her find her own people."

"However, at this point she may no longer need our help, sir."

"That doesn't mean she'd do a thing like this." He shook his head. "No, Data. All I see are a few ordinary quantum fluctuations, the kind that are common in any information system. You're reading patterns into randomness. A more likely explanation is that your neural-net algorithms are simply introducing some kind of error into the simulations."

"An error which manifests so differently in every case, sir?"

"A starship is a complex system, Data—these *Galaxy*-class behemoths more so than most. There's no telling how such an error could manifest itself."

Vejar came up alongside Picard. "Even so, sir, isn't it worth checking the possibility that Data's programming may have turned up some undetected weakness in the *Galaxy*-class software? As you say, they're very complex ships. Maybe they're just . . . too complex."

"She's right," Kolbe said. "They're untried technology. Who knows what could go wrong. And they're thinking of sending them out with civilians and children on board?"

"Mm, good point," Picard said. "Perhaps, like so many monumental constructions in the past, the *Galaxy* class may simply be a manifestation of hubris. The attempt to reach too far, too fast. Perhaps we simply don't understand enough yet to undertake a venture of such magnitude."

"Once we find the Manraloth archives," Vejar said, "will

we even need to go ahead with building those ships? Maybe the whole thing should be put on hold."

"I'll certainly pass that recommendation along to Starfleet."

"Inquiry," Data said. "Will you also 'pass along' the hypothesis that these simulated malfunctions indicate the presence of a modular virus? Would it not be prudent to mention the possibility?"

"Data, it is simply not reasonable. Ariel has been nothing but benevolent toward us. I trust her implicitly."

"Then perhaps she has been co-opted in some way by those within the stasis field."

"Data, *why?*" Picard asked, raising his voice. "The Manraloth were a peaceful race. They worked to ensure peace throughout the galaxy for literally millions of years."

"At this point, we have only anecdotal testimony to that effect from Ariel herself."

"And if she vouches for them, then we may rely on their integrity as well."

Data paused before speaking again. "Captain Picard . . . may I speak to you in private?"

*Now what?* "Very well, Lieutenant. In my ready room."

They adjourned to the small office adjoining the bridge. "Captain," Data began, "I did not wish to bring this up in front of the crew, at it may have infringed upon a confidence. But I am concerned that you may be allowing your personal relationship with Ariel to compromise your objectivity toward her."

Picard stared. The android's interpretations of events continued to grow more bizarre. Had he placed too much faith in this artificial man? "Data, Ariel and I are simply very close friends. True, we have shared a . . . companionable relationship for some time, as is often the way of things between consenting adults, but we have both chosen to move on from that. I have no particularly strong feelings toward Ariel one way or another, beyond my deep personal respect for her and fascination for the history and civilization she represents."

Data frowned. "I am . . . very confused, sir. Thirty-two days ago, at 0547 hours, you stated to me that you wished nothing more than to spend the rest of your life with Ariel, and that you considered it likely that you would propose marriage to her. I do not understand how that can be reconciled with your preceding statement, sir."

Picard was taken aback. "Did I say that?"

"I quote, sir: *'And I'll be happy as long as I get to spend the rest of my life with her.'* You subsequently added: *'Just five years ago, I thought I'd never want to settle down with one woman. Now I think there's nothing I want more.'*"

Picard stared. Data didn't simply quote his words; he recited them in Picard's own voice, as if lip-synching to a recorded audio file. Hearing the words in his own intonations reminded Picard that he had in fact said those things—and that he had meant them. "Well, Data . . . you see, the reason I said . . ." Data waited patiently for an explanation, but the more Picard tried to reconcile his feelings then with his feelings now, the more impossible it became. He remembered the depth of passion he had shared with Ariel, the profound, overpowering love. He had been willing to devote his life to her. He had given up his doctorate, had been willing to give up Starfleet, all to help Ariel pursue her dream. Because all he had wanted in life was to make her happy.

But surely that was it? What made her happy now was being with her people, going off to find the archive, seeing him where he belonged in command of a starship. If that was what she wanted, then naturally . . .

No. He remembered it now: the yearning he had felt, the echoing void in his heart when she had been away for even a few days. How could he now accept their parting so easily? How could he have allowed the depth of love he had felt for her to simply *slip his mind*?

He strove to remember the last time he had felt that passion, the first time he had felt companionable detachment in its place. "It was . . . four nights ago . . . Ariel came to the ship. We . . . she talked all night . . . talked about . . . I barely remember. But it was about . . . moving on. Moving on with our separate lives. And when I awoke . . . I thought I no longer loved her." But he still did—didn't he? Even the memory of it was dizzying in its power.

"Data . . ." He turned to the android, seeking his simple purity of thought, his structured, analytical view. "Could she have . . . brainwashed me?"

"Inquiry, sir: 'brainwashed'?"

"Conditioned. Hypnotized. Altered my way of thinking."

"Such external manipulation can explain a sudden change in behavior or perception."

"But she's not telepathic. Not in that way, only with language. Communication."

Data took on his faraway, thoughtful look for a moment before refocusing his gaze on Picard. "Interpersonal communication exists on many levels, Captain. I have only partially mastered verbal communication and still have much difficulty with emotional nuance, vocal intonation, body language, contextual social cues, and the like. And I am unable to respond to chemical cues such as pheromonal exchange. However, you have pointed out to me that understanding of communication can be improved with practice and experience."

"What are you getting at, Data?"

"Ariel is from a species with an innate ability to process and utilize communication on all levels. She is also several thousand times older than either of us. Therefore, it follows that she has had several thousand times as much practice at the use of her communicative gifts, and has thus been able to refine them to a degree no other known entity has achieved."

"So . . . she can alter the way we think . . . simply by the *way* she talks to us? Her choice of words? Data, that's difficult to credit."

"But do not humans do the same to a lesser degree, sir? In Starfleet training, is it not stressed that the manner in which you communicate your intentions is fundamental to achieving command authority? That 'it is not what you say, but how you say it'?"

"Persuasive speaking," Picard said. "Propaganda. Elevated to an art we have barely begun to imagine . . . just as Benjamin Franklin playing with his electrical parlor tricks could not have imagined you. It's staggering, Mister Data . . . the subtlety of it. The power to win any argument, resolve any disagreement, simply by persuading the other side that you are right. Through keen psychological insight, precise choice of words . . . I can't even imagine the method."

"Subsonic vocal modulation may be a factor, sir. Certain subsonic frequencies have been shown to have psychoactive effects. Pheromonal cues may be involved as well."

Picard shook his head. "The ultimate weapon . . . one that wins you a new ally for every enemy it destroys. Conquest so subtle that no one even knows they've been conquered."

Data nodded. "Ariel did claim that the Manraloth were key in organizing and maintaining a galaxywide civilization."

"One without war . . . without struggle . . . without dissent. Because the Manraloth simply *talked* everyone into playing along. The tongue is mightier than the sword."

The lieutenant furrowed his brow. "Inquiry: Did Ariel speak with you and the crew about the benefits of access to the Manraloth archive and the hazards of starship exploration?"

"Yes, Data, I believe she did." But Picard's mind was filled with another realization: If Ariel had talked him *out* of loving her, had she talked him *into* it in the first place?

Picard strode out of the ready room so fast he practically didn't realize he'd left until he was already on the bridge, with Data tagging along after him. "Open a channel to the planet," he ordered. "Picard to Kilif!"

*"Kilif here, sir."*

"What is the current status of Ariel? Is she still in a trance state?"

*"Negative, sir. She awakened several minutes ago."*

"I want her taken into custody."

A pause. *"Sir?"*

"You heard the order, Lieutenant! Restrain her and bring her back to the ship. And at all costs, do not allow her to talk you out of doing so. Do not allow her to speak at all!"

*"But, sir, it's Ariel."*

"Acknowledge my order, Lieutenant!"

*". . . Aye-aye, sir. Ariel is to be taken into custody and returned to the ship."*

"Mister Data, prepare a report of your findings to Starfleet."

"Sir?" Vejar asked. "With that Breen ship so close—"

"Good point, Number One. Prepare a class-eight probe. Upload Data's report, set it to begin transmitting once it's clear of the disputed zone."

"But, sir—"

"Commander, I'm now convinced Data was right after all. Now, I know you don't wish to believe that, but you have been influenced. All of us have. We must strive to separate our own judgment and beliefs from what Ariel has influenced us to think and feel."

Before Vejar could ask for further clarification, the intercom came online. *"Kilif to Portia!"*

"Picard here. Go ahead."

*"Ariel offered resistance, sir. When she realized we were coming for her, she broke and ran. I overtook her, but she twisted in a way I didn't think was possible and flung me into the wall. I got off a phaser shot, but she barely felt it."*

"Where was she headed?"

*"The transporter, sir."*

Picard exchanged a look with Data. "Number One, have a security team report to shuttlebay one immediately. Data, you're with me."

# 18

———

HALFWAY DOWN TO THE PLANET, THE SHUTTLE
rocked and alarms began to sound. At the same time, Picard
felt a familiar stinging sensation pass through his body. Data
convulsed and his head jerked back and forth several times
before he stabilized. "Oh, my God," Picard breathed. "She's
done it. She's tried to beam her people out—collapsed the
stasis field." He opened a comm channel. "Picard to Kilif,
come in!" There was no answer. "Picard to McCarthy!" Silence. "Damn. Picard to *Portia*. Medical emergency. Lock
onto all personnel on the planet and transport them immediately." He only prayed the radiation interference would not
do them more damage than they'd already suffered.

"Captain," Data reported, "I am no longer reading the stasis field. I am, however, reading a small spacecraft resting
atop the base."

"The ship that was inside the field," Picard said. How
many inside were left to die in favor of bringing out the
craft?

Rider's voice came over the comm. *"Portia to Picard.
We've retrieved everyone but Ariel. Her position is shielded."*
He paused. *"Lieutenant Kilif is dead, sir. The others are on
their way to sickbay."*

Soon, the shuttle was nearing the base site. Picard saw that the rocky ground around the base was glowing red-hot, cracks spreading out around it. It was a few hours before local dawn; the platycauds would still have been clustered around the base. "Data, scan for life signs."

"Scanning . . . Twenty-two Manraloth biosignatures detected inside the base. No indigenous biosignatures within four hundred meters. I am detecting small numbers of platycaud biosignatures at a greater remove, sir. However, the signatures are weak, many of them fading rapidly."

"My God, Ariel, what have you done?" Picard murmured.


The atmospheric containment field they had erected around the entry point to allow safe passage from shuttles was no longer functional, and the landing area was molten. The shuttle had to set down atop the base itself, its occupants then using its escape transporter to beam inside, a safe enough operation at point-blank range.

Phasers drawn, the away team ran toward the concentration of life signs. Ignoring the security team's efforts to keep him protected, Picard raced into the lead, flying around the last corner. There was Ariel before him, surrounded by twenty-one others of her people. They all showed damage to their skin and clothing and moved haltingly, and there was a trace of the charnel stench Picard remembered from the *Kingsley*, but they all seemed essentially intact. They came in different shapes, sizes, and colors, some with tails or enlarged ears or a coat of hair down the back, but it was evident despite their surface injuries that they all shared Ariel's butterfly-scale epidermis and intricate fractal stripes. All of them save Ariel were shirtless, male and female alike, revealing other differences. But nonetheless, every one was Manraloth. Ariel had beamed out only her own people, sacrificing the other species within the bubble.

All of the Manraloth were hugging and stroking each other gingerly, chatting with happy relief in a mellifluous language Picard had never heard. It was a hideous sight in the context of what had been done to make it possible. *"Ariel!"* he roared.

She spun to face him, her hair flying outward and slowly wafting its way down again. The sight no longer delighted Picard as it once had. Seeing his phaser pointed at her, a tall Manraloth male, silver-scaled with patterns of dark blues and bright greens, strode forward to shield her, even though he reeled slightly. But Ariel held him back. "Ngalior!" She exchanged a few fluid words with him, and came forward. "Leave now, Jean-Luc. Don't get in our way. This has grown beyond you now."

"Don't think you can tell me what to do! I won't fall for your manipulation anymore!" He shook his head. "I should've listened to you months ago, when you warned me that Ariel was a spirit of illusion and deceit. I named you more aptly than I knew."

"It was necessary, Jean-Luc. You would not have understood what needed to be done. I needed your assistance, your cooperation."

"Did you need me to love you to obtain those?! I would have helped you gladly, without needing to be tricked."

"I needed you strongly motivated, so you'd go back to Starfleet. Was it so bad while it lasted? And I tried to end it for you comfortably. To spare you the pain."

"Spare me pain?" he asked incredulously. "You have just killed my chief of security and injured a half-dozen others of my crew. You have killed over a hundred of your own contemporaries. You have slaughtered an entire population of platycauds, and deprived any survivors of the heat source they depended on for their survival!"

Ariel strode closer, showing an anger she had never let him see before. "If you hadn't forced the issue, I could've waited! A few more weeks and we might've found a way!"

"Forced the issue? And tell me, Ariel, how deep would your modular virus have penetrated into Starfleet's systems by then, hmm?" To his satisfaction, she was rendered speechless. "Why, Ariel? After all we have done for you, why would you attack Starfleet in such a vicious, insidious way? Why target starships with civilians and children on-board?"

"You think I wanted to?!" she asked, seeming agonized. "This is the greatest sacrifice I have ever had to make. I'll have to live with it long after your whole civilization has fallen to dust. But I had no choice. The alternative was so much worse."

"What about Coray? Was she a necessary sacrifice? Did she discover your manipulative talents and lose her life as a result?"

"She died just as I said—she was too reckless and used an untried formula against my explicit warning." She sighed. "At the time, I was every bit the ingenue I seemed. I didn't regain my memory until Centauri, just as you saw."

"Then you would have me believe that our relationship was sincere until then? How can I possibly trust in that, in anything you have ever told me?"

"Believe what you like, Jean-Luc. This is bigger than you and your bruised pride. Bigger than one life, bigger than ten thousand."

"There is nothing that can justify exploitation and murder on the scale that you have perpetrated it."

Ariel laughed, but there was no joy or malevolence behind it, only bitter irony. "Ohh, Jean-Luc, you dear, innocent little child. You have no idea, no ability to conceive of the true scale of my people's crimes." Her eyes glistened. "Did you never realize? When you saw how hard it hit me back on Centauri? I'm nearly *one million* years old. I've had twice the lifetime of your species to learn to cope with emotional distress. Can you imagine the magnitude of the horror it would require to break me like that?"

He faced her squarely. "Then tell me. Explain it to me in terms a child like myself can understand. What crimes did you commit? After you conquered the galaxy with kindness and gentle counsel, what did you inflict upon your subjects?"

Ariel stared, then shook her head. "You truly do not understand. That is not the nature of our powers. We can cajole and convince receptive minds, but we cannot control them. The fact that you overcame my attempt to influence you proves that. We were what I told you we were—peacemakers, guides, advisers to the races of the galaxy."

"Your peace. Your agendas."

"No. Theirs." Her gaze went unfocused, as though seeing infinity. "We are communicators, Jean-Luc. We connect to other beings, understand them . . . even evolve ourselves to be more like them. It is why we endured so long.

"Remember Professor Galen's conjecture? How the early civilizations in the galaxy lived alone for millions of years before moving on or dying out, never encountering another sentience? How billions of years later, when species finally began meeting each other after long isolation, they couldn't cope, and bloody wars and conquests resulted?" Picard merely waited. "Galen was right, Jean-Luc. For nearly a billion years, that was the way of things in the galaxy—long periods of a single race's dominance, broken by massive wars waged with weapons that could annihilate star clusters or erase whole civilizations from existence. Followed by long gaps of emptiness until a new starfaring intelligence arose and started the cycle over again.

"But then evolution produced a new adaptation: a species that had a special empathy for others, that could bridge the gulf of understanding. By now, more habitable planets were mature enough to produce intelligence, and our ancestors were able to build the first true interstellar alliance in this galaxy, over six hundred million years ago. Over the millennia, we refined ourselves into better communicators, better bridges, able to adapt to more new and exotic species—and with the galaxy no longer being torn apart by successive theomachies, more species were able to evolve to full sentience.

"As time went on, our technology improved and we made ourselves immortal, along with most of our longtime allies. But over the ages, those allies went through changes. Some grew tired of corporeal immortality and took other paths—undergoing introdus into virtual worlds, migrating to custom-built pocket universes, transitioning to incorporeality or higher planes of existence.

"But the Manraloth cherished our partnership with other races far too much. The paths these others took were too solipsistic for our tastes. We simply lived on, keeping our existence fresh by befriending more new species and evolving ourselves in new ways.

"And so, over the megayears, we became the eldest race in the galaxy. Simply by default, we came to be the warders, the protectors, the ones who watched over the younger races and offered them guidance."

"What kind of guidance?" Picard interrupted. "Starting when? Did you meddle in their affairs from the beginning?"

"Did we have a Prime Directive like yours? No. It is cowardly and criminal to leave young civilizations to struggle alone, to endure plague and warfare and superstitious hatreds."

"To develop their own identity, their own unique perspective on the universe. To find their own solutions to their own problems."

"We did allow them that. We gave them freedom to make their own choices and mistakes, but protected them from the worst ones. Of course it's wrong to do a child's thinking for her, make her dependent upon you. But it's just as wrong to abandon her in the wilderness. She may grow up strong if she survives, but she will be scarred forevermore. Scarred as you are now, all you younglings with your wars and occupations and buffer zones."

"What right do you have to treat other races as your children?"

"The right of all sentient beings to care for one another. To have an interest in each other's well-being." Ariel winced. "And that is where we failed. We grew too selfish."

"In what way?"

Her chevron brow twisted with irony. "Not the way you assume. We were always such a gregarious people. When one of our neighbor races would leave this plane of existence . . . we missed them. It saddened us to lose touch with them. We filled the void with new friendships, but still it hurt. And it happened again and again, over tens of millions of years."

She glanced over at her fellows, the diverse group of Manraloth who stood watching, listening, no doubt learning the language more fully with each moment. Already they were visibly more healed than they had been minutes ago. "But we are a race that evolves quickly. More a genus than a species, after all this time. Eventually, some of us evolved in our preferences as well. Some of our own people chose to evolve to other levels of existence, ones beyond our ability to perceive. The void was keenly felt among the rest of us. Over the next few million years, gradually, more and more of us went. Still a tiny percentage of the whole, but enough. Those of us who remained behind felt a greater cavity in our collective soul each time it happened. And when Manraloth chose the transition, many of the races that looked up to us were inspired to follow as well."

By now, the other Manraloth were clearly grasping her words, their faces displaying a panoply of angst, grief, and guilt as she spoke. She ambled closer to them and clasped the hand of the tall silver-blue male she'd called Ngalior. "Most of us could still not bear to give up our corporeal lives, to move on from our responsibility to the younger races. But we still longed to regain contact with those we'd lost.

"So some of our great minds devised a plan. The Manraloth were the great communicators, after all—the bridge between the races. Surely we could be a bridge between dimensions as well. If we could devise a technology to enhance our minds, let them tap into those other planes of consciousness, we could restore contact with those who had moved on. We would no longer have to be separated from them. And they could share their knowledge of the other realms of existence, opening up a brave new era of discovery."

She was silent for a time, her gaze going unfocused. Her hand slipped free of her comrade's grasp. When she spoke again, it was slow, deliberate, rigidly controlled. "That was the plan. Since we were spread across the galaxy, a loose, decentralized coalition, scientists on multiple worlds worked on it simultaneously, a friendly competition to construct a working interdimensional logopathic conduit. But the knowledge was freely shared throughout our galactic network, instantaneously disseminated through circuits that interfaced directly with our minds. And so the devices were completed on numerous Manraloth worlds at roughly the same time. And we, in our great collective spirit, spontaneously agreed that we would activate them all at once in a single, vast celebration."

The ironic cheer that had crept into her voice fell flat. "And so . . . the links were activated. The veil was pierced, and our minds were opened to the realms that lay beyond.

"And we drowned in them.

"We . . . could not have anticipated the sheer power, the complexity of the mental energies within those planes. Those energies flooded through the connections, searing their way into the minds of the Manraloth and other telepathic species. Those minds further amplified them, resonated with them, sent those energies further out through the galactic network. So not only telepaths were affected. The energy was beamed into every brain that was complex enough to respond to it.

"It affected these minds differently, depending on their development. Every sentient being whose brain was complex enough or properly attuned . . . was forcibly transitioned to an incorporeal state. The energy of the phase transition vaporized their bodies . . . and irradiated everything around them." Picard remembered the tetryon burns in the ruins on Tanebor.

"Every brain advanced enough to receive the signals but not enough to make the transition," Ariel went on, "simply . . . burned out. Every living thing with a neocortex. And many of the surviving plant and animal species were killed when the sentient populations on their planets turned en masse into glowing balls of energy and poured vast amounts of heat into their environments.

"Literally within minutes, all intelligent life in this galaxy . . . over a quadrillion individuals . . . was gone. Half of it forced into a plane it wasn't ready for . . . half of it simply killed. The entire galaxy was . . . depopulated."

Picard had no words for a long moment. Only Data could find them. "How is it, then, that you survived?"

"Those of us in remote, shielded locations, such as research bases in hostile environments, were partly protected from the effects. Our shields were designed to causally isolate us from exterior influences, and so we were spared the worst. But it was temporary. The beings whose energies were catalyzing this effect existed on a transdimensional level, and so the emanations seeped through. We tried enclosing ourselves within event horizons, but the energies pervaded all dimensions. There was nowhere we could escape to. The only thing we could do to prevent the change . . . was to prevent all change. To enclose ourselves in fields of zero entropy . . . detach ourselves from time itself. It was a step so drastic that even we could see no way to reverse it. But it was the one desperate chance we had. All we could do was hope that one day, new life would evolve from the simple forms that survived, discover us, and find a way to set us free."

After a time, Picard shook his head. "It doesn't make sense. There is no record of any such singular event. The extinctions in that era were spread out over millions of years. Many have demonstrable causes such as volcanism or asteroid impacts."

"What would happen," Ariel challenged, "if everyone in your civilization suddenly died or disappeared? Vehicles would crash, reactors would explode, delicate experiments would shatter and spill their toxins into the environment. My people built planets, Jean-Luc. We tailored stars, rechanneled subspace itself. When those energies flew out of control, the results were cataclysmic. Supernovae, gamma-ray bursts, gravitational shock waves that shattered planets and sent their shards hurtling through space. The cosmic turbulence would have taken millions of years to settle down entirely.

"So do not tell me that does not make sense!" she cried, striding toward him. "I have *lived* it. When I went to Organia, they showed me. The tale is legendary in the incorporeal planes. Their realm was flooded with trillions of refugees, half of them crippled or driven mad by their forcible transformation. Even beings of their power were overwhelmed by such a burden. Chaos reigned on their planes for millennia, sometimes spilling over into ours. Even more stars were destroyed, more planets shattered by insane, self-styled gods before they could be healed or imprisoned. Even today, some of those damaged entities survive in a weakened form, incorporeal predators who take glee in the suffering they can inflict on organic beings. Perhaps as some sort of twisted revenge against those who still possess what they had torn from them. Torn from them by us.

"And because of what the Manraloth did, you who evolved in our wake had no one to protect you from their assault. To guide you away from the chaos and war that have left such scars on your societies. You have lived your whole existence knowing such profound pain and horror, such injustice and cruelty. And we abandoned you to that fate . . . because of our own selfish need for contact.

"That is our crime. We, the Manraloth, who lived to protect and nurture the races of the galaxy, destroyed them all, and abandoned their successors to the wilds. That is what we must atone for now."

"Atone for?" Picard challenged. He shook his head

slowly, thinking. "If what you say is true . . . then I cannot begin to grasp the magnitude of such a tragedy, or of your guilt. If it is the truth, then I am truly sorry for your people. But how in heaven's name can you possibly atone for such a thing by committing sabotage and murder, by turning on your own allies?"

"Don't you see? The Federation is the greatest threat to the galaxy today!"

"Why?"

"*Because you are us.* Because you are at the beginning of a journey that leads to what we were. You are so irrepressible in your curiosity, your optimism. So eager to seek out new life, to forge new alliances, to embrace diversity in all its combinations." She smiled. " 'How noble in reason! How infinite in faculty! In form and moving how express and admirable! In action how like an angel! In apprehension how like a god!' You have it within yourselves to unite this galaxy, as we once did.

"And you have it within yourselves to make the same mistake. Go far enough along this path, and you will feel the same temptation—to unite not only the galaxy, but the multiverse itself. Oh, you may feel you have learned from our mistakes, that you can tackle the problem and make it work this time. You're so clever, so optimistic, you're bound to believe you can try. But the problem is just too complex. It has too many dimensions for us to master. Keep going on this path, and you will destroy life in the galaxy all over again. If not with our mistake, then with another act of cosmic hubris."

"So you intend to destroy the Federation?"

"No, Jean-Luc. To *tame* it. To contain its ambition. You need to slow down, to stop expanding. You need to stop imagining you can do everything and learn from the wisdom of your elders. Once you have the black-hole archives, and us to guide you through them, you will have that wisdom at your beck and call. If you wish to learn something, we will help you find it. If you wish to meet the other races of the galaxy, we will arrange the introduction. You will no longer yearn to quest, to expand. You will be content to let the galaxy come to you."

Picard stared at her in growing horror. "And the destruction of the *Galaxy* class?"

She winced. "A necessary evil. Sometimes behavioral modification requires the stick as well as the carrot. The *Galaxy* ships are the ultimate symbol of Federation optimism—vast, peaceful vessels of exploration, whole communities questing out in search of contact and discovery. Your society has pinned so much hope on its success that you would actually entrust these ships with your future, your children.

"If those ships die, and those children with them," she continued in a heavy tone, "then that eagerness for the quest will be tempered. You will think twice about your love of questing outward. And that will be our opportunity to guide you onto an alternative path." She gazed into his eyes. "I will mourn every being who dies on those ships. But they would have died hereafter anyway. And their legacy, their species, will live on. That is the life we must strive to preserve."

Picard sneered. "Your assertions of benevolence ring hollow when I look behind you and see only other Manraloth. Do their lives matter more to you than the other species you allowed to die in the stasis field?"

Her eyes flared. "You have no right to take me to task for that, Picard! It was your reckless arrogance and hamfisted technology that killed everyone else in my stasis field! My colleagues, my friends, people I loved. If you had known how much I loathed you after I remembered . . . how hard it was to pretend all these months . . ." She shook her head. "But you were only an ignorant child. I have to live with *choosing* to sacrifice the people in this bubble. I wanted to save them all, but I needed to save the Manraloth—the ones who had the most power to influence and persuade, the ones with the best chance of diverting you from your course and keeping the galaxy safe. The oldest ones, best qualified to safeguard all the rest. If your ship loses pressure, whom do you give an oxygen mask to first? Yourself, or the child next to you? It has to be yourself, because if you do not survive, you cannot save the child anyway."

"So all the others were only children to you?"

"I had to kill nearly a dozen Manraloth as well. To choose the ones best qualified to help and sacrifice the rest. I mourn the others' deaths no less than theirs."

Ngalior moved to her side. "We agreed. All of us. We would make . . . any sacrifice . . . for peace."

"Including the sacrifice of others who were not consulted in the matter?" Picard demanded. "You have no right, Ariel. You had your chance, and your time is done. We can take care of ourselves now."

*"My name is Giriaenn!"* She took several gasping breaths thereafter, as though she had been holding it in for months. No doubt she had. "I am Scholar Giriaenn Lilaeannin eb Vairan Gela-syr, Sisterdweller of the Worldring Vairashu Five in the Ranaeth Cluster. I live. My people live. And we *will* rebuild what we destroyed."

"Then why don't you? Why stand here yammering to me about your plans? Why not just kill us like you've killed so many others and be on your merry way?" He narrowed his eyes. "You need something from us—Scholar Giriaenn. Despite all your bombast, you still require some assistance from us ephemeral mites."

"Only the information you possess. We only know where our archives were, over a turn of the galaxy ago. We need your orbital correction data to help us find them."

He slapped his combadge. "Picard to *Portia*. Number One, tie in the main computer."

A moment later, the computer voice came over the channel. *"Working."*

"Delete all Manraloth-era navigational data from all ship's databanks immediately, authorization Picard Sigma Eight-One-Four. Alpha-level security protocols. Reformat all sectors containing the data. Acknowledge."

*"Acknowledged. Files deleted. Reformatting sectors."*

Ariel's—*Giriaenn's*—eyes went to Picard's side. "Data. You still have the information."

"Mister Data, I order you not to give them any navigational information. If they attempt to scan your neural net, delete the relevant files."

"Aye, sir."

"You're being very childish, Jean-Luc," Giriaenn said. "At most, you've only delayed us by a few years, a few months. The blink of a Manraloth eye."

He met her eyes without blinking his own. "Then I will find other ways to stop you."

"It's we who must stop you now, Jean-Luc." Giriaenn sighed. "I really didn't want to have to kill you, you know. As furious as I am with you, the bond we had was real for a time, and it helped me when I needed it. But you could stop us from saving your galaxy. You doomed yourself the moment you discovered the modular virus, the moment you forced me to show my hand." She sighed. "I just . . . felt you deserved to understand why it had to end. So that hopefully you could take some comfort in your sacrifice. I'm sorry you refuse to understand."

But Picard smiled, for he had heard Vejar issuing orders in the background over the comm channel he had left open. "You know what the problem is with being from a race of communicators, Scholar Giriaenn?"

"What?"

The transporter beam began to take him and his team. "You talk too damned much."

Picard came out of the transporter queasy but apparently intact. Counting his blessings, he thanked Chief Rider and ran for the bridge.

Twenty seconds later, he strode from the turbolift toward the command chair. "Ensign, take us out of orbit and set course for the ring system. We're about to come under pursuit from a ship much faster and more powerful than our own; our only hope is evasion."

"Aye, sir."

He threw a look at Vejar as he sat down. "And thank you for the timely rescue, Number One."

"I can't believe they fell for it," Vejar said. "A million years old, and they fell for an open comm channel."

"If the erstwhile Ariel is to be believed, they come from an age of peace and subtle persuasion; they have seen little or no open conflict in their lifetimes. We had better hope she was truthful about that, at least. Because if that ship is as advanced as I expect, our . . . feral cunning may be our only advantage."

"Manraloth scout ship now launching from planet surface, sir," Data reported from the science station. "Intriguing. It appears to have expanded in volume to accommodate the entire twenty-two-Manraloth complement."

Vejar stared at that. "How much bigger do you think it can get?"

"Not very much, Commander," Data replied. "It may have been stowed in a more compact configuration to fit inside the stasis field. I detect no change in mass aside from the addition of its occupants."

"That's some comfort," Picard said. "Perhaps their technology is at least somewhat distinguishable from magic."

But he spoke too soon. A second later, the fluid, birdlike Manraloth scout suddenly materialized in their path. "Helm, evasive! Full phasers, fire!"

As he hoped, the abrupt violence of the attack seemed to throw the Manraloth off long enough for the *Portia* to dodge and make a last dash for the rings. "Tractor beam!" called the relief ensign at tactical, but just then, the ship reached the refuge of the inner ring, and the beam caught particles of rock and ice, yanking them toward the scout at rapidly increasing speed. But the scout took the hits with no apparent damage and curved up over the ring system, staying parallel with the *Portia* as Kolbe ducked and wove between the particles. The large ones were kilometers apart or more, but at these speeds that was still a harrowing obstacle course.

Suddenly, boulders began to appear in their path where none had been before. Kolbe showed quick reflexes, swerving away at the last second, but more asteroids were teleported in front of them. "Full shields!" Picard cried, as one snapped into their path at point-blank range.

The ship smashed through the asteroid, spattering it across space and taking little damage. Again Picard thanked fortune for favoring fools such as he; the asteroid had been a loosely packed aggregate of rock and ice particles, more a dirty snowball than a solid body.

But Picard knew that fortune was a fickle mistress; he could not sustain this chase for long. He had to go on the offensive. "Tactical, lay down photon torpedoes in the ring field, zero velocity. Program them to track the scout and stand by to engage full thrust. And stand by on tractor beam."

"Aye, sir."

He waited a few more seconds, until they'd gained some distance from the torpedoes. "Fire full phasers at the scout."

"Firing."

Hopefully that would focus their attention on the *Portia* and away from the Easter eggs he'd laid behind them. "Engage torpedoes!"

The scout ship rocked from the combined barrage, but Picard assumed it would sustain little damage. Still, he'd only wanted to blind them. "Lock on tractor beam! Helm, accelerate toward the nearest solid asteroid and ram them into it!"

The ship shuddered as the beam engaged, but despite his fears, it moved forward. Data had said the scout's mass had not changed. For all its superior technology, it was still subject to Newton's laws; the *Portia* was far heavier and thus could yank the scout around like a toy, as long as the scout didn't brace itself with its engines. So for the brief moment that he had them off guard, he was able to drag them straight into the side of a sturdy silicate asteroid. *That should shake*

*them up a little. They call us primitive and warlike? Fine,
then that's what we shall be.*

But he had no hope that it would stall them for long.
"Disengage tractor. Helm, drop below the ring plane and engage at warp three. Get us some distance." *And please, let
them at least require some time to regroup.*

"Data, send your report to Starfleet immediately." At this
point, detection by the Breen was the least of their worries.

After a moment, Data shook his head. "We are being
jammed, sir. All frequencies."

"Damn." On the screen, the micronebula was slowly
drifting by, and inspiration struck. "Helm, divert course toward the nebula. Warp four."

In this miniature system, it took less than a minute to
reach the nearest part of the micronebula, the long streamer
that trailed out from where Adonis had smashed through it
centuries ago. But by the time they reached it, Data reported
that the Manraloth scout had cleared the rings and was pursuing at well above warp nine. "This nebula won't hide us
from them," Vejar told him.

"Hopefully it will do just enough," Picard replied.

Giriaenn watched the holodisplay sadly as Jean-Luc continued to dodge the inevitable. She had never anticipated that
he could be capable of such blunt savagery; for all his
species' turbulent legacy, all the viciousness in his beloved
Shakespeare and Dixon Hill, she had believed he represented a first step beyond all that, a more civilized kind of
human. She had hoped that he could even understand the
necessity of what she had to do. This, all of this, just made
the whole ordeal more painful for everyone involved.

Beside her, Ngalior clenched his big, silver-scaled fists
and shook his head, as discomfited by all this aggression as
she was. "Does he think he can hide from us?"

Shireilil walked around the holodisplay, her child-sized,
green-gold body passing through the miniature nebula. "Ooh!

That tickles. He's firing weapons to ionize the cloud. Thinks it will blind us." Giggling, she took a breath and blew away the static from the image, revealing the ship clear as day within—along with several duplicates. "Here. He sends out decoys." She peered closer at one, clasping it in her long-fingered hands and pulling aside the layers of sensor information. "Merely a tiny drone giving off a false warp signature. These too." With a sweep of her hand, she highlighted all the other fakes, leaving only Picard's proud *Portia*.

"Let's make a point to them," Ngalior suggested. "Rei, clear the air, all right?"

Shireilil giggled again, took another deep breath, and blew, sweeping her arms through the space before her. The ship read her intentions and made reality fit her gestures, its displacement beams sweeping the nebula away for a million kilometers around Picard's ship.

Merthiel gazed down from where he hung on the bars the ceiling had extruded for him, clinging by his prehensile toes and tail. Like Shireilil and several others, he was nude, having discarded the tattered clothing that hadn't healed as their bodies did. "Why not just teleport the android here? We could take him through their shields easily."

"And he would wipe the information before we could retrieve it," Ngalior told him. "Maybe a skilled positronicist could recover it, but we have none in our number."

"Still," Giriaenn said, having second thoughts, "we're no better off if we destroy him. We could capture him, deactivate him until we've carried out our plans. Once he can do no harm, we can revive him."

"Why take the trouble?"

"Ngalior, he is the only one of them who could live as long as us. And the only one who could be neutralized long enough and then revived."

The Manraloth traded looks, reaching a quick, unspoken consensus. It was agreed; they would take Data. "I'll work the displacer," Giriaenn offered. The ship obligingly placed a holocontrol by her hands.

By now, Picard was dodging at warp, firing more stings at the scout. Ngalior lazily dropped the scout in *Portia*'s path over and over, until Giriaenn chided, "Stop toying with them, Ngal. It's cruel."

"Sorry." With a gesture, he had the ship in a tractor beam. The scout was learning with experience, and made no error this time. Another gesture, and their shields were neutralized. Giriaenn squeezed her holocontrol, kneaded its tactile interface, and *Portia*'s warp core materialized in open space a thousand kilometers away. She stroked it once more, and Data and Picard snapped into existence before her with a whipcrack of displaced air. Ngalior stared at her, surprised at the latter inclusion. She told him with a look that it was her own business.

Picard looked around in surprise, but recovered quickly. "What have you done to my ship?"

"It survives, for now. I wanted to give you one more chance. Now that you've seen what we can do, now that you know you have no hope of overpowering us, let us try to convince you to cooperate. If we have your help, it will minimize the need for further loss of life."

He straightened with pride. "Every member of my crew is willing to die to protect the Federation from the self-righteous tyranny you represent. Perhaps you immortals have forgotten this, but there are some things worse than death."

Her fury at his mayfly smugness returned. "And you have no conception of death on the scale we're trying to prevent. If only you could begin to understand!"

Picard shook his head. "No, Giriaenn. It's you who don't understand. This is not your galaxy anymore. This is not a world you know how to cope with. Yes, perhaps we have grown up in more chaos than all of you. Perhaps it has left its scars. But it is our life, our reality, and we have been struggling our way toward solutions to its problems for thousands of years now. You, with your ancient, complacent civilization, you don't even remember what that's like. All you know is how to apply answers someone else already thought of. But those answers are ill-suited to the galaxy you have to live in now."

"The Manraloth began much as you did! We have the knowledge of our ancestors."

"Abstract, musty tomes. You haven't lived it. You've never known war, bigotry, strife, starvation at first hand. Your people bred those out of your galaxy before any of you were born." He shook his head. "And I commend your ancestors for that triumph. But you are too far removed from them. Too old, tired, and decadent. You have no answers for us."

Giriaenn took a breath to argue, but something was nagging at her. Hadn't he just chastised her for talking too much? "You're stalling," she said. "What do you think you're buying time for? There's nothing more your ship can do."

Picard smiled, his eyes on the holodisplay. "There's nothing more it needs to do. Except hold your attention."

Shireilil gasped. "The decoys! They have warped out of jamming range."

Giriaenn's heart sank. "No, Rei. Picard made himself the decoy. Now one of those probes is beaming the whole story to Starfleet, isn't it?"

"Even as we speak," Picard answered. "You've lost, Giriaenn. Starfleet will learn of your sabotage and remove the virus."

Ngalior was still trying to make sense of it. "You had a trick within the trick! You knew we'd identify the decoy probes and think that we'd outsmarted you . . . and you used that to get us off our guard. Impressive!"

"It's an old battle tactic, sir, hardly my own creation. There can be wisdom even the ways of us feral beasts."

Ngalior shook off his moment of admiration. "A wisdom bought at too high a price."

"I do not dispute that," Picard replied. "Which raises the question: What will you do with us now? Are you as peace-loving as you claim, or will you slay us anyway out of spite?"

"He's right, Ngal," Giriaenn said. "There's no point in further violence." She kneaded the holocontrol, and *Portia*'s warp core returned to its cradle, perfectly attached as though it had never been gone. "Go home to your people, Jean-Luc, and we will go in search of ours."

"And what happens when you find them?" he challenged. "What new attack will you launch on my Federation in the name of your version of galactic peace?"

"I don't know what we'll do next, and you couldn't do anything about it if I did. We've reached an impasse, Jean-Luc. So walk away, and live your brief, precious life while you have it."

His eyes were steel. "As long as you remain out there, I will watch for you. I will defend the Federation from you until my last breath, if it comes to that."

"I fear it must, one way or the other. We are patient, and we will simply outlast you." She turned to Data. "Are you sure you don't want to come with us, my friend? A bit more color in your cheeks and you could practically be one of us."

"No, thank you, Scholar Giriaenn," Data replied. "My loyalty is to humanity and the United Federation of Planets. And my . . . friendship . . . was with a person named Ariel. It has now become evident that she never actually existed."

"She did," Giriaenn said with regret. "But all too briefly." She kneaded the hologram again, and Picard and Data popped back to their bridge before they could see the tear glistening in her eye.

# 19

———

**THE DOOR SIGNAL SOUNDED FOR THE THIRD TIME.**
*"Captain?"* Vejar's voice came over the intercom. *"Do I need to call security?"*

After another moment, Picard gave in. "Enter."

The door to his quarters slid open, the light from the corridor knifing into the darkness where he sat. Vejar entered and stopped as she registered the gloom. "All right, then. Good idea. Saves power." She took another step and let the door close behind her, reducing her to a vague dark shape. "We're clear of the disputed zone, sir. Long-range scans showed the Breen investigating the Adonis system, but there's no sign they registered our presence. As Data predicted, the disruption of the nebula dirtied up the local space enough to obscure our ion trail." She paused. "I just hope the Breen leave the platycauds alone. They may be pretty curious about what caused that fresh molten crater. But hopefully the radiation will keep them out."

Picard reflected on that final mission to Adonis II, to retrieve the shuttlecraft and plant antimatter charges that would complete the work of melting the crust, sinking the Manraloth outpost deep into the mantle to conceal its presence from the Breen, just in case any of its damaged technology could still be recovered or reverse-engineered. Data had projected that the resultant breach in the crust would provide the platycauds with a heat source for tens of millennia at least—provided that the small surviving population was able to recover, that is. Conceivably, without the need to fling boulders for warmth anymore, those complex behaviors could be adapted to some other use—perhaps technology. Or perhaps warfare. Either way, Picard knew, it had to be up to them.

Kilif's body remained in the morgue, in stasis until their return to Federation space. The others had all recovered through Doctor Bowman's ministrations, though Jones and Deb'ni had suffered brain damage and the long-term consequences to their careers remained uncertain. But by a tragic fluke, the damage Kilif had suffered from the particle incursions had been in just the right places to be instantly fatal. Picard's letter of condolence to his family—including a wife, co-husband, and two small children, the younger of which was Kilif's—remained in stasis as well, and not simply due to the communications blackout as they fled the disputed territory. So far, Picard had found it too difficult to keep his own anger and betrayal from taking over the letter, distracting his attention from where it belonged, on the family's loss. He needed to remember that. Ariel's—*Giriaenn's, damn it!*—her sin was in forgetting that no single life was disposable, that a death that might be a single, incidental statistic on the cosmic scale of things could still be the greatest tragedy in some child's life. He knew he should be striving to focus on how deeply Kilif's family had cared for him and would miss him. But right now, he could barely find it in himself to care. After what Giriaenn had done, his own emotions felt alien and untrustworthy to him.

"Thank you, Commander," he said after a time. But Vejar still made no move to leave. "Anything else?"

"Sir . . . it's been six days, and you haven't said a word to the crew outside of orders. They're worried about you."

"The only thing they should worry about, Commander, is the performance of their duties."

She took a step closer. "Frankly, Captain, if you want to know what I think—"

"No, Commander. I do not."

After another moment, she snapped to attention in the darkness. "Understood. Sir."

"Dismissed."

She turned smartly and left him to the dark.

## Stardate 37334

". . . And so, for service above and beyond the call of duty, I hereby promote you to the rank of Lieutenant Commander, with all the privileges and responsibilities granted thereto. Congratulations, Mister Data."

Lieutenant Commander Data accepted Picard's proffered handshake. "Thank you, Captain."

Picard gave a polite smile for appearance's sake. He wished it could be just himself and Data, for the android would not be troubled by a lack of faked enthusiasm. But Quinn had insisted on a public ceremony. As Picard stepped aside, the admiral himself moved in to shake Data's hand. "My congratulations as well, Mister Data. You performed beyond anyone's expectations, and it's no exaggeration to say you've saved the entire *Galaxy* class."

"Thank you, Admiral Quinn. Inquiry: Have the remaining quantum code sequences been successfully purged?"

"They're persistent, I'll tell you that. As a matter of fact, Commander Quinteros informed me recently that they plan to scrap the entire software package and rewrite it from scratch. It should delay the launch of the ships by at least another year, I'm afraid. They were hoping to have the *Galaxy* ready to launch for the Bicentennial, but they'll just have to make do without her. Still, they will be launched, and they will be safe, thanks to you." Quinn patted Data on the back. "In fact, my boy, I'm certain there'd be a place for you aboard one of them if you wanted it. You've certainly earned it."

"Thank you, Admiral." He threw a look at Picard. "I do indeed want such a position. However, in the immediate term, I would like to request a science officer posting aboard a research vessel. I wish to gain additional personal and career experience. I will no longer be satisfied with isolated or unchallenging assignments."

Quinn held up his hands, laughing. "All right, all right! You're a go-getter, no question about that. I'll see what can be arranged. I think the *Trieste* has an opening."

"Thank you, Admiral."

After accepting a few more handshakes and platitudes, Data made his way over to Picard, appearing as pleased with himself as an emotionless person could be. "You were right, Captain. Asserting my personal goals and preferences does produce positive results. I have you to thank for teaching me that, sir. And I look forward to applying your lesson to the formation of interpersonal relationships as well."

Picard looked him over. "Don't thank me, Mister Data. You may have been better off the way you were. Emotional involvements are too great a liability. Be glad you can function without them." He left Data standing there, looking puzzled.

After a time, Quinn saw Picard standing on the periphery of the starbase lounge and made his way over. "Jean-Luc, this celebration is for you as well. This mission may have to remain classified, but I'm going to make sure all the top brass knows what you did for Starfleet and the *Galaxy* class. I've recommended you for the short list. Those ships are going to need fine captains when they're ready."

Picard shook his head. "No, Greg. Thank you for the offer, but no. I have other obligations." He drew Quinn further aside from the guests. "The Manraloth are still out there. They're few in number now, but there could be thousands of them still hidden away across the galaxy, with who knows how many other ships and technologies we can't even begin to counter. I have to find them and stop them before they recover those assets."

"Of course Starfleet will take steps to respond to the threat, Jean-Luc. We're reviewing our options now. But you've done your part. You don't have to let this follow you."

"Is there some doubt as to my competence?" Picard asked. "Because I let her deceive me, use me, is that it?"

"Calm down, Captain," Quinn said, a touch of command steel entering his voice for a moment. "No one's blaming you for that, and you shouldn't either. At least, no more than I'm blaming myself. She tricked me too, remember. And I'm a lot older and smarter than you." Quinn offered a smile, but Picard could find none to reciprocate with.

"In that case, Greg, I need to be the one. I know the Manraloth . . . I know Giriaenn . . . better than anyone. We need that advantage. We need every advantage we can get, because they have so many over us."

Quinn studied him. "All right. I believe strong personal incentive can be a good motivator—*if* you don't let it blind your judgment. I'm putting a lot of faith in you if I give you this job, and I won't be at all happy if you let me down. Is that understood?"

"Quite clearly, Admiral. And . . . thank you, Greg."

As Quinn patted him on the back and strode away, Picard reaffirmed to himself that he would not let Quinn down. He knew he was driven by personal concerns, but he also knew he could not afford to let them compromise his judgment or his discipline. He had to become as hard-shelled and unemotional as Data. From this day forth, he must have no desire save the defeat of the Manraloth.

# PART IV

## ABYSM OF TIME

———◆———

2363

# 20

---

CAPTAIN PICARD STRODE DOWN THE CORRIDOR of Starbase 324's administrative section, reviewing the latest tactical updates on his padd as he sipped his morning tea. He passed relatively few people, and as usual they gave him a wide berth, having learned from experience not to get in his way before he'd finished his tea—or at just about any other time.

The news from the frontier was the usual mix. The *Albany*'s captain had successfully brought both sides to the table in the dispute over Betelgeusian argosies' rights of passage through Mulzirak space. Conversely, the far-flung Caitian colony on Kirisha IV continued to be harassed by representatives of something called the Regnancy of the Carnelian Throne, apparently with the goal of enslaving its population. The Starfleet Intelligence operatives on Epsilon Canaris III suspected Klingon renegades were the source of the dissidents' weapons buildup. SI was proving less successful at the other end of explored space, still failing to track down the home territory of the Ferengi raiders or obtain firsthand data on their appearance or genetic profile, despite their implication in several thefts and hijackings over the past few years. And the ancient artifact unearthed on Vemlar IV, which had temporarily given the crew of the *Kyushu* the ability to communicate with their near-future selves and had nearly trapped them in a temporal Möbius loop until they had learned to stop second-guessing themselves, had now been secured by Temporal Investigations and was being shipped to the maximum-security vault where such devices were kept on ice—or so Picard read between the lines, because even at his clearance level, he wasn't supposed to know the facility existed.

All this was the routine sort of business that Picard supervised for Starfleet Tactical's Long-range Threat Assessment and Response Division—monitoring the frontier for signs of trouble, trying to head off crises before they erupted, keeping abreast of new advanced technologies that could endanger the peace, and researching countermeasures to same. Picard had worked hard to assemble a unit equal to those tasks.

The problem was that none of the news related to the core purpose of that unit: to hunt down the Manraloth and stymie them before they could strike again. Despite all Picard's efforts to foster diplomatic contacts with the known civilizations of the Alpha and Beta Quadrants in order to warn them of the threat and solicit information, no solid leads on the Manraloth had emerged in three years. The only thing in recent weeks that had even distantly pertained to them was the Mabrae's latest accusation that the Federation was keeping Manraloth technological secrets from them in violation of a diplomatic accord they themselves had declared void two years before.

Thus Picard was too distracted to respond right away when he heard his name called. He finally noticed it on the second or third repetition. "There you are, Jean-Luc," Marien Zimbata said, catching up to match his stride. "I need to talk to you."

"I'm on my way to see Admiral Hanson."

"This won't take long."

"The *Victory* passed inspection yesterday. Do you have further concerns about the mission?" Picard had spent the past week making sure Zimbata's vessel had been at its peak efficiency, its engines and sensor arrays up to the task of patrolling the Federation's most remote frontiers and scanning beyond them for new black holes, stasis-field echoes, transwarp signatures, or other hints of Manraloth activity. His time aboard the *Constellation*-class ship had been an uncomfortable reminder of the *Stargazer*, but he knew the powerful engines and sensors of the class made it ideal for his purposes.

"More of a personnel matter, Jean-Luc." The captain's large hand on his arm brought Picard to a halt. "I'd appreciate it if you'd stick to terrorizing your own people rather than dragging mine into it as well."

Zimbata kept his tone amiable, but Picard could sense the veiled anger. "All I did was to push your people to make sure the ship was at top efficiency. You do no less yourself."

"There's pushing and then there's browbeating. You could've gone easier on young Ensign La Forge yesterday."

Picard tried to place the name. "You mean my shuttle pilot? The fellow with the visual prosthetic?" He waved his hand in front of his eyes to suggest the shape of the device.

"Yes. The one you tore into about a four percent excess in the shuttle's power demand during acceleration. One that's well within the acceptable margin of error, I might add."

He still wasn't sure what the captain was talking about. "I may have made a passing remark about the inefficiency, but that was all."

"Not the way La Forge tells it. He acted like he was afraid of being drummed out of the service."

"He complained to you about it?"

"No," Zimbata said. "I found out when he came on shift exhausted and unshaven this morning. Turns out he spent the whole night refitting the shuttle's fusion initiators. It's a job that should've taken three hours at most, but he kept re-doing it in the hope of eliminating the very last of that four percent."

That piqued Picard's interest. "How close did he come?"

"He got it up to three percent *beyond* optimal. But that's not—"

"Impressive," Picard said. "And without any sleep? Why are you wasting this man as a shuttle pilot?" If there was one thing Picard admired, it was an officer who didn't give up, who kept at a task until it was complete, no matter the obstacles—unlike some of his staffers, who'd turned to whining about the lack of results and transferred out to assignments that provided more instant gratification. This La Forge sounded like the kind of officer Picard wanted working for him.

"It's not my first choice," Zimbata said. "He has great potential, and he's overdue for a promotion, but there aren't currently any openings on the *Victory*."

"Hmm." Picard thought a moment. An officer with such skills as a pilot or engineer would be wasted at administrative tasks under Picard, unfortunately, but another possibility occurred to him. "I hear the *Hood* needs a new senior flight controller. A post that would require a lieutenant JG at the very least. I could recommend your man to Captain DeSoto."

Zimbata stared a moment and smiled. "That's very generous of you, Jean-Luc. Maybe you're not the Scrooge people say."

Picard allowed himself a tiny smirk. "Humbug," he replied. "I'm simply concerned with ensuring that officers are posted where their talents can be put to the best use."

"Still, I consider it a favor. To him and to me. I've taken considerable interest in the lad's future."

"You can make do without him for now?"

"In fact, we were a bit overstaffed in his department. So it works out for everyone."

"Grand. Now, if there's nothing else, Admiral Hanson is waiting to see me."

The captains made their farewells and Zimbata returned to his ship. A few moments later, Picard was at J. P. Hanson's office, letting the admiral's aide know he had arrived. "Just come in, Jean-Luc," came Hanson's deep, gravelly voice from the inner office.

Picard entered the room, where Hanson was already out of his seat, leaning his stocky frame on the edge of his desk. He stared at Picard with arms folded, his bulldog features stern. "You did it again, Jean-Luc."

"Sir?"

"Scared off another counselor."

"I don't 'scare them off,' J. P. I simply don't have the time to go through the same old runaround."

"The only one running around is you. If you'd just co-operate a little and let them in—"

"So they could tell me what? That I blame myself for setting the Manraloth free? That I'm driving myself to atone for my mistake? That is nothing I don't already know and nothing I have a problem with. If it gets the job done—"

"You don't get the job done by burning yourself out, Jean-Luc. Or by making your staff cower in fear of your wrath whenever anything goes wrong." He smirked. "That's supposed to be my job. How'm I supposed to keep up my tough-guy image when you make me look like a pussycat?"

"Never underestimate the viciousness of a cat," Picard said, remembering how Giriaenn had purred—and quickly shoving the memory aside. "And I could do my job more effectively if you wouldn't keep handing me these distractions. It seems I only just got back from Daran V and now you want me to negotiate with the Alraki warlords? What if the Manraloth make a move while I'm away?"

"You've put a good team together, Jean-Luc. Besides," the admiral went on, rising to his full height, "it's been three years with not a peep from these Manraloth. I can't just leave skilled personnel sitting around waiting for something to happen. You're one of my best people, Jean-Luc. I have plenty of skilled tacticians, but you're a superb diplomat as well. And you've built up an expert team that's been invaluable in defusing a number of serious crises. So what you see as a distraction from your real work, I see as a valuable service to the United Federation of Planets. The other assignments will continue, Jean-Luc. I am not going to let you and your people go to waste just . . . just scanning the horizon for a sighting of your white whale."

Likened to Scrooge and Ahab in the same morning? That was a new record. "You'll need me when the time comes."

"*If* it comes. They're immortal, remember? And they have the whole galaxy to play around in. They may not return in our lifetimes."

"They're after the Federation, J. P. They feel they have to stop us before we advance any farther. They'll be back. I know it." He didn't mention his conviction that Giriaenn would be driven to confront Picard again while she had the chance—that it was as personal for her as it was for him.

"And you won't do the Federation any good if you work yourself into an early grave before that happens." Hanson thought it over. "Maybe you're right—I should get someone else to handle the Alrakis situation. Why don't you take some time off? Take a trip to Risa, maybe." At Picard's fierce frown, Hanson amended, "Or maybe a couple of weeks back home on Earth. Paris in the springtime . . . well, late springtime."

"Thank you for the offer, J. P., but that would simply be a waste of my time."

Hanson furrowed his craggy brow. "You know what the real waste is, Jean-Luc? That you're sitting around behind a desk like me. If—or when," he conceded, "the Manraloth do show up again, it'll take a starship to deal with them, maybe a whole fleet. You should be out there again, on the front lines."

Picard was shaking his head before Hanson finished. "I can do a better job here, where I can look at the big picture. Gather all the information I need to make an informed decision."

"In other words, you made one bad decision a few years ago and now you don't trust your command judgment in a crisis. You're afraid to get back on the horse."

"I simply prefer careful deliberation to acting on impulse."

"That's not the Picard I knew at the Academy."

"That Picard got himself killed a long time ago. I am what survived."

Hanson shook his head, exhaling a frustrated breath. "I hate to see you like this, Jean-Luc. You know they're still holding a seat open for you on a *Galaxy*-class ship. You may have lost the *Yamato* to Don Varley and the *Enterprise* to Tom Halloway, but the *Odyssey* will be ready within a year. And after all the diplomatic and strategic successes you've scored in the past couple of years, she'd be yours for the asking. But if you pass up this one, they may not offer you the next one."

Picard shook his head firmly. "No. Even if I did want a ship again, there's no way I'd take out one with civilians and children on board. It's just too dangerous out there. You and I know that better than most."

Hanson shook his head. "We really don't, my friend. We're not the ones out there."

# 21

---

## A MANRALOTH WALKED INTO A BAR . . .

. . . and thought, *How did it come to this?* Giriaenn looked around her at the raucous multispecies crowd—less diverse in body plan than she was used to, with more manraloids than in her day, but still wildly multifarious—and wondered if she and hers would ever fit into this time. All around her were tones of aggression, pain, intolerance, and ignorance. The unhealthy sexual urges she felt from various quarters, here as elsewhere in the city, compelled her to dress far more modestly than was her wont. Patrons vied with each other in ritualized small-scale combat, and those wagering on the outcome seemed ready to erupt in less structured, more earnest combat if the outcome did not go their way. Many others sought to intoxicate themselves into oblivion, hoping to pretend for a little while that their problems were gone rather than actually seeking help to solve them. Giriaenn wanted to go to them and offer her guidance. But there was little help she could give under the circumstances—not until her people found the means to rebuild their power base in this era. Not until they found the black hole.

It had been a matter of some debate among the survivors after leaving Adonis: whether their first move should be to seek out the nearest black-hole archive and mine it for a way to locate and liberate the other surviving Manraloth, or to track down the two other stasis bubbles whose locations the Organians had provided and hope their occupants had the expertise to free themselves. A few had even been so desperate as to propose traveling back in time to undo the disaster, forgetting or not caring that such an act would eradicate the entire current population of the universe and be an even more heinous crime. The argument had grown rather heated—at least by Manraloth standards—and Giriaenn had realized that the others were beginning to be overwhelmed by the impact of what had happened. For them, it had only been a day since their whole civilization had vaporized around them, and they had not had a buffer period of amnesia to ease their adjustment. For them, the shock was at once more immediate and more abstract, for none of them had seen the modern galaxy as she had.

So she had persuaded them to take some time. Time to mourn those they had lost, and then to witness the galaxy as it was, to learn of its inhabitants and recent history—to understand the pathologies its children suffered so they would truly grasp what was at stake and what was needed to mend things. They had found a vacant planet, a world of great beauty to reassure them such things still existed, and had taken weeks to grieve, to share stories of what they had lost, and to grow together as a family. Giriaenn had made love to them all in turn, and all of them to each other, to solidify the bonds that were now all they had in the universe.

And to do more. All of them were sterile now; immortals had no need to breed, save to replace individuals who had died from violence or chosen to leave corporeal existence. Being alone on this planet, an isolated population too small to survive on its own, should trigger their bodies to begin developing their latent reproductive organs, while frequent copulation and the associated feelings of mutual need and devotion should generate the right hormones and enzymes to nurture the process. This, of course, had necessitated adopting a less ecumenical approach than was normal and favoring partners of the opposite sex; but Giriaenn was somewhat accustomed to that after her time with Picard, since her need to appease his preference for monogamy had precluded her from seeking a proper balance of lovers. Of course it was possible for any one of them to evolve into a hermaphrodite, and in time they all might take turns doing so in order to maximize the number of wombs and genetic pairings available. But that would take considerably more time, so they were starting out with simple heterosexuality. She had found herself gravitating toward Ngalior; he had been the uploaded sentry at Adonis, and they had already begun to bond during their subjectively hasty mental communion. He had responded to her feelings in kind, and she was confident that when her womb finally quickened in another few months, Ngalior would be the father of her first child.

A clamor broke Giriaenn from her reverie. The open conflict she'd feared had begun to erupt at one end of the tavern. She wondered whether she should attempt to intervene, but then the bartender, a brown-complexioned, smooth-featured woman in an extraordinarily large hat, came out from behind the bar wielding a theatrically massive hand weapon and made threatening proclamations toward the fighters. It had the effect of breaking up the conflict, and moments later all combatants were on their way out, with no real harm done.

Still, it was such a crude, dysfunctional way to deal with conflict, Giriaenn reflected as she made her way to an empty booth at the far end of the tavern. And it would do nothing to solve the underlying problems of the fighters or the culture they inhabited. A culture that most of the occupants of this tavern shared regardless of their species, as denoted by the collars they wore: chain-link bands bearing polished oval stones of clear red-orange chalcedony, marking them as slaves of the Carnelian Throne. The ubiquity of those collars on this world and its neighbors had been a shock to Giriaenn at first, until she had sensed what lay beneath the word "slave" in this culture. Now it simply confused her.

The others had been just as confused by this feral age, and Giriaenn had spent weeks on that idyllic world bringing the others up to speed with what she knew about it, supplemented by the scout's long-range sensors, which let them observe other worlds for hundreds of parsecs around as though standing on their surfaces. After seeing the widespread conflict and ignorance, they had quickly reached the consensus that they must regain their role as the galaxy's mentors, and would most likely need to wield a firmer hand this time to keep these unruly children in line. Giriaenn had argued that the archive was key to that goal. The others had agreed, but had still pushed to rescue their fellows first. Twenty-two people and one small ship were not enough, especially in such a dangerous galaxy. The scout may have been far beyond what anyone else had, but they had still wielded it amateurishly and it was not made for battle. If one human with one starship had outwitted them, what might an armada do? They could not afford to let the Manraloth die out again. (Indeed, Merthiel had suggested that it might have already happened more than once. In the hundred million years since sentience had reemerged, surely Jean-Luc Picard had not been the first being to seek and find a Manraloth stasis field. Perhaps others of their kind had been destroyed in failed attempts to open the bubbles, but perhaps others had been retrieved alive and killed by the feral ones who had freed them.)

So Giriaenn had acceded to their logic, and they had gone to the next nearest stasis bubble, eight thousand light-years away in the Crux Arm (she still thought of the galaxy's geography in human terms, for it had been wholly different in her day). Soon after they had found it, though, they were attacked by a powerful force, a biocybernetic hybrid race of a far cruder sort than the Manraloth, traveling in awkward cubic ships. Despite their technological inferiority, they had wielded immense power and a relentless desire to "assimilate" Manraloth technology, while rejecting every attempt at communication and persuasion. Ultimately the damaged scout had broken free and fled, forced to abandon the stasis field. The cyborgs had taken the field into custody, but Giriaenn had not believed they would be able to damage it; the brief contact had made it clear enough that they were only borrowers rather than innovators, and could not wield an imagination on a par with Kathryn Janeway's. They would simply be stymied by the field and eventually dismiss it as "irrelevant." Unfortunately, they had taken the field with them through a transwarp conduit, and Giriaenn had known she was unlikely to see it again before her people had regained the resources to tame such a menace. The presence of such a threatening force in the galaxy had heightened their conviction that they needed to regain their power—and their numbers—at all costs.

The remaining known stasis bubble was nearly a quarter of the galaxy away from there, on the outer edge of the Perseus Arm. They had found it buried in the upper mantle of its now-dead planet, a world in a highly skewed, eccentric orbit around its star—perhaps knocked out of alignment by the galactic turbulence in the wake of the Manraloth's folly. It had taken days to excavate down to it with displacers, using manipulator fields to keep the semimolten pit walls at that depth from collapsing, and lift it to the surface. Unfortunately, no external portion of the facility survived for them to work with. They had made contact with the leading civilization of the region, the Le-Po, and had negotiated to obtain the transporter and other equipment they would need to make contact, as well as the assistance of the Le-Po's leading physicists. This time, they had taken great care before attempting to contact the interior, exploring every possible theoretical permutation they could devise for weeks while the Le-Po had struggled to keep up. They had hit a snag upon discovering that the Le-Po were attempting to employ Manraloth knowledge to develop new weapons. It had been the work of another week to track down everyone with such knowledge and persuade them to allow their recent memories to be erased courtesy of the scout's medical bay, then retire and retreat into lives of seclusion on isolated farming colonies. That had not resolved the problem, though, for the regime that had ordered the plan now wished to take them into custody and extract their secrets more forcefully. With a few words in the right ears, the Manraloth had manufactured a scandal involving corruption and violation of the society's sexual taboos, leading to the downfall of that regime in a mercifully bloodless coup (since Giriaenn herself had spent the previous night with the Chancellor, convincing him to step down without armed resistance).

After that unpleasant inconvenience, the Manraloth had needed to proceed without local help. Achieving no theoretical breakthroughs, they had finally agreed to go ahead with a modification of the strategy used at Adonis. Upon making contact with the severely slowed inhabitants of the bubble, they had instructed them to transfer their consciousnesses and genetic patterns into the base's computer memory, whereupon Giriaenn's party would beam out the computer core as a backup while simultaneously trying to retrieve their live bodies. With time slowed so drastically within the bubble, it had taken over two years of external time for all its occupants to transfer themselves one by one, during which time Giriaenn's party had continued to strengthen their mate-bonding, fended off Le-Po spies (since the new government had turned out no better than the old one), and worked to enhance their transporter's ability to lock onto the maximum number of bodies within the field.

Unfortunately, that last effort had been a mistake. Apparently, the more of a stasis field's contents one locked onto with a transporter, the faster the quantum dissolution proceeded, making it a proposition of diminishing returns. Ronael, operating the transporter, had intuitively sensed this as the field had begun to collapse, and had tightened the beam to retrieve only the computer core. But the damage had been done. Although the core had been able to repair itself afterwards, much of its memory had been lost. Most of the minds and bodies stored within it could probably be reconstructed by data interpolation and then rematerialized by a sufficiently advanced transporter such as the scout's. But the survivors would have impaired memory and mental function, and it was unlikely the non-Manraloth within the core could recover as fully as Giriaenn had.

Besides, where would they live? The scout had no room for over a hundred occupants, particularly ones who would need to be nursed back to health and reeducated. And many of the species in the core had special environmental or dietary needs. It would be irresponsible to restore them before the Manraloth had reestablished a support structure they could work within.

And so the most intact, viable Manraloth in the core—only nine, since there had been relatively few at this facility to begin with—were beamed back to life. But the other occupants remained in limbo. *At least they are free to think again,* Giriaenn thought.

After that, the Manraloth had decided to let the remaining stasis fields wait and concentrate on finding the black-hole archive. But first they had needed to improve their knowledge of the modern galaxy's mass distribution, rebuilding the data Picard had deprived them of. Even with that knowledge, it had proven more difficult than expected to localize the black hole. It seemed that singularities, plunging as deep through subspace as they did, were more affected by its irregularities than normal stars and nebulae, introducing still more error into their long-term orbital calculations. The well-ordered subspace highways that the Manraloth and their contemporaries had woven into the substrate of the galaxy (and the smaller satellite galaxies around it) had grown fragmented and decayed over time, their only remains being various subspace distortions and warps scattered throughout the galactic system, including a chaotic mix of anomalies peppering the Delta Quadrant and a set of interspatial fissures that converged upon the Small Magellanic Cloud like rapids flowing downhill.

The best they had been able to do was to narrow the nearest archive's location to somewhere within the Carnelian Regnancy. But it was a large territory, rivaling the Federation in size, and it was well-patrolled by powerful ships. The scout had long since healed from the cyborgs' attack, but its limited intelligence was wary of further confrontations, and so were the Manraloth. They had decided to infiltrate the Regnancy and win its cooperation in tracking down the archive. This society of conquerors and slavers was not one the Manraloth were comfortable dealing with, but they needed allies and they needed access. Hopefully the Carnelians could be persuaded to accept the same hidden deal Giriaenn had offered the Federation: trading their interest in expansion and conquest for free access to the archive's contents. And a power as strong as the Regnancy might prove useful for keeping the Federation in check.

So here Giriaenn was, a guest on the Regnancy border world of Coteul, befriending the local magistrates in hopes of winning the right to petition the upper tiers of the bureaucracy for their aid. It was proving oddly difficult. The Carnelians (a term that applied to subjects of the Regnancy regardless of species) were wary of outsiders, allowing them minimal rights or freedom of movement—which was why Giriaenn found herself lodging in this unsavory section of Coteul's capital. If anything, it seemed the nominal slaves had far more privileges than outsiders did. In fact, everyone she had met in the local government wore a slave collar, some with gold or silver chain, but all with the same carnelian stone at the front.

"You're wondering about the collars, aren't you?"

Giriaenn looked up to see the bartender standing over her. There was no mistaking her with that extraordinary hat, a yellow disk nearly as wide as the woman's shoulders. She bore the unadorned, neotenous facial structure that many manraloids, including humans, tended to converge upon over evolutionary time, but her scent and body language were distinctly nonhuman, at least to Manraloth senses. She also seemed more mature and seasoned than any human. Giriaenn instantly liked her. "Yes," she replied, noting that the bartender also lacked a slave collar. "As I understand it, slavery is a terrible institution, yet I see no sign of it here. The slaves seem content with their lives, even quite prosperous and successful, despite having to wear a mark of ownership at all times."

"'As I understand it'? You've never encountered slavery before?"

"It was unknown in my civilization."

"Sounds like a nice civilization. I'm Derian, by the way. I tend the bar." Something behind her gentle voice told Giriaenn that Derian was not the woman's real name. But Giriaenn herself had tried out various names during her long life, usually during her sojourns in radically different bodies. Perhaps Derian had simply entered a new life phase and was trying on an identity she wasn't used to yet.

But Giriaenn felt no need to hide her own identity. She had grown tired of doing so in the Federation. "I'm Giriaenn."

"Giriaenn. Nice name. Reminds me of someone I know."

"Who?"

"Oh, nobody. Just someone who likes to listen."

Giriaenn smiled. "And you like to talk?"

"No, I'm a listener myself. Call it a knack of my people. I travel the galaxy, I tend bars, and I listen."

"Sounds like an excellent way to get to know people."

"I think so."

"So what do you know about the Carnelians? How can they be so free when someone owns them?"

"Nobody owns them."

"But they're slaves."

Derian nodded, her hat bobbing alarmingly. "Slaves to the Carnelian Throne."

Giriaenn peered into her eyes. "You don't mean the government."

"No. Can I get you a drink?"

After studying her a moment more, Giriaenn said, "If you bring me a meal—something either replicated or wholly without meat—will you then tell me what you mean?"

"Sure."

Several minutes later, Derian returned with a local vegetarian delicacy and took a seat across from Giriaenn as the latter began to eat. "Once upon a time," Derian said, "on the homeworld of the Regnancy's founders, there was a king. He was the greatest conqueror his world had ever known. But once he'd conquered all the known world and was starting in on the unknown, he was called back to his capital to put down a huge rebellion. See, his armies were spread too thin with conquest, so they were too weak at home to suppress it.

"But the king returned with the might of his army behind him, and they battled the rebels all through the city. The battle raged right into the throne room, and the king fought off hundreds of rebels who tried to reach his throne. It was a magnificent throne, carved from a single enormous piece of clear white chalcedony." Derian furrowed her brow. "I guess quartz was rare on their planet, so they prized it more."

"I understand."

"But so much blood was spilled that day that the red soaked clear through the throne and turned it into carnelian. That's what the legend says, anyway. You'd have to ask a mineralogist if it makes any sense.

"Well, when the battle was won, the king looked around at all the blood that soaked his throne, his palace, his whole city. And he wept at the horror of it. He realized that if he kept on conquering, he'd just end up destroying the world as he knew it.

"So from that day forward, he vowed to use his reign only to do good, to give his people the best life he could. He ruled with law instead of the sword, promoted morality by his own example, used the taxes he collected to improve the cities and roads and hospitals and make things better for his people. And he lived a very long time and became the greatest ruler the world had ever known. And he kept the Carnelian Throne as a symbol, a reminder of what could happen if his rule ever strayed from the righteous path.

"He raised his heirs to be like him, but of course not all of them got it. Eventually they got decadent and corrupt, and the people suffered, and invaders came in and burned down the palace and shattered the Carnelian Throne. And the world went through chaos for a long time, an age of slavery and tyranny and massive bloodshed.

"But something happened after a few centuries. The slavers became so dependent on their slaves in the bureaucracy that the slaves ended up pretty much running the place. Slaves rose to become generals and governors, even conquer other lands and become their emperors, even though they were still technically slaves. And there was one slave empress wise enough to rule with mercy and justice, and so her kingdom became strong and prosperous and kept growing while the mean old slavers back home fell into decay and collapsed a couple of generations later.

"Now, this was a problem for the empress at the time— the granddaughter of the first one—since her authority was based on being the slave of a higher power, one the people would respect. But she remembered the Carnelian Throne and what it had stood for. It was a legend the whole world knew by then, a symbol of justice and righteousness that everyone respected. So with her original slavers gone, she declared herself and her people to be slaves of the Carnelian Throne. They say the collars she and her court wore were fragments of the original Throne." Derian shrugged. "These days they're mostly replicated."

Giriaenn was catching on. "So they weren't slaves to a state . . . they were slaves to an ideal."

"You're getting it. They were slaves to what was right. They had no freedom to disobey the commands of justice and morality and kindness."

"So when people wear these collars," Giriaenn said, "it's a declaration of obedience to law and righteous principles."

Derian nodded. "Which is why those of us without the collars are met with such distrust," Giriaenn went on. "We haven't yet agreed to abide by those principles."

"Right. We haven't yet earned the right to be enslaved."

"But the Regnancy still conquers other worlds. Requires them to submit."

Derian tilted her head, her hat brim almost touching her shoulder. "Well . . . they see it as bringing justice to chaotic worlds. It's more a symbolic conquest, really—at least when people recognize the benefits of 'enslavement' and play along with the rituals. If they fight back, the Carnelians assume they don't value justice and peace, and that makes them a threat that has to be controlled." She shrugged. "Maybe they get a little carried away sometimes, but nobody's perfect. I've lived in a lot of civilizations over the past few centuries, and the Regnancy isn't the best, but it's far from the worst. They mean well, and I figure that's got to count for something."

Giriaenn hoped so, since the Manraloth needed the Regnancy's support. She had to admit, it was a fascinating adaptation: taking something so vicious from their damaged past and turning it around into something constructive. It gave her hope that this strife-torn galaxy was eager for redemption after all. There was even a rough-hewn beauty to this tale of blood and horror.

*No.* She reminded herself that such beauty could be known only from a safe distance, when such horrors were well in the past. There would have been no beauty for those who had suffered and died in the thick of it. Until all such tales were safely in the past, this could not be a beautiful galaxy again.

She studied Derian. "So what about you? Are you hoping to earn the right to be 'enslaved'?"

The bartender pursed her lips and shook her head. "I've always preferred following my own rules. And I don't plan to stay forever. I'm looking for someone interesting to travel with."

Giriaenn smiled. "Is that why you've talked to me so much, my friendly listener?"

"It could be. Or maybe I was just letting you finish your meal." Derian looked her over. "Why don't you talk to me for a while? I have a feeling you'll turn out to be very interesting."

Giriaenn had been right: Guinan had been acting out of character when she had approached the Manraloth woman and told her the tale of the Carnelian Throne. Not because she had told the story; Guinan liked telling stories, though the ones about herself were not always entirely true. What was out of character for her was taking an active role in others' affairs. She would listen to others' problems and try to point them in the right direction to find solutions, but rarely would she take an active role in trying to influence large-scale events. Certainly nothing as large-scale as what the Manraloth planned.

But this time, there was more at stake for her personally. The future was heading in the wrong direction, and if she didn't nudge it back on track, she would lose her own past.

It had been 470 years now, by Terran reckoning, since Guinan had glimpsed her future. She had been a callow youth, fired by the restlessness that overtook many El-Aurians in their early one-hundreds, when she had rebelled against her father and run away from home. Or rather, *migrated* away from home. Guinan had undertaken to circumnavigate the galaxy, spending decades drifting from world to world, paying her way with her listening skills—which generally meant bartending, since she lacked the patience to earn psychiatric degrees on each new world and lacked the temperament (and stamina) for sex work. She had picked up a few husbands along the way, but the marriages had never lasted more than twenty years or so, and then wanderlust had overtaken her again.

Eventually she had made her way from the Crux Arm

across the Carina and then into the puny sliver of the Orion Arm. There, she had fallen in with a group of anthropologists who clandestinely studied life on primitive worlds, tracking their cultures over generations. They told her of one world they had been observing on and off for millennia, ever since learning of it from a group of Sahndaran refugees who had grown enamored of its people. Recently, they had learned that a species called the Skagarans was abducting the planet's natives as slave labor. They had intervened to halt the slave trade and were now conducting follow-up observations of the continent from which the slaves had been taken.

Finding that she could pass as a native of this world, Guinan had chosen to conduct some observations of her own, hitching a ride down to that continent with the anthropologists and going off on her own independent tour of the planet. She had found it difficult to operate on Earth (as it was called by the continent's current occupants) due to the natives' prejudices about her sex and, bizarrely enough, her complexion. She had endured rough treatment in various locales, but had borne it, learned from it, and used her listening skills to adapt and find her way to more tolerant climes. Eventually she had worked her way up to higher society, becoming something of a minor celebrity among the liberal intelligentsia, a symbol of their belief that humans of her coloration could "better themselves" after all. They still often made her feel somewhat like a performing animal put on show as a curiosity, but at least they were trying in their own way. And there were a precious few, like a gruff old writer named Samuel Clemens, who sincerely accepted her as an equal.

It had been in Clemens's company that she had encountered a being even more alien to Earth than herself: a pearl-skinned android named Data, who had recognized her though she had never seen him before. At first she had thought he was one of the operatives her father had occasionally hired to haul her back to the life he had planned for her. But to her astonishment, he had revealed that he came from her future, serving aboard a ship named *Enterprise*. He had been trapped in the past while pursuing alien parasites preying on the locals (what was it about this planet that drew so much outside interest?), and he had sought her help in defeating them.

Guinan's anthropologist friends had been off surveying some other world at the time, though she knew they would be back for her. So she and Data had been left to confront the problem on their own—until Data's crewmates had come back to find him. Their captain had been a striking, bald-headed human named Jean-Luc Picard, who had not only recognized her, but told her they knew each other very well in his time. When Guinan had been injured in a confrontation with the parasites, Picard had risked being trapped in time himself to stop her bleeding. He had saved her life, and told her that she would become very important to him five centuries in the future. She certainly had no doubt that his future was very important to her.

Soon, though, Picard had gone back to his own time, and Clemens had taken Guinan to the hospital. Eventually the anthropologists had returned for her, and she had begun the long migration back home, sobered by her brush with death. She had become immersed in family and parenthood, and as the centuries went on, she had almost convinced herself that her encounter with Picard had been a fever dream.

But then, after another of her bouts of wanderlust a century ago, she had come home to find El-Auria destroyed by a cyborg race, its people scattered. She had joined the survivors in their migration spinward, away from the monsters that had taken their home and families. After three decades spent wandering from system to system, they managed to obtain passage on two ships belonging to the United Federation of Planets. She had learned that the Federation's capital world was the very Earth she had visited centuries before, and she had begun to suspect her memories of Picard had been true.

Then the refugees had run afoul of the Nexus, a turbulent flaw in the weave of spacetime itself. They had almost literally died and gone to heaven, finding themselves in a timeless realm where they could live any life they could ever imagine and make their greatest wishes real. Being "rescued" from that paradise by the Federation's Starfleet, forced to live in harsh, imperfect reality while still vividly aware of the endless joy they had lost, had plunged Guinan and her fellow survivors into a depression so profound that she had barely noticed how familiar the human species was to her, and barely cared.

Eventually she had moved on with her life, giving little thought to her encounter in Earth's past. After the Nexus, where past, present, and future were all one, that single anachronism had no longer weighed heavily in her thoughts. Indeed, she had no longer cared much about anything in this life.

Then, three decades ago, she had met a young Starfleet captain named Jean-Luc Picard and had known it all was real. They had helped each other through a rough situation, and Guinan had been left with no doubt that this was the same man. Seeing him with so much potential yet to be realized, knowing the dignified, poised, and kind man he would become, gave her new (if vicarious) hope for the future. She had taken an ongoing interest in his life, doing what she could to nudge him toward becoming the man she knew he could be, while proceeding gingerly lest she create some sort of paradox and jeopardize her own past. He had come to value her counsel and support, while still never knowing just how much she valued him.

Lately, however, it had begun to go wrong. Ever since the *Stargazer* had been lost, Picard had been straying from his destiny. Perhaps if Guinan had been there at the time, she could have helped him through it. But instead she had come back three years late to find him in civilian life, burying himself in books and old relics. She had tried to revitalize his interest in travel and adventure by offering him an irresistible archaeological prize that would require roving the stars once again.

But her plan had backfired. His quest had awakened the Manraloth, they had betrayed him, and now he was obsessed with hunting them down. Her visits and correspondence with him over the past three years had left no doubt of that. He was back in Starfleet, but as far from captaining the *Enterprise* as he had ever been.

And Guinan knew the time was drawing close. In the past—her past, their future—Data and Picard had been circumspect about the specifics of their time. But the signs were accumulating. In his latest correspondences, Picard's pate was finally as smooth as it had been when she had met him in the past, his remaining monk's fringe nearly as white. Data had become a lieutenant commander three years ago, and the *Enterprise* was months away from launch.

What was more, she had been changed by her Nexus experience. A piece of her had never left that timeless realm, and that lingering connection gave her a special awareness of time. She sensed that the temporal currents around her own worldline were nearing a point of divergence.

But it was clear that Picard would not command a starship again until the Manraloth situation was resolved. Until the threat to the galaxy was averted—and Picard's own faith in his command ability restored.

So Guinan had found it necessary to hasten things along. Calling in some old markers from among the more ancient civilizations she'd encountered in her travels, she'd spent the past year tracking down the Manraloth, eventually finding them en route to Carnelian space. She had visited the Regnancy more than once in her travels, and had friends there who could keep her abreast of the Manraloth's movements and put her in a position to contact them. So it was that she had been tending bar (as "Derian," the name of a daughter lost when El-Auria fell) in the tavern near where the Manraloth had lodged. So it was that the local magistrate had arranged for them to lodge there in the first place.

And now Guinan had begun her efforts to infiltrate the Manraloth as Derian, much as Giriaenn had infiltrated Starfleet as Ariel. She would listen to them, chat with them, and learn what she could. Once she understood them, she would know what to do next. Perhaps, she hoped, to help them work through their problems and join the galaxy as constructive partners rather than benevolent conquerors. Perhaps, if necessary, to undermine them from within and exploit their weaknesses.

Either way, though, the endgame would not be hers to play. It had to be Jean-Luc Picard who made those final moves. He had to come out here, commanding a starship, and take whatever diplomatic or military actions proved necessary to resolve the Manraloth crisis. Guinan would do what she could to give him the knowledge and opportunity he needed. But Picard had to take the decisive action, whether with pen or sword, and rectify the mistake he blamed himself for. Only then could he move on and become the captain he was destined to be.

Guinan had never been so frightened in her life. She had been in danger before, but never had her fate—as well as the fate of so many others—depended so heavily on her taking the right steps. The Manraloth were no fools; their insights into others were much like her own, and they had thousands of times more experience. If she made the wrong move, told too big a lie or pushed too hard at the wrong moment, it would jeopardize everything.

And the odds were not in her favor. The Manraloth could afford to be patient. But Guinan was running out of time.

And so, she feared, was Jean-Luc Picard.

# 22

---

Stardate 40533

DEANNA TROI SAT STIFFLY ERECT AS ADMIRAL
Hanson paged Captain Picard to his office. Once he signed
off and offered her what he no doubt thought was a reassuring smile, she gathered her courage and said, "Admiral, I
must again protest this assignment. A counselor-patient relationship cannot begin with dishonesty."

"I'm not asking you to take him on as a patient, Lieutenant," the admiral replied. "I simply need an assessment
of his emotional state. His fitness to remain on duty."

"Then you should simply order him to submit to an examination."

"I have. Repeatedly. He goes, he lets the counselors question him, and they all come back with the same answer: that
he seems perfectly able to do his job, but they can't dig any
deeper. And I'm not satisfied with that. I don't believe a man
can go on the way he's been going without snapping eventually. And there may be no obvious warning signs. So I need
someone who can get a glimpse beneath his buttoned-down
surface. I need a Betazoid."

"Admiral, it is highly unethical for me to read a fellow officer like that without his consent."

Hanson leaned back and raised his brows. "You see, Lieutenant, that's the advantage of being a junior officer. I'm ordering you to do this, so you're off the hook. The ethical burden falls solely behind this desk."

"I'm afraid I don't see it that—"

"Lieutenant. Did you notice the part where I said it was an order?" His light, avuncular manner receded and his tone grew stern.

"Yes, sir," she said, subsiding. She berated herself for backing down so easily. But what could she do? She was only four years out of the Academy, and she'd spent more than half that time back home on Betazed conducting advanced psychology studies. Sometimes it seemed the only thing anyone valued her for was the empathy she had been born with, rather than the knowledge and skills she'd worked hard to acquire. She strove not to let her insecurities show, not wanting to undermine her patients' faith in her, but as often as not, her attempts at confident reserve simply made her seem uptight or haughty in the eyes of others.

At least her icy reputation helped defuse the lusty emotions that her male (and sometimes female) colleagues tended to emanate around her. Not that she had a problem with such things per se; since Betazoids could not easily conceal such desires from one another, they had developed a relaxed frankness about sexuality out of necessity. But among humans and other less emotionally mature species, sexual interest could get in the way of appreciating a person's other attributes. (Her mother teased offworlders relentlessly about their "pornographic fantasies" toward her, as if that were anything a Betazoid—particularly one as vain as Lwaxana Troi—would be offended by.) And Deanna very much wanted to be appreciated for more than the gifts of her genetics.

"You wanted to see me, Admiral?"

"Ahh, Jean-Luc, come in." Broken from her reverie, Deanna rose to attention and turned to face Captain Picard, self-consciously straightening the hem of the junior officer's skant she wore. The captain was less physically imposing than she'd expected, with a face that she felt would be very warm and gentle if he allowed it to be. His charisma was intense, though, and she could understand his larger-than-life reputation. "I'd like you to meet Lieutenant Deanna Troi. I'm assigning her to your team as a contact specialist. She's got excellent qualifications in xenopsychology, diplomacy, and linguistics." Deanna fidgeted at the admiral's lie of omission, masking her bitterness that he only pretended to commend her for the skills she truly wanted to be acknowledged for.

Picard looked into her dark, irisless eyes. "A Betazoid?"

"Only partly," Hanson replied. "On her mother's side. Her father was Starfleet—Ian Troi. An old friend of Elias Vaughn's, in fact."

"Is that so?" Picard asked, still looking at Deanna. His emotional control was profound for a human, but she felt his suspicion that he was being set up.

She strove to find her voice. "We . . . haven't spoken since I was a child," she elaborated. *Since he came to tell us Father was dead.* "I—I look forward to working with you, Captain Picard," she said, if only to change the subject.

"Yes. Lieutenant, tell me about your Betazoid abilities . . . as they relate to your work as a contact specialist." His gaze went to Hanson over the last few words. "Can you read thoughts?"

"No, sir," she said, sensing the admiral's scrutiny. "Only a . . . limited awareness of general mental state." It wasn't precisely a lie. But she had to resist an urge to fidget with her long black curls.

"No matter," Hanson told Picard. "She gets by just fine. A keen observer, very sharp. Hard worker. You'll like her." Hanson nodded at her. "That's all, you're both dismissed. Go to work," he finished with a grin. She threw a glare back at him as she and Picard left.

Deanna supposed the admiral would expect her to make small talk while trying to probe him for information. But she could find no words, and Picard was evidently content to remain silent as well. Once they had been in the turbolift for several awkward moments, Deanna could not keep her feelings bottled up anymore. "Hold," she called, and the lift came to a halt. "Sir," she said, her heart pounding in her chest, "I'm disobeying a direct order by telling you this, but I have a higher obligation to my profession. What the admiral didn't tell you is that my primary specialty is psychotherapy. I'm a counselor."

Picard sighed. "J. P. . . . I knew it."

"I'm highly empathic. The admiral assigned me to perform a covert assessment of your emotional state, sir." She took a breath, hoping she wouldn't faint from the lightheadedness she felt. "But I simply can't do it, Captain, orders or no. If I'm to be of any help to you at all, then I need to begin from a foundation of complete honesty."

Picard simply studied her for a long moment. Remarkably, she couldn't tell what he was feeling; his control was exceptional. Or maybe she was just too terrified to sense straight. She continued. "For what it's worth, the admiral was truthful about my other qualifications. I would like to work with you as a contact specialist. But if you feel you could use someone to talk to, I'd like to be available to fulfill that role as well. But only if it's what you want. I won't spy on you for Hanson."

The captain's brows went up slightly. "And what will you tell the admiral?"

It would be easy enough to prevaricate, to say that Picard had caught on and sent her away. But there was only one answer she could give the captain. "The truth," she said, holding herself rigid to keep her knees from knocking. "That I could not carry out his orders. That I told you who and what I really am. That my first duty is to my medical ethics and integrity, and if that can't be reconciled with my Starfleet duties, then perhaps he'd better just discharge me," she finished with her chin held high. Sure, it was haughty, but it felt strangely good.

Picard studied her for another moment, then said, "Resume." The lift moved again, and she watched him, waiting for the other shoe to drop. When the doors opened, Picard stepped out . . . and then turned back to the frozen Deanna and asked, "Coming, Lieutenant?"

She forced her legs to move before the doors shut on her, and then strove to keep up with his determined stride down the corridor—toward his offices, she noted. "So tell me . . . *Counselor* Troi," he said. "Just what can you discern about my emotional state? In your professional opinion, am I overworked, overly repressed, or on the verge of a breakdown?"

"It's too early to make a proper assessment, sir . . ."

"You're not making a report, Lieutenant. I'm asking for your opinion. A contact specialist needs to be able to make prompt assessments on the spur of the moment."

"Yes, sir." She evaluated her impressions. "I think that you're very driven. That you keep your emotions under tight rein."

"And you fear they might burst free at any moment?" His tone and aura were jaded, as though he'd heard the assessment before.

"Actually, no, sir." He came to a stop, surprised. She was grateful for the chance to rest. "I sense in you a level of mental discipline and self-awareness I have rarely encountered outside a Vulcan. You are not simply suppressing your emotions, but regulating them. This does create stress, but that stress is managed, kept at a reasonable level—one sufficient to keep you vigilant and intent on your goals, but not enough to threaten your stability. I assume you meditate?"

"Not as such," Picard replied in the most conversational tone he'd used since she'd met him. "I read. I listen to music. I go riding on the planet below. You know horses?"

"I'm aware of them," she said. "Mainly from fiction." Her father had loved the glamorized tales of America's Ancient West and had filled her head with them in the few precious years they'd had together. "So tell me, Captain, when you go riding or listen to music, are you able to put the Manraloth completely from your mind?"

After a moment, Picard shook his head fractionally. "Does that make me obsessed, Counselor?"

Interesting that he called her by her profession instead of her rank. "It makes you single-minded."

"Is there a difference?"

"Yes. Many mental illnesses are simply exaggerated forms of behaviors that can be normal, even healthy. Schizophrenia is an amplification of the imagination that inspires artists and writers. Autism is an extreme form of the rational, analytical thinking that can make great scientists."

"Well, then. It sounds as if I have no need of counseling."

"I didn't say that, sir." He stared at her again. "I said I think you're able to function. But only because of the exceptional discipline of your mind. I can believe a highly trained acrobat can survive a walk across a tightrope without a net. That doesn't mean I think it's conducive to his long-term health if he keeps it up indefinitely."

He sized her up for a moment longer. "I happen to agree with you entirely, Counselor Troi. But perilous times require the willingness to take risks."

"Yes, sir, they do. I know the power of communication, of persuasion. I don't take the Manraloth lightly as a threat."

"That is very wise of you."

"But, Captain . . . don't you think the risks we most need to face are the ones we can least afford to face alone?" At his returning skepticism, she went on. "As I said, you don't have to come to me as a counselor unless you want to. But I can help you by doing the job I've been . . . nominally assigned to do. I'm well versed in diplomacy and crisis resolution. And, Captain . . ." She held his gaze, unflinching this time. "I won't betray you."

He was unreadable, even to her. "You've studied my file."

"I'm very good at my job."

No change showed on his face, but she sensed a burst of amusement from inside him, and she knew it was all right.

"Come along then, Lieutenant," he said, striding forward once more. "We have work to do."

She hurried to follow. "And the admiral?"

"I'll take care of it," he said simply. But the surge of righteous anger she sensed—the wave of protectiveness on her behalf—left her blinking away tears.

Picard glanced over as Lieutenant Troi returned from the aft section of their long-range shuttle, still adjusting the sparkling headband she used to hold back her long, curly hair. During the talks on Epsilon Canaris III, she'd adopted a more severe style, her hair pulled back in a tight, austere bun. Now she had returned to her more wonted style, one that Picard privately allowed himself to admit he found far more appealing—although he refused to allow himself to pursue that line of thought any further. *It was purely an aesthetic assessment,* he assured himself.

Troi gave him a polite smile as she resumed her seat, but said nothing. After a moment, he said, "You've been awfully quiet since we left."

After a moment, she replied, "The truth is, I'm a little embarrassed. I'm supposed to be your adviser on alien cultures, but the way you dealt with those renegades . . . You showed insights into Klingon culture that I've never even heard of."

"It's nothing, really," he told her. "I used to know a couple of people who were raised within Klingon society."

"The Asmund sisters. From the *Stargazer.*"

"That's right. Anything I know about Klingons, I learned from them."

"Still, you wielded that knowledge brilliantly. And averted a second Canarian war."

He waved off her praise. "I just wanted to get this nonsense over with so we could get back to our real work."

Troi peered at him. "Why do you do that?"

"Excuse me?"

She was already shifting into what he thought of as her Counselor Mode. "You're so quick to embrace blame and penance for your failures—and yet so reluctant to reward yourself for your successes."

"Would you rather I were arrogant and cocky?"

"I'm not talking about arrogance, sir. I'm talking about letting yourself be happy when you've done well at something."

"I am pleased," he said, "that no more lives will be lost due to sectarian violence on Epsilon Canaris. That is ultimately all that matters."

"So it's not about you."

"Certainly not."

"Then why are you so insistent that you have to be the one to solve the Manraloth problem?"

He glared at her. "I thought we agreed—you wouldn't try to counsel me."

"I'm sorry," she lilted, not even pretending sincerity. "I was just trying to make conversation. It's going to be a long trip back."

She fell silent, leaning back in her seat and nonchalantly examining her nails. After a while, despite his better judgment, he found himself saying, "Who else could it be, Counselor? No one knows the Manraloth as well as I."

She was unconvinced. "That's your explanation for why other people need it to be you. I'm asking why *you* need it to be you."

He threw her a sidelong glance. "The fact that I unleashed them in the first place isn't explanation enough?"

"Well, it's the obvious one. A bit *too* obvious, if you ask me. And awfully convenient."

"Convenient."

"Yes—something you can whip out on demand, a confession you can use to show the Starfleet counselors that you're aware of your emotional stake in all this and are able to manage it in a mature and healthy manner."

"And you don't believe I am managing it?"

# CHRISTOPHER L. BENNETT

"Oh, you're certainly managing *that* well enough. That's what I told you the day we met, and that's what I told the admiral." Picard remembered that meeting, and the heated talk he'd had with Hanson afterwards. To his credit, Hanson had actually been impressed that Troi had defied his orders and stood by her principles—though Picard wondered if Hanson would have felt the same if Troi hadn't essentially achieved what he wanted in the process.

Picard waited for Troi to fill in the corollary to her statement. But she had gone quiet again, idly studying the readouts on the copilot's console before her. He knew she'd trapped him, but he gave in anyway. It would be a long trip, after all. "All right, Deanna. What do you believe I am *not* managing?"

She studied him for a moment. "I don't think you're able to accept the idea of failure."

He was taken aback. "Excuse me? I've spent every day for the last three years coping with one of the biggest failures in human history. I know all too well when I fail. Because when I fail, Counselor, I fail big."

"You sound almost proud when you say that. As if a more ordinary scale of failure were somehow beneath you."

"What are you talking about?"

She leaned forward. "Captain . . . I didn't say you can't accept the reality of failure when it happens. But it hasn't happened very often in your life, has it?"

"I've had many failures."

"And you can list and enumerate every one, can't you?"

"I certainly can. I failed the Starfleet entrance exam my first try. I nearly lost my life to a gang of Nausicaans through my own arrogance. I failed to save the research outpost on Chemenek IV. I lost many valued officers on the *Stargazer,* and then lost the ship itself."

"Exactly. The events we remember most readily are the exceptions to the pattern of our lives. And the pattern of your life is one of ongoing success at virtually everything you try. You were a star pupil in school, earning exemplary grades. The Starfleet entrance exam was your first setback, but you went back and fixed it the next year. And you were a standout pupil there too. You were the first freshman ever to win the Academy marathon. You were popular and admired, particularly among women. You were such an outstanding archaeology student that Professor Galen himself asked you to be his protégé."

"You have done your homework." As he said it, though, he realized he had told Troi quite a lot about himself in the past six weeks, even without her actively trying to counsel him. Despite her often stiff manner, she had a quality that made one want to open up to her. And her behavior on that first day had done much to win his trust. He was only now realizing the extent of that trust. Without it, he would never have let her get even this far.

"You could've had your pick of careers," Troi went on, "but you stayed in Starfleet. You took command of the *Stargazer* when her captain was killed, you triumphed over everyone's doubts, and you led that crew for twenty-two years. You took a sabbatical and, as a mere doctoral student, managed to unearth one of the great mysteries of the galaxy."

"Your point, Counselor?"

"Most of your life has been defined by a pattern of success. Especially in your early life. The patterns laid down in our youth tend to set our expectations for the rest of our lives."

"So you're saying I expect to succeed at everything?"

"No, of course not. You've certainly been tempered enough by life to know better." That, at least, he could agree with. "But I think your life experience has conditioned you to see success as a normal state of affairs. To feel . . . not so much that you're entitled to succeed, but that your success is simply the way things *should* naturally be. That's why you don't treat it as something worthy of celebration—because it's nothing more than living up to your minimal expectations about yourself."

"How is that not the same thing?"

"Because you assume that your awareness of the possibility of failure will enable you to ensure it doesn't happen. Or at worst, if you do fail, that you'll be able to learn from it, go back, and fix it. You see failure as an aberration that must be undone, a state of affairs inconsistent with the way your life is meant to be. And so you keep striving to correct it until that cognitive dissonance is resolved."

"You make me sound like a raging narcissist."

"No," she said, dismissing it after a moment's thought. "Just a man who holds himself to impossibly high standards. Narcissists always blame external factors for their failures and refuse to believe they did anything wrong. You not only accept but embrace responsibility for your failures, because you feel that the only way to restore the natural order of things is if *you* do it over and get it right this time. To take the second chance you deserve, in order to get the result you know you're capable of."

Picard stared at her, bewildered by her analysis. "Is it so unhealthy to be determined to make amends for one's failures?"

"Not necessarily. That determination enabled you to pass the Academy exam the second time, and to save the *Stargazer*'s crew after the ship was crippled. But what happens when the failure is one you can't possibly do anything to change? If you can't let go of those, you'll never stop punishing yourself for them. You'll just keep driving yourself to fix something that's beyond your ability to fix, and feeling responsible when you can't."

She gave him a sad smile. "Your problem isn't that you evade responsibility for your failures. Your problem is that you take responsibility, not only for the failures themselves, but for your failure to undo those failures. And if there is no way to undo them, that becomes a vicious cycle that can trap you."

"Are you saying I am obsessed with the Manraloth after all? That it's a futile effort?"

"I hope it isn't. Someone has to counter their plans, and I

feel very safe knowing that Jean-Luc Picard is taking on that responsibility. I do think you have too little faith in your ability to make decisions in the heat of a crisis, but so long as you remain in a desk job, that isn't a serious problem.

"But the very real possibility exists that the solution to the Manraloth crisis will not be found in your lifetime." She reached out and touched his arm briefly. "You still have the potential to do so much with your life. Are you ever again going to open yourself to those possibilities?"

They held each other's gaze for a moment longer. But then he turned away. "I appreciate your concern, Counselor. But you're off the mark here. I've never 'expected' to succeed. When I succeed, it's because I do the work—and get lucky. I've simply had a healthy share of good fortune in my life—along with no small abundance of bad fortune.

"I persist in pursuing the Manraloth because I am convinced that Giriaenn will not be willing to wait a human lifetime. She has an . . . investment in me, Counselor. She believes fanatically that she is right and she feels it necessary to try to persuade me of that.

"And there's a more basic factor. It won't take long for the Manraloth to find their black-hole archive. They may have found it already for all we know. And once that happens, they will consider themselves invincible, and they will be back.

"So yes, Counselor. The Manraloth will strike within my lifetime, and probably within the decade. That and that alone is the reason for my urgency."

Troi did not look wholly convinced, but she declined to press the issue. "If you say so, Captain."

"I do. Now let us hear no more of this." He went to the replicator to conjure a cup of tea, and wondered if perhaps his trust in Deanna Troi had been misplaced.

But her words continued to trouble him for the rest of the trip.

# 23

---

AFTER SIX CENTURIES OF LIFE, GUINAN WAS NOT prone to impatience. But the days of waiting for Picard at the Kartikeya outpost were an exception to the rule.

Partly it was the view. Kartikeya's night sky was dominated by the cluster of juvenile blue supergiants that humans called the Pleiades. From this angle, the cluster was stretched into a band across half the sky. It was so close that when one's eyes adjusted to the darkness, one could see the wispy reflection nebulae around the Pleiades, an ethereal blue river flowing across the heavens. For most people, it was a spectacular sight. But it reminded Guinan too much of the Nexus.

Mainly, though, she was eager for Picard to arrive so she could pass along her message and put him on track toward resolving matters with the Manraloth. But Kartikeya was out on the rimward fringe of the Federation proper, its closest outpost to Carnelian territory, so it had been the most convenient meeting place. She had summoned Picard while still en route, and he had almost refused, citing the demands of his work. But she had stressed the urgency without going into detail, and finally he had relented, saying, "But only because it's you."

Picard finally arrived on the *Cybele*, an *Ambassador*-class starship, but only as a passenger. When she beamed aboard the ship, he met her in its transporter room and clasped her hands warmly, saying, "Guinan. It's been far too long."

"I'm glad to see you too," she replied. "And I'm glad you're still glad to see me. Seeing as how I'm the one who sent you after the Manraloth in the first place."

Picard shrugged that off. "You couldn't have known what would come of that. I can't hold that against you."

"That's good to know," she said. "Considering what I have to tell you. Is there somewhere we can talk? Does this ship have a bar?"

He smirked. "The observation lounge will have to do. Come on."

"Well, all right," she said, following him out the door. "But they really should think about putting bars on starships."

Soon they reached the lounge. Mercifully, the ship's current orientation placed the windows away from the Pleiades, so only an ordinary starscape showed beyond the planet's rim. "So," Picard said once they were seated. "What's this urgent news you have for me?"

"It'll take a little time to explain." He nodded, encouraging her to go on. "Do you know of something called the Regnancy of the Carnelian Throne?"

Picard searched his memory for a moment. "Yes. They're an imperialist power, out near the Alpha Persei Cluster."

"A lot farther, actually. At least the core worlds are. But they have some remote colonies in that area, I think."

"As do we. At least one, a Caitian colony called Kirisha. It's been subject to repeated harassment by the Carnelians."

"Sorry to hear that." Guinan shook her head. She was wearing a smallish traveling hat today, so the gesture didn't create much turbulence. "The Carnelians can get a little overzealous at times, but their intentions are good."

Picard stared. "Guinan, they're trying to enslave the colonists."

"Well, that's a long story."

"Is this why you summoned me here? Something to do with the Carnelians?"

"Indirectly," she said. "The Regnancy is the place where I tracked the Manraloth to."

Picard jolted forward in his seat. "They're there now? Are you certain?"

She nodded. "I met them myself. They're good people, really. Just a little overzealous, like the Carnelians."

"Guinan, listen to me carefully. The Manraloth are very cunning and manipulative. They can influence your thinking—"

"Picard." She threw him a look. "I'm a listener, remember? I can hear what's going on behind people's words. The few times they tried to play me over the past few months, I made it clear I wasn't falling for it. Eventually they stopped trying. Realized I could do them more good if they were straight with me."

Guinan trailed off, realizing that Picard had grown very still. He had a look that she'd never seen in his eyes before. "Are you telling me," he said very slowly, "that you have known of their location for *months* . . . and did not tell me? That you have actually lived among them . . . done things for them? What have you done, Guinan?"

"What I always do. I listened. I let them tell me about their problems, and I offered a little friendly advice."

"Do not make light of what they represent," he snapped. "The magnitude of their 'problems' and their intended solutions is beyond anything we have ever faced."

"If there's one thing I never make light of, it's the value of talking through your problems with a good listener. It's usually a lot cleaner than the alternatives. Gets a lot fewer people killed."

"So, what, then? You believed you could counsel the Manraloth out of their fixation on destroying the Federation? They're fanatics, Guinan! Absolutely convinced of the rightness of their cause."

"They're the survivors of a race that destroyed its own universe. They're lost and desperate and full of pain, and they're looking for a way to fix it. You of all people should be able to relate to that."

His gaze was cold. "I have never tried to sabotage a fleet of starships. I have never condemned a species of intelligent animals to the brink of extinction."

"You've never seen all life in the galaxy wiped out before, either. Can you know what effect that would have on you?"

"Surely you're not condoning what they did."

"Of course not. But they regret it too. Giriaenn most of all." Picard visibly winced at the name. "She was probably more than a little insane after her memory flooded back. Anyone would be, after that. At the time, she thought it was the only way to prevent the disaster from happening again. She sees now how irrational that was."

"Does she?" The words were armored.

"We've had a lot of long talks across the bar. Not just Giriaenn, but the others too. All they want is to protect the galaxy. I . . . suggested . . . that since the Federation wants the same thing, they'd be better off if they worked with you instead of against you. If you keep fighting each other, it'll just take you both farther from your goals."

"And how did they respond to this . . . suggestion?"

She spread her arms. "You're looking at it. They sent me to arrange for peace talks. They want to meet with you."

"Do they."

"Don't misunderstand—it took me some doing. They still have trouble trusting people so young. And they're so close to reaching their archive—"

Picard barely stayed in his chair this time. "They've found it? One of the black holes? Another thing you conveniently neglected to tell me?"

"I was getting to it. There's an archive somewhere in Carnelian space. They've been negotiating with the Carnelian government for help in accessing it."

"They're in collusion with the Carnelians?"

"I wouldn't call it collusion. They could just go in and take it, but they prefer gentle persuasion."

"Until they don't get what they want." Picard rose from his seat and paced before the windows. Guinan noticed that the haze of the Pleiades was beginning to drift into view. "I never took you for a fool, Guinan."

She stared. "And I never took you for one. I know what I'm doing. I've been listening to them for months."

"And they're using you! Just as they use everyone, and discard them once they're done."

"They care about our well-being."

"Like they'd care for a pet. Not an equal. We're ephemeral creatures to them, Guinan, dead before they blink an eye. 'As flies to wanton boys are we to the gods. They kill us for their sport!' You can't forget that!"

"So you won't even give negotiation a chance?"

"How can I, when by your own admission they're negotiating to give advanced knowledge to a hostile power?"

"They promised me they wouldn't share the archive with the Carnelians until they reach an agreement with the Federation. They want to negotiate an arrangement for sharing the knowledge freely with everyone."

"You're a fool if you believed that. The Carnelians are their next weapon against us. Once they have the archive and the technologies it contains, the Federation will be enslaved within months. Our desire to expand and *connect*," he said with a sarcastic scowl, "will be thwarted, and life in the galaxy will be safe."

"You're wrong, Picard. Wrong about the Manraloth, wrong about the Carnelians. They're not tyrants. The whole 'slave' thing, it's a metaphor."

"A metaphor. One they impose through force of arms. They have emplaced *mines* around the Kirishan settlements to cut them off from their livestock and starve them into submission!"

"They probably see the colonists as a threat. They think the people are oppressed by their leaders and they want to wear the system down." Given how passionate Federation people were about democracy, Guinan thought, they wouldn't have been too open-minded about the Carnelians' symbolic conquest and enslavement. And the Carnelians would've taken their resistance as a rejection of the justice and righteousness that the Throne represented, and concluded that the colonists were enemies of justice. "It's a misunderstanding, Picard. And not the only one that's going on here. I asked you here because I thought you'd be the right person to negotiate with these people and work things out. Because I trust you to do the right thing."

His eyes burned her. "You dare to speak of trust? The one person in whom my faith has never wavered . . . and now you tell me this?"

She came to her feet, coming closer and holding his gaze. "I know I'm asking you to take a leap of faith here. But it's one you need to take. For you. For me. For everyone. If you've ever trusted me about anything, Picard . . . trust me now."

Their eyes met silently for a long moment more. But then his head shook fractionally. "You are a stranger to me."

He strode past, leaving her speechless. "Picard to security. Please send an escort to the observation lounge."

The voice of the *Cybele*'s captain came over the comm. *"This is ch'Regda, Captain. Is there a problem?"*

"I want our guest confined to quarters. I believe her to have been co-opted by the Manraloth."

A pause. *"You have evidence of Manraloth activity?"*

"Guinan has confirmed that they are present in Carnelian space." At least he hadn't said "confessed." "Get me Starbase 324, Admiral Hanson, Priority One."

*"Acknowledged."*

The security escort arrived, and Picard pointed to Guinan. "Confine her to quarters."

They moved toward her, but she held her ground, staring at Picard. "If you think I'm such a security risk, drop me back on the planet."

He shook his head. "I want you where I can keep an eye on you. Now, will you go quietly?"

"I might as well," she said, striding forward with dignity and allowing the guards to flank her. "I don't think things are going to stay quiet for much longer."

Supervisor Runac came up to Giriaenn and bowed his elongated, bovine head, a gesture not generally extended to those not "enslaved" to the Throne. "Emissary Giriaenn. My humble self has received news from those who serve Emissary Guinan's transport. They have delivered her to the Federation outpost and are now returning."

"Thank you, Runac." He bowed again, twitching his small, high ears. In her months here, Giriaenn and the other Manraloth had worked their way up the bureaucratic ziggurat and won the status of special emissaries, with some help from Guinan and her connections. The need for the "Derian" facade had fallen away before long. Giriaenn had recognized very early that the friendly Listener had some agenda and foreknowledge motivating her, and had suspected she was an agent for the Federation. But she had also sensed that "Derian" meant no harm and had allowed her to come clean at her own pace. As it turned out, she had merely been an independent party interested in peace. Giriaenn had no problem with that. And she, Ngalior, and many of the others had been genuinely moved by Guinan's words about the rewards of joining the galactic community rather than seeking to dominate it. Force was never a desirable option, and the Manraloth welcomed alternatives.

Runac made a low rumble in his sinus cavity, a nervous gesture in his species, the Gororm, who dominated the bureaucracy of the Regnancy's coreward reaches. "With respect, Emissary, would it not have been better for the couriers to wait and return with the Federation representatives?"

Giriaenn smiled. "You're concerned about being in the position of strength. You don't want them to come in their own ships."

"I humbly beg forgiveness, but yes. They are a warlike people, contemptuous of proper ritual. Their colony is a wild element intruding on our border, and they have shown themselves unwilling to be tamed."

Giriaenn patted his heavy, hooflike hand. "Don't worry, Runac. Soon you will have the wisdom of the ages at your disposal, once we achieve interface with the black-hole archive. The Regnancy will then be stronger than any rival."

He worked his low-slung jaw. "Perhaps. But as you have told us, it will take time for our humble selves to access and wield that wisdom. Therefore I fear I must advise you: if the Federation comes in force, we will have a fleet poised to counter them. The Regnancy must protect its slaves; that is our sacred duty to the Throne."

"No, there's no need for rash action. Guinan assures me she can persuade Picard to come in peace. Even if she fails and he comes in force, simply knowing that you have the archive should deter them."

"But we do not have it yet. Not until the ion storm clears."

Giriaenn winced internally. The storm was a frustration, a petty obstacle so close to their goal. Normally the scout ship's displacers could scatter any such phenomenon, but this one was particularly intense. The black hole had recently passed between a pair of blue stars less than a twentieth of a light-year apart, at an unfortunate angle that had taken it close to both stars in turn. Its magnetic field had clashed with theirs to produce intense turbulence that had ripped huge gouts of ionized gases from their atmospheres, and the plasma now roiled in a fierce, unstable vortex around the hole. As the gravitationally compressed gases were accelerated through the hole's magnetic field lines, they generated intense heat and radiation far beyond that of a typical ion storm. Worse, the black hole still dragged the blue stars' field lines out behind it, building up a huge magnetic potential at their tautest point, around the hole itself. This fired up the plasma to even more tempestuous extremes, spilling out gouts of high-energy exotic particles from strange quarks to verterons. The scout ship had the technology to disperse such energies in principle, but for a storm of this intensity it would take considerable time and would drain the small vessel severely. It would still be a few weeks—enough time for Picard to arrive. And Runac had a point; Giriaenn could not be entirely certain he would come in peace.

Still, it didn't matter. "They don't need to know that," she told the Gororm-Carnelian. "Like the Throne itself, what matters is the symbol. That should keep them at bay long enough for the symbol to become a concrete reality. Then you will be powerful enough to protect all the Throne's servants from the Federation or any other threats. And the Federation will learn the wisdom of giving themselves in service unto the Throne, so that they may gain the knowledge and power that we give unto it, and the peace and justice that it provides."

Runac clasped the stone in his collar and bowed. "We serve the Throne in all things."

"And the Throne is peace," she replied. Runac nodded acknowledgment and left.

*Peace,* Giriaenn echoed. It truly was all she hoped for now. Guinan was right about one thing: she had come to rue that first, mad scheme to sabotage the *Galaxy* class. True, the Federation still needed to be turned from its reckless expansion. But there was no need for rash and violent methods to achieve that goal. It would still be many generations before the crisis point was reached, and the Manraloth would have plenty of time, once they had the archive to tell them how to free the rest of their people. The archive itself, along with its sisters elsewhere in the galaxy, would be all the leverage they needed. The Federation might have rejected the prize at first, but the Carnelians and others would accept it. They would grow strong and content with the fruits of that prize, and then the Federation and other holdouts would have to subscribe to the archives as well if they wished to avoid being overshadowed. The galaxy would be tamed without any need for sabotage or murder. How could she have been so corrupted, so twisted by grief and shock, that she could not see that?

*No doubt because I lacked the companionship of my own people,* she thought, laying a hand on her belly, where she could feel the regrown womb inside. *Soon,* she told herself. Her body was now ready to conceive a child, and once matters were resolved with the archive and Picard, then she and Ngalior would have the time to make it happen. *And my children will grow up in a galaxy at peace. I will make sure of that.*

She simply hoped Jean-Luc would not get in her way. True, what she sought could be accomplished without mass murder. But if Jean-Luc pushed too hard against the advance of history, he might get himself crushed under its wheels. And those wheels might well be made of carnelian.

# 24

---

THE ALPHA PERSEI CLUSTER HAD A LEGITIMATE claim to being the most important place in the explored galaxy. Over thirty million years in the past, a massive burst of star formation had begun in the region, giving birth to the cluster. The intense outbursts from those forming stars, and the supernovae of the hottest, shortest-lived ones, had compressed the surrounding interstellar medium and triggered more star formation. The chain reaction had propagated outward and continued to the present day, creating much of the modern geography of the central Orion Arm: the Pleiades, the Orion Nebula, the Gum Nebula, the Antares Maelstrom, even the micronebula cluster near Adonis. Moreover, as those waves of star formation and supernovae had swept through the region, they had caused ecological catastrophes on countless worlds, wiping out old species and paving the way for new ones to adapt and evolve. Not long after the wave passed near Earth, the first hominids had emerged. Much the same could be said for the ancestors of Vulcans, Andorians, Klingons, and various others.

In recent times, however, the cluster had loomed less prominently on the cosmic stage. No great interstellar power currently claimed the region, and no major natural cataclysms were expected until Mirfak, the yellow-white supergiant at the cluster's heart, went supernova in a few million years. Now, though, it might become a nexus of galactic change once more. For it was at Mirfak that Picard assembled his fleet prior to advancing on Carnelian space. And it was at the Kirisha system on the far edge of the cluster, where the farthest tendrils of Federation and Carnelian expansion met, that they would no doubt meet the Regnancy and attempt to stop them from accessing the Manraloth archive.

Of course, Picard's orders from Admiral Hanson were to achieve that goal through diplomatic means if at all possible. The fleet was a precaution and a show of strength. But Picard knew the allure of the Manraloth's promises and expected to meet resistance from the Carnelians. Unless he could win their cooperation, it would be necessary to seize the black hole and defend it militarily—essentially occupying a portion of Carnelian territory. Hanson had been loath to authorize such a mission, reminding Picard of the quagmire it could open up. Rarely in history had any armed occupation gone smoothly. But the continuing reports of Carnelian attacks and minings of the settlements on Kirisha had helped persuade Starfleet Command that the Regnancy could not be allowed to gain the advanced knowledge of the archive, particularly if the Manraloth intended to help them wield it against the Federation.

If it came to a fight, the *Cybele* and its fellow *Ambassador*-class vessel *Thelian* would be the heavy hitters of the fleet, along with the two massive *Excelsior*-class ships, *Tecumseh* and *Malinche*. Marien Zimbata's *Victory*, already in the region on frontier patrol, offered more speed and endurance than raw power, as did the midsized *Korolev*-class cruiser *Puttkamer*. The final ship, the *Nautilus*, would help compensate for their limited firepower, bearing the rollbar weapons pod of the "classic" *Miranda* configuration, while sharing their advantages of speed and maneuverability.

Once assembled at Mirfak, the fleet set out at high warp for Kirisha. As they drew closer to the disputed system, Picard went to Guinan's quarters more than once to seek information about the Carnelians' likely strategies and weaknesses. But she refused to cooperate. "I could talk," she said, "but you wouldn't listen, so what's the point? You've made up your mind that anyone who associates with the Manraloth is the enemy."

"I'm not eager for combat, Guinan. I'll avoid it if at all possible. You know that about me."

"I know that about the Picard I met a long time ago. But you're letting obsession turn you into someone else. You're on the wrong path, Picard. And you've got to turn back before it's too late."

"You were the one who wanted me to come."

"But not with a warfleet behind you! I came looking for the diplomat, the explorer. He's the man we need now. The man *I* need. And I know you can still be that man."

"I'll be happy to," he told her. "Once the Manraloth are stopped. Until then, I simply do not have that luxury."

"If you go ahead with this, all you're doing is proving them right about us."

"They *are* right, Guinan. We modern mortals are not the placid, domesticated breed they know. We are fierce, unruly creatures. Give us power and some of us will use it to turn on our neighbors. And that is why any attempt they make to tame and enlighten us will only breed turmoil and force them to crack down harder. Far from elevating us, it will drag the galaxy down and them with it. That is why we must stop this before it starts."

"Then stop it. Here and now. Send the fleet home, come to them with me, and *convince* them."

"Try to beat them at their own game? I wouldn't have a chance. Our only advantage over them is our legacy of blood. And if blood is what it takes . . . then 'my thoughts be bloody, or be nothing worth.' "

Once the fleet arrived at Kirisha, they found an array of Carnelian warships awaiting them on the fringes of the system's Oort cloud. Picard ordered his fleet to a halt one AU out from the arbitrary border those ships defined, spread out enough to prevent the Carnelians from attempting an englobement. Then he accepted their hail.

The commander who appeared on-screen was a fierce-looking humanoid, his tall, bullet-shaped head bearing a solid bony carapace over his face, forehead, and crown, with textured blue-gray skin exposed on his chin and temples. Picard recognized him from intelligence reports as belonging to a species called the Brunyg. He wore a silver chain-link collar with a large red gemstone at the throat. *"I am Kunrud, Admiral of the Fifth Regnancy Fleet and loyal servant to the Carnelian Throne,"* he declared in a gravelly baritone. *"Your uninvited approach in force constitutes an act of aggression against the Throne. Cease your advance here, or we shall be forced to defend our territory."*

Captain ch'Regda, still in command of the *Cybele,* turned to Picard and nodded, deferring to him as commander of the task force. "I am Captain Jean-Luc Picard, representing the United Federation of Planets," he said, stepping forward. "We are here to apprehend members of a race called the Manraloth. They are wanted for acts of terrorism against the Federation, and their objectives pose a grave risk to the security of the galaxy as a whole."

*"The Manraloth are our allies and benefactors!"* Kunrud boomed. *"Unlike you, they have taken steps toward the Throne with all proper deference and patience. They have proven themselves friends of the Regnancy."*

"They have misled and manipulated your leaders. They possess great powers of persuasion which they employ to deceive and suborn others. I know they have offered you access to an archive of knowledge stored in a black hole within your territory. I assure you, what they offer is merely the bait in a trap, a lure to make you dependent upon them. They are as much a threat to you as they are to us."

*"You simply fear the Regnancy will gain the wisdom of the archive and use it to check your imperialism! You are already too late for that, Captain."* Thus Kunrud confirmed Picard's certainty that the Manraloth had lied to Guinan about holding the archive in reserve.

"We are prepared to show you proof of the Manraloth's duplicity. We ask that you escort us to their location and help us take them into custody."

*"And if we do not?"*

He paused. "We will do whatever is necessary to contain the Manraloth threat."

Before the admiral could reply, he was distracted by a signal from behind him. He moved away from the screen, revealing a bridge with an extraordinary centerpiece: a large, domed tank containing what appeared to be a large cephalopod organism inside, its tentacles blurring as it operated an array of controls along the tank's inner edges. It flashed intricate color patterns on its surface, which the bridge crew seemed to be reading like status displays. *A galley slave,* Picard concluded. *Bound in service as a part of the vessel itself.*

Kunrud studied one of its chromatophoric displays for some moments before turning angrily back to Picard. *"Your claims of benevolence are hollow! Even now, your occupiers attack our forces on Kirisha!"*

Picard stepped forward. "They are peaceful settlers, Kunrud! It was your people who emplaced mines to destroy their livelihood!"

"Captain," said the *Cybele*'s communications officer, "we are now receiving a distress signal from Kirisha."

"On-screen," ch'Regda commanded.

A Caitian female with dark gray fur and a white-streaked mane appeared on the main viewer, displacing Kunrud.

*"Starfleet, we need help! They've come for us, they're trying to take us! Take our children!"* The sounds of weapons fire and feline screeching filled the background. *"We need you now! Emergency! Can you—"*

The signal fritzed and cut out at the source, putting Kunrud back on the screen. *"Do not attempt to cross into the system! This is a matter of Regnancy security enforcement, and we will tolerate no interference!"*

"Tell your people on Kirisha to stand down," Picard demanded, "or you will leave us no choice but to defend our citizens!"

*"Do not attempt to cross,"* Kunrud repeated before signing off.

"Damn," Picard said. "Picard to all ships. Prepare to jump to warp seven on my command, on course for Kirisha. We'll try to jump past them. If they overtake you, break formation and try to draw them away. Defend yourselves as necessary, but do what you can to make sure at least one ship gets to the planet. Ready . . . *engage!*"

Of course, there was nothing the Carnelians could do to prevent the Starfleet ships from getting past their line in the sand. The imaginary boundary they defended was a surface trillions of square kilometers in area, mostly empty space. At warp seven, it took less than a second to shoot past them. But within a few seconds more, the Carnelians were at high warp as well, arcing ahead of the Starfleet ships and firing torpedoes to force them into evasive maneuvers. One by one, the ships scattered, luring the Carnelians after them.

Picard monitored their swooping courses on the *Cybele's* tactical display, looking for openings in the defensive line. With the eye of an experienced chess player, he saw a weak spot he could exploit. "Picard to *Malinche* and *Victory*. Sanders, target the ship at 57 mark 308. The only ship close enough to assist it is the one blocking the *Victory*. Zimbata, fake a retreat and drop to half warp power. Make them think you're no longer a threat. But maintain a constant distance from the colony. When you get an opening, kick in both sets of nacelles and blast through at top speed."

Both captains acknowledged. On-screen, the blip labeled *USS Victory NCC-9754* swerved off on a leisurely tangent while *USS Malinche NCC-38997* took a more aggressive course, vectoring toward a Carnelian ship like a hawk stooping on its prey. Picard had the *Cybele* harry the ship that had been pursuing the *Malinche,* giving George Sanders a free shot at the other. Sanders may have been a relative newcomer to command, but he showed no lack of skill or fortitude as he came in close enough to synchronize warp fields and engage with phasers. His ship took a pounding in return, but the *Excelsior* spaceframe was strong, designed to withstand the stresses of the abortive transwarp drive experiments of the 2280s and thus overbuilt for a conventional warp vessel.

Soon enough, the Carnelian blip nearest the battle vectored toward it. Moments later, there was a wide enough gap in the enemy's formation that no Carnelian ship could intercept the *Victory* in time. "Zimbata, now!" Even as he spoke, the *NCC-9754* blip made an abrupt dogleg turn and shot sunward. Picard then ordered the other ships to keep the Carnelians as busy as possible so that the *Victory* would be free from pursuit long enough to reach Kirisha.

Thanks to the *Cybele*'s skilled tactical officer, the ship they battled was soon adrift, its dorsal nacelle severed and the ventral one dark. Picard ordered a course toward the *Puttkamer,* which had fallen into a pincer maneuver near a large ice dwarf and needed reinforcements. As they traveled, science officer Borm consulted with ch'Regda, who then called Picard over. "I think you'll want to hear this, Captain. Mister Borm?"

"Long-range scans have identified a gravimetric signature consistent with a stellar-mass singularity, sir," the young Tellarite said. "Seventeen parsecs away, in proximity to Hipparcos 14047. Not in orbit, though; it's too fast."

"A black hole," Picard said. "But is it *the* black hole?"

"There's more, sir," said Borm. "The singularity is engulfed in a force-twelve ion storm. However, something seems to be breaking up the storm."

Picard stared. "Breaking up a force-twelve storm?"

"Yes, sir. It was probably a much stronger storm before. Something is dispersing the magnetic field lines, and there's plasma scattered across half a cubic light-year around the hole. I don't know of anything that could do that, sir."

"Sufficiently advanced technology, Lieutenant," Picard muttered. "We've found them." No doubt the storm was impeding Giriaenn's access to the hole, and she was using the scout ship's technology to dissipate it. "How long before the storm is down to force eight?" That was the threshold of serious risk for a heavy cruiser, but would probably be gentle enough for the Manraloth scout to handle.

"A matter of hours, sir."

And it was over a day away at maximum warp. "Damn. We have to end this battle and get to where the real emergency is."

But just then, security chief Hutzel announced, "Closing on the *Puttkamer,* sir. She's taken heavy damage."

"Drop to impulse and engage," ch'Regda ordered.

First things had to come first, Picard knew. He left it in ch'Regda's capable hands, and soon the ship attacking the *Puttkamer* was busy fending off the *Cybele.* The ship rocked under its return fire and moved to evade. Picard noticed that they were drawing close to the ice dwarf, in danger of being trapped in orbit. "Captain, mind your course."

"I am, Captain. See the surface topography? Suggests geysers."

Picard soon saw what he meant. This dwarf must be on a highly eccentric orbit, sometimes drawing close enough to the primary star to be relatively warmed, at least enough for the reservoirs of liquid ammonia, methane, and water beneath its surface to erupt free. There should still be liquid pockets remaining, waiting to burst forth. "Understood. Your strategy, Captain."

The Andorian played it well, luring the ship in close and then letting loose a phaser barrage at the weakest fissure in the planetoid's salmon-tinged crust of ice. An immense gout of superheated steam burst forth behind the *Cybele,* swiftly crystallizing. It had little mass or momentum in itself, but the pursuing ship slammed into it at over a thousand kilometers per second, and the kinetic energy of the impact was enough to knock out the ship's shields and send it swerving out into space. Captain ch'Regda seized the opportunity to jump to warp and break free of the battle zone—unfortunately, inward toward the star rather than out toward the black hole. Picard wanted to protest, but he saw it was the only opening ch'Regda had.

"Take us in to Kirisha, best speed," Picard ordered. Perhaps the *Cybele* and the *Victory* together could resolve the crisis on the surface faster, at least evacuate the settlers, so that the fleet could then break free and make its way to the black hole. Picard could only hope it would take the Manraloth time to gain any advantage from the archive's contents.

He could only pray they were not already too late.


"You must hurry," Admiral Kunrud implored Giriaenn. In her mind's eye, it was as though she stood upon the admiral's bridge, and he saw a corresponding hologram of her, even though she stood parsecs away on the scout ship as it worked to disperse the storm. "The situation is degenerating rapidly. The defenders of the Throne on the planet . . ." He hesitated, and Giriaenn could read his embarrassment. "They grew overzealous. When they saw the Federation fleet coming, they impulsively acted to take hostages as a brake on the invaders' wrath."

"You mean they panicked and are trying to hide behind civilians and children," Giriaenn snapped. "I'm very disappointed in you, Kunrud. You promised me that the Regnancy would not initiate conflict."

"I would have sent my own troops to resolve the situation! But the enemy fleet seized the excuse to attack. Two of them have already broken through the line, and we are taking heavy damage from the rest. We need your power to stop this before more lives are lost!"

"Not yet!" It was Ngalior, appearing beside her in her mind's eye as he was in reality, though unseen and unheard by Kunrud. "We're so close."

She took his hand, reminding him nonverbally, *We knew this might happen.* It was only the approach of the Federation fleet that had prompted the Regnancy bureaucrats into bypassing the last few stages of ritual and granting the Manraloth permission to access the archive. They had all known that their efforts might be interrupted if battle broke out.

Ronael appeared now, shaking her hairless, blue-striped head as she sensed Giriaenn's intention to head to the battle scene. "The dispersal has drained our systems," the four-armed technospecialist said. "Even if we take a sundive, it would take three cycles to recharge fully. And my girl is tired," she said, speaking of the ship. "She needs rest."

"Even at one-third power," Merthiel opined from his ceiling perch, "we're still a match for all their ships combined."

"For their energy," Ngalior replied. "Not their viciousness."

"We *must* go," Giriaenn told them. "Lives are being lost as we speak. We cannot stand by and let that happen!"

One by one, the others consented. Sensing their collective will, the scout halted its dissipation efforts and gathered its energies for the jump to transwarp. Giriaenn looked around her in amazement, wondering how she had ended up as the leader of her people. She had been many things in her life—traveler, nanosculptor, poet, body-swap adventurer, teacher, biologist—but never a politician or administrator. Yet the others had looked to her from the start as their guide to this frightening new galaxy, and had been content to follow her plans for reclaiming it.

Why her? Why must she be the one on whom the future of all the galaxy depended?

*Because someone must,* she answered herself. *What happened was the Manraloth's responsibility, and I share that obligation as fully as any other Manraloth. I am the one who survived, the one who was granted the chance to change things back, and so I must be the one who bears that burden. I cannot refuse it.*

*And I cannot fail.*


Kirisha IV had a young biosphere, at least where multicellular life was concerned. Like Earth in the early Devonian, its land surface had been colonized only by plants and small arthropods. Without animals to eat them, the plants had proliferated and filled the air with oxygen. But no trees had evolved yet; the surface was covered mostly in grasses, small ferns, and lichens. The planet's distance from its smallish sun made it cooler than Earth on average, with much of its moisture bound up in large icecaps. Thus, the bulk of its land surface was covered in dry grasslands with little indigenous animal life. It had been the perfect place for the Caitian settlers to recreate the savanna of their ancestors with a minimum of damage to indigenous life. That was why they had come out this far to settle. But now that very savanna threatened to destroy all they had worked for.

The Caitians lived in small, temporary settlements, migrating among them as they followed the herds of *shu'prra*—great mammalian beasts native to Cait, like purple bison with armadillo shells and long, retractable necks. The settlements had all the modern conveniences, but adapted to the needs of a migratory culture—an unusual mix of herding and hunting, trailing the free-range beasts, guiding them in the desired directions, and periodically sending out hunting prides to chase down and kill a prime *shu'prra*. Picard had read of the delicate balance they had to maintain between taming the animals enough to be herded and keeping them wild enough to satisfy the felinoid need for the hunt.

But the Carnelians had mined the savanna around the Caitian settlements, using a mix of land mines and aerial mines that hovered hundreds of meters up and swerved unpredictably, sending down disruptor blasts at anyone or anything moving directly beneath them. The Caitians could not get to their herds to save them from the danger. The *shu'prra* were adapted to the savanna environment and thus able to withstand the frequent grass fires started by the mines; they simply hunkered down under their fire-resistant shells until the flames passed. The shells even afforded them some protection from the aerial mines. But there was nothing to shield their underbellies from the land mines, and too many fires and disruptor strikes in quick succession could overwhelm their tough shells before they had a chance to regrow.

The crews of *Victory* and *Cybele* had been doing their best to persuade the Caitians to evacuate, but many were unwilling to abandon the *shu'prra.* They had little invested in their dwellings or any given patch of land, but the herds and the savanna were their lives, and many chose to stay and defend them against the Carnelian forces. As Picard monitored the battle in space from *Cybele*'s bridge, he also kept an eye on the reports from the surface on the mission ops console. The ops manager had even tapped into a local news video feed, with a running commentary from a Caitian reporter insisting that *"these crimes must be documented for the galaxy to witness."*

The bulk of Picard's attention remained on the fleet. The *Puttkamer* was out of the fight, doing its best to lie low in orbit of the ice dwarf in the outer system. Most of the action had shifted inward to the heliopause between the star's magnetic field and the interstellar medium, a border the Carnelians were defending fiercely. The *Nautilus* and the *Thelian* had taken significant damage, though they were still in the fight, and the two *Excelsior*s had each destroyed one of the enemy ships. But both sides were currently regrouping, the lull giving Picard a chance to check on affairs below.

Cries of *"Don't go out there!"* rose from the surface feed, followed by the sound of an explosion. "What's happened?" Picard asked. "Surface teams, report!"

The reply came from Mario Hernandez, the *Victory*'s security chief down on the planet. *"The fighting in the adjacent settlement spooked the herds this way, sir. Some colonists ran out to try to warn them off—a mine got them."*

*"One's still alive!"* came another voice, feminine and fraught with intensity.

"Can we beam the survivor aboard?" Picard asked.

*"No good,"* Hernandez answered. *"The mines generate a localized interference field— Hey! Lieutenant, get back here!"*

*"We have to help!"* It was the same female voice.

"Sir!" The ops officer called Picard's attention to the news feed. The camera operator had homed in on the action. Out on the savanna just beyond the settlement, two massive *shu'prra* lay dead or dying, and before them three Caitians lay next to a crater in the ground, bleeding out onto the flattened grass around it. A grass fire was starting to burn nearby. The camera pulled back, and Picard saw a lithe, shaggy-haired blonde woman in Starfleet mustard and black racing out into the minefield. But there was nothing reckless about her action. She kept her tricorder out before her as she loped through the grass, slaloming around the land mines with the ease and grace of an athlete. Hernandez issued a warning cry—*"Tasha, above you!"*—as an aerial mine swooped down, but the lieutenant was already reacting, leaping headlong over a mine and tucking into a roll as the disruptor blast detonated the mine she'd just vaulted. She came away singed, her uniform smoldering, and she slapped at the back of her head to put out a fire in her hair. Then, without pause, she started forward again, single-minded in her striving to reach the wounded colonist.

"Who is that?" Picard asked.

Zimbata's voice replied over the comm; he was no doubt

monitoring from his bridge as well. *"Natasha Yar, my assistant chief of security. A real tiger, that one. She'll go far if she doesn't get herself killed first."*

By now Yar had reached the surviving colonist and was applying a tourniquet to his arm to stop the bleeding. Then she struggled to lift the barely conscious Caitian to his feet and began dragging him back away from the fire. It seemed there was no way her slender frame could bear such a weight, but she refused to give up. Picard was transfixed.

Until Hutzel reported, "Sir! A new ship is closing . . . at incredible speed! Coming out of warp . . . or whatever . . . it reads as the Manraloth scout!"

Picard whirled. "Take us out of orbit! Intercept course!"

"We still have teams on the surface," ch'Regda protested.

"The *Victory* can see to them," he snapped. "You have your orders!"

Ch'Regda looked as though he might protest, but he subsided, his antennae sagging sullenly. "Aye, sir. Conn, put us on an intercept course with the scout."

"Once more unto the breach," Picard murmured.

# 25

———

THE CHAOS GIRIAENN NOW BEHELD IN THE KIRISHA
system was as bad as anything she had seen in nine hundred
millennia of life. No, it was worse. She had seen large-scale
death resulting from unanticipated natural disasters. She had
even encountered isolated pockets of violence, the occasional act of murder or terrorism, since even a peaceful and
united galaxy was too complex to run smoothly at all times.
A few times, she had followed the news as invaders from another galaxy or dimension had launched an assault on the
home galaxy or its satellites, only to be easily neutralized by
the might of Manraloth technology and either persuaded to
accept a peaceful settlement or permanently banished to
their home.

But what she saw before her now was *war*. An all-out battle between two evenly matched forces capable of harness-
ing immense energies of destruction. The brutality of it was
staggering. She had stopped monitoring mind-feeds from the
Carnelian fleet, for she could no longer bear to see the bodies of their crews torn into by fire and shrapnel or shattered
by blunt impacts as inertial dampers faltered. Even with all
her millennia of biocontrol, she had nearly vomited.

Once they fell out of transwarp, though, her spirits rallied. Now they could do something about it. They could separate these children and make them behave.

The scout emerged near Kunrud's flagship to find it under bombardment from a stocky, thick-necked Starfleet vessel. The shipmind read the name off its hull: *U.S.S. THELIAN NCC-26047.* "All right, *Thelian*," Giriaenn said, "that's quite enough." She summoned up the displacer control with a gesture, kneaded the hologram that appeared in her hand, and left the *Thelian*'s warp core and fusion reactors drifting in space well behind it while the ship coasted forward on momentum. *Now on to the next,* she thought, gratified at how easy it would be to save these people's lives.

Until Kunrud's flagship whirled around and fired all weapons at the *Thelian* before it could transfer emergency power to its shields. It was shocking how little time it took to blow apart something so massive and snuff out seven hundred lives.

For a moment, she was paralyzed by grief, her own and the others'. Then anger overcame it. With a thought, she was on Kunrud's bridge again, her hologram confronting him furiously. "Why did you do that?! We'd neutralized them!"

"They could still fire torpedoes!" the Brunyg-Carnelian bellowed in return. "I have to protect my crew!"

"They were no longer a threat! You could've stood down! They wouldn't attack you without cause!"

"It was you," Kunrud told her, "who warned us of the menace posed by the Federation!"

Just then, an explosion ripped through the bridge behind her. Giriaenn felt the searing heat through her hologram's skin before the comm system damped down its sensory response. When she reoriented herself a moment later, she found her hologram lying atop Kunrud, having coincidentally shielded him from the blast. But when she made it rise and turn to survey the rest of the bridge, she saw blood and burned flesh everywhere. Worse, she *smelled* it, and let out a gasp at the unimagined fetor of it. The shipmaster's tank was cracked, its nutrient fluid leaking out onto the deck, and the shipmaster itself was flashing alert colors on its carapace as its tentacles worked to summon emergency crew to the bridge.

"Are you going to stand there mewling," a recovering Kunrud said from behind her, "or help us?"

Squeezing her eyes shut, Giriaenn cut the transmission, clasped the displacer control, locked onto the attacking ship (*Tecumseh* was its name), and sent it as far away as she possibly could. But the displacer was still weak and could only send it a parsec. It would be back before long.

Had Kunrud been right? Had she played up the Federation threat too much in her appeals to the Carnelians, leading to the current hostilities? Was she as responsible for this whole war as she was for the death of the *Thelian*'s crew?

Ngalior sensed her guilt and came to her side, clasping her free hand. "You could not have anticipated how viciously they would respond to your influence. This is not your fault, Giri."

"It's my responsibility, Ngal. We have to stop them."

"We lack the power to displace them all."

An idea came to her, inspired by her old associates the Organians. "Can we induce heat in their control circuits? Make them too hot to touch?" She couldn't recall whether the Organians had done that for real or simply created the illusion, but she was only interested in replicating the results.

Ronael communed with the ship for a moment. "Yes, my girl. That'll work. Do it."

For a few moments, the ships drifted, no longer firing, and Giriaenn felt relief. But then the weapons started up again and the ships resumed their deadly games of chase. Little Shireilil darted her head around, taking in mindlink views from the bridges of the various ships. "They're using voice commands! They learned from the last time."

"Maybe we can neutralize their computers," Merthiel said.

"They'll just find more creative ways to fight," Ngalior replied.

"And there are more coming," warned Chieraial, silver eyes going wide in his gold-furred face as he monitored long-range sensor input. "Another Carnelian fleet, days away. Subspace messages going out to the Federation—it'll bring another fleet. And they'll just keep killing each other."

Giriaenn strove to think of a solution. She placed herself on *Cybele*'s bridge, before Picard himself. The sight of his face was painful bliss, but she had no time to reflect as he drew a phaser on her and fired. "I'm transmitting to you from my ship," she told him. "Please, just leave this space and the Regnancy forces will let you go. I'll make sure of that."

"We will not leave, Giriaenn! Not until the colonists on Kirisha are safe!"

"I'll see they're protected!"

"Like you protected the *Thelian?!*" She lowered her head, chastened. "You assume you are so much wiser than we, but you are out of your depth here. This is what your 'gifts' will bring to the galaxy, and it is why we must stop you!"

"This is your own chaos, Jean-Luc! Your own savagery seizing any excuse to express itself!"

"That's right, Giriaenn. And it's a chaos you cannot understand. Your solutions are not for us!"

"Then where are your solutions, Jean-Luc? At the point of a spear?"

Before he could answer, she cut off the connection, knowing nothing more could come of this. Not only was Picard past reason, but she was not free of blame herself. "Everything that's happening here is because of us," she told the others. "We abandoned them to this, stripped away everything that could free them from it. We *must* find a way to give it back!"

"All we have left is the archive," Ngalior said.

*The archive,* Giriaenn thought. Once it was one of the beating hearts of an information bloodstream that unified the galaxy. Any solution to any problem could be found by tapping the wisdom of the ancients.

"Yes," Shireilil said, sensing the direction of her thoughts. "We can find an answer in the archive."

"It's not enough," Giriaenn said. "Not if they won't listen. They have no experience with it, no sense of connection to—" She broke off.

"Giri?" Ngalior asked.

"That's it! Take us back to the archive, now!"


"Sir!" Hutzel cried. "The Manraloth scout is entering transwarp. Heading back to the black hole!"

Picard looked around the bridge. Only a few junior officers were hasty enough to be cheered by the news; the others realized it was more likely an escalation than a retreat. "Helm, pursuit course!" Picard ordered.

"We can't possibly pursue a transwarp ship!" ch'Regda protested.

"Maybe we can, sir," Borm said from the science station. "Whatever type of transwarp they're using leaves some sort of subspace wake, as though it temporarily stretches space out behind it. It's like it's making the distance much shorter, at least until the effect fades."

"Very well," ch'Regda said. "Helm, engage at maximum warp!"


"Thought is information," Giriaenn told the others, "and information is energy. The black hole's event horizon is the greatest sink of information in this galaxy." The ship told her and the others that Picard's flagship was following in their transwarp wake, but she knew it would quickly fall behind as the wake dissipated. The scout would reach the archive at least half an hour before Picard could. "If we can tap into the horizon, entangle with it logopathically, its energy will enhance our abilities. We'll be able to reach out with our minds and serve as conduits, linking every mind in the sector, enabling them to communicate freely through us."

The others stared. "To what end?" Ngalior asked. He

seemed nonplussed; it was unusual for a Manraloth to have trouble following another's intentions.

"This whole conflict is a misunderstanding. Each side assumes the other is a threat. If they can read each other, listen to each other directly, they can understand that neither one is an aggressor and stand down. At worst, if they keep killing each other, they'll experience those deaths and that should shock them into breaking it off."

There was silence for a long moment. Merthiel lowered himself down from his perch and stood facing her. "What you propose, Giriaenn . . . do you not hear the echoes? It feels like . . ."

"Like what we did," Shireilil said with unwonted solemnity in her girlish voice. "A quarter-billion years ago. Mass linking of minds . . . tapping into cosmic power . . ."

"I know," Giriaenn said. "Believe me, loves, I know the enormity of what I propose. But we are only linking corporeal minds this time, and on a far smaller scale."

"Still," Merthiel said, "something else could go wrong. Have we not learned by now the cost of overconfidence in our mighty schemes?"

"You think I haven't learned that, Mer? Look what our games with the Carnelians have caused! Look what happened to the *Thelian* because of us! This is all our mess! The whole state of the *galaxy* is our mess, and we must do something drastic to clean it up!"

Ngalior moved in beside her. "It could work," he said. "Even looking at it their way . . . if each side could sense the other's strategies and secrets, if each knew the other could sense theirs, would they dare continue fighting?" The others pondered his point, and Giriaenn sent him nonverbal gratitude for his support. "And once we've tapped them into the archive, we can help them find some precedent, some kind of agreement that can fit this dispute."

"That can fit a war?" Chieraial asked.

"A dispute over territory and rights," Ngalior said. "That's what they fight over."

"And they are still fighting," Giriaenn stressed. "And dying, more by the moment. We have no time to debate it. We must act now!"

One by one, just a few at first but then en masse, the others signaled their consent. As if joining in their consent, the ship dropped them out of transwarp back at the archive. "Let's do a sundive," Ronael told it. "Recharge what we can and feed it to the displacers. I know they ache, baby, but we have to clear enough of that storm to get through."

The scout dove headlong into the blue star's chromosphere, drawing in enough energy to leave a tiny, cool sunspot behind it once it breached the surface again. Another transwarp hop and it was back alongside the black hole. The ion storm around it was a work of art. Vast loops of actinic light caged the hole, arcing from pole to pole, limning the contours of its magnetic field. Red-violet flames danced and flickered for thousands of kilometers around it as the intense particle currents triggered auroras in the hydrogen clouds. The accretion disk glowed with rainbow light, red on the outside and up through orange, yellow, blue, into ultraviolet and beyond toward the center.

But it was an artwork they had to destroy, and they went about it methodically. The displacers seized great masses of plasma and teleported them into empty space. Meanwhile, Ronael reached all four arms into the virtual image to seize magnetic field lines and twist them, pinching them off into loops she then set free to expand and dissipate, taking some of the system's energy with them.

Once, Giriaenn reflected, the magnetic field would have been a tool, a structured adjunct that served as an interface and volatile memory, with vast amounts of data encoded in its magnetic matrix. But that elegant, fragile structure had been washed away by time; only the event horizon, the timeless core of the system, survived intact. Everything her civilization had ever learned or achieved lay waiting for her within, perfectly preserved for all time. And now it could live again. It was simply a matter of making the connection.

"The system was meant to be easy to use even without an interface," Ronael explained, "in case of field collapse. A basic, direct photon entanglement should access a directory at the substrate level of the horizon's coding. Then we just download the interface protocols for further access."

"We don't need them," Giriaenn reminded her. "Not right away. All we need is to link our minds with the horizon on the most basic level. We're using it simply as an amplifier. After all," she said ruefully, "we don't want to risk tapping into anything too complex." The others exchanged heavy looks.

"Fine," Ronael said. "Then let's get ourselves in interface first, then activate the entanglement. That way the hard part is only one step."

They all signaled agreement. The ship materialized interface couches for them all, and they eased back onto them. Giriaenn clasped Ngalior's hand in her right, Shireilil's in her left, and squeezed them encouragingly. "Let's bring back our world."

At first, all she sensed was the connection with the others' minds, the chatter of familiar inner voices as stray thoughts darted through their linguistic and logopathic centers. She urged them all to focus on opening their minds, reaching out—to each other, to the event horizon, to the thousands of children fighting and dying out there. She sensed many of them transmitting the same encouragements. *Set the self aside. We are conduits. We are guides. We live to bring others together in understanding. We are harmony.*

Then she felt an abrupt broadening of her awareness, a rush of new sensation, like the mental equivalent of jumping out of a small, silent hovercar and plummeting through wide open sky. The noise of it was shocking, a blast of mental static as the entanglement initiated. She almost shied away from it, but willed herself to face it, expecting to push through it and settle into a stable interface.

But the noise wasn't fading. It burst over her like a torrent, fiercer by the instant, pouring into her mind through every sense, every input, every aspect of her consciousness.

It flooded her mind from within and drowned her reason, her awareness.

She could not hear her screams, or those of the others. All that existed for her was pain.


Picard paced the bridge, staring at the oddly distorted warp streaks on the viewscreen. "How soon?" he asked, not caring how many times it had been.

"At least twenty minutes," Borm said. "The wake is dissipating, and we're slowing by the moment, even with our warp factor constant."

"Get whatever more you can out of the engines," Picard ordered ch'Regda. "We have to catch them." He had seen the changes in Giriaenn when she'd beamed her image before him: her hips were wider, her breasts fuller under her halter top. The Manraloth were adapting themselves to breed. An immortal race making more of itself. He had to stop it here.

"They've already arrived at the hole," Hutzel said.

"Can you get a visual?"

Long-range sensors probed through subspace, and the monitor extrapolated an image—a roiling storm of multihued light, scattered and splashed outward, with magnetic eddies swirling free like smoke rings. Picard was stunned at the sheer violence even a "peaceful" Manraloth scout could wield on nature itself. "Magnify!" The storm filled the screen, and Picard glimpsed (or did he imagine?) a tiny pinprick of a ship near the heart of the storm, hanging still where nothing should stay still. He strode forward to see more clearly, willing the *Cybele* to race faster into the raging fires of the storm.

But then the storm was in his head, roaring and battering him, deafening him with thunder, blinding him with lightning, sweeping him away. He screamed and could not hear it, could not hear anything but screaming. Could not see for the torrent of vision, his eyes stuck open by all the sights that crammed into them, filling his head to bursting.

His mind cried out for something to comprehend, a face,

a voice. Ariel's purring filled his ears, vibrated in his chest, but then Giriaenn's knife stabbed through his heart and out the front while Phillipa and Guinan held his arms, and he looked down at the blade and laughed as the blade began to burn him

And the burning engulfed him and he reached out to Vigo who took his hand and caught fire too and burned down

And the bridge was in flames and the ship burned down around him

"I told you this would happen," his father hectored as the fire engulfed him too, and his mother sat behind him shaking her head sadly

    as her tea set burned down along with her

                along with the *Stargazer* until

there was nothing left

    and he floated in space

    staring at Jack's lifeless face through the helmet

           through the helmet

was a formless gray mist that exploded outward

leaving charred bodies

    charred body reached out to him

took him in her arms

took him in her eyes

    fell into her eyes and they were blue fire and it burned

             it **burned**

                  Make it stop

                  Make it stop

                    · Make it stop


Tasha Yar cursed as her hand surveyed the burned strands on the back of her head. Just when she'd finally decided to try growing it out, this had to happen. Maybe she would go back to the tightly shorn style she'd worn on Turkana IV to make herself less appealing to the rape gangs (or at least give them less to grab her by). Reminder of her past or not, it was a practical style for a Starfleet security officer.

And Starfleet was what gave her life meaning now. It had freed her from the hell of Turkana, a hell she'd grown up thinking could be escaped only through drugs or death. It had shown her there was a better way of life, that Turkana was the exception rather than the rule. And so she served Starfleet and its ideals, driven by overwhelming gratitude, determined to prove herself worthy of its gifts and never let it down.

The Caitian she'd pulled from the minefield was in the *Victory*'s sickbay now, so she'd done her job. She just wished she could've saved the rest. But there were others she still could save, if she could get to them in time and break up the fighting. It was a tall order. But she was in Starfleet, and that meant she could work wonders.

But as she ran, her world exploded around her. For an instant she thought she'd stepped on a mine, but the agony didn't end, it just kept pouring into her, enough to blind and deafen but it just kept coming, overwhelming her

           the bombs kept falling, fires burning, her mother's body lay atop her and she heard Ishara wailing

           but she knew to stay quiet and hidden

                hide and go seek it was a game could save your life

            the cat meowed and she shushed it, don't alert the rape gangs, don't let it happen again

           Cats?

        *Caitians!*

    Yowling, screaming, panicking

                    running into the savanna

                        into the mines

    Focus, Tasha! Ithurtsithurts but block it out

                  done it before

          no more joy dust

             ithurtsithurts

        Life hurts—deal with it! No more joy dust

      No more dependence

Freedom              =             Starfleet

    OFFICER! Security

officer with lives to save.
Caitians running toward mines—STOP THEM
STOPITITHURTS
Focus! Get them out
Keep them safe
But the world is falling apart and it's very loud
So what else is new?
Job to do.

The storm whirled around Guinan, through her, threatening to dissolve her in its chaos. But at the center, there was an eye of calmness. A Nexus where all was serene, all was joy. Guinan reached out for it, reached in for it, found that link to the piece of herself that still was there, there in stillness, timeless and unchanging, an anchor. She seized that stillness, used it to shut out the chaos. She rested on the warm belly fur of her Tarkassian razorbeast, its soft purr filling her with peace.

She opened her eyes, and she could see again. Barely. The storm of images, sounds, smells, textures, memories still battered at her, but she willed herself to see, like forcing her eyes to stay open against a driving rain, ignoring the stinging, blinking away the blur. She was in her quarters. She was in her quarters on the *Cybele* and there was screaming outside. Perhaps not all of it was outside.

She breathed slowly, calmly, in time with the serene inspirations of her Nexus echo, that facet of her quantum self that had never left there because time never passed there. Now the screaming was only outside. Whatever had happened to her must have happened to the others. But they had no Nexus to give an eye to their storms. She had to get out and help—

Oh. The door was locked. No matter; she hadn't always made her living as a bartender. She knew a few things you could do to an electronic lock that weren't in the manual. They wouldn't work on a Starfleet brig, but she was only confined to quarters.

And then she wasn't. Looking down, she saw the posted guard writhing, screaming, tearing at her uniform. Guinan made an effort to calm her, but the woman was lost in her agony. Others down the corridor were in similar straits.

Guinan ran for sickbay, distantly noticing a breeze upon her head—she had lost her hat. Her mind raced. She knew this must be the Manraloth's doing. There had been a battle, and then the planet had been out her window, and the guard had told her they were defending the colony. Then they had abruptly raced back to the battle zone, and Guinan had known the Manraloth had arrived, for only that would draw Picard away from the rescue effort (a sad thought; the Picard she'd once known would not have left even for that). Then the stars had streaked into warp, but with an odd, elongated, almost tubular pattern around the ship. She'd realized that somehow they were chasing the Manraloth somewhere, riding in the wake of their drive.

Guinan understood how Giriaenn and her people thought. The raw violence of the battle would have horrified them. They must have tried something to stop it, something telepathic. But neither they nor their ship had the power for this. They must have tapped into something else—the black hole?

She couldn't figure it out now. What she knew was that it had gone wrong, inundating the crew's minds with an overload of psionic white noise, their brains being flooded through every possible input. Many of them tore at their clothes, their hair, their skin, trying to remove whatever it was that burned them through every nerve ending. If it didn't end soon, it would drive them mad. And not only them. This was too uncontrolled to be narrowcast. Every mind in the sector might be affected, maybe even beyond.

As she arrived at sickbay, Guinan struggled to remember what her seventeenth husband had told her—or had it been the fourteenth? The neurobiologist, the one with twelve fingers and the enormous collection of Znelfian fungal caps. Something about his research in shielding Znelfian agents from psi-projective attack, dulling their telepathic sensitivity by suppressing electron tunneling in the thalamus.

After feeding the right search terms into the sickbay computer, she found the drugs she needed—a thalamic inhibitor plus a mild sedative for good measure—and ordered the replicator to produce a batch for her. *You have to love Starfleet,* she thought. Their personnel were all so responsible and well-adjusted that the sickbay computers didn't need security codes to prevent unauthorized users from replicating any given drug—at least when it wasn't notably dangerous.

Of course, she couldn't be sure if a Znelfian treatment would work on other species. She sighed. "A bartender should always try out her new concoctions first," she said, and injected a dose into her neck.

A few moments later, she felt the pressure on her mind easing enough to make it less of a strain to think clearly, although it still felt like the mental equivalent of being inside a metal drum in a hailstorm. "Computer," she said. "If this drug compound has the desired effect on the El-Aurian brain, will it affect the other humanoid species on this ship the same way?"

"An equivalent dosage should have a comparable effect," the computer replied.

"Thanks," she said, injecting another dose into the chief medical officer's neck as he writhed on the floor. After hastily explaining the situation to the doctor, she hurried toward the bridge as he went to replicate more of the compound.

She found Picard lying before the main viewscreen, curled up naked in a fetal position, his uniform discarded beside him. He seemed nearly catatonic, but his fingers twitched rhythmically and tears poured from his eyes. She injected him first, then made the rounds of the bridge. By the time she'd injected the whole bridge crew and made her way back to Picard, he was stirring, clarity returning to his eyes. "How are you doing?" she asked, kneeling beside him.

"I . . . I'm . . ." He looked down at himself. "I seem to be out of uniform."

"That's okay. So am I."

His eyes fixed on the braids that fell free over her face and shoulders. "Haven't seen you . . . without a hat . . . in thirty years." He frowned, confused. "Are you even here? Are you real?"

"I like to think so."

He stared. "It's you, all right." He looked around, getting his bearings, and spotted his uniform. She looked away as he pulled it back on, saw that others in the bridge crew were doing the same with theirs. The uniforms were durable and had suffered only minor tears, fortunately for Picard's dignity.

"Are you better now?" she asked when he was dressed again.

"Somewhat. But not quite in my perfect mind. I still feel . . . the *noise* . . ." He peered at her. "You seem to have resisted it better than most."

"Not entirely. Enough to get to sickbay and replicate a psionic blocker. It's temporary, though. Somebody's got to stop this at the source."

"This is some . . . attack by the Manraloth."

"I think it's a mistake by the Manraloth. They probably wanted to do something to stop the fighting. Something to do with the black—"

"The black hole," he said, overlapping her. "Conn, time to intercept?"

The flight controller strained to focus her eyes on the console, and answered with some surprise, "Two minutes, sir!"

"Whatever they did," Guinan said, "it's gone wrong. If they could stop it on their own, they would've done it by now. I bet they're in the same boat everyone else is."

"Sir," Hutzel reported, "I can't make contact with anyone in the fleet. Anyone in the sector."

"The Federation?" Picard asked.

Hutzel shook his head. "Too far away for real-time contact. I don't know."

"You think it could spread that far?" Guinan asked.

"From what Giriaenn told me about what happens when Manraloth try to link minds together, it could spread indefinitely as each new brain affected becomes an amplifier, a transmitter."

"Maybe not," Guinan countered. "Not if those brains burn out first."

"Either way, it must be stopped." He strode toward the lift. "Mister Hutzel, assemble an away team."

Guinan jogged to get in front of him. "I have to go with you."

"It's not your place," he said curtly.

"Yes, it is. It's the whole reason I'm here at all. I know these people, they trust me. They chose me to mediate between you and them. You may need me to resolve this."

He studied her. "I appreciate what you've done for us just now. But I still don't know that *I* can trust you."

Guinan stared for a moment, then scoffed loudly. "That's rich, Picard! That's really rich. I told you what would happen if you came here in force. If you'd just trusted me in the first place, none of this would be happening now!"

Picard was visibly taken aback by her unwonted anger—and by his dawning realization that she was right. Seeing that he was on the verge of taking yet another burden of guilt onto his shoulders, she regretted her anger and chose to amend her statement. "I think that in your gut," she told him, "you still know that you can trust me. The problem is, you stopped trusting your gut."

After another moment's thought, he nodded. "Come on, then." She joined him and Hutzel in the turbolift.

As they rode toward the transporter room, Picard looked at her and spoke softly. "Tell me . . . how did you manage to resist the madness?"

She was silent for a long moment. It wasn't something she wanted to talk about. It was just too joyous to bear remembering. "Let's just say . . . that there's a part of me where I'm always at peace."

He absorbed her words. "That's an enviable thing."

*No. It really isn't.*

# 26

———

THE MANRALOTH SCOUT WAS DEEP IN THE ION
storm when the *Cybele* arrived. At first, the transporter chief
was unable to get a lock. But then something unexpected
happened. "A lock has . . . been established," the Aulacri
chief said, his tail twitching in surprise. "But not by me. It's
as if someone . . . opened the way for us."

Picard frowned. "Then perhaps they are more in control
of themselves than we assumed."

"But they're still asking for our help," Guinan said.

He took her point, but remained wary. "Phasers on maximum stun," he told Hutzel. "Energize."

Once they materialized on the Manraloth ship, though, it
was clear that none of its occupants had been in any position to act. All of them—roughly thirty, by his quick esti-
mate—lay on a ring of interface couches, paralyzed yet
trembling as if in seizure. "Then who set up the transporter
lock?" Hutzel asked.

"The ship," Guinan said, glancing over its consoles. "It
sensed we were trying to get here, and in its own way it
asked for help."

The fourth member of the party, a medtech named Westmore, was scanning the Manraloth with her tricorder.

"Their neural activity is off the charts. It should've killed them by now."

Picard found Giriaenn and called Westmore over. "Give her the inhibitor."

"We don't know if it'll be effective—"

"We have to break their link one way or the other. Do it."

Westmore complied, injecting the psi-suppressant. After a few moments, Giriaenn's tremors stopped and she opened her eyes. *"Irieu—"* She focused on Picard. "What happened?" She sat up, looking around at the others. "The entanglement . . . it's gone wrong."

"You tried to link your minds with the black hole?"

She nodded. "To amplify our logopathy, bring your minds together. I don't know what went wrong."

As Westmore moved on to inject the others, Picard told Giriaenn, "Whatever it is, it's flooding the minds of everyone for sectors around with overwhelming sensory input. If we don't stop it now, they'll all go mad or die from the strain."

Before he finished speaking, Giriaenn gestured, and some kind of free-floating hologram materialized by her hand. She stroked it in a certain way, then reported, "The interface is deactivated."

But none of the others' status changed in the moments that followed, aside from those Westmore had injected. "They should've woken up by now," Giriaenn said.

"Picard to *Cybele*," he said, hitting his combadge. "Any communications from the rest of the fleet?"

After a moment, ch'Regda's voice replied. *"Negative. Not from the fleet, not from anyone within range."*

The Manraloth next to Giriaenn, a dainty green-gold pixie with long waves of candy-floss hair, was looking around her as though scanning an unseen vista. "They're in agony!" she cried a moment later. "Everywhere I look, out to Kirisha, past the blue-star cluster . . . and it's spreading!"

"How can that be?" Giriaenn demanded. "The link is off!"

Another female, four-armed and blue-striped, shook her hairless head. "It does not matter anymore. The link just created the entanglement. Now all those minds are entangled directly with the event horizon."

"How do we stop it, Ronael?"

"I don't see a way. The horizon's time-frozen, unchanging."

Giriaenn shook her own head, her fiery hair swirling around it. "That's exactly why this couldn't have happened. It should have been there! The interface, the archive. The answers." She leapt off the interface couch, which obligingly dematerialized, allowing her to pace through where it had been. "All the collected knowledge of half a billion years of civilization! It has to be there!"

Picard caught her eye. "What about the quarter-billion years since?"

Ronael gasped. "A quarter-billion years of the black hole sucking in all information, all energy that fell into it. With no one to regulate the input. No one to order it."

"The information is still there," Picard realized. "But it's buried under two hundred and fifty million years of random noise. Lost in the static."

The Manraloth stared at each other, thunderstruck. "Everything?" asked the large silver male whose name Picard recalled was Ngalior. "All our knowledge . . . our art, our history . . . gone?"

"Listen to me," Picard barked. "There are more pressing concerns! We must find a way to break this entanglement or *trillions* of lives will be destroyed!"

"There's no way," said Ronael. "Except by destroying the archive itself."

"Is there a way to do that?"

Ronael pondered it for a time, then lifted her head to speak—and stopped. Picard caught the look Giriaenn had given her. "What is it?" he asked them both. "Is there a way?"

"No," Giriaenn insisted.

"No," Ronael echoed, looking away. "I was wrong. It would never work."

"What would?" Picard asked.

"It would never work," Giriaenn repeated.

He moved closer to Ronael, peering into her eyes. "There is something. You do know of a way to destroy the archive."

Hesitantly, she told him, "We could use the scout's drive . . . collapse the singularity out of our continuum."

"We *can't!*" Giriaenn cried. "There must be another way. The information is still in there, under the noise. If we could evolve the right algorithm, we could reconstruct it."

"There's no time!" Guinan said. "You told me yourself, Giri—the Manraloth live to nurture others. There are a lot of others going insane out there. There's more at stake than preserving your history!"

"But it has all the answers. Answers that could help you all, that could restore the galaxy to peace and health. We can't give that up!"

"You have to!" Picard said.

"No! It's the only thing left that we have to help you with. The archive and the ship, and you ask us to destroy them both!"

"Yes, we do," Guinan said. "Because that's how you can help us now."

"It's only temporary! There has to be another way. We *need* to find another way!"

Picard studied her, suddenly understanding her. "That's right, isn't it. *You* need to find a way. A way to make amends for your people's great mistake. And you can't allow yourself to let go of that sense of obligation, no matter what the cost."

"It *was* our mistake, Jean-Luc. We have to make amends for what we did to you."

"Is that really it, Giriaenn? Or are you just so accustomed to your life of ease and success, your effortless ability to shape the galaxy as you saw fit, that you can't accept the reality of failure? That you feel you must get it right the second time around, just because you expect to be able to get it right?"

She stared at him. "What do you mean?"

The words had meant little to him when Deanna Troi had said them two months ago. But now, seeing how trapped

Giriaenn was by her own guilt, he understood what she had meant. "I mean that, sometimes, we must learn to accept that we were simply not meant to succeed at everything. We must accept our failures . . . and we must forgive ourselves for them. Otherwise . . . otherwise," he went on ruefully, "we may become so obsessed with our efforts to repair our mistakes that we are blinded to other priorities and end up causing more harm. First to ourselves, and eventually to others." Guinan saw the apology in his eyes and gave him a tiny smile.

Picard moved closer. "Giriaenn . . . we have all made horrible mistakes in our past. But—as a wise woman named Ariel once told me—our intentions were noble and giving, and so we must forgive ourselves. We must stop living for the past, or we can never reach forward to seize the future."

"And if there's no future," Guinan added, "then there's no one to preserve the lessons of the past. It's time, Giriaenn," she said, though her eyes strayed to Picard. "Time to stop waiting for the past to resolve itself and start looking forward to the future."

Giriaenn turned to gaze into Picard's eyes. He had never seen her so lost, even when she had first awakened with no memory and no name. He stroked her striped cheek, hearing the tiny rustle of butterfly scales. "Help us now, Ariel. Live for the moment . . . and let the past rest."

She stared, unblinking—but only for a few seconds. "Ronael, do it," she said. "Everyone, get ready. We're abandoning ship."

The Manraloth assembled in a group, save for Ngalior, who retrieved a small orb that he cradled like a child, and Ronael, who stroked the scout ship's wall with both left hands, seemingly as much to comfort it as to enter commands. "Thank you, dear one. Good-bye."

A few moments later, they were all crowding *Cybele*'s bridge, the command crew reacting in alarm. "It's all right," Picard assured them.

"Not exactly," said Ronael. "We're far too close. Wait a moment . . . there."

A surge of sensation passed through them, barely noticeable over the mental background roar of the event-horizon chaos, but the image on the viewscreen changed. "Sir!" the flight controller cried. "Suddenly we're a dozen light-years from where we were!"

"It should be enough," Ronael said. "At least until a dozen years from now."

On-screen, the black hole and the ion storm around it were still visible in real time thanks to subspace sensors. Suddenly, the gases of the storm began to distort. No, Picard realized—it was space itself that was distorting, warping the background starlight in expanding ripples, pushing the plasma outward in concentric spheres. Spikes of violet energy shot out from the core of the effect as if through tears in space. Then, suddenly, it all collapsed in on itself and exploded outward in a blinding burst of white light.

Once Picard's eyes and the screen cleared, he saw nothing where the black hole had been, aside from a subtle rippling of space that might have been his imagination. But the nearby blue star had changed; it now glowed white-hot on the side facing where the black hole had been, and a haze was starting to appear around it, an expanding ring of atmosphere. Whatever had happened to the black hole had released enough energy to heat the surface of the star far beyond its already intense temperature and blow away whole layers into space. Some fraction of the energy must have propagated faster than light to affect the star so promptly. Not surprising, given the multidimensional turbulence of the event.

"It's only a fraction of the informational energy the horizon contained," Ronael said. "But I fear it will pose something of a radiation hazard in this sector for years to come, as the wave front expands. We should advise all travelers to stay clear, and check for nearby inhabited worlds that may be endangered."

# CHRISTOPHER L. BENNETT

"But the immediate threat is gone?" Picard asked.

"Calls are coming in from the fleet," Hutzel told him. "They sound pretty shaken up, but they're alive."

Picard nodded, then ordered him to begin clearing the crowded bridge, escorting the Manraloth to guest quarters under guard. Then he moved to Giriaenn, who stood apart at the side of the bridge. "How could we not have known this would happen?" she asked. "Nothing like this was ever reported before. If this had been possible, we would've known."

"How would you have known?" he asked gently.

"Because—" She broke off. "We would've been able to look it up in the archives." She shook her head. "Oh, we were such fools!"

"For hundreds of millennia," he told her, "you were accustomed to operating within an extremely well-established support network. You lived your lives by building on what those before you had achieved."

"And that won't work anymore, will it? Not in your world. You have to make it up as you go." She offered him a feeble smile. "And that makes you more resourceful, doesn't it? Better able to cope with the unknown. The unexpected."

"We generally manage." He sensed Guinan coming up behind him, but she simply listened.

Tears glistened in Giriaenn's eyes. "We don't have the answers for you, do we? We can't help you. You need to face the universe on your own . . . never knowing what lies ahead."

"It's hard, isn't it?" Guinan asked her. "To realize your children are all grown up. That no matter how much you still want to protect them, all you can do for them anymore is let them go." She smiled. "But I'll tell you something. As much as it hurts, there's nothing that makes a mother prouder than knowing her kids are ready to make it on their own."

Giriaenn gazed at Picard and smiled sadly. "You are ready, you know. I see that now. But we had nothing to do with it."

Ngalior came forward and took her hand. "Maybe we did, Giri. From what I've learned of the worlds they evolved on . . . well, they would've just been developing multicellular life during the Manraloth Era." He turned to Picard to explain. "When we came upon worlds like that, we usually declared them off-limits for colonization. We wanted to give their biospheres the chance to evolve new forms, to add to the diversity of the galaxy."

Picard looked at the Manraloth with new awe. "So we may owe our very existence to you. To the fact that . . . you left us to evolve on our own."

Giriaenn smirked. "Is that your subtle way of telling us it's time to go away?"

"But where can we go?" the tiny female asked. "There's no one left but us, and the other stasis bubbles around the galaxy. And we don't have any way to free them safely."

"We'll just have to start over," Giriaenn said. "We have nothing left except ourselves. We're orphans now. Exiles."

"Some of you may survive," Picard suggested. "You told me yourself—when the Cataclysm happened, every being with an advanced enough mind was forcibly evolved to an incorporeal plane rather than dying. Surely that happened with the Manraloth."

Giriaenn stared. "But by now, they would have long since evolved into something else—something unrecognizable."

"Maybe," Guinan replied. "Maybe not. Your people stayed the way they were for a long time on this plane. Who knows how time passes up there? Out there? Whatever."

"If you can evolve yourselves to adapt to different environments," Picard said, "or . . . to breed, then can you not evolve your brains as well? To tap into the psionic fields that allow such a transition?"

Giriaenn shook her head. "No. That way is not for the Manraloth. It means turning our backs on everything we love about our existence. Everything we cherish. It means leaving behind all you lovely species, all the opportunities to connect with you."

"I understand your reluctance," Picard said. "No one likes to give up the life they've always known. But that life is already gone for you." He paused. "Every other ancient race save yours has . . . left this existence in one way or another. Maybe it's right that every species eventually moves on and clears the stage for the next generation."

She stroked his cheek. "But I don't want to go."

He took her hand and clasped it. "Don't think of what you'd be losing. Think about the new adventure that lies ahead. Your people learned everything there was to learn about this dimension. You could call it up from an archive, have it at your fingertips in seconds. Out there, beyond this existence, who knows? It would be a whole new realm to discover. The chance to explore something completely new. That's nothing to fear, Giriaenn! Taking that leap into the unknown, being surprised by what's beyond each new horizon—there's nothing more exhilarating! Nothing that makes you feel more alive!" He realized he was grinning.

And as he saw himself reflected in Giriaenn's deep blue eyes, he realized that he'd found something he hadn't noticed losing. For the first time in years, he felt complete.

# 27

---

IT TOOK SEVERAL WEEKS OF DIPLOMACY TO WRAP
things up with the Carnelians. Fortunately the efforts of the
Manraloth, along with a word Guinan planted here and
there among her friends in high places within the Regnancy,
did much to ease tensions. After the surge of madness, no
one in the sector was eager to continue fighting, and the
causes they'd fought over seemed somewhat pettier—at least
for the moment.

Picard's participation in the mass funeral for the many
Regnancy subjects lost in the battle also served to mend
fences. The Carnelians were a people who placed great
stock in rituals and symbols, and once Picard had publicly
enacted the rituals of atonement and apologized personally
to the family of every victim, they showed a remarkable
willingness to forgive him. It was cathartic for him as well.
And Admiral Kunrud, in turn, apologized to Picard as the
representative of the Federation—hundreds of times, as Picard ritually spoke on behalf of the families of each and
every officer killed on *Thelian, Puttkamer,* and the rest of

the fleet. He would pass along Kunrud's words of atonement to all the families in time, and could only hope they would be as willing to forgive and move on as the Carnelians were. There was much to be said for ritual in matters such as this.

It also helped that the Regnancy leaders were grateful for Starfleet's assistance in resolving the crisis. Picard offered whatever additional support they needed in tending to the long-term mental-health consequences on their outlying worlds near the Alpha Persei Cluster, as well as the efforts to shield worlds endangered by the radiation front expanding from the former black hole. But the Carnelians were a proud people, especially when it came to taking care of one another, and the Regnancy had abundant resources of its own. Picard was confident that the worlds of the region would be in good hands. However, the Carnelians' cleanup efforts would leave them too busy to continue expanding toward the Federation, at least for the next decade or so. And if their leaders stood by the precedents Picard and Giriaenn negotiated, then their future interaction with the Federation would probably be far more peaceful.

As for the Kirisha colony, the mines were gone and the grasses regrowing quickly. The Caitians had been returned to their settlements and granted official status as Cohorts of the Throne, free to live as they wished without interference by the Regnancy.

Picard actually enjoyed his stay in Carnelian space. It was a complex, ancient culture with a rich and fascinating history. But soon enough, the time came for him to lead what was left of his task force back to Federation space—after first saying his good-byes.

One good-bye was to Guinan, though he hoped it would not be permanent. "Are you sure you won't come back with us?" he asked as they stood together in her opulent Regnancy guest quarters for the last time.

"I'll get back to the Federation eventually," she replied. "But I have some business to wrap up here first. Might take months."

"I've made a decision," he told her.

"I'm listening."

"For years now, people have been telling me I should take command of a starship again. I've finally decided I might as well stop arguing and do it—if only to shut them up." They shared a laugh. "Pending the results of the inquiry into the Kirishan incident, of course," he added.

"The *Enterprise*?" Guinan asked.

Picard stared at her. "How did you know I'd been offered the *Enterprise*? Admiral Satie only extended the invitation this morning. Captain Halloway's retirement was quite unexpected."

Guinan gave him an enigmatic look. "Just a good listener, I guess. So are you going to accept?"

He was still puzzled, but he let it slide. He had learned to respect her unique insight. "I haven't decided. You know how I feel about children underfoot."

She smiled. "You don't know what you're missing. Trust me—you want the *Enterprise*."

"Well." He cleared his throat. "I'll tell you one thing: whatever ship I do get . . . I'll try to arrange for them to install a bar."

"Oh! Then I'll definitely have to come back. Eventually."

He gazed at her, smiling. "Thank you, Guinan. Thank you for . . . so much. Somehow you always manage to set me on the right path. When I have enough sense to listen."

"I'm just reminding you of who you already are."

He shook his head. "I wish it were that simple. I still . . . cannot believe how far I let myself stray down the path of vengeance, when I have always striven to be a man of peace. I never would've thought myself capable of it."

She graced him with a beatific smile, as patient and unjudging as ever. "It can happen to anyone. I think that when you've been angry for a very long time, you just get used to it. It gets . . . comfortable. Kind of like old leather. After a while, you can forget you ever felt any other way. You forget it's even there."

He nodded, taking in her words. "I suppose so. But that's all the more reason for vigilance. I must rededicate myself to peace. I must resolve to use force only as an absolute last resort—even after surrender."

"That doesn't sound very Starfleet," Guinan said through a Cheshire-cat smile.

He smiled back. "My time with the Carnelians—and recent events in general—have shown me that at times there is great strength in submission."


Picard's other farewell—a harder one, in many ways—was to Giriaenn. He was still ambivalent toward her; though he could sympathize with the need that had driven her, the fact remained that she was a dangerously manipulative being who had exploited his deepest heart and soul, violated them in ways he could not forgive. Despite recent events, he still could not rely on the veracity of anything she had said about herself, her motives, or the ancient past she came from. Any part of it could have been a lie to serve her ends.

Yet this woman had meant so much to him over the past few years, one way or another. It was strange to think that she would soon be gone from his life—from this plane of existence—forever. But he found it fitting. It was a time for new beginnings. The past several years had contained wonders, but there was much about them he would just as soon forget. He was ready to put the past behind him and live for tomorrow. And saying one last good-bye to Giriaenn, however difficult it was to face her again, was the perfect closure to his old life.

"I can almost feel it happening," she told him. "Shireilil

and Ngalior have already made the transition. . . . I can sense them waiting for me on the other side."

"How is that possible?" he asked. "I thought that contact with the minds on those planes was . . . well . . ."

"Incredibly destructive? It depends," she told him. "There are many levels beyond this one. Tapping into the higher of those levels was what caused the disaster. So far we are only wading into the pool."

He smiled despite himself. "As I recall, you learned very quickly how to swim."

She clasped his hands. "Thanks to you, Jean-Luc." She smiled. "What I said about you once was true. You humans—you truly are 'the beauty of the world, the paragon of animals.' You could equal us one day. Perhaps even surpass us—and avoid our mistakes."

"Then perhaps your kind and mine will meet again one day. This time on a more equal footing."

"I have no doubt of that. I only wish you could be there when it happens."

She moved to kiss him, but he stiffened and she halted, stepping back. "I'm sorry for what I did to you, Jean-Luc. Please don't let it harden your heart to others."

He spoke very softly. "Do not presume to speak to me about my heart."

She grew wistful. "So sad. Your lives are barely long enough to let you heal."

"Yes, well." He straightened his uniform. "On that note, I really must be getting back to the *Cybele*. Erm. Good-bye, Giriaenn, and good luck to you."

Her vivid brows drew together. "You know . . . I think Giriaenn has had her day. I'm about to begin a whole new life, to start over from innocence. For that, I think I should be Ariel. She took to that better than Giriaenn ever could."

"I think," Picard said, "that is a wise choice." Despite himself, he felt a surge of nostalgia, remembering the Ariel he had fallen in love with—that exuberant mix of naïveté and brilliance, poise and playful abandon—and wanted to believe she had been real, if only for a time. Wanted to hope that in some way, she could be real again.

She sensed his regret and smiled. "'Be cheerful, sir.

> Our revels now are ended. These our actors
> (As I foretold you) were all spirits, and
> Are melted into air, into thin air.'"

"'We are such stuff as dreams are made on,'" he replied.

She took his head in her hands and gave him one last gentle kiss, which he accepted passively. "Dream well, my Prospero. And make your dreams real."

When he opened his eyes—with no memory of having closed them—she was gone. Only her crumpled dress remained upon the floor, hot to the touch. His first impulse was to call down a science officer with a tricorder. But he chose instead to allow her this one mystery. He simply laid the dress upon the bed and beamed back to the *Cybele*.

But her butterfly sparkles remained upon his cheeks.

# 28

---

ONCE THE TASK FORCE REACHED STARBASE 52, Picard faced his second court of inquiry, investigating the battle of Kirisha and the loss of the *Thelian*. This time, he was quickly exonerated with no call for a court-martial. It was clear that the Manraloth's actions had exposed the *Thelian* to destruction, and that Picard's able leadership had kept the rest of the fleet largely intact, as well as resolving a far greater crisis. In Starfleet's eyes, that outweighed whatever error he may have made by going to Carnelian space in force. "If you hadn't," Admiral Hanson told him after the inquiry, "matters would've escalated after Kirisha, and we would've met the Carnelians militarily before long anyway. And with a lot more bad blood in the way of making peace."

Picard was still surprised, however, that they wanted him to take the *Enterprise*. He hardly felt he deserved a command of such prestige (due to its class and historic name, it was being considered a sort of "flagship," a symbol of Starfleet as a whole). But he remembered what Deanna Troi had said about accepting rewards graciously, and undertook to consider the offer in earnest.

The *Enterprise* was certainly tempting, though not because of its prestige. The appeal to Picard lay in its mission:

an extended survey of the Cygnus Reach, probing into the great unknown beyond Deneb, the most distant point Starfleet had yet reached in the Alpha Quadrant. The challenge of being out there beyond where any had gone before was highly provocative. And yet he was still uneasy about the prospect of taking civilians and children out into unknown dangers.

But then he reviewed a letter he had received from Donald Varley months before, not long after his old friend had taken out the *Yamato*. Picard had not been ready to hear its message then, but now he listened. "A *Galaxy*-class vessel is not just a starship, Jean-Luc," Varley had told him. "It's like a university town in space. A whole community, not just of officers and enlisted, but scientists and scholars. Instead of having officers do the exploring and leaving the scholars to figure it out afterwards, we take them right to where the discoveries are.

"And they're made for long missions, up to fifteen years away from port. You can't ask civilians to give up their lives and families for fifteen years. Hell, you shouldn't ask that of officers. Yes, there's a risk, but it's the only way a mission like this is even possible.

"And there's more," Varley added. "Out there, on the frontier, we're the face of the Federation to everyone we meet. Maybe the only face they get to see. Do we want them to see a military force? Or a community of explorers and their families? How would we rather have them think of us?"

Picard reflected on the tragedy that had resulted when he and the Carnelians had been too quick to see one another as threats. He was certainly not naïve enough to think that simply going out with peaceful intentions was enough, or that alien crews could instantly distinguish between soldiers and civilians. The ship's intentions would not prevent an ambush like the one at Maxia Zeta. But the conflict with the Carnelians had come after first contact—after the window for establishing good intentions had been opened and, perhaps, missed. It was in cases like that where the approach of the *Galaxy* class could make a major difference.

Moreover, Varley's characterization of the ships as flying university towns was enticing. Starfleet was where he belonged, but there was a part of him that still felt at home in academia, surrounded by like-minded scholars and students with whom he could explore intellectual and artistic pursuits. What could be more rewarding than to have the best of both worlds?

With all that to recommend it, the simple fact that there would be children on board was not enough to break the deal. After all, it was the first officer's job to handle day-to-day interactions with the crew. He would simply have to choose a first officer who could handle children and serve as a buffer between him and them, as Miliani Langford had on *Cleopatra's Needle.*

And that brought him to the next hurdle: selecting his command crew. Much of the *Enterprise*'s crew was already selected, particularly the engineering team that had built the ship and would stay with it upon its launch, headed up by the able lieutenant commanders Heather MacDougal and Michael Argyle. But captains generally preferred to pick their own key staffers whenever possible—at least captains who had earned the privilege, as anyone veteran enough to get a *Galaxy*-class ship had done. So most of the key posts in the command staff were still available.

It was a given that Deanna Troi would be his ship's counselor. She had proven her worth as a contact specialist, a skill that would let her serve in a capacity beyond that of a typical counselor, advising him in interactions with aliens as well as monitoring the mental well-being of his crew. Moreover, she had proven her worth as a confidante, and not merely because of her unusual insight into his psyche. A counselor had to be privy to the captain's most private thoughts, as a vital check on his judgment and state of mind. He could think of few people he would be comfortable opening up to in that way. Troi had earned the right to be one of them.

Another easy choice was Lieutenant Commander Data, who had proven so invaluable on the *Portia,* and who had already requested a post on a *Galaxy*-class ship. The principal scientific posts were filled, but the post of operations manager would be ideal for a person of his abilities, and he could double as the second officer.

His next choice was equally easy, though he had to clear it with Marien Zimbata first—simple enough while the *Victory* was still undergoing repairs at Starbase 52. "You remember that favor you said you owed me, Marien?" he asked as they met for afternoon tea.

"Yes?"

"I happen to be in the market for a security chief. And I recall a very impressive young lieutenant named Natasha Yar."

Zimbata sighed, though he did not seem surprised. "It's a favor I'm happy to grant, for Tasha's sake if not for mine. After what she achieved on Kirisha, she deserves it." According to reports Picard had read after the crisis settled, Yar had not only saved that colonist from the minefield, but had actually been able to resist the mental overload to a limited degree and save several more colonists from running into the mines before she too had succumbed. The young woman's devotion to saving lives was extraordinary, and that was an ideal quality for the defender of a ship bearing children.

"Thank you, Marien. I'll take good care of her."

"I'm sure you will. But why is it that whenever one of us does the other a favor, I lose a good officer?"

That reminded Picard of a dedicated young man named Geordi La Forge. He resolved to see if he could persuade Robert DeSoto to give him up.

Picard realized he was beginning to find this rather exciting. He looked forward to the adventure that lay ahead, knowing he could assemble the best crew possible to adventure by his side.

His excitement faded, however, when he learned the post of chief medical officer had been filled.

"Beverly Crusher," Deanna said. "As in Jack Crusher?"

On the screen, Picard maintained his reserve, but Deanna could read the tension in his body language, even though he was far too distant for an empathic reading. He was calling from Starbase 52, while she, the newly minted Lieutenant Commander Troi, was laying over at Vulcan en route to Earth. He would meet her there in another couple of weeks, shortly before the *Enterprise* set out on her mission. It was less than ideal for a captain to board his ship for the first time so soon before her launch, but not unprecedented.

Finally, Picard answered her question. *"She was Jack's wife. I had to bring him to her when he died. To her and her five-year old boy."* He fidgeted. *"The boy will also be aboard."*

"That's difficult," she said. "But I sense there's more."

He gave her a rueful look. *"Let's just say that . . . if Jack hadn't gotten there first, I would have pursued her myself. Not that I ever did, mind you."*

"Of course not. But now that she's been single for, what, a decade now? It opens up certain possibilities."

*"It does nothing of the kind, Counselor. As far as I'm concerned, she is still my best friend's wife."* He took a calming breath. *"I am simply . . . concerned that it might be difficult for her to serve under the man who—a man who would remind her of Jack's death. It's not fair to the boy either, of course."*

"So you protested to Starfleet."

*"I tried. But I was told it was already a done deal. Apparently she was in great demand, and Admiral Hidalgo feels lucky to have beaten out Starfleet Medical for her services. I couldn't talk the admiral out of it."*

"Well, do you have any doubts about her abilities as a CMO?"

*"Not at all. Professionally, she's the perfect choice."*

"So it's just the personal side that bothers you."

He pulled himself even straighter, if that were possible. *"There is nothing personal about it at all. She is a fellow officer and I will treat her as such."*

Deanna looked at him sadly. "Captain . . . don't close yourself off to the possibility of new relationships. Just because you've been burned in the past doesn't mean it isn't worth taking a chance on again."

*"Perhaps someday, Deanna. But not yet. Not so soon. And certainly not with a member of my crew."* He sighed. *"Better to focus on other priorities. Things I know I can do well."*

"Very well. If it's what you're comfortable with." Deanna knew she couldn't force it. In a lot of ways, he had made his peace with Giriaenn (or Ariel); but he had loved her deeply, and her betrayal and loss had left scars that would stay with him for a long time to come. When she looked at him, she saw an aloof, inhibited, lonely man. But perhaps that was judging him too much by her own standards. If this detachment was what he needed to heal, then she should accept it and work with it.

Besides, it might not be such a bad thing. Picard had a difficult task ahead: commanding a ship with so many of Starfleet's hopes and ambitions riding upon it, while guiding and protecting an enormous, diverse crew. A certain asceticism, a duty-driven life without the distractions of close relationships, could serve him well in fulfilling that awesome responsibility—so long as he had her there to keep him stable. And he was still able to take unreserved pleasure in his work and his pursuit of knowledge; perhaps that would be enough to complete him for now. He might not bond very closely with his crew, but then, that was what counselors were for. Or first officers.

*"Oh, by the way,"* Picard said, his reserve giving way to enthusiasm, *"I think I've finally found the perfect first officer."*

Speak of the devil. "That's wonderful!"

*"Yes. I'd almost given up hope, after going through all those files—just the usual boilerplate, statistics, and hollow letters of recommendation. Nothing that made any of the candidates stand out. All the really top-rate commanders are getting offered their own ships already, or are unavailable on deep-space assignments."* Picard had already con-

veyed to her his disappointment at the unavailability of one
Kathryn Janeway.

*"Anyway, I was just about to set this man's file aside
when I noticed a reference in his disciplinary jacket."*

"Disciplinary? Something he did *wrong* caught your eye?"

*"Wrong, perhaps, but for the right reasons. He refused to
let his captain beam down to Altair III when a seismic up-
heaval endangered the research team there. He all but had
DeSoto put in irons to keep him from putting himself in unnecessary danger. Risked a court-martial and the end of a
skyrocketing career because he knew he was right."* He
shook his head. *"I'm amazed Robert never told me about it. I
suppose he was too embarrassed."*

"So you want a first officer who'll disobey you?"

*"When he knows I'm wrong, yes. Which is something
that happens more often than I like to admit."* He studied
her over the screen. *"I couldn't help but think of how you
risked your career to defy Admiral Hanson's orders when
you knew they were wrong. And I couldn't help but think of
how many people had to fail to stand up to me in order for
the Carnelian incident to go as badly as it did. I want someone at my side who's not afraid to put me in my place. And
I believe William Riker is that man."*

Deanna clamped down tightly on her reaction. "Will—
William Riker." *Imzadi!*

*"You've heard of him?"*

"Of the *Hood*. Yes, of course." How could she have not
placed Captain DeSoto's name? Denial, she supposed. "He's
had an impressive career." Her first impulse had been to
protest the decision, to try to talk Picard out of it. But she
knew that would be foolish. Whatever resentment she might
feel toward Will Riker for placing his career over their relationship, for jilting her on Risa two years before in favor of
accepting the first-officer post on the *Hood*, was her own
issue to deal with. Being on the same ship with him while
he remained in that same career-driven mode (and she knew
him too well to believe that could have changed so soon)

would be a difficult reminder. But she had chosen to move on with her life, and if anything, she should strive to be supportive of his career goals as a friend. Certainly she had no business objecting to the posting when she'd just chastised Picard for objecting to Beverly Crusher.

And who knew? There might be a chance for them to rekindle what they'd once had. It would certainly be interesting to find out.


Picard was still finalizing the last few crew assignments when he arrived at Starfleet Headquarters shortly after Christmas. He'd just managed to finagle the services of Shawn Rider from the Adonis expedition as his transporter chief, barely edging out a promising CPO named Miles O'Brien, whom Picard had assigned as a relief flight controller instead, believing he could benefit from a wider range of experience. Rider was actually considering retirement to a research career, but Picard had managed to talk him into signing on for one more tour.

Also keeping Picard busy were his ongoing efforts to familiarize himself with the intricacies of the *Enterprise*, his late-breaking mission briefings, and so on. Apparently the exploratory push into the Cygnus Reach had been made possible by the establishment of a new starbase on Deneb IV, to which Starfleet was in the final stages of negotiating access. But some in the Fleet were raising questions about how the planet's natives, a backward people called the Bandi, had managed to build such an advanced facility so quickly. It looked as though his first mission would be a slightly covert one, to unearth the mysteries of the poetically named Farpoint Station before advancing beyond it into the unknown reaches.

Moreover, it seemed the mysterious Ferengi had been reported in the region, showing them to be even more widespread in their travels than Starfleet had believed. Yet there were still no reliable descriptions or contacts. One of his open mandates was to be alert for Ferengi presence and attempt to initiate contact—while not being too aggressive about seeking them out, just in case they were as deadly as the rumors claimed.

With all this going on, he hadn't even managed to see the ship itself, which was still undergoing final performance trials in the Kuiper Belt and would not come into port until early in the new year. At least his hectic schedule of interviews and briefings gave him an excuse to decline Marie's invitations to visit the homestead in Labarre for the remainder of the holiday season. He was fond of his sister-in-law from her letters, but had no interest in hearing more of Robert's lectures about the glories of the past. He'd had quite enough of the past in recent years.

So it was that Picard was in a distracted and somewhat surly mood when the time came for his interview with a junior-grade lieutenant named Worf. It worked out nicely, though, for Worf (a name he'd been too distracted to place at first) turned out to be Starfleet's first Klingon member. If anything, he took Picard's gruff attitude as a compliment.

Still, Worf was not pleased when Picard declined his request for a security posting. "But, sir! Surely I have proven myself in battle. I am a capable security officer."

"Yes, I read your file. Believe me, Lieutenant, I have no doubts as to your abilities as a warrior. However . . . a Starfleet officer needs to be more than a warrior. As Sun Tzu said, supreme excellence lies in achieving victory without fighting." A paraphrase, true, and a subtle shift from Sun Tzu's original meaning, but it served him here. A Klingon would not be receptive to Surak or Schweitzer, but Worf's reaction showed he knew and respected the author of *The Art of War*.

"If you wish to advance in Starfleet," Picard went on, "you need to broaden your experience. To learn every aspect of starship operation." He consulted a padd for a moment. "Mister Worf, I am assigning you as the main bridge watch officer. Your responsibility will be to supervise multiple stations, including engineering, environmental, sciences, and mission operations. You will also relieve conn and ops when needed and stand watches when command officers are off shift. There is no better post for gaining a broad range of command experience."

Worf glowered, trying with little success to conceal his disappointment. "Yes, sir," he said through his teeth.

"Do not see this as a setback, Mister Worf, but as an opportunity. I have great admiration for the discipline, dedication, and integrity of the Klingon people. I believe those attributes give you the potential to be not only a fine warrior, but a fine leader as well. I wish to give you the necessary grounding so that you may pursue whatever career path you eventually choose—whether security or something else."

Worf puffed out his chest, heartened by the captain's words. "Thank you, sir. I will do my best to learn all I can."

"Mister Worf, aboard the *Enterprise* you will be *expected* to learn all you can."


Just before the new year, Picard received a communiqué from Guinan, still wrapping up her affairs in Carnelian space. A few days before, he had finally managed to get off a brief letter filling her in on his crew selection and other events. In her reply, she told him it would probably be close to a year before she made it back to Federation space, but that she looked forward to meeting the rest of the crew he'd assembled. *"You chose well,"* she told him. *"These are the right people, Picard. The right people on the right ship. I guarantee—you'll go far together."*

# INTERLUDE

## Timelessness

ARIEL HAD BEEN REBORN AGAIN. IT WAS HER THIRD birth, her third childhood—though the first was so deep in the past that she had entirely forgotten it. Just thinking the thought, though, opened a conduit to let her witness the event as it occurred. In these dimensions, time was just one axis on the map of her former universe as it lay spread out before her, one continuum out of many floating side by side, each with its own parallel quantum facets ever multiplying along the axis of time.

With existence on this level, a realm where matter, energy, and thought became one, came the knowledge of how she and her kin could reach back and undo the catastrophe they had caused, and yet at the same time there came a more visceral understanding than ever of precisely why that should not be done. Each event was part of the tapestry of the universe—even of the multiverse, in this case, for that event had been so pivotal in the history of the higher planes.

So far, she and the others (who now communed more profoundly than they ever could have within the confines of neuronal meat, although there was a raw intensity to the flesh that she still lamented losing) had yet to encounter any of the Manraloth who had come before them, though they sensed in the conceptual winds that others had felt their presence. She could see their passage in the timestream, could even go back and speak to them if she wished. But there was still so much to learn about how reality worked on this level before she could feel comfortable taking such strides. Besides, she wished to meet them as they were now. Living in the past was a trap; it was time to move on.

Of course the Manraloth had not abandoned the past. In their communion, the commitment was still strong to find a way to free those trapped in stasis, and to heal the damaged minds within the computer core—minds that they had carried with them inside their psionic matrix when they sublimed, but that still were not ready to function on their own, especially not at this level. Healing them might be easier than freeing the stasis bubbles, though; the fields had been designed to shield their contents from interference on all dimensional levels, and the Manraloth had built them well. Still, Ariel and her people would not rest, would not attempt to move higher in the hierarchy of existences, until they had liberated all the surviving Manraloth and elevated them to this, the next step they should have taken ages before.

They were not alone on this level, either. Ariel and her kin had already made friends here, communing readily with the beings who inhabited this plane, just one level above the four-dimensional, and with others who passed through it on their journeys between planes. Many who lived here still kept an eye on the physical universe, whether out of curiosity about the dramas played out there or out of nostalgia or protectiveness toward what they had left behind. She had met a race of Travelers who still retained a link with corporeal existence, each member starting out in that form before evolving to other levels, since they valued the journey more than any single place. She had heard tales of a secretive people called the Douwd, beings to whom imaginative thought defined reality, so that they lived lives of illusion and pretense, rarely revealing themselves for what they were—although the one thing they would never do was use their deceptions to harm others. She had shared a brief communion with a multifaceted entity called the Voyager, a composite of minds—both organic and artificial—that had once existed on the corporeal plane before coming together to transcend its limits and seek new discoveries. It came as no surprise to Ariel that it was partly a child of humanity, imbued with their passion to seek and explore. The Voyager's joy at learning all that was learnable helped bolster her courage for the journey that lay ahead for her.

But then there was the trickster. This was a being from a continuum of existence that was beyond her grasp even on this level, yet one who could not resist meddling in the mortal plane, poking the anthill with various sticks for his own petty amusement. The Manraloth had known him even in their own time, and had feared him at first, until they learned how to cope with him and realized he was actually rather pitiful, his people decadent and sterile. It was to the Manraloth's discredit that it had taken them so long to realize they had fallen into the same trap.

If the trickster sensed these thoughts in Ariel as he approached (and surely he must, for this dimension and its denizens were as flat and exposed to him as fourspace was to her now), he gave no sign of it. He simply offered the hyperdimensional equivalent of an oily smile and said, "Ahh, there you are. The last stragglers of the race that destroyed their galaxy. What took you so long? Looking for a way to finish the job?"

"Don't start with us, trickster," she told him. "From up here, your taunts look pettier than ever."

"Oh, don't get me wrong," he told her. "I admire what you did. Shook things up around here like nothing's done in billions of years. The chaos was *so* entertaining. I look forward to seeing what new disruptions you'll bring to these stuffy climes."

"Wait in vain, then."

He sensed her intent and radiated regret. "Aww. You're still so dedicated to peace and communication. Bringing people together, ohh, so poignant and sappy and dull. You learn so much more about people when you get them angry!"

"Well, you would certainly know."

"That's why I spend so much time slumming on the mortal plane, you know. They're so much more primitive down there, such slaves to their impulses. So much easier to get a rise out of them."

"Even if it kills them?"

"They kill themselves off sooner or later anyway, so what's the difference?"

Ariel faced him proudly. "You're so wrong about them. Even some of the youngest among them have immense potential." She shared with him her experiences with humanity, with the Federation, with Jean-Luc Picard. "Such a short time ago they were slaughtering one another over skin coloration and territory, and now look what they have achieved. They could be here with us before you know it. The Travelers tell me some of them are already on the verge."

The trickster scoffed. "Them? Those lowly, ridiculous creatures? So enslaved by their predatory instincts that they slaughter their own kind by the millions? So locked into their own skulls that they don't have an inkling of true reality?"

"They're young, that's all. But look how much they've accomplished already. Mere moments ago, they were an insular, violent people, but they've come so far, broadened their understanding so much in an incredibly short time. They will reach our level before long."

"As if *you* were anywhere near *my* level. As for them, they're barely above the level of pond scum."

"Look at what just one man among them has accomplished. Jean-Luc Picard made a difference in matters far beyond his scale, matters of cosmic significance. He convinced the oldest race in the galaxy to change its ways. He may have saved the galaxy in doing so." She continued ruefully. "It took someone of his youth to correct the mistakes we elders made in our arrogance."

"Out of the mouths of babes?" he asked, plucking all her knowledge of human language and culture from her mind in an instant without bothering to ask. "Hmm, well, you may be onto something," he confessed. "They're an utterly clueless people, but sometimes fools and infants can stumble upon useful possibilities without even realizing it. Perhaps I'll pay this Picard of yours a visit. Put his species to the test through him. If they do have the potential to intrude upon our shores in the near evolutionary future, then they may be a threat. A few noble speeches and lucky breaks don't cancel out a grievously savage history."

Ariel bristled. "If you're to put them on trial, I demand to speak in their defense."

"Your testimony has already been noted for the record. You put so much stock in this Picard? Then let's see if he can withstand the trial on his own. If you're right about him, you should have nothing to worry about."

"If there were any chance of this trial being fair, I might believe that."

"It will be as fair as life itself," the trickster said, and Ariel knew just how unfair that was. "But don't worry. I'll give him the chance to prove himself, though I won't make it easy. After all, who knows?" he added, more to himself than to her. "It's a long shot, but even he could be the one."

"The one for what?"

"Stick around, you'll see." The trickster pondered, growing giddy with anticipation. "Yes. I shall go down among them and subject them to the trial. I shall take their form—only merciful, it's the only thing their pitiful brains can comprehend—and present myself as: The Inquisitor!" He paused. "No, that's too complicated for them too. Fewer syllables. The Questioner? No, make it as basic and simple as they are—I'll call myself *Q!*"

Ariel laughed. "A bit obscure, don't you think?"

"Oh, but it's so perfect! It can stand for so many things. The quintessence of existence, the quoin that holds up the arch, the quantum that is the quiddity of all things."

"The quidnunc who quibbles over every quirk. Queer, yet quotidian."

"Ohh, you cut me to the quick with your querulous quips! No, Q it shall be. I, Q. We are all Q!"

She sensed that he was dying for her to ask, so she asked. "And what will you tell them if they ask why you name yourself after that letter of their alphabet?"

"You really want to know?"

"Not really."

"Oh, go ahead and ask!"

She would have sighed if she still had lungs. "Very well. Why are you Q?"

Even without a face, he bore a devious grin. "Because U will always be behind me."

# EPILOGUE

—◆—

## JANUARY 2364

**Stardate 41124**

"CAPTAIN?" PICARD LOOKED UP, BROKEN FROM A reverie, as Tasha Yar came forward from the aft compartment of the shuttle *Galileo* and resumed her pilot's seat. "Will this be your first time on a *Galaxy*-class starship?"

"Yes," he replied. "Of course I'm familiar with the blueprints and the specifications. But this will be my first time on board."

"Well, then if I may be so bold, sir, you're in for a treat. The *Enterprise* is quite a ship."

"I'm sure she is," he answered. "But she has quite a crew as well."

Yar blushed and turned away, her girlish modesty a striking contrast to the fierce professionalism he'd seen her display on Kirisha. He noticed that she'd cut her hair more severely since then, buzzed nearly to the scalp at the back and temples, though longer on top. By now she should have been able to grow back what had burned away in the minefield, but apparently she had chosen to keep the close-shaven style for practical reasons. Or perhaps for aesthetic reasons, he thought; it was quite a flattering look for her features.

"*Enterprise to shuttlecraft* Galileo," came a voice over the comm. "*You are cleared for arrival in shuttlebay two.*"

Yar reached over to open the channel. "Acknowledged, *Enterprise*." She turned back to the viewport in anticipation, then grinned as the shuttle came about and the McKinley Station drydock came into view. "And there she is."

And there she was, wrapped in the drydock's arching superstructure as though gently clutched inside an eagle's talons. He had seen it in blueprints and holos many times, but they had not prepared him for the immense reality. The *Enterprise* seemed to flow toward him as the shuttle circled in around its bow. As stubby and bloated as it might have seemed in miniature, in reality it was a study in elegance, less a starship than a freeform sculpture expressing the *idea* of a starship. Its saucer broke over the shuttle like a tidal wave; he gazed upward and it was a vast plain, a city that he flew underneath. The engineering hull below curved like a gentle hillock in the landscape; the deflector dish at its bow was a pair of parted lips, feminine and welcoming. The dorsal between hulls spread outward like a mighty oak to hold the immense bulk of the saucer. As the shuttle flew past the dorsal on its port side, Picard could see tiny faces peering out from its skyscraper wall of windows. Some of them waved, knowing who was aboard the *Galileo*. It was a longstanding Starfleet tradition for captains to board their new ships by shuttle. And now Picard truly understood why. In the seconds since he had first glimpsed the lady *Enterprise*, he had begun a love affair with her.

A moment later, almost shockingly, they were out from under the saucer and coming around to the rear slope of the dorsal, by itself nearly twenty stories high. *You could go skiing down the back of this ship*, Picard thought.

Then the shuttle finished its turn and he could see the light of shuttlebay 2 pouring out. It seemed so tiny for a shuttlebay, but the reality was that he still struggled to grasp how vast the ship was. In moments, the shuttlebay filled the forward port, and with a gentle nudge it passed through the atmosphere containment field. Yar deftly spun it around so that its aft hatch faced the honor guard who stood assembled to meet their captain, then lowered it to the deck with a jarring bump. She blushed fiercely, but he gave her a reassuring look, appreciating her enthusiasm.

Picard rose and moved to the back of the shuttle as the hatch lowered, revealing his assembled crew. Or what there was of it. Due to the vagaries of schedule and starflight, the *Hood* had been unable to return to Sector 001 in time. Instead, they had rendezvoused with a ship carrying Doctor Crusher and her son, and would meet up with the *Enterprise* at Farpoint Station to deliver them, along with Commander Riker and Lieutenant La Forge. Meanwhile, both MacDougal and Argyle were back at Utopia Planitia, assisting Commander Quinteros and Doctor Brahms with emergency repairs following a construction accident on the *Odyssey*. They would be back in time for launch, but for now his honor guard consisted only of Troi, Worf, assistant CMO Asenzi, assistant flight controller O'Brien, and assorted personnel he had not yet learned to recognize. Commander Data was aboard, of course, but currently held the conn. All in all, it was an understated welcoming party.

But it would do. And its modesty did not keep Tasha Yar from striding forward and announcing in regimented tones, "Commanding officer, *Enterprise*, arriving." A crewman sounded an antique bosun's whistle, piping the captain aboard, and the crew snapped to attention. Yar preceded Picard down the ramp, as tradition dictated a security officer should do even in as safe a haven as this, and he followed a moment later. His boots struck the deck, and he was aboard his ship at last.

But he did not pause to absorb the moment, or any such sentimental nonsense. The podium stood waiting, so he stepped up to it smartly, laid the padd containing his orders upon it, activated the screen, and intoned: "'To Captain Jean-Luc Picard, Stardate 41124.8. You are hereby requested and required to take command of the *U.S.S. Enter-*

*prise* as of this date. Signed, Rear Admiral Nora Satie, Starfleet Command.'"

With his captaincy now formally affirmed, he stepped down and approached the ranking officer, Lieutenant Commander Troi. The handshake they exchanged was traditional, but his smile was sincere, as was hers. "Welcome aboard, Captain Picard," she said.

"Thank you, Commander. I am . . . very glad to be here."

The interior of the ship was as remarkable in its way as the exterior, if only for the sheer size of it. The quick tour Deanna gave him on the way to the main bridge only gave a taste of the rich environment and diverse community that was the *Enterprise*. He knew he would enjoy having the run of its science labs, arboretum, art galleries, and library databases. Deanna told him of upcoming concerts and plays that he was tempted to sample, although he remained uneasy about interacting closely with the crew and civilians on a social level. She also waxed poetic about the advanced and spacious holodecks the ship was equipped with, and though Picard found them somewhat more frivolous than a good book, he was willing to concede that they might be useful if he wished to get a bit of riding in during a long haul through deep space. Or perhaps—just maybe—to sample the world of Dixon Hill from the inside.

The main bridge, when they reached it, was almost disturbing in its luxury. For a moment he thought the lift had taken a wrong turn and deposited them in a crew lounge. But the console layout was unmistakably that of a starship bridge, and a highly advanced one at that. Deanna led him down to the command alcove while Yar moved smoothly to the tactical rail and Worf took ops at the front, next to Rene Torres at conn. But he looked skeptically at the overly cushy command chair, wondering if he'd be able to stay awake in it. "Where is Commander Data?" he asked.

"In your ready room," the relief watch officer told him.

"He heard something about a lion in there? He wanted to see it."

"Lion*fish*," Picard corrected him. Deanna had suggested that he get some sort of low-maintenance pet for stress relief, and he'd given in and gotten a fish. He was actually growing to like it. So it was with some haste that he made his way into the ready room to ensure that Data hadn't suffocated it out of excess curiosity.

Instead, Data was simply watching the fish as it swam, tilting his head back and forth and moving his mouth in mimicry. Registering Picard's arrival, he turned, his mouth frozen open until he remembered to shut it. Then, to Picard's surprise, he smiled. "Captain! Welcome aboard. I am very pleased to see you again."

Picard shook his proffered hand, staring at him. "Mister Data . . . it's good to see you too. Have you . . . learned to feel emotion?"

Data's expression grew wistful. "Only to mimic it, I fear, sir. I find it makes it easier for my crewmates to accept me. I've also been practicing a more informal speaking style." He frowned in his small, staccato way. "And, Captain . . . I would appreciate it if you would not . . . inform the crew about my lack of emotion. I believe it would make it more difficult for them to accept me."

Picard frowned. "Of course I will not violate a confidence, Mister Data. But if I may offer a suggestion . . ."

"Certainly, sir. Your input is always welcome."

"Data . . . you shouldn't have to pretend to be something you're not in order to get people to accept you. You should give them a chance to know the real you, not some façade you erect to meet their expectations."

Data tilted his head, considering. "Perhaps in time, sir. When the rest of the crew has had a chance to grow more comfortable with me, perhaps I will resume . . . being myself. But I shall . . . traverse that bridge upon arrival. Sir." He recited the mangled metaphor in a very stilted way, yet seemed quite proud of the accomplishment.

"Mister Data," Picard said, smiling despite himself, "I have no doubt you will prove yourself an invaluable member of this crew. It is good to have you aboard."

"Thank you, sir. It is good to be aboard."

"You're dismissed. Man the bridge, Commander."

Data acknowledged the order and exited, leaving Picard alone in his ready room. Well, almost alone. He strode over to the floor-to-ceiling window that gazed out onto the stars. Below him, the surface of the *Enterprise*'s saucer stretched back like a plateau and dropped away, with only the stars beyond. Their patterns from here were ancient, familiar, the same stars he had gazed on as a child yearning to know what lay beyond them. Now he had been to so many of them, learned so much about their history. And yet he felt his search for answers was just beginning.

Turning to the tank, he said to the lionfish, "I'm ready. Are you?"

Taking silence as consent, he nodded and headed back out to the main bridge. Data rose from the command chair as Picard approached and said, "I relieve you, sir."

"I stand relieved."

"Report."

"A full crew complement is now aboard, sir. Commander MacDougal reports full readiness in engineering."

"Grand. Thank you, Commander." Data relieved Worf at ops, and Deanna smiled broadly as Picard lowered himself into the command chair at last. Unexpectedly, it was warm, though not as warm as if a human had sat in it. After a moment, he decided it was sufficiently comfortable but not too much so. He flipped the side consoles open and tried them out, finding them acceptable as well.

But Deanna was still watching him, mirroring the expectancy of the crew, so he faced forward and spoke. "*U.S.S. Enterprise* to McKinley Station. Requesting clearance to depart."

"*Acknowledged, Enterprise. Clearance is granted. And our hopes and dreams go with you.*"

"Acknowledged, McKinley. And thank you. Picard out."

On the viewer, the talons of McKinley Station rose away. "We are clear to maneuver, Captain," Torres announced.

"Very good, Mister Torres. Thrusters, ahead full. Take us out of orbit."

"Thrusters, aye."

Without any sensation of movement getting past the inertial dampers, the curve of the Earth began to recede on the viewer. Picard was impressed that such a mass could accelerate so swiftly.

Once they were clear of Earth's orbital space, Picard ordered full impulse, and the ship performed just as smoothly, the deck still feeling as stable as if it were on solid ground. *A city in space indeed,* he thought. *Now let's see what she can really do.*

"Set course for the Deneb system, Mister Torres. Stand by for warp."

"Course set, sir," Torres announced after a moment. "Engineering reports ready."

"Ahead warp factor two," Picard ordered. "Now let's make those dreams real." Deanna smiled, and Data turned around quizzically. Raising his finger like the starter of a race, Picard swept it forward as he ordered:

"Engage."

*Exeunt omnes.*

# Acknowledgments

———

Thanks to Marco Palmieri for once again giving me the chance to tell a *Star Trek* story I've wanted to tell for a long time. And thanks to David Mack for paving the way.

The events of Chapter 1 are based on the TNG episode "The Battle" (teleplay by Herbert Wright, story by Larry Forrester), as well as the novel *Reunion* and the short story "Darkness" by Michael Jan Friedman. Most of the *Stargazer* crew characters mentioned here were created by Friedman. I'm indebted to Michael Okuda and Michael Schuster for technical details on the *Stargazer*. (Any more Mikes and we could hold a press conference.) The log entry in Chapter 1 was written by Mike Okuda for a viewscreen graphic in "The Battle," although I may have misread one or two words in transcribing it from a screen capture. Mike was quite helpful with my questions, but unfortunately the original graphic no longer exists.

The *Stargazer* court-martial and Phillipa Louvois were established in "The Measure of a Man" by Melinda Snodgrass. For assistance in figuring out the legal and procedural details of the court-martial, thanks to Dayton Ward, David Mack, Jim Fisher, and the Ex Isle BBS posters known as CJ Aegis, D'Monix, G-man, and Life for Rent.

The lyrics to "Beyond Antares" were written by Gene L. Coon. Jeri Taylor's *Mosaic* provided information on the state

# ACKNOWLEDGMENTS

of Cardassian affairs and Kathryn Janeway's status as of 2358–9. Certain events in Part IV, the Interlude, and Epilogue are based upon references in the TNG episodes "Encounter at Farpoint" by D. C. Fontana and Gene Roddenberry, "Legacy" by Joe Menosky, "The Next Phase" by Ronald D. Moore, "Time's Arrow" by Menosky, Michael Piller, and Jeri Taylor, "Second Chances" by René Echevarria, "The Pegasus" by Moore, "All Good Things . . ." by Brannon Braga and Moore, and *Star Trek: Generations* by Rick Berman, Moore, and Braga. Donald Varley (Thalmus Rasulala) appeared in "Contagion" by Steve Gerber and Beth Woods. Admiral Quinn (Ward Costello) was introduced in "Coming of Age" by Sandy Fries. Admiral Hanson (George Murdock) comes from "The Best of Both Worlds" by Piller. T'Lara (Deborah Strang) appeared in *Deep Space Nine*: "Rules of Engagement" by Moore, Bradley Thompson, and David Weddle. The *Malinche*'s Captain Sanders (Eric Pierpoint) appeared in *DS9*: "For the Uniform" by Peter Allan Fields. Torres (Jimmy Ortega), MacDougal (Brooke Bundy), Argyle (Biff Yeager), and the nameless transporter chief played by Michael Rider appeared in early first-season episodes of TNG.

The 2364 scenes in "All Good Things . . ." contradict several details of earlier episodes (including whether Picard had seen Yar before, Yar's hairstyle, O'Brien's post, and the stardate on which Picard took command). Since the altered events there have no effect on later timeframes, it is reasonable to conclude that those portions of "All Good Things . . ." occurred in an alternate timeline. Thus, where contradictions arise, I have chosen to adhere to what earlier episodes established.

Thanks to Delvo of Ex Isle for helping me figure out what would remain of the B'nurlac, and to Tristan of the TrekBBS for a quick Trek-continuity answer when I needed one. Thanks to Keith R.A. DeCandido for helping me keep the Interlude consistent with his novel *Q&A*. And thanks to cover artist Stephan Martinière for inspiring the look and feel of a pivotal moment of discovery.

# ACKNOWLEDGMENTS

The concepts explored in this book owe much to the "transhumanist" science fiction of authors such as Vernor Vinge, Iain M. Banks, and Greg Egan, particularly Egan's novel *Diaspora.* The descriptions of the magnetic field of a black hole owe greatly to Gregory Benford's novel *Eater.* And thanks to Alfred Bester for demonstrating how to achieve better madness through typography.

My description of the Alpha Centauri planetary system is based on simulations by Elisa Quintana et al. in the paper "Terrestrial Planet Formation in the $\alpha$ Centauri System." The description of Proxima Centauri's role in the system's geological and evolutionary history is extrapolated from a suggestion made by Dr. Greg Laughlin on the Systemic blog on July 5, 2006 (http://oklo.org/?p=107). The description of the hot Jovian planets in the Tanebor system is based on the paper "Albedo and Reflection Spectra of Extrasolar Giant Planets" by David Sudarsky et al. The correlation between hot Jovians and water-rich worlds was codified in "Exotic Earths: Forming Habitable Worlds with Giant Planet Migration" by Sean Raymond et al. (*Science,* Sept. 8, 2006). Thanks to SolStation.com for information on the appearance of "brown" dwarfs. The existence of planets and particulate disks around brown dwarfs has been confirmed, though a Saturn-like ring system around one is my own extrapolation. The concept of a black hole event horizon as an information sink is based on Dr. Leonard Susskind's proposed solution to the black hole information paradox formulated by Dr. Stephen Hawking, with added inspiration from the *Gene Roddenberry's Andromeda* episode "The Banks of the Lethe" by Ashley Edward Miller and Zack Stentz (although I have taken some slight liberties with the physics for story purposes). *How to Do Archaeology the Right Way* by Barbara A. Purdy was my chief source for archaeological practice and terminology. The Kirishan *shu'prra* were loosely inspired by the rattlebacks in *The Future Is Wild* by Dougal Dixon and John Adams, a speculative book and TV series about the future evolution of life on Earth.

# ACKNOWLEDGMENTS

The Celestia space simulator was invaluable in determining the galactic itineraries and vistas described in this book (particularly the location of the final confrontation), with geographic help from *The Guide to the Galaxy* by Nigel Henbest and Heather Couper (for the real stuff) and *Star Trek Star Charts* by Geoffrey Mandel (for the not-so-real). Memory Alpha and Wikipedia were invaluable references as well.

Last and hardly least, thanks to Patrick Stewart, whose illustrious career as a Shakespearean actor influenced this novel as much as his iconic portrayal of Jean-Luc Picard did. And thanks to the Bard himself for saying it all so well.

So, good night unto you all.

# About the Author

———◆———

Christopher L. Bennett is a lifelong resident of Cincinnati, Ohio, with bachelor's degrees in physics and history from the University of Cincinnati. His love of science and science fiction was inspired by his discovery of *Star Trek* at the age of five. By age twelve he was making up *Trek*-universe stories set a century after Kirk's adventures (an idea years ahead of its time), but soon shifted to creating his own original universe, and eventually realized this was what he wanted to do for a living. His first sales were a pair of original novelettes published in *Analog Science Fiction and Fact,* but since then he has established himself as a *Star Trek* author, following up his debut eBook *Star Trek: S.C.E. #29: Aftermath* (now available in a trade paperback reprint of the same name) with the critically acclaimed novels *Star Trek: Ex Machina* and *Star Trek: Titan: Orion's Hounds*, ". . . Loved I Not Honor More" in *Star Trek: Deep Space Nine: Prophecy and Change*, "Brief Candle" in *Star Trek: Voyager: Distant Shores*, "As Others See Us" in *Star Trek: Constellations*, and *Star Trek: Mere Anarchy Book Four: The Darkness Drops Again*. He has branched out beyond *Star Trek* with the publication of *X-Men: Watchers on the Walls* and the upcoming *Spider-Man: Drowned in Thunder*.

More information, original fiction, novel annotations, and cat pictures can be found at http://home.fuse.net/ChristopherLBennett/.